SETAN SERIES:
BOOK 1

The Claiming

SANDY WEST

LOCH SATICAMA
PUBLISHING

Copyright © 2025 Sandy West

www.lochsaticamapublishing.com

Cover: Miblart

Editor: Rachael Swanson

ISBN-13: 979-8-9996528-0-5 (eBook)

ISBN-13: 979-8-9996528-1-2 (print)

ISBN-13: 979-8-9996528-2-9 (hardcover)

First Edition: August 2025

10 9 8 7 6 5 4 3 2 1

Dear Reader,

As you know, some languages don't translate well. Example: Unlike English, many languages lack direct equivalents to "yes" and "no". They may change a verb or noun to show an affirmative or negative. The name of one object may not appear in another language.
Translating Setan into English runs into this problem.

Therefore, to make reading easier, any unusual word or word that doesn't have a direct translation will use the English variant or continue using the Setan version, where the meaning is obvious, so the reader doesn't feel like they are reading disjointed sentences.

Thank you for reading this book. I hope you enjoy it.

Sandy West

Acknowledgements

Thank you to everyone who believed in me. All my love to my children, who supported me. Thank you to my beta readers, including the one who didn't finish (you know who you are.♥). Another thanks goes out to my editor, Rachael. Once this series is done, I'll get working on *that* book.

Chapter One

IT WAS A RISK, but their group decided to travel through the forest for what little protection it offered. Quietly and deliberately, they moved forward, minimizing any sound. The canopy overhead was empty, skeletal branches reaching out to the gray sky, offering them little cover. Their sole solace lay in the sparse, interwoven clusters of evergreens. During breaks, they would spread out under them, trying to hide themselves from view. Today, the early morning fog was slowing them even further.

The fog is thick. Too thick.

Siana stumbled over the forest floor. The rope around her waist tightened, slackening again as she regained her balance. The backpack tugged her arms in protest. When a hand gripped her arm, she laid hers briefly over it, silently showing she was okay. Jacob released her as they continued walking. He was a dark shape, only visible when he came close. She couldn't see the others. Only the slight crunching of leaves told her they were there.

The group moved at the speed of a turtle. The pace was driving her crazy. She just wanted to run, to get there—wherever "there" was—but with their numbers, it wasn't possible. Larger than normal, their group had to take precautions. In any case, running wasn't a good idea. The couple behind them were barely audible. Newcomers, they joined thanks to the woman's engineering position and the man being an electrician. She had glimpsed them but never had a chance to introduce herself or talk. The journey began once the group was complete; they were the last to join. Although she could hardly see the others they were trailing, there were approximately eight more individuals in the lead. The couple in front of her carried two children. Two boys around four and seven. Stomach tightening, she didn't want to think about them.

The younger the child, the greater the chance of discovery.

The belief that children were a death sentence caused others to object to the family being part of their group. These two, however, displayed exemplary behavior. They were quiet and never threw tantrums. The others yielded after a few days spent near them. That their mother was a doctor and their father a teacher also helped. The supposition they were close to the end of their journey helped too. They hoped to arrive before the children grew frustrated. Though, despite extensive walking, they behaved well. Siana was conflicted. Part of her wanted to allow them so they had a chance; the other part wanted to leave them to give Jacob and herself a better chance. She hated making these decisions. Decisions that meant life or death to another.

She sensed Jacob's slight hesitation before she felt herself being pulled to the ground. A low, almost imperceptible rustling to her right, the brush moving slightly, indicated he was searching for a hiding spot. Siana didn't question it. He was more right than wrong. The rope tightened as he moved away. She followed. It slackened as she drew closer. Branches lightly scratched her face as she moved across the damp leaves to lie next to him under what felt like bushes. A sound distinct to the blocking blanket reached her ears, a green and brown combination of fabric and metal threads designed to hide heat signatures and help block the tracking devices. There was almost a slight metallic hum as she quickly helped him unroll it to cover themselves. It was an act of practiced necessity.

How many times have we done this? How many more before it's over?

The latter question made her weariness worse. She pulled the last corner of her side over her head.

A Faraday cage for humans.

The thought amused her. She realized how tired she was, because it wasn't funny at all.

Why do I always have to pee?

Annoyance filled Siana. She landed in an awkward position. A slight adjustment to take the weight off her hip, and she felt the unexpected pressure of Jacob's hand on her side. She understood. Any movement, any sound, could be a death sentence. The blocking blanket, as they called it, could only do so much. Concentrating on controlling her breathing, trying to slow it to barely life sustaining levels was the hardest part. That feeling of needing to take a huge breath of air was something everyone needed to overcome, especially since their hunters would target anything falling within the human respiration rate. Uncontrolled breathing resulted in death. She still had trouble doing it, but she was getting better. Jacob usually positioned himself in front of her, preventing her breathing from being detected. He, of course, was great at it.

When the screams began, they froze. It was the sound of those who hadn't heard the warning in time. The lucky ones didn't have time to scream. Instant death came to them before they fully registered what was happening. Their deaths usually alerted the others to their discovery. It was utter pandemonium —breaking branches, the shrill whine of disruptors, the frantic cries of people desperately trying to escape. Just before the voices stopped, a child started crying for his dad.

Siana corrected herself. *The hardest part was listening to them.*

For a pediatric nurse, hearing a child cry was actually a positive sign. Now? Not so much. Even weeks later, tears still welled in her eyes each time a child's silence became permanent. Early on, she almost got herself and Jacob killed. A desire to help, to save lives, motivated her. Nursing school resulted from her compassionate nature, yet this same nature almost caused her to expose them frequently. In the end, Jacob made her realize they couldn't help others if it meant hurting themselves. This unfortunately meant listening to their deaths, something she still found difficult.

"Don't set yourself on fire to keep others warm," he said. "You can't help anyone if you're dead. I know it's hard. I know it. You have to steel yourself against it."

It was challenging. Extremely difficult. The children's cries of fear and pain were especially disturbing. She didn't think many children remained.

Mankind's future. Gone.

The end of humanity felt inevitable to her. Like hamsters on a wheel, they were going nowhere. Despite everything, she refused to surrender.

A warming sensation on the back of her neck interrupted her thoughts. Confused, she concentrated on it. The tracker, implanted in the back of everyone's necks courtesy of their government "for their protection," was disabled. The thin metal chokers around the survivors' necks blocked any potential reinstatement. Another little Faraday cage, specifically designed to block tracker signals.

Why does it feel like it's heating up?

It was growing increasingly uncomfortable. In a slight shift of her head, she attempted to ease the feeling, though she knew it was inescapable. She gritted her teeth to stifle any sound of pain. The heat was almost unbearable. She shifted subtly, hoping to go unseen, but it made no difference.

A sudden, intense dizziness overcame her. Though she desperately wanted to alert Jacob, her body wouldn't respond. Panic resulted from feeling paralyzed. A growing, intense pain engulfed her. A deafening roar in her ears drowned out all other noises. The breathlessness made her desperate to shed the blanket. Her body felt increasingly crushed, like garbage compacted. A scream wouldn't come, even if she wished it.

Darkness.

Chapter Two

THE PAIN!

A splitting headache threatened to overwhelm her. It felt as if rabid dinosaurs were tearing her body apart.

They found us?

Nausea rose. Her stomach tried to give back the few berries they'd found on today's trek. Teeth gritted, she breathed deeply to avoid vomiting, then slowly opened her eyes as warmth replaced the chill.

Was she hit?

Blinded by the light, she squinted her eyes shut.

When did the sun come out?

Despite trying to suppress it, a low moan escaped her lips.

Jeez, it hurts!

Siana was unaware of how much time passed as her body struggled to recover. The wetness in her jeans signaled her bladder was empty. Her jumbled thoughts prevented her from making sense of what had happened.

Focus. Take stock. Triage.

The pain made it difficult, but slowly—too slowly—it became bearable. Her gloved hand could feel the hard roughness of the earth beneath her. Again, she tried to open her eyes, this time succeeding. Time had moved her into shade. She inhaled deeply, then looked up to see a bright blue sky. Arched over her were lavender- and blue-leafed trees. Birds singing. A warm day.

Wait a second. Lavender? Warm day?

Puzzlement overcame Siana. The season was fall: foggy, gray, cold.

Think. What happened? Jacob!

She sat up to find her brother, but the world swam before her eyes. Instead, she rolled over, losing the battle for the berries. She fell beside the mess onto the purple, blue, and green grass. Her only thought was to concentrate on not dying, because it certainly felt like she was. She lay there until she could function, sure she had blacked out again. Time's passage brought her back into sunlight. As she squinted, she saw the sun approaching the horizon, its rays slicing through the trees. Driven by thirst, she soon moved. Cautiously, she turned onto her side and attempted to sit up once more. Instead of a full rotation, the world cooperated by staying on a slightly tilted axis. There was an emptiness on her back.

The backpack. Where is it?

She rose slowly, pleasantly surprised when she managed it. She quickly located the backpack, snagged on a low branch.

What the heck?

She eyed it, perplexed.

How did it move from her back to the tree? For that matter, where the heck was Jacob?

She grabbed the backpack, concern for her brother overriding her distrust of the backpack's traveling ability.

"Ah!" A soft whimper of pain escaped from her. Her mouth clamped shut instantly; she listened closely for approaching drones. Not hearing them, she relaxed a little. Her quick move caused pain to radiate through her body. She put the pack down between her feet in a slow, deliberate manner.

In the unhooked side pocket, she found a blue metallic bottle. To avoid causing further pain, she carefully removed it. She felt heartened by the sound of water sloshing. The first small rinse cleaned her mouth of the berried-bile taste. She spit it out. Siana took another sip, this time swallowing. She waited, not wanting it to join the berries. Once she kept it down, she drank enough, hopefully quenching her thirst, but avoiding overloading her stomach. From the tree line, she looked around but couldn't spot the others.

Where are they?

She expected signs of a struggle or death, but the scene was peaceful. Warm. Colorful.

Definitely not what I'm used to. Where am I? How did I get here?

Her confusion only deepened when she looked around. Trees encircled the large, flower-filled field she was in. The flowers looked normal, but the trees indeed had lavender-colored leaves tinged with blue, their bark grayish.

What kind of trees have leaves like that? And the grass...

As Jacob was the botanist, she was determined to ask him. He would likely spend days studying it all.

He'd been interested in plants for as long as I can remember.

She checked her bag's contents after replacing the bottle, verifying their belongings were still inside. She got out her phone, replaced the battery, then snapped several shots of the field and trees to show Jacob. If he wasn't in the area, she knew she couldn't do them justice with words. She put the phone in an outside pocket. Despite the initial determination to overcome the pain of putting on the pack, which elicited some disgruntled thoughts, she soon abandoned the attempt. Her arms felt like she'd done a month's worth of arm lifts within an hour. She opted to carry it by the strap, carefully assessing her pain level. It still hurt, but it was doable.

As she recalled the tracker activating, a hand went to the back of her neck. She'd always hated the thing. Only the government's threat of not being able to work, eat, or purchase items without one made her accept it. The device felt warm to the touch. The surrounding area hurt, but it lacked a sense of activation.

Strange.

Her hand searched for the choker. Fingers brushing the coldness of the links, she discovered it had lowered and exposed her to the tracking devices. As she hastily covered the tracker again, her heart pounded in her chest with the chilling certainty that they had likely found her.

Siana ensured her brown knit hat was still on her head and that her other clothes were undamaged, although the day's warmth would probably make her remove her winter hat and jacket soon. Auburn tendrils curled playfully around her eyes. She adjusted her hat, tucking her hair back in to keep it out of her face.

Once positive she and her clothing were okay, she started calling softly, "Jacob."

She walked the field's edge, the scent of wildflowers enveloping her, her pack dragging a little behind. She braced herself to speak, knowing it was the only way to find him, her heart racing in anticipation. Though birds sang and insects buzzed, Jacob was nowhere to be seen. No one, in fact, answered her. Her pain levels were decreasing. She decided to go further into the woods, and again circled the exterior of the field, quietly calling for him. Her confusion grew, a knot tightening in her stomach.

This is weird. Where is everyone?

She enlarged her search area again, though trying to maintain visual with the field through the trees proved a bit of a challenge.

"Jacob." No response other than an orange bird, upset at her disturbance.

She pressed on, her search expanding, until the field disappeared from view, the trees closing in, forcing her to halt.

No point in getting lost.

The increasing sense of unease overshadowed Siana's attempts to remain calm.

He was here somewhere. He has to be. We had been right next to each other.

She felt her waist, remembering the rope. It wasn't there. Her hand felt only the clothing she wore. There was also no sign of the rest of the group. Since it was an attack, belongings of the dead should be scattered.

This is getting creepy. Where are they?

Breathe. She could mentally hear Jacob's voice. It was his go-to when she was stressed. As she went back to the field, her anxiety increased. She knew something had happened, but she didn't know what. The sense of being alone combined with the fact she had just been with her brother and others had her on edge.

Was he dead? Was I? Where was he? Where am I? Panic started rising. *I don't want to do this alone. Please, Jacob, answer me.*

Unexplained events fueled her growing fear. She tried to contain it, but the emotional beast didn't obey. Again, she fruitlessly searched, knowing he wasn't there, yet not wanting to believe it. Siana's lower lip trembled as she fought back tears, her hands clenched into fists. She didn't want to be alone. She wasn't good at it. From childhood adventures to adult challenges, they'd always been together, their bond unbreakable.

"Jacob!" It was a last desperate bid, even though the shout may cost her life.

It echoed, but no one called back. She yelled once more as loud as she could, but this time with a hint of hopelessness.

Nothing.

She waited another minute. As her emotions overwhelmed her, tears started to trickle down her cheeks. The world tilted slightly, and she swayed. The lack of food and whatever was happening made her body want to collapse.

A snapping twig, close behind her, made her jump. She spun so fast the trees swam before her eyes; a wave of nausea threatened to send her toppling. Instinctively, her feet moved apart to keep her balance. A man, aiming a crossbow at the ground, emerged from the woods. Her first thought was that it was the man from the couple behind, but that man had brown hair, brown eyes, a beard, and was her height—it wasn't him.

This one wore dark pants and boots, along with a tunic-like shirt that buttoned at the neck. The clothing was unfamiliar, yet she understood the survivors' resourcefulness in making and using what they could. Thick blond hair fell to his jawline. Insipid gray eyes stared back at her. His pallor reminded her of a ghost. His height was what most caught her attention. He was a tall man. Exceptionally tall. Of all the men she'd seen, he was easily one of the tallest. He spoke as he approached her. At first, she wasn't sure she'd heard correctly. She inched closer, head tilted slightly, straining to hear him. He said it a second time.

That's not English. Was a tourist trapped when it all began?

She didn't care where he was from. Though relieved to not be alone, a sense of unease lingered, making her cautious. Appearances could be deceiving. The man's expression shifted as he approached. In short order, he was standing before her. His eyes scanned her from head to toe. She recognized the look, a knot reforming in her stomach. As he reached for her jacket, he said something else, pulling it open on one side. She pulled away warily, her eyes never leaving him. She herself was five foot ten, yet this man towered over her.

Where is Jacob?

Jacob, unlike her, knew how to fight. People often bullied them growing up because they were redheads. He usually protected her.

The man's gaze fell upon her left hand. As he licked his lips, a sense of foreboding filled her. She started backing away, unable to take her eyes off of him. In a single motion, he discarded his crossbow, lunged forward, and seized her. How he moved so fast, she didn't know. With a sharp tug, he yanked her hat off, pulling out strands of her hair, eliciting a pained wince. His grin, as her hair cascaded down her back, sent a chill down her spine. She recognized his kind from their journey and immediately felt a sense of danger.

I need to get out of here.

As she released her pack, aiming a punch, the stranger seized her wrist. His foot went to the rear of hers. The impact of her backward fall momentarily knocked the wind out of her. The force of his weight landing on her worsened the situation. With her arms pinned, he used his body to keep the rest of her from moving. With one hand, he could hold both her wrists above her head; the other pulled her shirt up. He reached under and seized her breast, chuckling while she struggled to break loose. He bent over her, his hand moving down to unbutton her pants. She pulled one hand free, attempting to hit him, causing him to laugh again.

He's enjoying this.

The soreness in her arms prevented her from being effective. Her weakened state wouldn't give her the power she needed to land a hit effectively. She was aware she couldn't succeed, yet she fought with all her might as he tried to push her pants down.

He's too strong.

No longer caring about getting caught, she opened her mouth and screamed.

Chapter Three

AS LORICA AND his guards were riding, they heard another sound. Gently halting their mounts, they watched the forest, waiting. Curious glances passed between them as they listened. This is Devereaux land; others weren't supposed to be here. They only heard the sweet sound of birds singing, tiny flashes of red, orange, and blue as the birds moved quickly through the branches. Lorica's eyes narrowed.

"If that *blotzen* Talon is poaching again..." His tone promised retribution.

As he turned his *storjen* toward the sound, they trotted while dodging low tree limbs, the undergrowth flattening under hooves. His guards followed instantly. Shortly after, Lorica's pace decreased. He gave his captain a quick look, and the male shrugged. They lost the direction of the sound. Guided by a piercing scream, they galloped toward its source. Lorica grew up in these woods, and while sound could deceive, he had enough experience to know where the louder one came from.

That sounds female. Why would a female be on our lands? More to the point, why would a screaming female be on our lands?

Together they rode, Lorica mentally hurrying his mount. If Talon were here, and there was a female, it wouldn't end well. They rarely lived with him around, and a dead female on their property would be a big headache. His mount jumped over a fallen log and came to a stop in a field. Lorica recognized it as the one his mother used to take them to for picnics.

A smile stretched across his face as he saw *Bund* Talon. He was really in the mood to cause him some damage, especially since the arrogant *mut* liked to treat House Devereaux lands as his own. To be sure, his elder brother would be very angry if he harmed Talon. The *blotzen* meant little to him; as House Head, Tamek's focus was on safeguarding their House.

The law is the law. Tamek's voice resounded in his head. Lorica inwardly rolled his eyes. Malk, his mount, snorted. The fighting on the ground drew his attention. Unfortunately, it looked like Talon had indeed dragged a female onto their property.

Lorica yelled Talon's name, drew his short swords, and dismounted. Despite Talon's poor fighting ability, his guards, fond of combat, gladly accompanied him.

Lorica, sword in each hand, advanced on the scrambling *mut,* his gaze then shifting to the female. Her green eyes, filled with tears, made it obvious she hadn't chosen to be there. His timely arrival was clear as both still wore their trousers. Talon turned tail and ran, thrashing through the trees, forgetting his crossbow in his haste.

Typical.

Lorica wanted to chase him, but he had to deal with her first. After re-sheathing his swords, Lorica drew near, observing the female's jaw drop before quickly closing. Aware of the impression he made, he approached her, ignoring it. Her size was far less than the average *Setan* female.

She looks like a child. Surely Talon hadn't sunk that low. Then again, I wouldn't be surprised.

As he moved closer, she retreated. He came to a halt and watched her wide eyes briefly stare at their mounts before turning back to him. He had no intention of scaring her any further. His guards would approach her from behind after supposedly chasing Talon away, although that's being considerate.

Hopefully, there were a few discolorations on the cretin by the time they finished. Adding some color could enhance that monster's appearance.

From a short distance, he studied the figure. If he hurried, he could catch her, but he preferred her coming to him. Talon had already terrified her. Lorica coaxed her gently, a smile on his face. Despite his best efforts, she refused to come to him. He stepped forward, and she stepped back. He paused, puzzled by her silence.

Sure, Talon scared her, but being alone, she could have predicted this. Had she had someone else, he could have protected her. Besides, revealing her name wouldn't hurt. It could only help her, especially if she had family nearby. Lorica felt insulted. Most females who met him usually fell over themselves trying to get him to claim them, even though he wore the ring.

"Are you alone? Is there a male with you? Where is your family?" He kept his voice low and friendly.

Another confused look was all he received.

Maybe she wasn't very intelligent?

His captain voiced Lorica's thoughts. "Is she a simpleton?"

Lorica shrugged, but didn't discount it. After all, he wasn't getting any answers, and the female continued to look scared and confused. He sighed. Night was falling quickly, and he couldn't leave her unprotected out here. Now that Talon knew she was here, he'd skulk around to get her alone again. Despite the bruising his guards would give him, Talon was an animal in heat around a female.

She needs to be brought to the house, which means she needs to be caught.

It was clear, from her edging away, that it wouldn't be without a fight.

With a grim set to his jaw, he turned to his captain and said, "She's on Devereaux lands. We can't leave her here, but I don't think she's going easily."

The captain agreed, dismounted, and both began moving to opposite sides of the field, flanking her. Her understanding of their intentions was clear to him.

She's not a complete simpleton.

To appear less threatening, he adopted a friendly, relaxed posture, crouched down, and slowly approached her, extending a hand in greeting. At least, that's what he hoped. Rarely did he need to pursue females; he'd been told he was very handsome. He continued, ignoring Malk's amused noise. Lorica tried his utmost to persuade her to approach him. He tried again and again, his words soft but urgent, but she wouldn't budge, the space between them a firm barrier.

With a sharp turn, she fled. Lorica sighed in disappointment. Perhaps his appearance was starting to decline. A snort, bordering on a chuckle, from Malk caused Lorica to glare at him. He refrained from pursuit. He knew that the other guards were trailing her. Unfortunately, judging by the boot sounds, they hadn't gotten close enough before she ran. He waited near where she had entered the woods, in the event of her return. His captain stayed where he was. His guards soon called instructions, their voices echoing through the trees, but Lorica struggled to identify their location. He ran a hand across his face.

Please tell me a female child did not outmaneuver my guards.

The calls escalated into shouts. Silence fell after a small scream. Worried, Lorica was on the verge of entering the woods when his guards arrived; one carried the unconscious female, wrinkling his nose, while the other carried her bag. Lorica stayed calm. He knew they wouldn't hurt a female—male, yes—but he wasn't sure why she would be in such a state.

A guard quickly said, "We caught up to her, seized her arm, and she fainted."

Lorica took her from the guard and quickly learned why he had that expression. The stench of unwashed body and urine overwhelmed him. Lorica almost gagged. He laid her on the ground and inspected her for any injuries. Her bruised wrists, clearly Talon's doing, were the first thing he saw. Her gauntness most surprised him. Rare as they are, most took care of their females. Others, like his family, did what they could to protect those who had no one. Of course, there were the Talons of the world, but still.

Who has been neglecting her?

19

Once he located her family, he would investigate them. Her hair caught his eye, and he instantly knew she would be a highly sought-after prize. Neither her red hair nor her curls were typical. He moved her overcoat and saw she was definitely not a child, despite her unusually small size. Her origin remained unknown to him. Her presence on Devereaux lands complicated matters for the family. He had no choice but to take her to his brother. Given her smell, he made one of his guards carry her.

Chapter Four

WARMTH AND SOFTNESS surrounded her. She considered snuggling into it and ignoring her alarm, even though it hadn't gone off yet. Maybe she should call out? That would be mean. They were short-staffed as it was.

Wait, no. That's not right.

With a groan, she opened her eyes, rubbed the sleep from them, and squinted at her blurry surroundings. She was lying in a bed.

A bedroom? What happened? Where am I?

Despite not wanting to, she forced herself into an upright position. She wanted to burrow under the covers, a luxury long forgotten.

When did I last sleep in a bed?

By tossing the blankets aside, she discovered she was in her birthday suit. She froze, eyes widening. In horror, she recalled the stunning dark-haired man in the field, wondering if he or his companions had removed her clothes.

I meet the most attractive man I've ever seen, possibly get undressed by him, and I look like a yeti.

She realized this shouldn't be her top priority. Given the first man's actions, she suspected the second man of similar intentions and immediately examined herself for signs of assault. Only arm bruises and no further injuries. She recovered herself, recalling her last memory. What she'd seen so far flummoxed her. The mounts, the color of the trees, how tall the men were, the unknown language—it was all so confusing. Where was she? More importantly, where was her brother?

The door interrupted Siana's musings, slowly opening in and two women appeared. A portly, older woman, who was beaming at her, entered first, followed by a thinner woman closer to Siana's age, carrying a silver tray. It smelled like food, and Siana's stomach rumbled. They wore identical brown trousers, hip-length tunics, and turban-like scarves that partially concealed their ears.

Who are they? Nurses? Servants? She anxiously monitored them.

As the younger woman set the tray down on the small, round table beside the bed, near the draped windows, the older woman approached Siana, clapped, and spoke cheerfully. Upon Siana's lack of response, she tried again. As Sia puzzled over the woman's words, she saw her scrutinizing her face. A slight frown creased her forehead as she pinched her lips together and turned away. The older one seemed to give instructions to the younger. Siana tried hard, but she couldn't figure out what language it was.

Is the older one the boss?

The latter drew back the drapes on the windows. Sunlight filled the room, causing Siana to blink. The setting sun was her last recollection.

How long have I been out?

The older one turned back to her. With a beckoning hand, she signaled for Siana to follow, but she stayed put. The situation's strangeness caused her to hesitate. Her lack of awareness regarding location and companions made her uneasy while unclothed. The elder spoke to the younger, and the younger vanished behind a door. A similar dark wood door with carved scrolling throughout sat to the right. They were rather big. Strangely, neither door possessed a doorknob. Sage green painted spaces separated identical scrolled wood panels evenly across the room's walls and ceiling.

As the older woman gestured for Siana to stand, Siana shook her head, pointing to her body to explain her predicament.

The older one looked perplexed. Her face cleared. "Ah!"

She went to the large wardrobe opposite the bed and took a dressing gown from inside. It was plain white and looked like cotton. Siana's relieved expression caused the other woman to break out another huge grin.

She looks quite proud of herself for figuring it out.

Siana put on the soft robe, tying the sash securely before swinging her legs over the bed and adjusting the folds for comfort. She spotted her backpack, its straps askew, lying at the bottom of the wardrobe.

That's a relief.

The woman gestured; she should rise. Though Siana swayed while complying, the elder woman caught her and prevented a fall. Once steady, the elder woman guided her to the table. The table's light wood stood out against the walls.

Matching chairs, wall-colored upholstery, were placed side by side. The delay caused her stomach to protest audibly. The woman pulled out a chair for her, and Siana cautiously sat down.

This smells good!

Although the aroma of the food was incredibly tempting, she knew she hadn't eaten properly in days and that overeating would lead to the same fate as the berries—wasted. With a practiced hand, the elder poured a fragrant liquid from a small, ornate metal carafe into a waiting cup. As she watched the steam rise, the delicious smell of the tea filled the air. She decided to wait for it to cool.

The plush cushions had sunk beneath her, a stark contrast to the hard ground she'd recently called home. The experience felt surreal. Although hesitant, she accepted the offered food because she knew her body needed it. She couldn't rule out the possibility of poison, though. Once she understood the situation, she planned to seek help immediately to find Jacob. He was out there somewhere, and she wanted her brother back.

His words echoed in her mind: *If you are in an unfamiliar situation, remain silent. What you hear may surprise you.*

She didn't really have a choice. If she didn't understand them, there was a good chance they wouldn't understand her. The past several months taught her that silence was the key to survival. All survivors had adopted it as a habit. A single misplaced word, and the drones would detect it. It suddenly occurred to her that they were all speaking. All of them.

How did they remain undetected while living in this house?

Despite the silence rule, they weren't quiet. The man in the field shouted. Although she screamed, no drones materialized. The elder woman was speaking normally. As time passed, she grew increasingly bewildered.

We should all be dead by now.

Fork-like utensil in hand, she eyed her plate after the servant unveiled the food.

It looks like... eggs?

She wasn't sure. They were red, so she was really hoping it wasn't some sort of blood dish. Gingerly biting, she discovered it was indeed scrambled eggs. The red color was off-putting, but she was too hungry to be picky. The bread beside it radiated a cozy heat and was covered in a spread of a grayish hue. It honestly looked unappetizing as well. With a small, tentative bite, the flavor of sourdough lingered on her tongue, mixed with an unfamiliar taste. It wasn't jam, jelly, or butter. It had a creamy texture. Not unpleasant. She didn't know what it was, but hunger was a stern mistress. She ate with gratitude, praying nothing bad was in it. With the steam lessening, she picked up her tea, took a small sip, and let out a sigh.

Heaven.

She didn't know what kind it was, but it was wonderful.

Jacob would know.

She had so many questions: *Where is my brother? Where am I? How did I get here? Did that man bring me here? And, more importantly, who the heck undressed me?*

Given her present company, she assumed they did.

To her dismay, she could barely eat half of the food and only finished one cup of tea. The older woman encouraged her to eat, obviously worried about such a malnourished frame, but Siana shook her head and patted her belly to let her know she was full. The elder woman cocked her head, studying Siana for a short time before nodding and beckoning her to follow. As Siana rose from her chair, she noticed the sunlight glinting off a piece of jewelry on the woman's left hand. Siana's bladder spoke up. She cleared her throat, then wondered how best to make her point. Her subtle squirm caught the woman's attention. The older woman gestured for her to enter the right-hand door. Siana glanced in.

A bathroom! She almost cheered. *When was the last time she'd been able to use an actual toilet?*

However, this one was unusual compared to her norm. To the right of the doorway, a wide, marble-like tube extended from the floor. A brown, circular, cushioned seat encircled the top of the tube. Opposite the door was what she took to be a sink made from the same material as the tube. Siana hurried to the tube, assuming that's where she did her business. As she turned, she realized she was alone.

Good. Privacy.

She sighed in relief as her bladder emptied. Upon examining the room, she realized the walls had identical material covering them. However, there wasn't any toilet paper or cloths. With a searching glance, she saw a nozzle-like thing emerging from the wall near the tube, but out of reach, and a smaller one above the sink.

I guess I'm drip drying.

It wouldn't be the first time. Sometimes on their travels, whatever group they were with just didn't have or couldn't find what they needed. Drip drying was preferable to poison ivy.

The door swung open, admitting the younger woman. Adjusting her robe closed, at first hesitant, Siana showed she required something to clean herself. The woman looked at her in confusion, then pulled the nozzle from the wall. It connected to some sort of hose. She offered it to her. When Siana turned it in her hand, perplexed, the woman stared at her. She held the nozzle in front of Siana's face, demonstrating how to turn it to the setting needed. Taking one of Siana's hands, she pushed a small button on the side, and it activated. Aiming it at Siana's hand, she showed her how to use it; it washed and dried at the same time.

Well, that's cool.

The younger woman waved her hand at Siana's lower half, then turned her back. Understanding, Siana used the nozzle as intended, feeling refreshed and clean afterward. It was something she hadn't felt in months.

After Siana stood, she used the nozzle on her other hand, cleaning it. Once finished, she tapped the younger woman on the shoulder. The woman took the hose and showed her how to retract it into the wall. She beckoned Siana and led her to the sink.

From a wicker-like container on a nearby shelf, she gave Siana a twig. A further look of confusion crossed Siana's face. The woman's slightly exasperated expression was evident as she mimed chewing on the stick. She finally spoke to her. When Siana looked puzzled, she pointed to her throat and shook her head.

Don't swallow it. Got it.

Cautiously, she put the twig in her mouth and glanced at the other person to make sure she was doing it correctly. The woman gave her an encouraging nod. Siana began chewing. It didn't seem to have any flavor. The woman mimed moving the stick around and chewing. Siana copied her and realized her teeth felt clean wherever she chewed. She did so more enthusiastically.

Clean teeth. Another luxury. Odd how the basic necessities had become luxuries.

The woman seemed to assume Siana was an idiot and led her through using the smaller nozzle in her mouth. This time, it only rinsed, and she spat into the sink. Once finished, she took Siana's hand and led her out of the toilet room, through the bedroom, and into the door next to it. Flat gray stones, warm to the touch, formed the floors of both the toilet and bath rooms. This room felt warmer. A long, low tub, matching the toilet, occupied its center. Heated water filled it. Hands opening her robe caused Siana to grab it and hold it closed. This time, the woman gave her a fully exasperated look and scolded her. Too bad Siana didn't understand a word. She did, however, understand the intention behind them.

Do I care about modesty or an actual bath? she asked herself while the girl bored holes into her with her golden-brown eyes.

The bath won. Siana shed her robe, eased into the water, and settled down with a sigh of contentment. She blushed, noticing the woman's amused expression at her response. The woman put her robe in a nearby basket, then retrieved soap and a cloth. Siana felt her beginning to wash her back. She objected, twisted around, and tried to take the items to use herself, but found her hands being lightly slapped away as she was scolded again. Getting the idea she would lose this battle, she gave up.

Finishing her back, the woman unplugged a nozzle from the wall. Following some adjustments, she lifted Siana's chin, causing her to look at the ceiling. With warm water flowing from the nozzle, she started washing Siana's hair. As the maid massaged soap into Siana's scalp, she would occasionally glance at her face, studying it. It was a little disconcerting. Again, grabbing the nozzle, she rinsed off her hair. Siana didn't mind; she'd always loved having her hair played with and styled. She missed having that luxury. Since she wore her hair up at work most days, Jacob saw it as a waste. He didn't quite understand it wasn't the hair; it was the pampering.

Once finished, the woman fiddled with the nozzle and began using it near Siana's hairline, working her way to the ends. As she worked, she moved Siana's head to where she needed it. Siana wasn't sure, but it felt like her hair was being dried. Finished, she took a hair clip from her pocket and put Siana's hair up, clipping it near the top of her head. She gave her the cloth and soap, then left. Siana wasted no time washing the rest of her body. She absolutely did not want the woman doing it for her, especially when she saw how dark the water was becoming.

I know I'm dirty, but holy cow, that is nasty.

She knew wherever she was, they had money. The two women seemed more like servants than nurses. Only the wealthy could afford completely marble-clad bathrooms with servants.

It could be a survival compound. A new thought occurred to her. *Let's hope it's not a brothel.*

She knew the AI wouldn't have allowed that to survive and immediately dismissed it. Then again, how had these people survived living like this? The door swung open; the older woman walked in, followed by the younger. Outside the tub, the older one's hand pushed something, causing the water to drain. She gestured for Siana to rise.

Apparently, modesty isn't a thing here.

Slowly rising to avoid falling, Siana attempted to cover herself. The elderly woman seemed to understand but mostly disregarded it. Again, pulling out the nozzle, she repeated what the younger woman did, but this time it was her body being rinsed and dried. It felt good. Siana thought the elder hesitated when she reached her groin, but she used the nozzle down to her toes. With the task done, she helped Siana out of the tub and guided her out, while Siana desperately wanted her robe.

In the bedroom, both women started helping her get dressed. As she tried to dress herself, the younger woman knocked her hands away.

For a maid, the younger one seems a bit physical.

First, she donned men's boxer-like underpants, a supportive fabric across her chest, and a short-sleeved, emerald-green cotton dress reaching her lower calf. The rounded collar nearly reached her neck. Guided to a desk chair, the older woman fastened her dress while the younger slipped on ballet shoes. Dress and shoes were the same color and a little too big for her. Finishing, the elder woman commented, departing.

The remaining woman opened a drawer and took out what appeared to be hairpins and a comb. Siana's curls cascaded down her back as she released the clip. The woman picked up a section to study it. Returning the comb to the drawer, she then used her hands to comb Siana's hair. From the same drawer, she retrieved a bottle, and after applying some of its contents to her hands and rubbing them, ran her hands through Siana's hair. The oil had a faint lavender scent. She stepped forward, examining Siana's face. The servant moved behind her, picking up sections of hair to loosely French braid.

I miss being pampered. While manicures weren't her thing, she enjoyed massages and hair styling.

Once finished, the maid stepped away and examined her work. Seemingly satisfied, she put the remaining items away. The woman stood before Siana, studying her.

Finally, pointing to herself, she said, "*To betz* Brigitte."

Then the woman indicated Siana with a questioning expression.

She had to process what she'd heard. As she saw the woman waiting, she pointed and asked, "Brigitte?"

Brigitte smiled and nodded.

Siana pointed to herself and said, "Siana."

In response, she received a warm smile.

Brigitte pointed at her and repeated, "Siana," and received a nod.

Brigitte, using her hands, imitated the size and height of the older woman. "*Metz* Atwood," she said.

Siana repeated, "*Metz* Atwood."

Brigitte gave her a pleased smile.

Siana wasn't sure if *Metz* was a name or title.

Metz Atwood came back soon after and spoke to Brigitte. In exchange, Brigitte disclosed the name of their guest. The woman's expression showed surprise.

Turning to the still sitting woman, she asked, "Siana?"

Siana nodded.

Metz Atwood clapped her hands together in delight. She quickly left after speaking to Brigitte. Brigitte gestured for Siana to follow, and they exited the room together. Siana hoped it wouldn't lead to her doom. Though she was at least well-fed and clean.

Chapter Five

TAMEK'S FACE WAS A mask of frustration, his jaw clenched tight, eyes narrowed in anger. He paced the morning room, having forgotten his breakfast. His silver hair, which fell just below his shoulder, followed behind him, the two front braids falling down the sides swinging independently with each turn, his loose hair following like the train of a dress. His late arrival last night prevented Lorica from updating him sooner.

They rejected his petition for a law change he was passionate about, and then a female arrived at their doorstep. This wasn't good. In fact, it would cause them serious issues. Others would gleefully use those issues to their advantage against them. They were one of the few houses that opposed certain laws when it came to females.

He spun to face his younger brother. "Are you sure she isn't a child?" *We can work with a child.*

Lorica leaned forward, resting his arms on the heavy wood table. "Unless she's a well-developed child, I'd say no despite her small size. However, it may be possible she's defective. She seems like a simpleton. She couldn't answer any of the questions I asked her or"—Lorica's face turned thoughtful—"didn't want to."

"If we can't find her family, we'll have to see how much she knows and can learn, especially if she's simple. We'll have to gain her trust so we can find her a claimant. Since she'll be under our House, it will become our responsibility," Tamek said, voicing his thoughts out loud.

He noticed Lorica hungrily eyeing his untouched food. Lorica's longing look changed to impassive as he caught his brother's gaze. His brother loved riling him, and stealing his food would do it, but he had to be smart enough to know now wasn't a good time. Plus, he'd already eaten before Tamek had come down.

He refocused his thoughts. Their laws required females, once they had reached maturity, be claimed by a male. Death of the claimant was the only exception to the law against remaining single. The scarcity of females meant that any eligible one would have many claimants vying for her affections, including males as determined and ruthless as Talon.

Tamek thought over what he was told by Lorica and Mrs. Atwood. They'd told him about several physical variations between her and other *Setan* females that were noticeable. He worried about her safety above all else; her imperfections might unexpectedly help her. Her discovery on their land, with no male present, placed her under their protection. It became their duty to locate a suitable mate for her, keep her from the Talons of the world, all while ensuring her well-being and providing for her care.

However, given House Devereaux's stance on these issues, her presence could put them in a critical position. They opposed claiming and the way females were treated. Tamek was House Head. He would take her safety seriously. Anything less was unthinkable. As he let out a harsh breath, the weight of such a task heavy on his mind, Brigitte entered the room, trailed by someone he took to be their new house guest.

With an assessing look, he admitted she was attractive. He'd give her that. Attractive, though not breathtaking. A touch of sunburn marked her skin, yet her eyes were clear and widened when he came into her view. He brushed that off as insignificant. The High and Middles would line up for that hair alone—if she was within those circles. The thought of filtering through males clamoring for her made him want to take an extended holiday to the deep country.

Given the condition of her skin, he doubted she was High. They tended to be quite particular about their facial skin. Lorica also wasn't exaggerating. Her small stature compared to theirs made him doubt her suitability to be claimed. His quick, purposeful strides took him across the room to stand in front of her. She stepped back, eyeing him warily. He gave her a measuring look. He at least knew her name, thanks to Mrs. Atwood.

***

When Siana first entered, the wall of windows caught her attention. Floor to ceiling, uncovered, the expanse outside visible to all, the greenery showcased between the panes. Majestically tall, green hedges, vibrant and lush, seemed to strain to look at those in the room. A round wooden table with matching wooden chairs encircling it stood in front of the window. A red and blue rug covered almost all the wood flooring. She didn't notice the men until she had fully entered. Incomprehension filled Siana as she stood, eyes wide, staring at the man standing near the table. This man's height exceeded the first's by at least half a head.

However, what caught her attention were the pointed ears visible between the strands of his long hair. She glanced at Brigitte and realized she, too, had pointed ears, but the scarf wrapped around her head hid them. Siana hadn't noticed them because their outline was barely visible. She also failed to notice the blond tendrils that had come loose from her head wrap. The man at the table, whom she recognized as the one who saved her, had thick hair that hid his ears. In her distress, she had fainted before she saw the men with him properly. The one with armor, who had stayed, wore a helmet.

I must be dead or comatose. Elves? Seriously? Maybe I've read too many fantasy books because, come on, elves? What is going on?

As the taller one approached, his silver robe the same color as his swinging hair, she stepped backward. He appeared to be on the verge of walking right over her. His intense blue gaze, less brilliant than the other man, seemed to penetrate her very being. His features strongly resembled those of the other, implying they were related. The swift movement of his hand made her flinch; a wave of unease washed over her as she recoiled. Though she leaned away, he slowed, and hesitantly reached out to gently touch her rounded ear. He gazed into her eyes, his brow furrowing with thought.

Brigitte stepped forward. Pointing to the man in front of her, Brigitte said, "Tamek." Her voice was calm while Tamek gave her a disapproving stare.

Pointing at the man seated at the table, she said, "Lorica."

She received a surprised eyebrow raise from him.

Pointing to Tamek again, she said, "*Bund* Tamek." Then, "*Bund* Lorica."

They had titles. Mister? There wasn't enough context to know.

Brigitte turned to her. "*Okoos?*"

Okoos? What did that mean?

Brigitte repeated herself and actions. Again, she looked at Siana, raised her eyebrows, and asked, "*Okoos?*"

I don't understand. Wait...

Thinking for a minute while everyone watched her expectantly, she tried to decipher the word.

Understand? Is that what she's asking?

Pointing to the man in front of her, she said, "*Bund* Tamek?"

Brigitte nodded.

Pointing to the dark-haired one, she said, "*Bund* Lorica?" Her voice caught slightly as she stumbled over his name, but she managed to say it correctly.

Brigitte nodded, smiling. "*Toda Okoos.*"

Great. She added an unfamiliar word, but that's okay. I need to learn their language, so I can find my brother. Context clues. If "okoos" is understand, then "toda" is... Hmm, it wasn't a question. It was a statement. You understand. Maybe?

To aid her memory, Siana softly repeated each name and word to herself, a nervous energy driving her.

The silver-haired one said something to Siana.

Bund Tamek, she reminded herself.

His brow furrowed as he said something else to her. It sounded like a question, but Siana wasn't sure. He repeated it.

She nervously looked around the room as they all stared at her. Looking back at him, she hesitantly gave a shrug and a small shake of her head, hoping he'd know she didn't understand.

Tamek let out a sigh and said something to Brigitte.

Brigitte motioned for her to follow, and Siana left the room with her.

***

"She obviously didn't understand me, but she was taught our names." Tamek was glad she could learn, though he'd wanted to question her to begin with. Her taking instruction helped, but did they have time?

He turned to Lorica, asking, "Did anyone see you bring her in?"

Lorica shook his head. "Just mine and the House's guards. I deliberately kept her hidden. Out of everyone, Kell would be the best person to figure out what's going on with her. Honestly, he has a lot more patience and kindness than you or I. We also need to hide her quickly. Given her size, and his issues, he may be the best claim for her."

***

Siana, having gone through the house's enormous double doors—nearly twins of her bedroom's—followed the maid outside. Her eyes took in the grounds. They were beautiful. Lush, bluish-green hedges divided the area into sections. Some held flowers, others looked like fruit trees, and another looked like the entrance to a hedge maze, which was the direction Brigitte led her. Five rounded white steps, steep for Siana but perfect for the homeowners, led down from the house. Even Brigitte, with her shorter stature compared to the others, was considerably taller. Siana, considered tall for a woman, felt surprisingly short.

I'm going to end up with a sore neck.

The steps led to what appeared to be a circular driveway inlaid with white-looking bricks, which they followed to a path of similar stone "bricks." Siana briefly turned back to glance at the house. It was a perfect imitation of a French Château; crenelations topped the walls, and a vast courtyard, filled with the scent of flowers, stretched out before ending in the hedge maze. The entrance to the maze led to a series of shadowy alcoves, where Siana found benches placed thoughtfully among the high hedges, each one promising a quiet rest. At the start of their walk, Brigitte began by pointing to various things, saying their names, and having Siana repeat them while they wandered the grounds.

Just like you would with a child.

At one point, she told Brigitte, after she'd said her name for the millionth time, "Sia."

Brigitte looked confused.

She said, "Sia. Siana," and shrugged, showing she didn't care which.

Brigitte, eyes brightening, smiled and repeated, "Sia."

Time slipped by. As midday approached, her head swam. Siana felt guilty when she thought about not looking for

Jacob and the field, but she had to learn. That was the primary goal: learn the language, figure out where she was, and find Jacob, hopefully, with these people's help.

If they were good, she reminded herself. So far, they hadn't given her any reason to believe otherwise, but she hadn't been here long.

Brigitte guided her toward what she thought were stables; the warmth radiating from the building and the animals moving within enveloped her as she approached. The path changed from smooth, worn brick to rough, uneven stone, a noticeable shift under her feet. She noticed the extensive use of wood. The stables were no different.

Was it wood from the grounds?

Entering, the smell of fresh bedding and manure hit her. Several beasts of various colors occupied open stalls. She saw their heads resembled those of birds, yet they lacked feathers. They had shaggy fur, six hooved legs, intelligent eyes, and short beaks. The four present watched her curiously. Siana became captivated by them, holding a stall wall to steady herself as she swayed.

When she glanced at Brigitte, she saw the concern on the servant's face as her eyes stared back. A warm, supporting arm encircled her shoulders, and Brigitte guided her out of the stables, down a wildflower-lined path, and to a white brick patio with a charming, round gazebo.

A warm wood table and chairs were set up inside. Brigitte gave her a small, almost apologetic smile, eyes worried. Her hand raised as she made a "stay" motion, then she gestured she was going to get food and drink.

Siana gratefully nodded. She wasn't sure she could make it back to the house in her weakened state. As Brigitte was leaving, Siana closed her eyes for a minute, tired. The cooling sensation of the gentle breeze made her pause and savor the moment—a rare sense of relaxation.

I could easily fall asleep here.

She gave a small smile, wondering when she last felt safe enough to sleep outside without a watch. They were usually rotating guard duty while others in the group slept. Only the children managed a full night's sleep. It was imperative that the guard woke anyone who snored or made any other noises.

A man's voice interrupted her reverie. Gray eyes, familiar ones, stared back at her as she opened her eyes. The nursing part of her decided the whites of his eyes looked unhealthy. Yellowish, almost like his liver was failing. He again said something, but she didn't understand him. When her mind finally processed it, she knew who he was. She stood, her heart pounding, then moved away from him. She glanced at the gazebo, noticing the fabric used as screening, the dark wood and the only exit directly behind him, a tantalizingly close yet frustratingly out-of-reach goal.

He smiled. It wasn't a kind smile; it was predatory, unnerving. It made her skin crawl. Despite his further comments, her expression betrayed a lack of understanding. With a quick grab of her arm as she tried to run past, he pulled her close and pinned her to him. With her face pressed against his shirt, its smell made her nose itch. He murmured something in her ear as he caressed her buttocks. The shock of seeing him vanished as the hem of her dress lifted; then, still weak, she fought back. His grip felt like steel. She tried to escape, knocking over a couple of chairs. A hand groped beneath her dress. She fought to evade him and block his move at the same time.

He spun her around, bending her over the table with his weight. Air hit her legs as his hand lifted her skirt. Desperately kicking back at him, a hand tried to find its way into her underpants. Siana clamped her thighs together so he couldn't touch her, but her position gave him some access.

Despite pushing with her arms against the rocking table, its unstable surface and his heavy weight pinned her down. She cursed her weak and tired body as she reached back, desperate to scratch any reachable spot. Her hand felt hair and her fingers fumbled for even a single strand. He pulled his head away right as she gained hold, and a few strands stayed entwined around her fingers. A sharp sting on her backside let her know he didn't appreciate it, and she heard him say something as she cried out in pain.

Tears starting, she tried letting her legs buckle so she could get under the table. He held her firm. Upon hearing his pants being undone, she bent down and clamped her jaw on the closest arm. He let go, yanking his arm away from the pain, and she took advantage. Throwing herself backward, she knocked him off balance, both falling. The cold stone of the patio felt rough against her hands as she pushed herself up and ran for the door.

Her body was still too weak, but she tried to run as fast as she could. Desperately trying to remember the way to the house, she ran for the tall hedges. If nothing else, maybe she could lose him in the maze. Scarcely a few feet into it, a hand grabbed her hair. She felt herself being tossed sideways. Harsh hands grabbed the front of her dress, tearing it, pulling her slightly off the ground. He raised one to strike her, but he couldn't follow through. *Bund* Tamek had grabbed it.

Chapter Six

"*BUND* TALON!" THE garden resonated with *Bund* Tamek's commanding voice. Talon, yanking his hand back, slowly stood, rubbing where Tamek had grabbed, defiant. Siana stood unsteadily, adjusted her dress, and hastened to her rescuer. Brigitte moved past him and grabbed her hand. Out of the corner of his eye, he saw Lorica motioning for them to leave. The two females raced back to the house.

Short of breath, full of indignation, Tamek masked it. Keeping control of his eye color proved more of a challenge. Brigitte had run inside, shouting furiously that Talon was on their grounds and moving toward their visitor. Because she knew their laws prevented her—a Low—from touching him, she ran home. Lorica and he had scrambled to get here. He saw the stark terror in Siana's eyes; her disheveled dress and hair were a testament to the struggle. Talon's hand was a blur of motion about to land. Instinctively, he had grabbed it, barely restraining himself from breaking it.

Talon has set his sights on her, but to have the gall to come so close to the house uninvited and attack a female on our lands, under our protection, is unconscionable.

The male may not know she was now under their protection, but that gave him no excuse for his actions, especially since he had to trespass to do it. Siana being on their lands was enough to show their protection, and Talon knew this.

Talon rose with an expression Tamek was more than familiar with. His previous outburst at Talon had occurred before the Convocation—their ruling body. Talon's brother had taken Tamek's claim, killing her. Talon had defended his brother, making horrible comments about Usala. Tamek's striking of the male led to a sanction by the High Chancellor. The laws prohibited violence in the Hall. Technically, Tamek had punched him in the face, breaking his nose, and wanted to do so again. Facing him, under similar conditions as before, he swore it would not end the same way, by the hit or the female.

Tamek fought to keep his face and eyes stoic. If Talon thought he was getting a reaction, it would just add fuel to the fire. With his gaze fixed on the male before him, he prayed his younger brother would control himself. A quick glance showed Lorica was furious. Talon once again was acting like he owned their lands.

Lorica, turning his face temporarily out of Talon's view, murmured, "He almost succeeded. I will place one of my guards on her. It will give them a reason to do their worst to him."

"What are you doing here?" Tamek asked in a forced monotone, not responding to his brother's words.

"Why, a little bird told me you brought the unclaimed female here. I came to see for myself. After all, she screamed so nicely in the field, and any solo unclaimed female is up for grabs." He shrugged nonchalantly. "I want her. With her small size, I'm sure her screams will be"—he licked his lips—"more delicious."

Only a fool wouldn't understand his implication. The brothers were well aware of Talon's enjoyment in causing pain to females. Both brothers also knew Talon had someone in their midst. Since Talon's lands were next to theirs, that meant it could be anyone. He'd arrived quickly. Tamek began going through possible suspects in his mind and made a mental note to have one of his guards investigate. He knew Lorica would do the same. They'd start with Brigitte. She most likely saw something she didn't have time to impart.

"That doesn't give you the right to come uninvited and try to claim her. She is under our protection. You know our laws," Tamek stated. *Which the male frequently got away with breaking because of bribery, though that seemed to be changing.*

"We-e-e-ll," Talon said in a singsong voice, "you know what happens when you leave your females unattended." He gave Tamek a fake smile, which turned genuine when the head of House Devereaux stiffened.

Tamek saw Lorica's face darken. He half hoped he would kill the male, especially after that comment, but that would cost them their House. Neither would give Talon that satisfaction.

Lorica asked, "Did you not notice she's defective? She's also a simpleton. Surely you realized she couldn't understand you. Are you blind in addition to being stupid?" Talon's body tensed. "Besides"—Lorica shrugged—"Kellan has already staked his claim. That's why she's here. You and I both know that's the best he'll be able to do."

Though Lorica sounded disdainful, Tamek knew he looked up to their eldest brother. He also knew Lorica hated saying that last part. Guilt still ate at their youngest sibling over the accident.

Tamek lacked the mental strength to tolerate the male in front of him at that moment. In addition, he feared fulfilling both brothers' wishes. He'd be glad to either murder the male or deliver him to Lorica's soldiers. They'd long been sick of him.

"As Lorica stated, she is already claimed. Her family and ours have an agreement," he lied. "We're waiting for Kellan to return to complete the deal. Now leave and do not return to our lands without permission again. The Convocation has already warned you about it."

***

Talon narrowed his eyes. He hated the youngest Devereaux. Lorica was known as the most handsome male of their race. Smooth skin, long, dark, wavy hair, his blue eyes were luminescent.

No one had the right to look that good.

He wanted to take a knife to his face, but that would probably only enhance it. Even females who were already claimed about fell over themselves to get his attention. He was also almost positive Lorica had Talon's younger brother killed over a female, of all things, but he could never find proof.

"I don't believe you. What female would accept someone with that appearance?"

Both brothers kept their faces composed.

He sneered. "I return; then what? Nothing! You are a coward and will always be one." Talon gave a smug look at

Tamek. He well knew Tamek wasn't a coward. It had taken weeks for his nose to heal.

Talon saw the red flash in Tamek's eyes and knew he'd gone too far with the Head of the House.

I need to leave before someone breaks my nose, or worse.

He began to leave, then paused and said, "If she remains unclaimed at the end of one lunar cycle, I will petition the Convocation for a *Yendali*. She will follow Usala's path if unclaimed, but this time with me."

This time, both brothers' eyes went red. Talon hurriedly took his leave, knowing that if he pushed his luck, it was possible Lorica's foreign guards would do much worse than bruise his torso. Besides, he had to plan how this latest claim's death would go. Now that his family no longer had control of the Hall, he wanted to draw it out. Who knew when he'd get another chance?

***

Brigitte hurried Siana to her room. Both women were shaking.

Brigitte kept repeating, her voice quavering, "*Iz avi. Iz avi.*"

Siana had no idea what it meant, but for now, she didn't care. The urge to scrub herself overwhelmed her. Each recollection of his touch triggered an urge to retch. Not once, but twice. A few times, Jacob and she had witnessed aggression and violence, yet this felt far more disturbing. Survival of the fittest was the primary rule then; a world devoid of law. Today felt like a game.

As they entered the bedchamber, Siana saw Brigitte wave her hand at the door after it closed. Brigitte grabbed Siana's hand and pulled her further into the room. As Brigitte's hands moved through her hair, hand combing and pinning it up, Sia trembled uncontrollably.

What kind of place is this? I want my brother.

A desire for the familiar caused tears to form and her breathing to accelerate. Hands on the back of her neck caused her to jump before she realized the buttons were being undone and she was stripped down. Her underpants had a tear. Siana heard a low gasp as she removed them. Anxiously, she looked back and saw Brigitte staring at her backside. Looking down at herself, she couldn't see anything without a mirror.

If it's looking that bad already, he must have hit it just right.

Brigitte wrapped a soft, blue robe around her and motioned that she'd be back. Siana gently sat and waited.

Why? Why was that man set on hurting her? Who was he? Thankful as she was for her hosts' timely arrival, Siana didn't understand why the man was on their property. Was he related? A trespasser? She needed a weapon.

Wait. Where's my knife?

Before she arrived, she had attached her hunting knife to her pants. She needed it and had completely forgotten about it. She'd also kept a pocketknife in her back pocket while on her survival journey. It was a simple one her father had given her before cancer took him. She hoped it wasn't lost.

I don't remember seeing either at all since I arrived here.

She became lost in her own thoughts, trying to sort what she'd learned so far. The opening door surprised her and brought her back to the present. Catching sight of Brigitte studying her, carrying in a tray with a carafe on it, Siana questioned whether this was typical of this place or simply her bad luck. Jacob would have beaten the crap out of the man on sight. Granted, she didn't know what the brothers—she assumed they were—were doing.

Brigitte showed her a jar of salve and motioned what it was for. Siana didn't argue, and stood as Brigitte opened the robe and massaged it gently on the bruising skin. Afterward, she set the jar on the desk. Brigitte then guided her to the table. She poured Sia the tea she'd brought, urging her to drink up.

Again, she said, "*Iz avi,*" with a sad smile.

Is she saying I'm sorry? She probably feels bad about leaving me alone.

As she sipped her tea, she recognized the chamomile flavor. After a hectic shift, she would make herself a cup before bed. It was a welcome reminder of home. Brigitte poured her another cup and urged her to drink it after she finished the first. Siana gladly did so as *Metz* Atwood entered the room. In her hands, she carried the clothes Sia arrived in, though they looked a lot cleaner. She looked at them with a questioning stare, then realized.

Unexpected guest. They probably have nothing else for me to wear now that that ass ruined what I was wearing.

Slowly standing to check her old clothes, she found they were all there. The black jeans held nothing. Neither knife was with the clothes.

How do I ask about them?

Brigitte helped her change back into the clothes, eyeing them curiously as she did so. She seemed particularly taken with the zipper on the pants. She urged Siana to sit back at the table and poured her a third cup. Siana didn't really want it, but Brigitte's concerned look made her give in and drink it. Both were watching her.

They probably think I'm going to have a fit of vapors or whatever they have here.

Metz Atwood said something to Brigitte, who answered her. They spoke too fast for her to catch any words to decipher. Her head spun, and the world tilted as a dizzying wave crashed over her. With a glance at her teacup, the thought occurred to her that she may have overdone it.

Two attacks within two days are too much for anyone, even when not including elves, starvation, bots, and an estate tour.

The weight of sleep pressed down on her, her head heavy and her eyelids drooping.

"*Iz avi,*" Brigitte murmured, her voice barely audible, echoing as if spoken from a faraway land. Muffled. Looking at her, Siana's vision became blurry.

They drugged me. I need to get out of here. Damn me for trusting them.

Standing, she took a step to escape; the floor rushed up to meet her. *Metz* Atwood had been waiting and caught her. Siana's last sight was her sad face as she said in the gentlest of voices, "*Iz avi. Tona nempor pend toda.*"

Chapter Seven

SIANA SLID IN and out of consciousness.

Someone moving her limbs.

She made a noise.

What's happening?

A woman's voice making comforting sounds.

A man's voice.

People talking.

Someone lifted her.

She tried to raise her head.

A man's soft voice. "*Iz avi. Jeno.*"

I don't understand.

She felt herself being put inside something hard. *A box?*

Wake up.

She was moving. It wasn't comfortable, but she couldn't speak to tell them.

Hot. She tried to open her eyes. *Dark.*

So sleepy.

Through her eyelids, the dark lightened.

Cool air brushed over her as she was lifted out of the box by multiple hands.

Strong arms cradling.

An outdoorsy scent.

What's happening?

A sound of fear escaped her.

A man's soothing voice reassured her.

Sleep called, and she couldn't resist answering.

Siana's eyes opened; she was somewhere new. With blurry vision and a head full of cotton wool, she rubbed her eyes, each movement slow and labored. Her lids didn't want to stay open. She rubbed her eyes again, the blurry world slowly coming into focus as she woke. It took a minute for her mind to start working.

They drugged me! Why?

Her brain tried to work out the "whys." She looked around as she tried to sit.

"Ow." She winced. The bruise on her backside reminded her to be careful.

Despite the absence of windows, low-level lighting revealed bare, undecorated white walls. Curiously, she couldn't see any light fixtures. The bed, along with the table and chairs in the corner, were functional. All of them were made of light brown wood. Metal spindles were on the headboard and footboard. Gray blankets covered her. She was relieved to find she remained dressed.

The opening door startled her. A woman, completely in burgundy, from her head wrap to her shoes, bustled in. Her loose slacks and short-sleeved tunic flowed freely. Over her arm, she had something cream in color.

Seeing her awake, she smiled and nodded at Siana, who warily returned the nod. The woman came over to her, pointed to herself, and said, "*Be* Tess."

She said, "Siana," as she pointed to her, showing she knew her name.

Siana nodded while wondering if that was her full name, her first, or if a title was involved.

Be Tess beckoned Siana to stand.

Suspiciously eyeing the new woman, she did so. She did not have a good track record with these people. Her entire body felt like it was in molasses. Moving was somewhat difficult. The woman guided her to a door and gestured for her to go inside. As she peered around the entry, she found it was the toilet. She provided Siana with a cloth and privacy. Simple wood formed the toilet's tube and seat. Wood planks covered the floor.

Less luxurious than the other place.

She didn't care. After using the restroom and cloth, she saw a basket and threw the item into it. She stood and stretched to get her body moving again. Her mouth felt like she'd been munching on one of her dogs, and she desperately wanted the taste gone. Walking to the sink, she spotted a basket of twigs and took one to chew on. She realized there were no nozzles in this toilet. There was, however, a pitcher with water, a bowl, and a cup. She was used to this. Rarely did any of the camps Jacob and she stayed at have running water. People usually fetched water from a stream or a river. Siana poured a bit of the water into the cup, rinsed her mouth, and spit it back in. She didn't see a place to put what remained of the stick, so she laid it next to the bowl.

As she was setting down the cup, there was a quick knock at the door and *Be* Tess entered without waiting for a response. She brought another pitcher containing warm water, which she poured into the bowl. The woman reached into the cabinet under it, pulling out soap, a cloth, and a larger cloth. She placed them next to the bowl, mimed a thorough washing, and indicated the gown hanging on the hook by the door.

Even though she had bathed yesterday, she felt grimy from the travel while she slept and that man's attack, so she would not argue about it. Some people bathed to relax, but for Siana, it had the opposite effect: it woke her up.

It didn't take long for me to get used to bathing again. Was it force of habit taking over or the ease of convenience?

Be Tess encouraged Siana to undress, collecting the clothes as she went. Siana stopped when she reached for her underwear, but the woman pointedly stared at them, at Siana's face, and back at the undergarments, raising an eyebrow and giving her a look that clearly said "I'm waiting."

She could easily be a drill sergeant. I swear these people have never heard of modesty.

Siana turned her back and stripped down.

A horrified gasp from behind made her realize her bruise was worse than she initially believed. When Siana finished, Tess gave a satisfied grunt, threw the clothes into the basket, lifted it, and left. Siana quickly washed everything she could before the woman came back and she lost her privacy.

I haven't bathed this much in weeks. I bet Jacob would love to have a bath.

He liked to sing when showering, which he wasn't great at. He wasn't ear-splitting terrible, but he did like to hurt her ears occasionally. Siana felt it was deliberate. He was so bad that once, when they were teens, she'd shut off the hot water to the bathroom. His yell had her watching her back for weeks. As she smiled at the memory of his indignant face, she reached for the sleeveless gown.

I wish you were here to help me figure out what's going on.

As concerned as she was about finding him, she knew he was resourceful. As a botanist for the government forestry service, he'd run into many a problem that had to be solved in the field. Truth be told, he was probably doing much better than her and was most likely already searching for her.

I hope we don't miss each other in the search.

She slipped the gown over her head. She realized many had worn the garment. Though not transparent, the fabric was becoming noticeably thinner. The chest area was open almost to her navel. Down the front, evenly spaced mismatched ties extended from an inch below the collarbone's top to an inch from the bottom. The hemline reached just below her knees. She expected the dress to be too big, given her size, and it was.

This front is too open for my liking; I feel a draft and exposed. It feels like it's going to fall off. Granted, the ties keep it shut, but still. And seriously, no underwear?

She had just realized all she had to put on was the gown. At least, it was long enough to cover the important parts.

Maybe she just forgot about it and will bring it in a minute.

Be Tess knocked, and once again entered without waiting. After eyeing the gowned female, she gave another satisfied grunt, and waved Siana to follow, which she hesitantly did. They walked through the bedroom, but there was no underwear in sight.

As she followed *Be* Tess through the doorway, Siana found herself in a room that felt oddly familiar, the worn wooden floorboards creaking softly beneath her feet, a slight smell of something she knew in the air. Wood shelves and cabinets, some worn from age, lined three of the four walls, which were white on the top half and deep red on the bottom. On the remaining wall was a simple wood exterior door with a small window next to it, giving her the barest glimpse of the outside. Tables lined the remaining wall space, each holding various items. A long, narrow wooden table in the center of the room caused her concern, and something metal hung from the middle of the side facing her. A small stool stood at the end.

What is that table for?

Books on a nearby shelf caught her eye. After looking at them, she slowly walked around, examining each shelf, while the woman just watched her, and she realized why it seemed familiar: it was an infirmary.

Chapter Eight

SIANA NEARLY JUMPED OUT of her skin. How on earth she hadn't seen the man standing in the corner, next to a bookcase, was beyond her. He wasn't exactly small. She should have immediately noticed his impressive height. His facial features reminded her of the men at the house, and she stared.

His hair was long and black, darker than *Bund* Lorica's. From each temple, two neatly plaited braids extended to the back of his head, the dark strands catching the room light. Each side also had a braid hanging down in front, with the rest of his hair loose. It fell to just below his shoulders, with the braids landing slightly above the rest. His blue eyes sparkled and watched her with interest. The lines at the corners showed he laughed a lot. His skin was darker than the others, which only accented his eyes. Unlike the others, he had a bit of a five o'clock shadow. Part of her brain admitted he looked like her type. She'd always been a sucker for facial light and dark contrasts. Her preference was light or bright eyes, dark hair with darker skin. *Check, check, and check.*

The raised skin and borders of a scar streaked across the left side of his face from his eye and temple, down his face, covered his cheek from lip to ear and disappeared into his shirt. Siana recognized the scars. At some point in his life, he had been in a fire. While it didn't look like he'd worn compression garments, the scars seemed to have healed well. While plainly visible, she had seen worse, but she wondered about their treatment. Their lack of advanced technology was evident from the infirmary's rough-hewn wooden tables and absence of advanced equipment. Aware he knew she was seeing the white, angry marks on his skin, she deliberately redirected her attention to his eyes.

His kind smile, crinkling the corners of his eyes, made her heart skip a beat. His face lit up; it was like his mouth had thrown a party and his entire face was invited. His features were reshaped, his expression softened; it completely changed the way he looked. He wasn't bad to begin with, but that smile, a flash of white teeth against tanned skin, was completely captivating.

The man pointed to himself. "Kellan."

Siana dutifully repeated his name, wondering who and what he was.

That somehow made him smile wider. He pointed again at himself. "*Lodan* Kellan."

He didn't have Bund *like the others, so maybe not closely related?*

Pointing at her, then at the end of the table, he said, "*Zel.*"

Siana wasn't sure what he was saying, and it showed.

He pointed to the stool, then to himself, a small smile playing on his lips as he uttered, "Kellan, *zel*," the words sounding oddly melodic, as he sat on the stool. With dawning understanding, she cautiously moved to the end of the table. He quickly scooted the stool and himself out of the way, the legs scraping on the wooden floor.

Siana, keeping a suspicious eye on him, hitched up her skirt and, with a step onto the cold stool beneath the table, sat on the edge. Kellan encouraged her to scoot back a bit and reached out to examine her ears. Siana leaned away, her face revealing her suspicion.

He sat back and said something to *Be* Tess. Her eyebrows shot up in surprise as she looked at him. Turning on his smile, he tilted his head slightly, seeming to plead with her. He received narrowed eyes in refusal. He smiled even more and said something. *Be* Tess rolled her eyes and huffed.

With a loud, affected cough, she dramatically clutched her forehead, her other hand fluttering in front of her mouth, a gesture of mock fragility. She shuffled toward him, slumping over.

Kellan, looking suitably horrified at her state, cried out. He hurriedly, exaggeratedly, grabbed a device from the table behind him. Arms swinging wide, he placed it on her forehead. Aghast at the reading, he pretended to swoon, forearm on his forehead. He examined her eyes dramatically, made a big deal out of her throat, walked in a manner reminiscent of a cartoon character to a cabinet, pulled out a bottle, showed it dramatically to Siana, handed it to his "patient," and she said, "*Velta toda, Lodan!*" and walked away looking normal. The over-the-top melodrama unfolding before her was so reminiscent of an old vaudeville show that, despite her caution, Siana had to hide a smile behind her hand.

Kellan, looking quite proud of his performance, turned to Siana and asked, "*Ookos?*"

If she was right, *Lodan* Kellan was *Doctor* Kellan. So, *velta toda* was thank you? Or goodbye? With a twinkle in her eyes that showed amusement, she repeated the phrase in their tongue. Doctor Kellan's disarming grin about split his face. She could watch that smile all day.

His face turned thoughtful, and he addressed *Be* Tess, eliciting an annoyed response. He pleaded with his boyish grin. She gave in again. Siana felt like she gave in a lot. She was older, so it felt like a mother and son relationship, though they didn't look alike as far as facial features went. His cheekbones were higher, and there were no similarities.

Once again, she pulled her coughing act. Kellan looked at Siana, then at *Be* Tess. He pointed at her, then at Siana. With his hand on his chin, he appeared to be pondering the problems of the world. *Be* Tess moved spots and pretended to be cheerful and talkative. Again, Kellan pointed between the two, furrowed his brow, and made his contemplative face. He pointed at Siana, looked at his upheld left hand as if in deep thought, then his upheld right hand, moving them up and down as if weighing them, his head tilted, eyes up, as if judging them.

He wants to know if I'm sick or healthy.

In other words, she was about to get a physical. Siana nodded, a slight tremor in her hands betraying the uncertainty hidden behind her calm facade.

He clapped his hands together with excitement, glancing at her hands, then looked away, keeping his smile. He motioned to *Be* Tess, said something, and clapped while she took a bow. Then he bowed while she clapped. Siana chuckled at their antics, gave in to the humor, and softly clapped for them both. It felt so *normal*. Not like life had been recently.

As long as the result finds Jacob. Her smile faded.

He moved to stand before her, bending and offering his warmest, most charming smile, his breath ghosting her face.

He definitely knows how his smile affects people.

Doctor Kellan stepped back and dramatically cleared his throat, which got Siana's attention. In a comical display of preparation for her exam, he cracked his knuckles with a loud *pop*, shook his hands vigorously, performed a couple of squats, and topped it all off with a playful wiggle of his eyebrows. It had the desired effect, and she gave him another amused smile. She'd bet a year's worth of supplies he was a hit with the kids.

As he drew near, he halted, arms outstretched, his eyes carefully studying her face.

Was he waiting for permission?

He placed his hands on her head; the warmth of his skin seeped through her hair, and she didn't stop him. He said something to *Be* Tess, and she gathered paper and what looked like writing supplies. With a soft sigh, she began taking notes as Kellan's practiced hands moved over Siana's body, the silence broken only by the rustle of paper.

With a gentle, but firm touch, his experienced fingers traced the contours of her skull, feeling for any irregularities. Their movement was slow and deliberate across her forehead, down her nose—a playful boop interrupted the process, causing her to start, eyes wide—and then across her cheekbones, ears, and jawline. He examined every inch of her head with his eyes and hands. Occasionally he'd say something and *Be* Tess would write it down. When he moved within her eyesight, she watched him. His serious expression was at odds with his earlier playful attitude.

He moved to her side, his touch featherlight as he inspected her left ear, his fingers following its contours. Siana realized it felt good and not in the doctor/patient sense. A certain area started waking up. He inspected the right ear after finishing. She made herself breathe normally. It had been a long time since a man had touched her like this, and she was definitely feeling it. He moved behind her, gently nudging her head forward, the soft strands of her hair falling away as his fingers traced the curve of her neck. The back of her neck was one of her erogenous zones, and it only intensified the sensation. As he felt her tracker, he paused. He tried to manipulate it a bit, but stopped when Siana tried to pull away, obviously uncomfortable. As he spoke, Siana heard the writing tool moving.

He probably thinks I have a tumor. Do they have tumors?

With his fingers, he continued to trace her spine to her lower back. He walked them back up, found the bottom of her ribs, and began tracing the outline with hands on opposite sides, stopping under each arm. Hoping he didn't feel her breath catching, Siana tried to bring herself under control. Again, he walked his fingers up her spine and began pressing around her shoulder blades. Reaching for her chin, he moved her head back to its normal position. As he moved to her side, he gently lifted her left arm, tracing the delicate curves of each digit with his fingers to test their flexibility. She was watching him as he intently studied it. Slowly, he moved up her arm, bending the elbow, and moving the arm at the shoulder. Lifting her arm, he examined her underarm pit.

She was embarrassed at her hairiness, then wondered if they shaved themselves.

Not shaving might be normal here. However, only the doctor had facial hair.

She watched him as he repeated everything with the right arm. With every gentle touch, her desire grew. Siana had to fight to control her body's response.

What the heck. Why are these feelings so strong?

He hesitated before moving in front of her. He theatrically lifted her left leg after extending a hand and kneeling. She gave him another amused glance, relaxing a little more. Even though his acting was a bit much, it was funny, but the mystery of her situation continued to bother her. He gave her his boyish grin again, sat on his stool, and began examining her leg, starting at her toes. He treated each leg as he did her arms, bending and flexing to see her movement and feeling her bones where he could. Siana adjusted her skirt to cover herself as he lifted her leg higher. As his hand neared her upper thigh, she subtly moved, acutely aware of the throbbing bruise on her buttock. Gently, he put her leg down, before turning his attention to the other leg. Again, she shifted uncomfortably as his touch reached mid-thigh. A comment to *Be* Tess caused her to frown.

What did he just say to her?

Doctor Kellan sat on the stool at the end of the table, motioning for Siana to move closer. He raised the stool, so his face was level with hers. She was shifting her position without hurting herself and didn't see how he did it. The stool seemingly just rose on its own. With a gesture toward the child's drawing behind him, he signaled for her to look. His hands, warm and tender, guided her face. She kept her eyes on the paper. His face was so close she could smell his breath, though she couldn't figure out what it smelled like. It wasn't bad.

His fingers gently pulled her lower lids down as he inspected her eyes. Out of the corner of them, she could see his brow furrow, blue eyes looking slightly confused. Moving closer, he examined her right eye more closely. He pointed at the wall to her left, and she turned her head to focus on it. He moved so close to examine the side of her eye that she thought his nose might touch her cheek. After a minute, he shifted her head so she looked back at the paper.

He moved the stool and studied her left eye. The furrow of his brow became deeper. He and *Be* Tess were having a conversation, but there wasn't really any context for her to pick out possible words. He had her look at the wall to her right while they continued their conversation.

When he finished examining her eyes, he had her face forward. He pointed at his mouth and opened it with his tongue out. With a nod of understanding, her mouth opened in mimicry after she swallowed. This exam resembled her usual exams. A glow came from below her nose, which she assumed was a penlight of sorts.

Do they even have those?

Again, they discussed while she tried to catch their words. The light quickly faded, and he sat upright, concern clear.

What's that look for? She mentally ran through probable outcomes that would cause a doctor to frown during an exam involving her mouth. *Cavities? It wouldn't be surprising, considering oral hygiene was minimal while on the run.*

After studying her eyes again for a few seconds, he said something to his assistant, and took Siana's hands in a light grip, which she found uncomfortable. He wasn't hurting her; it was just the feeling of having her hands restrained by someone she didn't know. With a reassuring smile, he caught her gaze before the room plunged into darkness.

Chapter Nine

SIANA STIFFENED WITH A gasp. As a teen, she had once visited caves in a national park with her family. The guides had recommended everyone hold hands, because they were going to shut off the lanterns they'd brought. They warned that the intense darkness would confuse their senses, and holding hands would maintain their group's stability. Parents were warned against holding their children unless absolutely necessary. They could drop them from the change in their senses. When the lights went out, the darkness was absolute. Not a speck of light. You couldn't see the shape of your hand in front of your face. Children began crying. She had immediately felt off balance and panicked, though her mother had her left hand and Jacob her right. The guides quickly turned the lanterns back on, but everyone seemed shocked at how dark it could get. This felt exactly like that.

Her heart pounded in her chest, but she tried not to panic, gripping Kellan's hands as he held hers, his touch a comforting warmth. The dark was such that she didn't care anymore if she was holding a strange man's hands. A light in two areas grew. Two glowing eyes now marked the spot where she knew *Be* Tess had stood. As she glanced at the hands holding hers, she noticed another pair above them. Horror gripped Siana. Only one being she knew of could do that.

How could I be so stupid?

She'd heard rumors of areas where bots ran human experimentation, but it never occurred to her she might be in one. People usually dismissed it as just a rumor. They did not need to run experiments when they had access to all the world's information. However, it looks like the rumors were true, and Siana had fallen for it.

Of course I would! You idiot. Elves don't exist. This was all a setup.

A cry escaped Siana's lips as she violently pulled her hands away from the man, her heart pounding in her chest. The sudden brightness of the lights being snapped on caused her to cover her eyes. Through her squinting against the light, she saw the doctor, with a look she didn't recognize, reach for her hands. Fear choked her cry as she kicked out, the impact of her foot echoing against his ribs. While he tried to keep his balance, she jumped off the table and ran for the door. There was no knob, and it wouldn't open. Banging on it didn't move it. She threw herself at it. It didn't budge.

How is it locked?

Turning, she saw a presumably confused and concerned man with his hands outstretched, trying to placate her. She knew it was a lie.

His voice was quiet. "*Iz avi. Tona nempor pend toda.*"

Siana knew she was in trouble and stayed away from him. Their size, compared to hers, put the odds of her winning in a very low realm of possibility. They could easily hit her with a disruptor, and the fight would never exist. Turning, she frantically looked around for a weapon.

It's an infirmary. Surely there are scalpels.

She moved quickly and made it halfway through the wall of shelves before she caught sight of a small knife. She could hear him talking to her as she scrambled through the items but ignored it. With the knife in her hand, she felt like a child playing with a toy; however, she would take anything to improve her chances. Siana raised the knife. Her eyes narrowed, trying to project an image of menace. He had been moving toward her slowly, but he froze at the sight of the knife.

Good! He's afraid of getting his wiring damaged.

The thought held a tiny measure of comfort. Now she needed an exit strategy. Since Be Tess's back was turned toward her, Siana dismissed her as a threat. She expected them to flank her, but since she only had to deal with "Doctor Kellan," she focused all her energies on him.

When his face tightened and his eyes narrowed, she paused, noticing the subtle yet menacing shift in his body language. A grim set hardened his features, his jaw clenching, eyes narrowing. He drew himself up to his full height, which she would not lie, was a bit intimidating, but she braced herself anyhow. Her refusal to let him touch her was clear. She needed to get out, survive, and find Jacob. Especially if he was in a simulation as well.

Kellan's powerful strides, heavy and determined, brought him swiftly to her side, the sound echoing in the stillness. A gasp escaped her lips; the sheer unexpectedness of it shocked her to the core. He didn't hesitate, didn't stop. He was a man on a mission. She knew she wasn't much of a threat, but honestly, this was insulting. Weapons usually stopped most. He completely ignored it.

Her fear and instinct surged when she saw his hand reach for her. After making contact, she felt the knife hit something, but he didn't stop. No sound escaped him. He remained stoic, offering no reaction. He just grabbed her arm. His forceful grip squeezed her lower right arm, causing her to cry out in pain as his thumb pressed into her wrist, cutting off circulation and numbing her hand. Her grip loosened, and with a clatter, the knife fell to the floor. She swung her other arm, aiming a punch at him, her muscles tense and ready to strike. While she knew the basics of fighting, Jacob always took care of her. Now, fighting on her own, her body was still recovering from starvation. Her punch had little power.

A dizzying sensation washed over her as she felt herself spin around. He stooped down, wrapped his left arm around her waist, trapping her left arm between them, his right still held her other arm, and lifted her effortlessly in the air. She kicked backward at his legs as hard as she could. She might as well have been a fly biting at a horse.

Bite.

With a jerk of her right arm downward, she nearly took a piece of his. He pulled back right before her teeth connected.

Out of the corner of her eye, she saw blood on his arm. *I knew I got him!*

The bit of satisfaction she felt disappeared when she realized he was carrying her to the table.

They're going to experiment on me.

A primal instinct of survival kicked in, and she became a wild, trapped animal. There was no thought. Only the desire to live. To survive. She screamed, tried to bite, grabbed anything she could, pinched anything she could grab, used her nails, anything to get away. She fought with everything she had. Right as they reached the table, she felt his arm lose its grip on her waist. Her feet hit the ground, and she almost pulled out of his hold. As he trapped her by dropping his body onto hers, she folded over the table. Siana froze as her mind flashed back to the gazebo. He lifted her as he stood and spun her, so his back was to the table. Jacob's advice about remaining silent as much as possible, the habit of quiet to avoid attracting bots, vanished.

She yelled, "Get your hands off me!"

She felt him slightly pause, her shout ringing against the walls, but he lifted her off the ground again. Out of the corner of her eye, Siana saw the woman rushing toward them with a canister in her hands. She struggled to keep her face away as she realized it had a face mask on top. If they could drug her, who knew if she'd live?

She almost caught *Be* Tess in the stomach with a kick, using her captor's body for leverage. The other woman's dodge showcased practiced skill. Pulling her right arm away from him, Siana almost slapped the canister out of the other woman's hands. She saw the "doctor" try to grab her free arm. She reached for his hair and grabbed a handful, pulling it again. He kept hold. Letting go, she instead tried to find his eyes. She fully intended on blinding him if she could, though she wasn't sure she could pierce bot eyes.

It happened so fast, Siana barely had time to react. She felt her feet hit the floor, and they went behind her. Falling forward, she just got her right arm out in time to catch herself from face-planting. Kellan swept her arm aside, turned her face sideways, and threw her onto her stomach, her cheek against the cold wood floor, his weight pinning her. Her left arm remained trapped beneath him; his left arm braced him, and his right held her head down. She heard him exclaim something to the woman.

Siana screamed and shouted at them to let her go. She struggled, using the floor to leverage her body, but couldn't shift his weight. With a snapping bite intended for him, she turned her head, only to be thwarted by his steel-like arm. She could barely move. Swinging her right arm, she intended to hit him. Instead, she tried to scratch the other woman as she came close, but she simply grabbed Siana's arm and knelt on it, causing her to cry out in pain.

The canister's approach, a quick descent, filled Siana with a chilling dread that caused her to hunch down, her face hidden against the uncomfortable wood floor. Together, they restrained her enough to put the mask over her nose and mouth. Siana heard a hiss as the canister opened. Her eyes welled up as she held her breath. She wasn't going down without giving it everything she had. Out of the corner of her eye, she saw the woman's arm reach out. A sharp, sudden pain caused her to gasp and inhale. Only one breath was necessary. The sickly, sweet scent filled her nose and mouth. Dizziness soon followed. Still trying to fight, she felt her sluggish body giving in to the drug. Siana let her tears flow. She'd lost.

Chapter Ten

They exchanged relieved sighs. Their patient had gone limp, eyes closed, though Tess held the mask on until the drug had fully taken effect. Kellan lifted himself off and knelt next to her, thinking while waiting for her to be completely unconscious. Kellan knew the effect his smile had on people. He didn't know why it had that effect, but he put it to good use whenever he needed to. It worked especially well with scared females and children. He'd used it on his new, frightened patient.

Siana's smile lit up her face, and her green eyes sparkled. He felt a pull where he had felt nothing for years. It took him by surprise, but he kept his face smiling. He agreed with his brothers on one thing: that hair was going to have claimants lined up around the estate. They had red-haired females, but not her color of red. Corkscrew curls swung around her shoulders, which he'd never seen. Most hair was straight, at most wavy like Lorica's. Normally, hair would be up for both male and female—though Lorica flaunted that whenever possible, much to Tamek's dismay—but he wanted to see if there were any differences between them, so he had *Be* Tess leave it down. It lay behind her body like a cape.

Tamek's message warned him about how small she was. He had placed a small step stool on the floor so she could get on the table easily. He expected an even smaller female based on the letter's wording, but while this wasn't true, she was still smaller than average. It concerned them all.

Thinking back, Kellan didn't understand what happened. She was completely terrified. Everything was fine until they lit up their luna lines so they could see. He had trouble seeing hers in the light, so he had Tess shut them off so he could see if Siana's were weak. Only she'd never activated them. In fact, she was acting like she'd just seen them for the first time. His suspicion grew, and he disliked the direction of his thoughts. He had felt her desperation when fighting and wished he knew what went wrong.

Any hope of being nice left when she found a knife, and he realized she would not give up. He could have probably outlasted her, but that wasn't a good option. Someone was going to get hurt, more than they already had, and it was most likely her. Kellan had been holding back. He didn't want to hurt her. Regretfully, he did what he needed to do.

As she bent over the table, her freeze reminded him of Tamek's letter detailing Talon's two attempts to take her. Even if he needed to subdue her, he didn't want to be equated with *him*. He stood and spun both of them around, so his back was to the table as she shouted. He kept his grip on her, but Tess and he stared briefly at each other in surprise. It was another language. Kellan confirmed his worst suspicions. She was not a simpleton, nor was she *Setan*.

What was she?

When she first became frightened, Kellan noticed Tess had calmly walked to a table opposite Siana. The one thing he liked most about his nurse was that she had no qualms about doing what she felt was best for her patients. She truly cared, and if taking a hard line was necessary, she didn't hesitate even if she knew the patient would never forgive her.

I wish I could explain this is all for her protection.

Once they were positive she was unconscious, he lifted her skirt to check the mark Talon had made. It was an ugly purple. Immediate anger filled him, catching him by surprise. The harm wasn't lasting, though healing required time. He carefully rolled her over, making sure not to trap her limbs. With his arms gently lifting her, he stood and carried her to the table. She was so light it took little effort. Only a glistening, dark spot on the polished wood marked where her tears had fallen. Regret filled him. This went in the worst possible direction it could've gone, barring serious injury or death.

I'm so sorry, Siana.

They laid her down, straightened her torso, checked that her hair wasn't caught underneath, and straightened her gown. He and his nurse quickly set about putting her arms and legs into the rests that doubled as restraints, which they engaged in case she woke early. Tess grabbed a cushion and slipped it gently under her head, pulling her hair to the side as she did so. He observed her distress mirroring his own. He watched her stroke their patient's head.

"Maybe if she'd been able to understand us, we could've eased her fears." His voice was quietly contemplative.

"I don't know. The way she reacted when she saw our eyes illuminate makes me think she may not have listened to us," Tess said quietly with a sad frown.

He nodded. They literally had no way of knowing if that's what set her off. They guessed it was their eyes, but until they could talk to her, they couldn't be sure. To do that, she had to learn their language. To achieve this, she required social interaction; however, he prioritized ensuring her health posed no risk to others. Because she was a small female, he also had to check if anyone could claim her. He had doubts.

Both took deep breaths and hurried to finish the exam before she woke. Kellan was glad he'd chosen to accomplish half already. He hadn't been sure whether to do her chest or legs first and chose legs. Now he was glad he did. The harder part was next. He untied the front of the exam gown and folded it back, exposing her. He repeated what he had done to her earlier, checking for illness, injury, and bone structure, noting her breasts were similar to a *Setan* female. One had a bruise which he assumed came from Talon. His nostrils briefly flared, and he saw Tess glance at him.

He checked her heart rhythm and Tess wrote her beats. He continued his exam down to her hips. After that, Tess assisted him in raising the leg rests, separating and lifting her legs as was common practice, so he could examine her most private area. Kellan was partially glad Siana was unconscious for this part. He didn't know how she would've taken it. They may have had to sedate her anyhow. Having moved the stool closer, he sat and lifted the skirt, illuminating his eyes so he could see better. The sight took him aback. If he had any doubts she wasn't *Setan*, they would be gone now.

When Tess came around between the patient's legs, behind Kellan, she came to an abrupt stop. Tearing her gaze away, she inquired about Kellan's intentions.

He gingerly touched the coarse, curly hair. *Setan* private hairs were soft and straight. He then gently touched folds of skin that *Setan* females didn't have. The skin felt dry. From the drawer built into the table's end, he retrieved a small oil bottle. He wanted to examine her, to understand her, not to cause her any harm.

At least not any more than I have.

Kellan requested sketches as a reminder, and Tess gathered her supplies. His adrenaline was finally decreasing, but he wasn't sure if he would remember the details. Kellan used a light amount of oil on his hands and carefully examined the folds. As he leaned forward to sniff, a musky scent reached his nose. He smelled nothing sour, like disease or infection. Opening the folds revealed unfamiliar and unidentifiable extra parts. When Tess came back, he closed the folds, moved aside, and let her sit to sketch what they saw.

While she drew, Kellan studied the sleeping female. He worried about her but was determined to help within the law. Since losing his *Bund* status, he wasn't sure how much that would be. If he felt she would accept him, he'd claim her himself. His injuries had left him smaller than most men, and he was determined to overcome her fears, no matter what they were. He didn't know why, but he felt protective of her.

Maybe because of how terrified she was?

Once Tess had finished, Kellan reached over her and opened the folds. Tess began sketching again.

Her voice was quiet. "She's so different."

With the back of her sketching implement, she pushed a fold further out for better visibility. The female had the back opening of a *Setan* from which all waste emptied. What looked like her passage opening was above that, which worried both of them. A *Setan* female's was larger and more obvious. Kellan would examine it after Tess finished, checking if their fears were valid. Another much smaller opening was above that. Neither knew what it was for.

Tess asked, "Is that her *sereto*?" pointing at something above the smaller opening.

Kellan wasn't sure. "I don't know. If so, why is it external?"

His nurse shrugged and kept drawing

Once Tess was done, Kellan took the stool again. His concern escalated upon examining his patient's opening. Adding a bit more oil to his fingers, he carefully inserted one into her passage. It confirmed her opening was small. Too small. His fears about her future grew. He gently added another finger and tested to see if it would stretch. It did for a small amount, but not nearly enough. He withdrew enough to add a third finger. It wouldn't fit unless he bunched them in a more triangular shape. Even then, he couldn't fit them in more than halfway without possibly tearing her. It was nowhere near the size needed.

"A claiming will kill her!" Tess's loud concern elicited a soft whimper from the table, reminding her to lower her voice.

Kellan knew she wasn't wrong.

This just keeps getting worse.

With the cloth Tess gave him, he wiped his fingers, then added fresh oil and continued his exam. Moving upward, the next opening was too small for anything he could think of.

No, wait. Some animals had two openings for waste. It's possible this smaller opening was for that purpose.

Until she could speak their language—if she ever spoke to him again—he'd have to wait for an answer.

Higher up, he encountered a small bump nestled in the deeper folds. It certainly looked like a *sereto*, but why was it on the outside? *Setan* females had it inside their passage, so both males and females received pleasure at the same time. It made claiming much easier when both were being aroused and pleasured. He oiled and inserted a finger again to double-check. Moving and pressing his digit against her, he determined it was absent. He realized her passage may be too small as well. Trying not to curse, he knew the female before him was in danger, and there wasn't much he could do to help.

Standing, he walked to a bowl and washed his hands. Tess handed him a clean towel, then washed the oil off Siana. They lowered her legs with a silent, shared concern, the weight of their worry palpable as they carefully aligned her limbs. The hushed atmosphere added to the solemnity.

Tess fetched the outfit she had prepared earlier. They worked together, the soft rustle of fabric accompanying the process as they dressed Siana in her undergarments, trousers, short top, and stockings. Tess washed the salty residue off the female's upper face.

Kellan lifted Siana, her head against his chest. He carried her from the infirmary, having unlocked the door with a wave of his hand as he cradled her, and wondered about the limits of their ability to keep her alive.

Chapter Eleven

HER EYES FELT HEAVY. Was she dead? *No, it wouldn't be fair to feel like this if I was dead.* She remembered. *There was a fight.*

She didn't think she was dead; the pain in her arm and soreness from fighting confirmed this. Her eyes flew open as she remembered the pinch.

That witch.

Gingerly, she sat up, rubbing the already purple, throbbing bruise that mirrored the color of her backside. The bruising on her bottom made sitting difficult. Her foggy mental state, a consequence of the ordeal and drug, made remembering a struggle. She remembered she cut the doctor's arm.

He bled. Bots can't bleed, can they?

Jacob was usually up-to-date on upgrades, and he had said nothing about it. She didn't think they could. If that was true, then he wasn't a bot, which left her more confused about where she was. She strained to remember anything else. The doctor's face when he saw the knife. Fighting. Her on the floor. The smell of the drug. Then the world went dark. That was all.

Jacob, I wish you were here to help me figure this out.

She noticed a glass of clear liquid on the side table beside her bed when she glanced around. She eyed it suspiciously, but the dryness in her throat demanded relief. Reaching for it, she sniffed it before taking a tiny sip. It had no smell or taste. She assumed it was water. As she looked around, she knew she was in an unfamiliar room. In fact, it wasn't a room at all. It was a large, square canvas tent. Without thinking, she had a bigger drink, then stopped to scold herself for carelessness, but her mind was a jumble.

I don't understand what's going on. Was this a simulation? Was it real? Where is my brother? If they weren't bots, why did their eyes glow? What did they do with my backpack? She last saw it in the bedroom at the house. *Where was it now? How did she get here? What did they do when they drugged me? So many questions, so few answers. I have no more ideas than when I "got" here.*

The thought depressed her. No answers meant no Jacob. She no longer wore the thin gown, as evidenced by her throwing off the worn wool covers. The serviceable trousers and tunic were soft from wear. Her mind was blank; the only conclusion she could reach was that *Be* Tess was the culprit. Suspicion that the doctor helped lingered. Her clothes were brown, not her favorite, but at least she was fully clothed.

Beggars can't be choosers.

Siana set the now empty glass—what was that about being careful?—on the table, she swung her legs off the bed, and slowly stood, making sure she wouldn't fall over. Her stocking feet felt some sort of carpet under her toes. It wasn't a large tent by any means, no bigger than her former bedroom back home. The space at the foot of the bed held a wooden crate. The heavy lid groaned as she lifted it, revealing blankets and more clothing. Slowly lowering the lid, she drifted to a simple desk and chair. Three small drawers lined up under the top. What looked like hair ties, hairpins, a comb, and hand mirror were in one. The next one was empty. The third held twigs, cloths, and some sort of padded material. Out of the corner of her eye, on the other side of the bed, opposite the flap, she saw a small standing set of shelves. It held a couple of books she couldn't read on the top shelf. The middle shelf held a metal cup, plate, bowl, and utensils. Next to that was a set of cookware that looked similar to cast iron. The bottom shelf was empty.

A sudden shout pierced the quiet, making her jump; she hurried toward the flap, the sound echoing in her ears. Near the entrance sat a pair of work boots, leather and scuffed. Having grabbed them, she sat back on the bed to put them on. They were a bit big, but usable. She quickly tied them and moved toward the flap. Hoping it wasn't locked, like every other entrance had been, she opened it. As she stepped outside, a refreshing, cool breeze caressed her skin, carrying the sounds of birdsong.

I need to get out of here and find my brother.

The moment she glanced around, that idea vanished from her thoughts. It was a far cry from the estate. The encampment was alive with activity; people moved with purpose, their footsteps muffled by the earth. Several tents of various earthy colors formed a ring around the edge of a clearing. It seemed someone intended the tents to blend in with the surroundings.

It reminded her that Jacob and she were camping when it started. He had talked her into taking time off so they could have some brother-sister time. If he hadn't, she would've died in the hospital when it collapsed. Internally, she briefly mourned for her unlucky former colleagues. The chattering voices brought her attention back to the camp. On the left side, just past two other tents, was a solid-looking building. It had a strange symbol on the front.

Is that where I was drugged? That they drugged her to force her to comply bothered her to no end. *When did bots start doing that? Why haven't they killed me?*

Nestled in the center of the clearing was a rock fire ring, gray and worn from countless fires, with ash still visible. Logs with worn tops placed around it showed it was probably a community gathering spot. Smaller rings were near each tent. As she looked around, she also spotted one near hers.

How do I get back to the field?

A woman waved at her to get her attention and hurried over. It wasn't until she came closer that Siana realized it was Brigitte. She was wearing clothes similar to hers. A mix of excitement and trepidation, a nervous flutter in her chest, warred within her as a knot tightened in her stomach. Remembering Brigitte was the one who helped drug her to begin with, she stayed where she was. As Brigitte caught sight of Siana's face, her pace transformed from a jog to a slow walk.

As she approached her, Brigitte said, *"To nimba."* She clasped her hands to her chest, and bowing slightly, she repeated, *"To nimba,"* anxiously looking at the other female's face. Siana's wariness was palpable, a heavy blanket of fear and distrust hanging in the air.

With a sweep of her hand encompassing the bustling camp, its sounds and smells, Brigitte declared, *"Toda rembit."*

Not understanding, Siana had no response.

Brigitte tried dropping to her knees with her hands clasped together. *"To nimba."* Her voice was pleading.

Siana's mind was a jumble of conflicting emotions and thoughts. It seemed like Brigitte was apologizing. It also meant what she thought was an apology earlier wasn't. With the image of Brigitte's sorrowful face and the taste of the tea lingering in her mind, she acknowledged that Brigitte likely had no alternative. After all, she was technically a servant. She may have lost her job if she disobeyed. This was all quite confusing.

What would I do in her place?

She realized she couldn't answer that without knowing more about the woman in front of her and where she had woken up. What she knew is she needed someone by her side to help her learn. If she stayed on guard, kept her resentment hidden, but let Brigitte believe she forgave her, she could use her to figure out where she was and how to get out.

Unless she's a bot.

What choice did she have? So far, Brigitte was the only person she knew in this... world? Simulation? She refused to count the other two. Brigitte also ran for help when that man showed up at the gazebo. Because she needed help to return to the field, she cautiously offered the other woman a chance but remained wary. Hopefully, she could talk the woman into leading her to find her brother—once they could have a conversation. She gave her a cautious, small smile.

Brigitte's relief spread across her face. She jumped back to her feet and clasped Siana's hand. "*Velta toda!*" she said.

Siana put it together when *Be* Tess said it earlier and realized it had to be "thank you." If so, her earlier comment was "you... something." She made a goal of buckling down on learning.

83

Brigitte beckoned her to follow. "*Yenon.*" Sia assumed it was "follow" or "come." Again, only time would tell.

As Siana slowly walked behind Brigitte, she glanced around. More lavender-colored trees. The top of her head was warming from the sun. Other people had noticed them and were milling about with curiosity. Brigitte turned and quickly used her hands to comb Siana's hair down to cover her ears. She gave Sia a meaningful look before turning back to her path.

What? Do I have offensive ears?

A low noise sounded, and everyone began moving to a large single-story building Siana hadn't seen. She couldn't see it from her tent because the infirmary hid it. As she drew closer, both buildings looked to be made from identical wood materials. Wide vertical boards over other boards gave it a sort of board and batten look. She didn't know what material the roof was made of. It didn't look familiar.

A woman appeared next to Siana and said something. Brigitte immediately turned back and spoke to the woman. The woman said, "Ah." She smiled at her, then bowed her head to Siana.

Pointing to herself, she said, "Norita."

Siana glanced at Brigitte, who gave her a slight nod, and introduced herself. "Siana."

The woman said, "*Ofena*, Siana," and smiled at her.

Another woman called to Norita, who waved goodbye and ran off to join her friend. It seemed as if Norita knew Brigitte.

Ofena would be "hello" or "welcome"?

Siana followed her into the building and discovered it was some sort of eating hall. Tables and seats of various types were strewn about. The hall appeared furnished with whatever they could find.

If it works, it works.

She'd gone dumpster diving a few times. One time, she found a puppy. She named him Koana, but her brother called him Trash Panda because of the black circles around his eyes and where he'd been found. The name stuck, though they used Panda. Her Shepherd mix, Cooper, hadn't been thrilled.

Brigitte again motioned for her to follow and joined a line of others. An older man handed each of them an unidentifiable plate of food and a metal cup of water. She followed Brigitte, and they found and sat at a small table with benches. It was the smallest unoccupied table. Looking around, she realized it was all women eating.

While Sia tried to eat, Brigitte taught her a language lesson. From the surrounding items, she learned the words for eat, table, bench, chair, cup, water, food, and the *gente*, a fork-like object. Between bites, Brigitte made her repeat each word over and over. Brigitte kept it simple. When Siana could confidently repeat each one, they took a break to finish their meal in silence.

Siana was trying to figure out a way to get back to the field when a deep voice spoke. She froze. Out of the corner of her eye, she saw Kellan give Brigitte a resigned look, said something to them both, and sat at a different table.

Brigitte turned to her, and said, "Brigitte, Siana *climpton*."

Siana just looked at her.

Brigitte, picking up Siana's hand, pointed to herself, then Siana, and repeated, "*Climpton.*"

I have no idea what that could mean.

Brigitte, giving a slightly exasperated sigh, just added, "Kellan, *climpton.*"

Siana took her hand back, ignored her, and went back to finishing her meal. She didn't care to learn what that word meant. While returning her dishes, Siana observed many women conversing with Kellan. He was laughing easily and talking without a care in the world. She narrowed her eyes, wondering if anyone had subjected them to what she had experienced, or if they were all bots. Just then, Kellan glanced up and caught her glaring at him, giving her a regretful gaze. She turned away and left with Brigitte.

Siana felt like a child following her mother. Brigitte took her around camp and introduced her to several others, all women, with Brigitte adding comments Siana didn't understand. She learned *ofena* still seemed to be "welcome" or "hello." Everyone said it after Siana introduced herself. After a careful study of each, she saw no indication they were bots.

By the end, her head was spinning with names and words she had no hope of remembering. She was even having trouble remembering what she'd learned during the meal. One thing she remembered: every woman had jewelry encompassing her left hand. None of it gave her any clues about where she was, and they all just seemed like normal people.

I honestly don't know what to think.

On the way back to her tent, Brigitte swung by a small building. An outhouse. Siana, accustomed to such things, used it without difficulty before continuing after Brigitte finished.

Brigitte walked ahead and began preparing a fire. Sitting on the logs near her, Siana took the time to study the woman and her surroundings better.

One thing she noticed was the forest. Nestled among the lavender trees were others with red leaves and a few with green and blue. A few even looked like palm trees. It was one of the most colorful forests she'd ever seen. It was thick and surrounded the encampment. If she walked through it, she could see herself easily getting lost. No one seemed to carry any weapons, so she did not know how to arm herself against them or predators.

That's a problem. Hopefully tomorrow something will show itself, and I can get out of here. I need to find my stuff as well. She hadn't seen her backpack.

There were a few paths leading in and out of the camp, but it was difficult to tell where they led once they disappeared into the trees. Once she was able, she'd have to discover where they went. Siana sat on the log, trying to figure out her next step, and Brigitte joined her. Through a bit of acting, she learned Brigitte would share her tent. At first, she was leery about it, but Brigitte pointed at each tent and then pointed at the occupants. Most were already sharing. The bed was large enough for both, so that wasn't the issue.

Is she staying with me as a guard?

The sun was going down, and the air was cooling. *Be* Tess showed up and gave Brigitte a lantern. She gave Siana an apologetic smile as she left, but Siana turned and refused to look at her. The two women sat in silence for a bit. While Siana had questions, she wasn't sure how to ask them. She tried one. Siana, reaching over, felt the chains on Brigitte's left hand.

She asked, "What is this?"

Brigitte started at the unfamiliar words, giving Siana a curious look. When Siana repeated the question, Brigitte held her hand up. Siana watched the firelight reflect on the bronze chains and jewels.

Brigitte said, "*Murjer eh rembit.*" Her voice was hesitant, as if she wasn't sure she understood the question.

Siana was uncertain of the meaning. She had said that last word earlier but had gestured to the entire camp. She racked her brain yet couldn't think of a word for both an encampment and jewelry. They fell silent again, each lost in their own thoughts.

Siana glanced at Brigitte. *Maybe I should try. She understood the meaning of the question. Maybe I can get her to understand I'm looking for my brother. But what if they're bots? If I can make her understand about Jacob, and she is a bot, that puts him in danger. He'll need secrecy if he finds me and needs to get me out of here.*

Her lips tightened with frustration. She didn't know how to tell if they were friend or foe. She needed to discover that as soon as possible. There was nothing she could do until she knew. She wouldn't put her brother in danger.

Darkness fell fast. Before Siana knew it, Brigitte was a shadow shape in the blackness. The lantern next to Brigitte's feet lit, illuminating the area. After picking it up and handing it to Siana, Brigitte turned and kicked dirt over the fire.

Pointing toward the tent, she said to Siana, "*Jeno.*"

Unsure of why they couldn't sit outside, she held up the lantern to light her way and entered the tent.

Is she afraid of predators?

Brigitte covered the fire and then walked in. With a movement toward the chest, she opened it, retrieving nightclothes. Reaching behind the chest, slightly under the bed, she retrieved a bowl and pitcher that Siana hadn't seen earlier.

With a quick raise of the pitcher, Brigitte uttered, "Water," before departing.

Knowing she remembered the word's meaning made Siana happy, and she vowed to learn as much as possible quickly.

Brigitte returned as Siana was flipping through a book she couldn't read. Brigitte beckoned her, repeating a word she'd said earlier in the day. Siana, having guessed "come" was the translation, felt a sense of satisfaction as she watched Brigitte beckon her forward, the word echoing softly within the tent.

That's another word I've learned.

They both shared the water and washed up. After taking the bowl, Brigitte left the tent. Siana heard the water being dumped in the fire pit. Away from the entrance, she quickly began changing. Entering and putting the bowl back, Brigitte did the same. When Siana saw Brigitte remove her underpants and hang them up to air out, she did likewise. Before things went south, she normally slept without underwear, so it didn't faze her. Both girls draped their clothes over the chairs and climbed into bed. One hand wave later, and the lantern turned off. As she fell asleep, Siana wondered how she was going to find her brother.

Chapter Twelve

A FEW DAYS AFTER Brigitte arrived, the sun woke Siana. The cheerful chirping of birds and the distant murmur of voices filled the air. The smell of eggs cooking wafted into the partially open flap. She also smelled...

Siana shot up and out of bed, rushing toward the entrance. *It couldn't be.*

She almost ran into Brigitte, who had entered with a mug of steaming liquid and handed it to Siana. Brigitte's eyebrows rose as Siana fairly danced in front of her. With a shrug, she returned outside to complete their breakfast.

Siana clasped her fingers around the cup. In her hands, she held the extremely rare cup of coffee. With the cup held to her face, a deep breath made her realize how much she missed waking to that smell. There wasn't any milk or sweetener, but she didn't care. She was so, so grateful for this cup of wonderful. Carefully sipping the hot liquid and savoring it, she began gathering her clothes.

A cramp and warm liquid leaving her body interrupted her happiness. *Oh, no.* Siana checked her thighs. *Crap! Why? I need supplies. Do they even have periods? Not if they're bots.* It had been a while since she'd had one. Malnutrition and fight-or-flight 24/7 had caused hers to stop. Honestly, she hadn't missed it.

Not knowing how these people handled it, she called out, "Brigitte."

Siana, embarrassed, pointed downward when the woman entered. Brigitte moved around the bed in order to see. Upon seeing the blood, her face registered understanding. Brigitte went to the desk and pulled out the cushions Siana had seen when she first arrived. She showed her how females used the cushioned pads, grabbed a cloth, wet it in the bowl of water she had poured earlier, and then handed it to Sia. Once that was taken care of and Siana got dressed, they went outside to eat the eggs, which, left unattended, were burning.

Brigitte had taught Siana how to care for herself after meals: where to dispose of food, how and where to wash her dishes, and where to return them when dry. Siana briefly thought of hiding the metal eating knife, but it really wasn't sharp enough to do any damage or be of any use. She took care of her dishes. It was obvious from day one that everyone took care of themselves, mostly. Brigitte also made it quite clear through actions: here Brigitte wasn't her servant, she was her roommate, though she frequently slipped back into servant mode.

With their dishes put away, Brigitte took a breath, which caught Siana's attention. She seemed to be thinking about something troublesome, but her face soon cleared. She smiled, took Siana's hand, and started walking, waving and greeting everyone they encountered. Siana copied her. She had trouble remembering everyone's name, so the morning ritual helped. She learned "hello" and "good morning," which meant *ofena* was actually "welcome."

They had gotten into a small routine of walking around camp after eating. Technically, Brigitte took her around camp. If it were up to Siana, she'd be investigating paths. To get

Brigitte to walk down them proved a futile endeavor. Anytime she tried, she was told no and pulled back into camp.

During one attempt, Brigitte, seemingly a bit annoyed at her repeated tries, motioned to the camp and said, *"Rembit."*

Once, she thought about just running, but she had no supplies, and no way of knowing where she was or how to get back. Acting rashly could get her killed. She also needed her backpack and had no clue where it was.

When Siana realized they were heading to the infirmary, she understood Brigitte had been keeping her distracted so she wouldn't notice. Avoiding its occupants had been her primary goal for the past several days. Any time they came near her, she'd go elsewhere, whether or not Brigitte liked it.

As she tried to pull away and turn back to the tent, Brigitte grabbed her arm, pointed to her lower half, and said, *"Tefzo.* Doctor Kellan."

Siana had interpreted it earlier as "pads," but she didn't know if that was the actual meaning. It didn't matter. All she needed to know was it meant what she needed. With only a few in the tent, and if she understood correctly, they needed to go to the building for supplies. Her heart beat faster and she felt a chill. She didn't want to. Brigitte's face held sympathy.

Does she know what happened?

Brigitte's tone was reassuring. *"Iz avi.* Kellan *nempor pend toda."*

She gently tugged Siana's hand, but Siana dug in her heels. Brigitte stood, holding her hand, obviously waiting for her to acknowledge she needed to go to the infirmary. Sia really didn't want to see them, but she needed pads. Another cramp hit her. *And maybe pain relief.* She also knew she had to talk to and be near them to discover their motives.

Who am I kidding? I'm just flat out scared of them.

Kellan and *Be* Tess's acting antics popped into her head. *They were funny, but was it an act?*

She took a deep breath and forced herself to think logically. If they intended to harm her, they had ample time to do so while she was drugged. After cutting him with the knife, Kellan bled, so the odds of him being a bot were low. It was possible the ability to make their eyes glow was natural to them. The days seemed quite short. Darkness here seemed absolute often and fell quickly. It would be a useful ability.

An evolutionary response? Maybe it's not out of character for this world or people who can lock and unlock doors or turn lights on and off with a wave of their hand. Was it a form of magic?

Frustrated, she didn't know what the right move was, who to trust, or if any of this was even real.

It could be an opportunity to study them better, but I really don't want to go in there.

Pointing at Brigitte, she motioned toward the building, and said in their language, which she learned was called *Setan*, "You."

Brigitte, with a determined face, shook her head.

A silent plea filled Siana's gaze as she looked at Brigitte, but Brigitte remained unaffected.

Dang it. Go in or bleed all over myself.

With a grimace, she decided against free-bleeding and offered Brigitte a small, anxious nod, her heart still pounding. Brigitte gave another encouraging smile and clasped her hand tightly, silently letting her know she had support. As they approached the door, *Be* Tess opened it. Siana couldn't stop herself from glaring at the woman. Her arm still hurt. *Be* Tess gave a welcoming sweep of her arm, pointedly ignoring the look, and stepped back so they could enter.

***

Kellan knew who was here. They had watched the females approach. It obviously was very difficult for their feisty friend, but she made it through the door. Kellan was surprised that Siana, whose face was full of distrust and suspicion, actually managed it.

She's inside. That's all that matters for now. It was an opening.

He'd been trying for one for the past several days. He kept his distance as Brigitte greeted them.

Brigitte encouraged Siana to greet them. She refused. Brigitte glared at her with that stubborn look of hers. Kellan had seen it many times.

Siana let out a begrudging sigh. She muttered, "Hello," in their language.

Brigitte prodded her, and Siana gave her a look. Brigitte, undeterred, nudged Siana again. The two glared at each other while Kellan watched in amusement, wondering who would give in first.

Siana gave a resigned, "Hello, *Be* Tess, Doctor Kellan."

Kellan smiled, crinkling his face into happiness, but Siana turned her glare to him. *Be* Tess looked absolutely thrilled.

"What can I help you with?" Kellan asked the maid.

"Siana started her cycle. She needs supplies."

"She has a cycle. Tess, note that."

Tess nodded but picked up a basket and began filling it with what their guest needed.

Kellan looked curious and said, "I wonder how long it lasts."

Brigitte answered, "That's something only she can answer. Given the language barrier, we'll have to wait until it's over or she understands enough to tell us."

Kellan nodded in agreement. He realized he was impatient to know more about her race, but he didn't want to push it. He'd already broken her trust, which he needed to regain, and he wasn't sure what else would scare her.

When Tess gave Brigitte the basket, Kellan noticed Siana cautiously staring at her eyes. He realized Tess also noticed, seeing her linger. He engaged Brigitte in conversation while he watched their patient. While still fearful, he also saw a bit of curiosity on her face.

Should I or would it scare her more?

He took a chance.

Chapter Thirteen

"SIANA?"

She turned to Doctor Kellan with wariness and realized he looked unsure of himself.

He stopped and had a brief conversation with Brigitte.

Brigitte put down the basket and faced Siana. "You..." She seemed to search for her words.

Instead, she pointed at Siana, then walking over to Kellan, pointed at his eyes. Turning to face him, she acted like she was examining them. She turned back to Siana and raised her eyebrows in a questioning manner. Kellan made a show of opening his eyes wide.

Do I want to examine his eyes? Why yes, yes, I do.

At the same time, she didn't. What if they did something else to her?

After all, I don't know what they did while I was unconscious. However, this was such a good opportunity that passing it up would be foolish. But do I want to get that close to him?

The thought of getting within his reach made her leery, but this was her chance to get a better look at him and his eyes.

Hopefully, she could tell if they were real or not. Siana decided to conquer her fear and hesitantly nodded. With a hop, Kellan landed on the table, his braids swinging, folded his hands, and waited expectantly. Siana grabbed Brigitte by the arm and brought her with as moral support. *Be* Tess brought over the step Siana had stood on before. When she got close to him, she hesitated. No one said anything or moved. They patiently waited with no sign of rushing her.

Siana looked at Brigitte, who gave her an encouraging nod. "*Iz Avi.*"

The meaning fell into place. "It's okay" or "It's all right." *Same difference.* She had an actual phrase to use. Just learning it made her a bit proud. Each time she previously heard it fell into place, and the phrase made sense within those contexts. With the memory of Kellan's repeated reassurance during the exam and her subsequent loss of control, she relaxed a little. Just a little. She was thinking she had misunderstood his intentions. He was most likely just a doctor who was trying to perform a physical.

Or was he? Was he just playing at it?

She didn't want to alienate people who were willing to help her. Not knowing the truth was going to drive her insane. She needed to know. Siana slowly stepped onto the stool. Leaning forward gave her nothing to hold on to.

Kellan reached down—causing her to step away—and pulled up the metal leg rests to give her something to lean on, separating them so they were on either side of her.

She couldn't stop the suspicion in her gaze as she noticed they also bent. *Did he...?*

She turned that gaze to him. Kellan's expression was calm and innocent.

Too calm and innocent.

She had a growing feeling he'd done a more thorough exam while she was unconscious. With her hands on the rests, she moved closer to him. Kellan didn't look at her. He kept his gaze on the paper attached to the wall, and his hands in his lap. She leaned closer and noticed him surreptitiously adjusting the bottom of his tunic to cover an obvious bulge, then gripped his hands together, digging his nails in.

Am I turning him on? Can bots mimic that? I don't think so.

The thought of him being aroused by her made her braver. It felt like she had more control. It also gave her something else to test. She wanted to make sure it was real, though the idea made her feel a little naughty. As she leaned closer, she "accidentally" let her hand briefly brush his lap. His sharp intake of breath told her he was indeed trying to hide himself from her view.

His gaze moved to her eyes and was so intense she felt her breathing stop for a split second as her body again reacted to him. She took a slow, deep, measured breath, then refocused, examining his eyes. At first, Siana saw nothing different. They definitely didn't look like a bot, but she wasn't an expert. She got as close as she dared, but saw nothing at all that gave any hint they were any form of tech. They looked similar to hers. In fact, they looked duller than they did yesterday.

She leaned away, giving him a questioning look. His eyes began to shine with a small glow. Now she could see fine lines marking through and around his iris. They didn't match with a bot's eyes. If they were, their tech had come a long way. The nursing side of her was very interested in knowing how they worked. It had to be some sort of evolutionary response to the darkness.

***

Out of the corner of his eye, he saw her gaze turn curious.

Good.

When he saw her coming, he and Tess both turned their lines all the way down. She obviously saw something wasn't the same. He had looked back at the paper when she started inspecting his eyes. Now he turned his lines on a low level. It was just enough for her to notice, and she came closer again. He turned the lines up a bit more. She backed up for a second but came closer again. She pointed her finger up. He obliged as much as he dared in a lit room. Her curiosity became fascination. When she pointed up again, he shook his head, pointed to the lights, and then feigned bright lights blinding him.

Was she brave enough to turn the room dark?

Though it took a minute to decide, she was and waved a hand at the light. She didn't know how to do it, but *Be* Tess understood and turned them off.

Kellan felt Siana sway from the change in her senses, but restrained himself from touching her. She put one hand on his thigh to keep herself grounded, much to his chagrin. She yanked her hand back, but stopped when she swayed again. He wouldn't let her fall, but he also didn't want to scare her, so he didn't move. He could see her in front of his eyes, but wasn't sure how well she could see.

She said something in her language. He did not know what "high beams" meant, but guessed she wanted him to bring the lines up all the way and did so. He noticed her eyes squint in the brightness; her expression then shifted to one of wonder. He slowly lowered his lines to a point where she no longer squinted, and then he waited for her inspection. Her hands moved slightly on his thighs as she shifted, as she seemed to forget her fear, and he was very glad the room was dark. He knew what she was seeing. His eyes were a brilliant blue and his lines were a slightly brighter shade. The combination kept the wonder on her face.

Siana turned to the general location of Brigitte.

"Brigitte?" She said another word in her language.

Brigitte, obviously guessing correctly about the word, turned hers up. Her eyes were normally a golden brown, and her lines were a yellowish tone. Kellan knew Lorica loved Brigitte's lit eyes. Her golden tone was rare. *Be* Tess lit hers up as well. Hers were shimmering gray.

Kellan was having a bit of an issue. Siana had leaned into his lap to keep her balance after she turned. Her arm was barely brushing his private area, and he was trying to think of anything horrible to keep it under control. He was failing. All he wanted to do was pull her on to him.

Honestly, he did not know what to think. He had felt little after the accident despite a few females who willingly looked past his scars, and at his family home, offering to be claimed. Many *Bund*, he knew, would accept that if they received what they wanted, but he craved more than being a mere bag of *terin*. More than a transactional relationship. The attraction wasn't there either. Lorica accused him of being old-fashioned. If he was, he wouldn't apologize for it. He knew what he wanted and wouldn't accept anything less. He also knew the female in front of him intrigued him more than any other had. Why, only time would tell.

***

Siana motioned for the lights.

There was absolutely no sign their eyes weren't real.

It only increased her confusion. Their pupils were smaller than a human's, so they wouldn't let in as much light as hers would in the dark. It also gave them an advantage over her. Where she had a limit on how much she could see, they could turn their eyes up to compensate for the smaller pupils. She also realized she didn't see many lights at night, which meant they used their eyes instead. To fully understand, she'd need a biology course on their race.

Is this why Brigitte has me go into the tent at night? Because they all use their eyes? Given how I reacted before, it wouldn't be surprising they'd avoid me seeing them again.

Tess slowly lit the room while everyone else lowered their eyes.

Turning, Siana gave Kellan a thoughtful look.

With a grin, he playfully wiggled his eyebrows at her. Her smile spread before she could stop it, but it quickly disappeared as she caught sight of his injured arm. He had hidden it under long sleeves, but his movement revealed the bandage. Kellan followed her troubled gaze.

If he wasn't a bot, I hurt him. If he really was just trying to examine me, I hurt him for no reason.

Guilt nibbled at her.

Kellan quieted his tone while pulling his sleeve down. "It's all right. You *churtuea.*"

Her troubled gaze shifted to his face. She realized she'd understood most of what he said. She wasn't sure what the last word was. Frightened? Scared? It was the same thing, and it would fit.

A knock interrupted them, and an elderly woman entered as *Be* Tess opened the door. Siana recognized her as the person behind the counter in the eating building. Following behind her was a man about the same age.

"Ah, *Metz* Berdon." He nodded at the female before turning to the male. "Berdon." Kellan welcomed them in.

Realizing their visit was over, Siana and Brigitte moved toward the door, Brigitte grabbed the basket as they passed. They nodded their thanks, greeted the older couple, and exited the building.

As she walked back to her tent with Brigitte, Siana was confused. More and more, she was thinking she'd somehow landed in a different world.

I really don't think they're bots.

Then again, other rumors said that different bots—who vowed to save mankind—were setting up areas of relative safety. They might have moved her to such an area, and they might have changed their appearance to one appealing to humans, but aside from their glowing eyes and small pupils, their eyes resembled human eyes. They ate food. She'd heard Brigitte using the outhouse. All signs pointed to this being real.

My current options: bots are using me in an experiment, different bots moved me to safety, or I'm in another world. If the latter, how did I get here? If they could do that, wouldn't they move everyone?

She thought about it.

Maybe not. That could overwhelm a new world with numbers. Then again, how would the second one happen? And where was Jacob? Did he even come with me? Is he still there?

She remembered how the tracker glowed and burned her before she passed out. Was it possible it was used to transport her? If so, any of the options were possible, though she was discounting the first one. She had a hard time believing bots bent on destroying them would be kind, as these people have been. There was also Kellan, bleeding. Though it wasn't beyond the realm of possibility if they'd somehow designed themselves in such a way. What disturbed her the most was the possibility that Jacob wasn't here. Her choker had slipped. If his hadn't, he'd still be on their world. Fear flashed at the thought.

Siana hated this feeling of uncertainty. She wanted answers, but only time would reveal them. She didn't know what to do but wait and gather information. To be safe, she had to assume Jacob was here until proven otherwise. With a renewed focus, having pulled herself from her thoughts, she scrutinized the encampment as Brigitte put the basket into their tent. She didn't see a garden or animals, though she witnessed everyone eating.

Where was the food coming from?

Brigitte rejoined her and led her to a bigger tent. They waited outside until a woman and man appeared. It was the couple from the infirmary. After introductions, Siana realized *Metz* was the equivalent of Mrs. She found herself being assigned chores, with Brigitte "interpreting"—which mainly comprised showing or acting things out. They allowed her several days to acclimate, but now she had to contribute. That day, she found herself on laundry duty.

Brigitte hurried to their tent, retrieved their dirty clothes, and guided her to the makeshift riverside laundry. Norita and her friend Giselle were already there. There were several piles of clothing laying on a blanket with what looked like a tag on them. After their greetings, Norita, Giselle, and Brigitte showed her how they did laundry within the camp. It was backbreaking work, and they didn't finish until near sundown. By the end, Siana wished she knew how washing machines worked, so she could invent one.

That night, after Siana prepared for bed, her cramps became worse. She attributed it to the stress, though it would've been nice had she been one of those who skipped their periods instead.

My cramps haven't been this bad since I was a teen.

Brigitte walked in and found her leaning over the desk, one hand on her abdomen.

"Okay?" Brigitte asked in *Setan*.

As she turned her head to look at her, Siana could only shake her head.

"I go Kellan."

Turning, Brigitte exited the tent. Upon returning, she had an unreadable face and a carafe of tea.

Siana reversed the question. "Okay?"

Siana was glad she was conversing. It may be a single word, but it was more than she'd started with.

Her new friend smiled in response to Siana using their language, but her smile held something unidentifiable. "Yes."

Something's wrong.

As Siana sat at the desk, Brigitte poured her a cup, urged her to drink, pointed at the cup, and held up three fingers.

She sniffed it before taking a sip. She recognized raspberry with a hint of something else. With her mother's interest in herbals, and Jacob's botany and herbal interest, she knew raspberry leaf tea was good for the uterus, though there was some disagreement about drinking it while pregnant. If she had to guess, she'd say something was mixed with it for her cramps. Given that she was told to drink three cups, she doubted it was strong. Siana downed all three, one after the other, and Brigitte encouraged her to lie down. Sia, changing into her bedclothes, climbed onto the mattress. Soon after she laid down, she felt the cramps subsiding and fell asleep.

In the morning, her cramps were better, but she expected them to worsen throughout the day. Her body was catching up on not having periods for a while. If so, she hoped she could get more of the tea tonight. Her cycle was going to be wreaking havoc for a bit because of the roller coaster of stress, physical toil, and emotion. After entering the toilet, and sitting, there was a slight burning as she urinated. Concerned about a potential reaction, she examined the material on the pad. It wouldn't be the first time. She also reacted to latex and spermicide, which she found out the hard way. That was not something she wanted to repeat.

That night, Brigitte brought her more tea. Siana gratefully drank it all. She didn't know what pain meds were in it, but she was getting some of the best sleep she'd had in a long time. She got herself into bed and waited for it to take effect. The minute it did, she was out like a light.

***

As Brigitte watched her, guilt washed over her. She felt what they were doing was wrong, but she also knew it was in her new friend's best interest. If she was recalled and handed over to someone else, she would die. They needed to make sure that didn't happen. Even if Kellan succeeded in winning her over, he could kill her. This helped prevent that. If Siana found out, things would go badly. With their language barrier, they wouldn't be able to explain why they were doing this. She would never trust them again, and she would end up dead.

Or worse—with Talon.

Technically, it was the same thing, but Talon would take his time, enjoying every ounce of pain he could cause just as he and his brother had done with Usala. Though they had no proof, it was one of those things that was known. Tamek had been beside himself when he'd heard the news of her claiming and death. None of them wanted that time repeated. Brigitte's mind warred with itself. She didn't want to be in here or be a part of this. It made her angry at everyone, including herself. She felt trapped.

If I'd kept my station, maybe I could have done something.

She knew it was a false hope. Even as a High she had little power, but maybe by now she could have changed even a bit of their laws. Inwardly, she ranted at Lorica. Though forced into it, she knew it had been her choice to go Low. She heard footsteps and opened the tent flap.

Chapter Fourteen

KELLAN SAW THE LOOK Brigitte gave them and gave her a helpless look in return. The same unspoken understanding hung in the air; they couldn't just sit her down and explain the complicated situation to her. This was something they couldn't act out. There were too many variables. She would have too many questions. This was the best they could do until they overcame the language barrier. Unfortunately, by that time, it may be too late. They were working on borrowed time.

Be Tess carried in a small box, setting it on the desk. Turning, she and Brigitte pulled back the blankets covering the sleeping female. Gently and carefully, they turned Siana from her side onto her back. Kellan lifted her hips. The females laid a thick cloth under her and removed her underpants. Brigitte carried it, laying it on the desk, while Tess pushed her nightdress up to her waist.

Kellan set Siana down on the cloth, then opened the box and took out a cylinder that was rounded at the tip, slowly increasing its girth until most of it was the same size.

"What size did we use last night?" He kept his voice quiet. He couldn't believe he was doing this; a cold guilty dread washed over him, but he didn't see another option.

Tess said, "I believe it was a number two." She was obviously not comfortable with this despite it being her idea.

He had the wrong one. He put it back in the box and removed the next size up. Kellan removed a bottle from his pocket. Brigitte opened it, since he only had one hand available. He used it to apply numbing oil to the cylinder; meanwhile, she assisted Tess in parting Siana's legs. Once accomplished, Brigitte went to fill the pitcher with the warm water they had heating in the infirmary.

While Siana slept, they used the instruments to try to stretch her opening gradually. Kellan loathed the task, the weight of their laws pressing down on him. If Talon got hold of her, because of her size, she'd die. This was their best bet to help her.

Early in the morning, Kellan sent Brigitte with a bit of *Wotal* to add to Siana's coffee to mask the pain she might feel when she woke. Hopefully, the oil lasted all night and wouldn't wear off until it took effect. Luck was on their side, and Siana acted like nothing was out of the ordinary.

That night, he noticed her flow was lighter.

"We're running out of time. Her cycle is almost over. Once it's over, she may refuse the tea."

Hopefully, she didn't, but they had to prepare for that eventuality.

Kellan chose the largest cylinder he felt he could safely use without tearing her. It was closest to the smallest *Setan* male—which would be him—so he prayed her body would accept it. It was still not large enough, but if her body could handle it, it would minimize later tearing and possibly keep her from dying. He knew despite their actions, injuries were inevitable. They couldn't change the physical size difference.

She whimpered in pain as he used it, but he didn't stop. She was asleep and *Monta* would block any memory of it. They used it for surgery for that reason. Tess had realized it took an unusually large amount of *Wotal* to induce sleep, especially considering her size. Siana also woke sooner than others. They attributed it to her race. It was determined to use *Monta* as well. If she woke up, she wouldn't remember doing so.

They also couldn't dally as they didn't know if she would stop drinking the tea. This time, he left the cylinder inside her for a longer span of time. He knew her body would contract to near normal soon, but also knew repeated usage would gradually stretch her just as repeated childbirth would stretch a female. He wanted to help her as much as possible. As long as she drank the tea, they could keep this up and really give her a fighting chance. They didn't have the luxury of explaining or waiting until she could understand. Still, he felt awful doing it.

The next night, as she once again slept, they did their normal preparations, but this time *Be* Tess said, "We don't have a larger size. You plan on claiming her. Just do it now."

Brigitte and he both stared at her in shock.

Kellan refused. "I'm not forcing myself on a sleeping female."

Tess pointed out in disbelief, "What do you think we've been doing every night?"

"We're performing medical procedures to help her body accept a *Setan* male without her dying."

Tess gave him a look that told him to stop splitting hairs. "Did you rehearse that? Or is it what you tell yourself to deal with the guilt?" She continued, "I know you want to claim her. Everyone can see how you look at her. The only one who doesn't know is her." She swung her hand at Siana's prone body. "You might as well do it. She won't remember even if she wakes up. You're worried about hurting her, and the infirmary is right there." She pointed in the general direction. "Get it over with, and everyone can stop worrying about her future. When she tears, we'll keep her asleep until she's healed. By then, it'll be too late for her to object."

He refused, his gaze fixed on Siana's drugged form. "Yes, I'm worried, but I'm not at that point yet. We just met, and she fears me. I want my claim to be accepted. I don't want a claim who doesn't trust me. As long as we stay here, I can take my time. I can get to know her, build a relationship, and prepare her body to accept mine. We can work on it slowly, preventing her from dying."

Besides, it wouldn't do Talon any good to call a Yendali if the female wasn't there to inspect.

Tess sighed. "I hope you don't regret not doing it now."

Kellan's voice was quiet but firm. "I won't. I refuse to be like the others."

Kellan ignored what he truly believed to be medically necessary, even though he hated himself for doing it while she was drugged. Each time had been an internal battle. The gruesome image of her, torn and lifeless, overcame his reluctance. He was talking about males who ignored whether the females consented or were hurt. Males like Talon. Some even enjoyed bringing them into the Hall and doing it publicly before the *Bund* and Convocation, no matter how the female felt.

He caught sight of Brigitte out of the corner of his eye. She was a good example. Lorica tried forcing her to be claimed in the Hall. At the time, he didn't stand with his brothers. He still didn't, but he didn't publicly go against them. Back then, he was a young hothead and wanted to show off to the other *Bund* that he'd claimed someone from a well-known High family. Lorica didn't understand her refusal to be claimed publicly. She tried to explain it was humiliating. That their first time together should be private and special. Unfortunately for him, she knew the law better than he did. Ultimately, her actions humiliated him.

They still haven't forgiven each other.

With Siana in mind, he longed for a claim that would accept him. His lowered position, his scars, all of him. He hoped she would be the one. The reason eluded him. There was something about her that lit a feeling in him he'd never felt. There was so much he still didn't know about her, though. They needed to find out all they could. The thought of tearing her body open with his made him physically ill. Hopefully, she would continue drinking the tea, and he could find larger sizes to help her. They prayed that in the morning she wouldn't realize what they were doing.

Chapter Fifteen

SIANA WIPED THE SWEAT off her forehead with the back of her arm. Today was going to be another hot one. They had all traded their trousers for pants that came down to their knees, but she had kept her long ones on, knowing she'd be kneeling in the dirt. All of her clothing was the same: brown headscarf, brown shirt, brown trousers.

They all wore similar clothing, simple and serviceable, but the colors varied. Almost all looked aimed at blending in with their surroundings. The only ones who wore burgundy were the medical duo. Siana had wondered if it was a color meant for infirmary personnel only. Most of the women wore scarves to protect their hair, but Siana wore one to cover hers and her ears.

The few times she'd been left alone, she tried searching the camp. They kept most supplies locked up, probably to protect them from wildlife, and she had found no weapons yet. There was an unlocked shed nearby, but it only held rudimentary tools for gardening. She'd hoped to find an axe, but she didn't. It was confusing, because they had firewood.

How did they cut it?

Movement drew her attention. Her eyes followed Norita as she walked down the dirt path to Siana. This morning, they were working in the garden. It was outside of camp, closer to a small river whose water was the clearest she'd seen. The rocky bed glowed almost copper in the sunlight.

I wouldn't mind jumping in right now, she thought as she waved a welcome at her friend. She knew she'd have the opportunity later.

She resumed pulling weeds, refocusing her attention. Even with two people working, it would take them all morning to clear only a portion of the garden. It was an extremely important job since they relied on it for much of their food, but lately their population was low, so the chores outnumbered the people.

Siana wasn't sure how long she'd been here. The days blurred with repetition. She'd found her place within the camp relatively quickly, used to changing groups back home. People were killed, and others took their place. You learned to adjust quickly to various personalities.

She'd also noticed the population of the camp changed. There were at least eight or more women when she'd arrived, but they started leaving. The first time she'd noticed it, a family comprising a woman and two men appeared. The woman and one man appeared to be older than the second man. They had talked to Norita's friend, Giselle. After a time, Doctor Kellan appeared, and they all left. They were gone for a long time. Eventually the doctor reappeared with Giselle, who packed her belongings, and left with the people after sad farewells.

She asked Brigitte, but didn't understand what she was trying to tell her until Brigitte said, "Mrs."

At that, Siana understood the girl had left to be married. This happened randomly. Sometimes it was just a man who appeared, other times, families of various sizes. All looked to be in different states of income. Because of chores, she usually had to leave before they did, failing to see which path they took. Siana wondered what the camp's actual purpose was but never found enough clues for a solid conclusion.

Before a few left, she saw the jewelry they were wearing removed. They put a new one in its place. She learned it was called "banding." Out of all of them, Siana was the only one without it. She'd repeatedly tried to ask Brigitte why, but she'd only shake her head. Eventually, Siana gave up. It didn't matter. As soon as she could find a suitable weapon, and a way to pack supplies, she planned on leaving to find her brother. Her backpack was also missing, and she wanted it. She still hadn't discovered where all the paths led to.

The first path she'd traveled had been to the laundry area. Discovering the south path led to the garden took that off her list. The easterly path led to a small makeshift barn with goat-like creatures and some version of chickens. Two other paths had yet to reveal themselves.

One of those has to lead out of here.

It was difficult to explore. Every time she tried to walk down one, someone—usually Brigitte—stopped her, shaking her head and just saying, "No."

When Siana showed she wanted to explore the path, Brigitte refused her. Siana tried acting out about Jacob, but the only thing Brigitte seemed to understand was that Siana wanted to look around, not that she wanted to look for someone. Siana was becoming frustrated, feeling almost like a prisoner.

Thinking back to the women who'd left, it was now just Brigitte, Norita, the Berdons, Doctor Kellan, *Be* Tess, and her.

She had helped clean and seal the empty tents and learned they were all the same inside. Brigitte had moved to her own tent once she was sure Siana could handle being on her own.

All meals were now held together in the eating hall, and Siana frequently found herself sitting next to the doctor. Over time, she had lost her suspicion of everyone. There was literally no sign of anyone being anything other than what they appeared.

So how did I get here? Where was "here"?

She had been treated with nothing but kindness and compassion. When they were all together eating or around the fire at night—now that she wasn't scared of their eyes— sometimes Doctor Kellan sat close enough to touch her. She got the feeling it was deliberate. He never paid attention to only her and spoke to everyone, so she felt she was being a bit too suspicious about it.

The mid-meal sounded, and both women looked up with relief. It seemed to be heating up for the hottest day yet, and they could both use a break. They were free to take one any time they needed, but by agreement, they wanted to do as much as possible before they stopped. Doctor Kellan had forbidden any laborious activity during the hottest parts of the day, especially if it was in full sun, which the garden would be by the time the meal was over.

After washing up in the river, they made their way up the path. Those already there welcomed them into the hall. Kellan told a story that she couldn't understand, but the acting he did got it across to her. He had everyone laughing so hard Mr. Berdon fell off the bench, which caused them all to laugh harder once they knew he was okay. Siana wished Jacob was here. She bet he'd try to outdo Kellan with stories. Her smile faded, and she stared straight ahead. She barely registered Kellan and Brigitte glancing at each other with concerned eyes.

After the meal, Brigitte motioned Siana aside, a troubled look on her face. She said to her, "I go."

"Go?"

"Brigitte go."

"Go where?" she asked in English before she caught herself, but Brigitte understood.

Brigitte thought for a second and said, "*Davned.*"

She tried again when her friend didn't understand. "Mrs. Atwood." She drew a house with her hands.

Home. She was going home.

She was losing her friend. Despite the language barrier, they had grown closer. Brigitte's kindness and pushing had helped her overcome some of her fears, and she had taught her a bit about their world, including some of their language. Mainly how to use the things Siana came across, but, to her, that was a big help. The thought of being on her own caused panic to lightly rise in her. Later, Siana tried to hide her tears as she waved goodbye to Brigitte's retreating figure.

***

Brigitte's eyes held tears as she was leaving. Kellan knew she didn't agree with their plans, honestly neither did he, but right now it's all they had. They had to keep Siana hidden until she accepted Kellan, since everyone agreed he was the best claimant. That wasn't the part she disagreed with. What she disagreed with was their back-up plan.

Upon approaching Siana, he saw the others had gone to the shade to cool down. He put an arm around her shoulders. She stiffened, then relaxed. He looked down at her, giving an understanding smile as he used a finger to wipe away a tear from her cheek. Kellan gave her a gentle squeeze as they both watched as Brigitte disappeared from view.

Siana looked at him again. Her sad and quiet tone tugged at him. "Brigitte no go."

She talked on the level of a small child, but she was making progress, albeit slower than they would like. After a short time, her difficulty with the local language was clear. Despite learning small words, she struggled to understand and pronounce the larger ones and the more complicated concepts.

He responded to her statement by softly rubbing her upper arm. Pressure on the side of his chest and lower back caused him to look down. She was leaning against him, her arm around his back. He couldn't stop his smile as warmth filled him.

Her head snapped up as she looked at him with wide eyes, then stepped back causing him to remove his arm.

***

With a glance upward at him, he seemed both pensive and anxious as Brigitte departed. He didn't seem to look directly at her retreating figure, but more in her general direction. Siana wondered what he was thinking.

She hadn't realized she'd leaned against him, nor did she notice she put her arm around him. It seemed like a natural thing to do, and she did it without thinking. She'd bolted up when she realized what she'd done. A small part of her didn't want him to let go. Because she felt lost, she longed for physical connection with another. Not knowing what else to do, she turned toward her tent and escaped the heat of the day.

In the morning, Siana walked to the dining hall for breakfast. It felt odd walking alone when Brigitte was normally with her. Norita was already leaving, so she knew she was late, but didn't worry about food. They'd hold a plate for her. It might be cold if she was late, but that was on her. It was a relief having food available for each meal after months of having to scrounge and forage. Again, she was surprised at how quickly she adapted. She saw Doctor Kellan was arriving late as well. Hopefully there hadn't been an emergency.

"Hello, Doctor Kellan." She was determined to use her language skills and improve.

"Hello, Siana." He looked like he was thinking. "Kellan. No doctor."

"Kellan." That would make things easier now that she didn't need to say his title constantly.

"You eat?" he asked.

She shook her head. "No."

He motioned ahead of him. "We go eat."

Nodding, she preceded him into the dining hall. Today, there was some sort of porridge, honey, and toasted sourdough. Much to her disappointment, her favorite item was nowhere to be seen.

Kellan asked, "You okay?"

With a pretend dramatic slump of her shoulders and a sigh, she said, "No coffee," her face portraying utter misery.

Amused, his gesture indicated the carafe that remained. "Tea."

"Tea." She sighed, her nose wrinkling slightly.

Chuckling, he said, "Tea is good."

Grudgingly, she agreed.

Coffee would've been better.

That evening after dinner, Kellan came up to her. "Siana, come."

That earned him a puzzled look from her.

He motioned to her. "Come."

After following him out of the building, he directed his gaze toward a path she had not yet explored.

Yay! Wait, we're alone.

When she hesitated, he turned to her. "It's okay. Come."

After they'd gone a bit, she wondered where he was taking her.

Stopping, she turned back to see how far they were from the camp. His understanding gaze met hers when she looked back at him.

"It's all right. I'm..." He was obviously struggling for words.

Siana reminded herself that if he was going to hurt her, he could have done so many times already. Yet, it never hurt to be cautious. With an anxious look, she approached him. He gave her an encouraging nod, turned, and kept walking. As they walked down the dirt path further from camp, she began getting more nervous.

A progressively louder background noise sparked her curiosity. As she rounded a bend, she discovered a waterfall. The pool it fell into was on their level. As they drew closer, she saw the water was clear, with purples and blues coating the walls under it. A strong, unidentifiable smell emanated from it. Steam rose from the water, and small whitish stone cliffs surrounded it. Though not huge, the waterfall and cliffs could inflict serious injuries if you fell. She began walking closer, but Kellan stopped her by holding his arm in front of her.

Pointing to a mark on the cliff wall, he said, "No go. Water hurts. Look. Understand?"

Darn, that water looked so perfect for a soak. What a shame.

Nodding, she wondered if it was like the pools at Yellowstone. People liked to leave the marked trails against posted rules and touch the water. They usually discovered the hard way it wasn't a smart move because of the water temperature and some pools held sulfuric acid.

That's what I smell. Sulfur. It is like Yellowstone.

Kellan moved to the side, sitting on the grass where the spray didn't hit while still watching the fall. As she sat near him, she watched it intently. This world had unique beauty, and some were like her own world. Colorful birds, lizard-like creatures, and foliage made this area feel almost tropical. Yesterday, she could've sworn she saw a bird similar to a parrot. She really wished her brother were here to see it, though she doubted she'd get him out of the forest.

As they sat there, neither felt the need to talk. They just let themselves be, though Siana was wondering how to get the idea of looking for her brother across to Kellan. She really wished she had her cell phone. The pictures of Jacob would go a long way. Though she still didn't know if he was here or still in their world.

We were together. It would make sense if he was also here, but my choker had slipped. If his hadn't, where would he be? And why didn't the blanket block the tracker?

Remembering the beginning of the end, she realized the man who gave them the blankets had said they helped to block them, not that they completely blocked them.

The sun was setting quickly, and the air chilled. Kellan stood. He offered Siana his hand; she took it, and he helped her to her feet. He didn't let go, which caused conflicted feelings.

I can't get involved. Not until I know where Jacob is.

She gave a gentle tug, and he released her hand. They began walking in silence back to the camp. Lost in thought, she didn't realize Kellan had pulled ahead of her. Soon, it became dark, and she couldn't see the path.

She stopped, a slight quiver in her voice. "Kellan?"

It took a minute before she saw lights coming her way. His glowing eyes still made her start at first sight, but now she was glad for them. When he reached her, he took her hand in his again.

"I'm sorry." She kind of felt like a burden.

She saw his eyes shake back and forth.

Now that's freaky.

"No sorry. It's okay." His tone was reassuring.

As he held her hand, their return to camp began.

"Thank you." It's all she could think to say.

His thumb stroked her hand as he said something she didn't understand. When his thumb stopped, she found herself disappointed. She lectured herself not to get involved with him.

I'm leaving.

She wistfully thought about having a partner. As far as her love life, being alone wasn't something she minded. It was more about having a normal life again. Having the possibility of a future without her current uncertainties.

As he escorted her to her tent, he opened the flap and wished her good night.

"Good night," she said. At least, she assumed it was good night. It was definitely said when parting company at the end of the day.

She noticed the lantern was lit as she entered her tent. The way it lit at sundown, and how it went out again hours later, was unknown to her. She had inspected it and didn't find a light sensor. Grateful for its glow, she began preparing for bed.

A couple hours later, Kellan quietly checked her tent to see if she was sleeping, waved his hand, and the light went out. He walked back to the infirmary to get his own sleep.

Chapter Sixteen

OVER THE COMING DAYS, she began taking walks with Kellan after dinner. Sometimes they went back to the waterfall and just sat. Other times, he took her to see various plants or animals he found. While he named them, it didn't help her with conversation. They rarely spoke. If she tried, he didn't. It was making her uncomfortable. She didn't know if he just didn't like to talk, or if he assumed she didn't want to because of the language issue.

How am I supposed to learn if he doesn't speak?

A couple of accidental brushes occurred between them. His expression suggested he welcomed the touch. Though she longed to touch him, she reminded herself she was leaving.

One rainy day, after the evening meal, he said, "Siana, stay."

Curious, she repeated like a parrot, "Stay?"

Pointing to a chair, he said, "Sit."

She bit her lip, knuckles white, to keep from barking out loud. He gave orders instead of asking.

She sat back down, humoring him. He hurried away and soon returned with a wooden box.

"You know *Yepja*?"

With a shake of her head, she looked at the container. It didn't give her any clues to work with. He opened it, a bit excited. It was a board game.

"You want to try?" He looked so hopeful, she almost laughed.

Why not?

"Okay."

The sheer delight on his face mirrored a child's Christmas morning happiness: wide-eyed and brimming with anticipation.

I guess he doesn't have anyone to play with.

It was a game similar to checkers. It wasn't quite the same, and what he didn't know was she kicked Jacob's butt many times. She was a checker expert. The first game was her learning. The language barrier made it take far longer to figure out than it should have. By the second game, she had gotten the hang of some of it, and she began figuring out strategies. When they noticed it was getting late, they called a halt for the evening. Together, they cleaned it up. Kellan put it away and walked her back to her tent, lighting the way. She realized it was quite handy to have a walking flashlight.

The following evening, after a supper of stew and bread, the rain returned, and she noticed his hopeful expression. Nodding, she watched with amusement as he jumped up and jogged to the cabinet. His childlike eagerness was endearing. They played a couple of rounds, and she finally fully understood all the rules. With the language issue, they again took a while to play each game, and it became late. Again, Kellan walked her to her tent after. A lingering look suggested he wanted to say something but ultimately decided against it.

"Good night." He turned and left.

To her, it felt similar to dating, though she was probably reading too much into it. Siana found herself wishing for a good night kiss and promptly began lecturing herself again.

The next night, he asked her to play instead of taking a walk. With a smile, she allowed her game flag to fly, gave Kellan a run for his money, and won the first round. He looked like a proud father when she did. The second game went the way of the first. He won the third game, obviously realizing he needed to play seriously. They played once more. Siana was winning when he dropped a round metal thing he'd been fidgeting with. She didn't know what it was. She grabbed it as it rolled by. When she sat up and handed it to him, she went to move her piece, and it was missing.

"Kellan." She drew his name out in an accusatory tone.

"What?" His innocent act was over the top.

"Give."

"Give what?"

She reached over and took the piece back from his pile.

He looked insulted and shook his head, though he wasn't hiding his "cheating" at all.

Later, she went to get a drink of water and returned to find his pieces rearranged to give him a clear advantage. He was intensely interested in his own nails.

"Kellan!" She didn't know whether or not to laugh.

"They do it." He gave an innocent shrug, gesturing at his pieces.

Such a blatant lie caused her mouth to hang open, and she graced him with a disbelieving look.

"No, or I not play." She gave him a pretend stern look, crossing her arms and adding a foot-tapping for good measure.

He shrugged, his hands wide, huge innocent eyes looking at her. "What?"

She looked at her chair to sit down and saw a piece of hers get snatched.

"Kellan!" She laughed in disbelief. *Such outright cheating.*

From her standing position, Siana saw that his hand still held it. Holding hers out, palm up, she said, "Give."

He stood up, pushing his chair back with a shrug. "Give what?" he said in a teasing tone.

"Give, Kellan." *The man seriously had some guts.*

He backed away, raising it high above her grasp. "You not have. Too small."

Her jaw dropped. After she closed her mouth, she thought, *Challenge accepted.*

He saw her face and ran around the tables. Giving chase, she demanded he give it back. He refused. They chased each other around the dining hall, laughing as they ran, with

Kellan knocking chairs into her way. They had a stalemate when they both were on opposite sides of a large table, going back and forth. She stopped and smiled at him. He froze, clearly wondering what she was up to. She hopped on the chair, stepped on the table, and jumped at him before he could blink. He caught her so she wouldn't get hurt, lost his balance, and fell, with her landing on top of him.

Siana's eyes widened in horror. "I'm sorry." Still laying on him, she reached up and checked his head. "You okay?"

He coughed, stuck his tongue out, and "died."

Apparently, he's not that hurt, but I could swear he hit the floor hard.

With a decision to check for injuries, she lifted one eyelid to check his pupil.

When he saw her concerned face, he acted without thinking. He leaned up, gave her a quick kiss on the lips, then "died" again.

Siana froze. Though unexpected, she wanted this, wanted his touch, but she knew it wasn't possible. She had to find her brother. She also wanted a normal life. A partner. Her career back. Maybe children in the future.

I'm starting to feel trapped between finding Jacob and wanting Kellan and what he represents.

He opened his eyes, saw her face, and then apologized.

With a shake of her head, she slowly rose and departed from the dining hall, hiding the emotions at war within her.

***

Kellan was lecturing himself. He'd thought they had something starting, but clearly she didn't feel the same. He sat up, rubbing the back of his head, and made a mental note to have Tess check it.

Maybe she just wasn't ready?

He pushed himself up from the floor to clean up the mess from the game and the chairs he'd knocked over.

Maybe it's my scars?

He hoped not. She never seemed bothered by them, but it's possible she hid her distaste.

Thinking back on the weeks since her arrival, Kellan had discovered she had good qualities he'd like in a mate. Her kindness and care for others were clear; she willingly helped with any task, however disgusting, and she didn't seem to mind living in the camp, a place he often inhabited. Sometimes, he saw a spark of fire in her eyes that she seemed to keep hidden. It intrigued him. There was more to her than she showed. With the shortage of females, he counted himself lucky to find one—granted, she didn't know it yet.

Worried, he knew if he didn't claim her, things wouldn't go well. Tamek's previous message stated Talon hadn't requested a *Yendali* yet, but Talon was notorious for ninth-bell calls or, more alarmingly, for stealing a female and forcibly claiming her, usually resulting in her death. Not from the claiming, but because of what he did to her afterward.

She was under House Devereaux. Claiming is one law House Devereaux was trying to change, but until they did, they were bound by them. Originally started to protect females from unscrupulous males, it had morphed into something else. Slowly walking the game back to the cabinet, he grew more concerned. Siana wasn't at the house, but the Convocation could call for her return. He had to claim her before then. Tamek had a plan to stall, but they could only stall for so long without risking their positions. Without their positions, they could change nothing. He closed the cabinet and walked to the open door of the hall. He watched her leave the outdoor toilet.

If Tamek had to stall, it would force Kellan to sedate her and get the deed done. Every fiber of his being didn't want it to come to that, but if he had to do it to keep her alive, he would, though he didn't know if what they had done to her worked. It's possible he could kill her. He cared for her, and he couldn't stop the gruesome mental image of her being torn apart to death from filling his mind. His fists clenched. The memory of what they had done and planned to do, despite their objections to the law, haunted him.

As he watched Siana return to her tent, Kellan wondered, *Are we really any better than Talon?*

He decided he'd try to talk to her in the morning. Maybe, with her increased language skills, he could get her to understand something of what they had to deal with. He shut off the light and went to his room in the infirmary.

***

Siana got ready for bed, even though it was early. Her thoughts were in chaos. When he kissed her, quick though it was, her body answered. She didn't know him well, but what she knew, she liked. So far, he had ticked all her boxes. From all appearances, he was a kind man. His removing the knife from her without thought for himself showed he could do what was necessary to protect himself and others. His apparent liking of her was evident in the kiss and his body's reactions, though she knew men could react to a sandwich. For just a minute, she thought of what could be. She let herself imagine a partner, a home, a family.

That wouldn't be fair to him or me.

Once she found Jacob, there was no guarantee they'd stay here. Finding her brother was her number one goal after learning to communicate. Leading Kellan on wouldn't be nice. She also didn't know their customs. Plus, she still didn't know where she was. Until she did, she couldn't allow herself to get involved with anyone. The only thing she knew was that the place and language were called *Setan*.

She was becoming frustrated with the language. It was hard when they forgot and started speaking beyond her comprehension without trying to help her understand. They did it a lot. When she was here, Brigitte spoke to her. After she left, they spoke around her. Now she understood how an old friend of hers felt. She was deaf. Because nobody knew sign language, Siana tried to include her after noticing she had been left out of many conversations. Siana had learned a little, but the friend had moved away soon after, and she hadn't continued.

It sucks being left out.

She climbed into bed, leaving the blankets off. Though the days were cooling, she was hot. She closed her eyes, pushed everything from her mind, and tried to sleep—a task easier said than done.

Chapter Seventeen

AFTER VISITING THE OUTHOUSE and dressing for the day, Siana stayed in her tent. Her thoughts were still all over the place, and she wasn't sure she wanted to interact with others. She was concerned about Jacob. Time slipped away faster than she liked, and she remained no closer to finding him because her situation trapped her.

Because she had a day off from chores—everyone rotated days off—she could take her time and think. She wondered if the infirmary held a map, though she wasn't sure she could figure anything out without knowing their geography. She did not know where she was, where their estate had been, or where the field was.

It wouldn't hurt to look. Maybe I can make them understand I want to know where their home is. I know that word. At least, it would give me a starting point.

That plan changed when a knock sounded on a pole of her tent. She hoped it wasn't Kellan. She did not know how to act right now. The object of her thoughts was standing there when she opened the flap. Once he saw her, that grin lit him up. He seemed genuinely happy she opened her tent flap. Slowly stepping outside, she found a hot mug in front of her face.

With a surprised look, she gratefully accepted the gift. He'd brought her coffee.

A peace offering?

He spoke first. "You okay?" His face returned to seriousness.

She stopped blowing on the coffee long enough to say, "I'm okay."

His grin came back. She refused to look at it.

"I'm sorry," he said.

She shook her head and gave him a small smile as she said, "No. No sorry."

He motioned toward the logs near her fire pit before walking over to sit down. Despite a longing for sugar and milk, she joined him, sipping on her drink. He kept fiddling with the bottom edge of his tunic. A small wave of calm washed over her as she saw his nervous fidgeting.

"You sad at me?"

She could see he was struggling to find words.

"No." Her look of confusion caused his brow to furrow.

"You *nete*?"

"*Nete?*"

In his usual dramatic style, he stood, scrunched his face, stomped around, and growled.

With a smile at his mummery, she shook her head. "No, I not angry."

He sat down next to her, looking relieved. Gently lifting her left hand, he softly stroked the back. She could feel a slight tremor in his hand.

He's really nervous.

"Siana like Kellan?"

Oh, hell. This is what I wanted to avoid. What do I say?

If Jacob and she stayed here, she could have a future with him, but if they left, she couldn't be with him. She was honest.

"Yes, but..."

How do I explain this? She needed her phone. She needed a picture of Jacob.

Facing him, she tried to explain. "Kellan, I—"

A shout interrupted them. A local, looking frantic, had run into the encampment. Upon seeing Kellan, the man ran over. Kellan spoke with him, then jogged to the infirmary. Siana only understood the man needed the doctor.

Hey, that's something. At least I got that much.

Kellan returned to her, his assistant accompanying him. He took the mug from her hand, much to her dismay, and set it on the log seat. With complete seriousness, he held her left hand. From his pocket, he produced a simple silver band. He slid it on her middle finger, where it automatically resized itself, causing her to start. He then put a matching one on his own. As she looked at it, puzzled, he turned his hand upside down and briefly joined his ring to hers. Her ring made a noise.

Siana watched in astonishment as three silver chains emerged from the ring and traveled down the back of her hand. When they reached the middle, they each moved in a separate small circle, then continued toward her wrist. Within each circle, a unique stone appeared. What looked like a tiny ruby appeared in the first one, an opal in the middle one, and a sapphire in the third. As the chains, which appeared to have a life of their own, reached her wrist, a silver band began encircling it. The chains joined to the wristband, and the noise stopped when the bracelet was complete. As she moved her hand, the chains, glove-like, stayed on her skin without pinching or pulling.

Holy crap, this is tech or magic. Given their ability with their hands, she'd guess the latter.

During her time at the camp, she'd learned the only things the hand motion worked on were wood-based objects. It seemed the *Setan* drew power from it. Their ability to draw light from wood explained its extensive use. Even her lantern was made of wood. The light she had seen in rooms had come from wood trim.

Once the low noise from the ring stopped, Kellan took her hand with his and laid his other one over the chains. *"Rembit."*

Still puzzled, she glanced at him, then she looked back at their hands.

"Siana." His serious tone wasn't his normal voice. The stare he gave her made her understand what he said was important. He searched for words. "No off. Understand?"

She realized, giving him a surprised nod, that she was banded. Unsure of its meaning or the reason for the change, she now possessed her own hand jewelry. It felt lighter than she expected. While it would take some getting used to, it wasn't uncomfortable. It was definitely pretty.

But why?

Upon examination, the ring revealed openings perfectly sized for the jewels on Kellan's ring, which were identical to those on her chains. That they had matching jewelry made her slightly uneasy. This implied a connection between them, and she wished she understood its purpose, especially after that quick kiss and their recent aborted conversation. Kellan got her attention, and she focused on him.

"Tess, I go. Come back." He used his fingers like people, showing them going away and coming back.

Siana nodded. She watched them leave with medical bags, then went back to studying her jewelry, trying to find a way to remove it if she needed to. He'd told her to not take it off, but if she was injured, she'd need to. No matter how much she examined, twisted, or turned it, it was solid, as if all one piece. There appeared no way to take it off.

So why did he tell her not to?

Chapter Eighteen

SIANA WAS GATHERING EGGS from the chicken-like creatures—they had fur, not feathers, and were tripods, which made them funny to watch—when she heard the yelling. Quickly finishing, she held onto the basket and rushed back into camp. The elder couple was rushing into the infirmary. Siana followed the trail of blood like breadcrumbs. Upon entering, she noticed Norita holding her arm. Her nursing skills kicked in. After setting down her basket of eggs, she hurried to Norita's side to examine the injury. The cut wasn't large, but it was bleeding steadily. She realized the elder couple were calling for Kellan.

"Kellan, *Be* Tess go."

The couple nor Norita were thrilled to hear this. They'd been gone for a couple of days now. Siana had missed their walks and game nights. Even meals were quiet without Kellan around.

The injury, on closer inspection, proved not to be too deep. It just needed a few stitches. She remembered *Be* Tess needing to do sutures for someone else. Siana had returned a basket of clean pads when an accident had happened. She had stayed out of curiosity and in case *Be* Tess needed help. Kellan had been elsewhere.

Where did she get those from?

Siana searched the area where she thought the suture thread was. After finding it, she looked for the bottle she had also seen. Mentally reviewing the steps Kellan's assistant had taken, and how the oil was used to numb the skin, she then retrieved soap, a clean cloth, and water. She washed her hands and cleaned the wound. Norita resisted at first.

Siana told her, "It's all right."

Whether it was her words, or the fact she seemed to know what she was doing, the injured woman allowed treatment. She prepared the items, doing her best despite the items being unfamiliar and her stitching skills being rusty from disuse. Norita held her arm still as Siana worked. Three did the trick. After she finished, she searched for the wrap she saw used on the previous injury while Norita inspected her arm. She found it, then wrapped the wound, cut the material, and sealed it with paste from a jar she had watched *Be* Tess use.

Concerned, she asked Norita, "All right?"

The patient, with a relieved smile, nodded. Siana noticed the elder couple was looking at her with something akin to shock. Norita jumped off the table and gingerly moved her arm. Siana made a "careful" motion with her hands.

She received a nod of understanding, and Norita left the infirmary before Siana could figure out where any pain relief was, calling out, "Thank you."

While she cleaned up the trash and blood, the elder couple murmured to each other. Siana's questioning look prompted a bow, smile, and departure from them.

***

Kellan felt the same shock the couple had felt when he discovered Siana had stitched up Norita's arm. Upon his return without Tess, who remained with the patient, the couple informed him that his claim tended an injury on their granddaughter. They were concerned about it being done correctly.

Upon entering the infirmary, he found it unchanged. There was no immediate sign of recent use. He set off to find Norita, doubting the couple's assertions. He found her with Siana, both laughing at the antics of a *toob* climbing around a tree and making noises at them.

As he walked toward Norita, he asked, "Are you okay?"

"Yes."

They had a brief conversation, and he carefully undid the bandage and inspected Siana's work. He asked the injured female more questions, which she answered. He re-wrapped the injury and turned to Siana.

Kellan was stunned. She stitched the injury as skillfully as he or Tess. It was clean and well wrapped. When asked, Norita told him the steps Siana had taken as well as she could remember. It was almost perfect. The only thing Siana forgot was a bit of *Wotal* for the pain. Norita informed him she would've refused it anyhow. It made her sick, plus it didn't hurt that much. When Kellan turned to Siana, he hesitated. She looked like a child awaiting a scolding. He schooled his face into a smile.

Kellan motioned toward Norita's arm, and said, "Thank you."

He motioned for her to follow him. "Come."

***

Siana followed with some trepidation. Norita waved and went into her tent.

After he led her into the infirmary, Kellan stopped. He turned to her. "Siana doctor?"

She shook her head.

"Siana *Be*?"

She shrugged, but nodded. She didn't fully understand what a *Be* was. Though suspecting it was a nurse, she wasn't completely positive about what the position entailed. She didn't want to claim to be something she wasn't, but she didn't want him thinking she was an untrained hack treating people.

His eyes, as he stared at her, held something she couldn't place. She swore they changed color for a split second as he moved closer to her. Like a feather, his finger stroked her cheek. Her breath quickened, even as she told herself to step away. This couldn't happen. Her body ignored her, a fire starting deep inside, willing him to touch her.

Kellan opened his mouth to say something when they heard a low whistle. He motioned for her to stay before going outside. Siana, a little sexually frustrated, curiously moved to look out the window, but Kellan walked out of view. He wasn't gone long. When he returned, he looked worried.

Kellan grabbed Siana's hand. "Come." Hurriedly, he dragged her to the edge of the woods. "Stay."

She watched him rush toward Norita's tent. He disappeared inside for a minute, then exited with her running behind him. Kellan swung by the elder couple's tent, poked his head inside, said something, and then turned back toward Siana. Kellan, running past her, motioned for her to follow. Both women ran behind him as he raced through the woods. Norita seemed to know what was happening, judging by her fearful expression, but Siana was clueless. She tripped on a tree root, fell, and Kellan ran back to help her up. They continued to run as if their lives depended on it. She was wheezing when they broke into a tiny clearing.

Lorica waited, hair tied back, catching his breath.

Did he run here in front of us?

Seated on his mount, he held the reins of another.

His urgency unmistakable, Kellan motioned to both females. "Go! Go!"

Norita jumped on the back of the closest mount, wincing at the use of her arm. She turned and took off with the beast. It was clear she knew what the plan was and where to go.

Lorica motioned for her to come to him. "Come!" His tone was urgent.

Not understanding why, she hurried over. Lorica reached down, grabbed her, and quickly lifted her by her arm while Kellan pushed her up. Siana caught sight of his face and the relief he showed when he saw her banding.

What's going on?

As he reached, arching his back, he dropped her behind him in a heap, causing Malk to shift his back four legs in protest.

Lorica brought him under control and told Siana to sit. She obeyed while trying not to fall off, Kellan attempting to steady her. Once she was on, Kellan moved away. Lorica reached back and grabbed each of her arms, wrapping them around his waist. As soon as he finished that, he said something she didn't hear and urgently said something to his mount, who bounded forward. The sudden movement caused her to tighten her hold, and the wind rushing by made her bury her face in his back.

Jeez, this thing is fast.

Once she became used to the movement, she raised her head to look around. Her scarf, caught by the strong currents of air, unwrapped itself from her head and landed in a tree. The pins held her hair in its bun for now, but spirals played with the wind around her face. They were galloping through the woods, man and mount seemingly as one.

Upon encountering a road, he turned right and continued galloping. Lorica's muscles moved and rippled under her arms as he controlled and guided his mount, his body and arms shifting. Its body was wider than any horse she'd seen, and she had a feeling she'd be quite sore by the end of the journey. The ride was jarring for someone not used to it. For right now, her primary concern was not bouncing off, though with six legs, the ride was smoother than she expected. She couldn't help but wonder what had set off this chain of events.

***

Kellan ran back to Tess; her surprise was apparent.

Partially bent over, trying to catch his breath, he waited until he could breathe easily before he said to her, "Lorica appeared. Someone leaked the camp's location."

"The females?" Tess's brow furrowed with apprehension.

"I got them out. I warned the Berdons as I was leading Siana and Norita into the forest."

"Do we know who?"

He shook his head, using the nickname he usually called his brother. "Lor may, but we didn't have time to discuss it. He was barely ahead of them. Norita went to the caves. Lor is taking Siana there as well. I'll go get them once it's over."

After catching his breath and drinking some water, Kellan walked back to the camp, acting like he'd been out on a stroll. The mercenaries had searched the camp before departing, leaving it empty. Tent flaps that were previously sealed were open, some items strewn outside. The eating hall door was swinging in the breeze. He saw Mrs. Berdon kneeling on the ground by her mate. Kellan hurried over to see how he was. He had sustained minor injuries during the soldiers' "questions."

"Norita?" Mrs. Berdon quietly asked, worry for her granddaughter clear.

"She's safe." They deliberately didn't share where the females hid with the couple. The less information people had, the better.

The infirmary, to which he led the elder, was largely untouched. He wondered if it was because they knew who owned it. The elderly couple shared what little information they had: they were looking for unclaimed females, not a specific one. That both bothered and relieved Kellan. It meant they weren't looking for Siana. Then again, they could've been saying that to not tip their hand. Either way, the camp's compromise signaled the end of their time. The couple cleaned up the soldiers' mess after dealing with the elder male's injuries, while Kellan went to the caves for the females.

Kellan's temper flared. Only Norita was in the cave. When questioned, she hadn't seen Lorica or Siana at all. That *blotzen* took her home.

Why? Why would he do this? It puts her in danger. I can't claim her.

His younger brother hadn't really been on their side when they challenged the laws, but deliberately putting a female in danger wasn't something Kellan expected him to do. Especially one that was under House Devereaux's protection.

It probably had something to do with Brigitte.

Lorica got tunnel vision when it came to her. Kellan guessed Brigitte was livid he'd called her back—most likely missing her—and that his taking Siana was an appeasement. Kellan decided Lorica better be ready to appease him, or he may just break his pretty nose.

My claim.

Though he knew Siana hadn't agreed yet, he decided he wasn't letting anyone else touch her. Earlier, he'd wanted to lay her on the exam table, cover her with himself, feeling her body against his. For a split second, he thought about it. Thought about drugging her, claiming her, and it had nothing to do with keeping her safe. She was his. The thoughts were concerning. It wasn't normal for him.

At least she has my claim on her. Lorica won't get into trouble if they're stopped. An unbanded female with a ringed male was just asking for a trip to the Hall.

Chapter Nineteen

SIANA DID NOT KNOW how long they'd been riding when Lorica suddenly veered off into the trees. Both ducked to avoid branches while he took them away from view of the road. He found a rocky outcrop and backed his mount in behind it. He hid them as best he could. She went to question him, but he shushed her. Then she heard it: mounts and voices.

Apparently, their ears were for more than looks.

Something hit her face, shocking her; instinctively, she caught part of it, giving Lorica a what-the-heck expression.

Lorica impassively pointed at her bare hair.

She reached up, covered her locks with it, and sat as still as possible. She understood if the sun hit it, it would shine within the dark forest. The men passing didn't seem to be in much of a hurry. Their voices carried as they laughed and talked among themselves. Lorica was like a statue, though she was more impressed his mount was the same. Neither made a sound nor moved an inch. As she looked at him, she noticed short swords on each side of his saddle and a crossbow near her knee.

For man or predators?

Given everyone's actions, she leaned toward the former.

A few minutes after the men had passed, Lorica motioned for her to get down. She did so gladly, but her legs almost buckled. She wasn't used to this.

Lorica, who had already dismounted, steadied her. As he walked away, he said, "Go toilet."

She stood, waiting for him to finish. He looked back at her and said, "Siana, go toilet."

Siana glanced at him, realized what she'd done, and immediately turned away. She did not know why she was being modest about it. It's not like she hadn't seen others use the bathroom before. Not thinking, she said in her language, "Okay, I will." She went to find a private area.

***

Lorica didn't know what she said. He knew it was an affirmative, but that was it. He liked the sound. To him, it had a softer quality than his language. Then again, he really had nothing to compare it to other than Falon, whose language was harsh and guttural. Given his boredom, maybe he would ask her to teach him the language. It could be fun talking about the *Bund* without them understanding. He wondered if they had curse words. He'd like to use a few of those on certain people as well. A mischievous grin lit up his face at the thought. It seemed he'd forgotten he belonged to their ranks.

***

Siana made sure she was alone before finding a spot to pull her bottoms down and off. She'd never gotten the hang of not splashing her clothes while peeing in the woods. Though it put her in more danger, eventually she had given up and just taken it all off. Jacob had told her to dig a hole, and it would help, but at some point, they'd lost their little spade, so she adjusted.

She looked around at the leaves, praying she wouldn't find their version of poison ivy; then, she pulled a few that looked promising to wipe with. After redressing, she realized she wouldn't be able to clean her hands. She got nothing on her, but she did not know what she was touching. Plus, it was just basic hygiene.

Which meant he couldn't either unless he had something in his pack.

Upon returning to the mount, she found he had already finished and was searching in his bag. She held up her hands and motioned like she was washing them, but he shook his head. She'd had to deal with that before, so it wasn't a tremendous surprise. Not ideal, but life happens. He pulled out a cloth containing something, unwrapped the top half, held it by the covered end, and held it out to her. It looked like jerky. She pulled out a piece. She sniffed it, and ignoring her discerning stomach, took a bite. It was unexpectedly delicious; she ate it with joyful abandon.

***

Lorica gave her an amused look.

She was like a child discovering things for the first time.

Malk made a noise in agreement. Lorica gave him a warning look, and the *storjen* rolled his eyes.

Lorica had Malk with him when Tamek explained Siana's reaction to *Setan* eyes. Tamek had just read Kellan's latest letter. No one was sure what she'd do if she knew about their mounts. They both figured it wouldn't be as upsetting, but held off showing her. Malk had agreed to behave, to hide his intellect, after an argument with his rider. Lorica knew she wouldn't be able to hear Malk anyway, as she was not his rider, but they wanted to play it safe.

He watched Siana walk around, sometimes stretching her legs, looking at everything around them. A light brown mound seemed to catch her eye. As she walked back to Lorica, she beckoned him. He followed her, catching sight of the creature. He stopped, got her attention, and shook his head.

Pointing at it, he said, "*Shel*." Then he said, "*Shel gond*."

As he watched her approach it, he knew it was the perfect moment to teach her those words. Upon joining her, he saw her realization that saving the creature was impossible.

Slowly, he swept his hands along the beast. He said, "*Shel*."

Pointing at Malk, Lorica said, "*Storjen*."

Again, to the creature. "*Shel*." Back to Malk, who was giving him a side eye. "*Storjen*."

***

After Siana repeated the words while pointing at the animals, for a second, she thought the *storjen* had given her a nod of approval.

That's not possible. She laughed to herself.

At that, she felt like the *storjen* had taken his approval back. She stared at it, confused.

Lorica pointed at the dead animal. "*Shel gond.*"

As she turned her attention back to the deceased, she understood. The *shel* was dead.

***

Lorica noticed Malk shift and shook his head.

Not now. He projected the thought to his mount.

Malk looked back at him, eyes disappointed. *Storjen* ate quite a bit, and Lorica knew his friend was hungry. The *shel* was more than enough for a meal. Lorica had an idea, and it was Malk-approved. He decided to just be honest.

Pointing to Malk, Lorica said, "*Storjen* name Malk."

Siana turned to look at the majestic beast. It held her with a steady gaze. "Hello, Malk." She greeted him in *Setan*.

He nodded his head at his name.

Lorica said, "Malk eat *shel*."

They both watched as Siana's eyes widened while she processed what she'd been told. Lorica removed his bag from the saddle.

***

Studying Malk, she could see his beak was like a bird's. Birds ate many creatures, fruits, seeds, and vegetables. He also carried them a long way at high speed and was no doubt tired and starving. While she had no desire to watch, she couldn't begrudge a creature its food, nor could she condemn its eating habits. What she knew equated to less than nothing about this world, and she had much to learn if she was to find Jacob and learn to live in it. She nodded, walked some distance toward where they'd come from, putting her back to the beasts. Lorica joined her, and together they walked back to the road. Siana did her best to ignore the sounds behind her.

Lorica said, "Malk eat. Come to you and me."

She just nodded, trying to keep the mental picture the sounds were creating out of her head. The creature was deer-like in shape and size. She wasn't sure how long it would take Malk to eat it.

While walking, a thought occurred to Siana: if Malk ate *shels*, what prevented him from eating people? They were certainly big enough to consider people prey. If horses were omnivores, humans would have a difficult time not becoming breakfast. She racked her brain, but the only thing she could come up with was some type of synergistic relationship. She stopped, lost in thought.

Malk seemed to understand her feelings and Lorica's words. Which meant they needed to be highly intelligent to understand, right? Maybe even empathic?

Lorica turned to her. "You okay?"

She responded, "I'm okay."

He nodded, and they continued their walk.

A short time later, they found a flowing creek and moved off the road to drink. It was as clear as the river had been.

No pollution here.

Lorica took an empty canister out of the bag. After topping it in the creek, he pulled a cup from the bag, shook it under the water, then swept water from the creek, and handed it to his traveling companion. Siana gratefully drained it, refusing to think about it floating around his bag. He motioned to the water, showing her she should drink what she needed. Carefully, she squatted on the bank and refilled her cup. She almost fell in when Malk's head appeared next to her, and he drank his fill.

How on earth did I not hear him?

Once finished, they began walking again, her eyes taking in her surroundings. Other than the colors, the forest looked like any on Earth. If the leaves had been green or if she had seen fir trees, she could easily forget she was in a different place. The birds, songs echoing, were loud and their songs were also similar.

Soon her feet were hurting, because of the oversized boots, and she was disappointed because they hadn't remounted the *storjen*. Instead, all three walked together.

***

Lorica noticed her sideways glances at Malk.

He said, "Malk eat..."

How do I explain that one shouldn't ride him right after he eats? Well, we could, but there was a good chance he'd give back the food, and no one wanted to see that.

Malk huffed as if insulted he would ever do such a thing. His burp belied that. Siana gagged as the smell hit her. Even

Lorica covered his nose with his hand, eyes glaring at the beast. Malk had the decency to look embarrassed.

***

Sometimes walking or riding, and hiding when Lorica deemed it necessary, they continued to travel. When they rode, Malk alternated between moving speeds, sometimes at a trot or walk, sometimes at a gallop. Siana swore he would burst into a gallop when he felt her relax, almost causing her to fall off. Finally, Lorica sternly said something to him, and he stopped doing it.

He definitely understands what Lorica is saying. A symbiotic relationship? No, that implies they need each other to live, but something was definitely between them. Wait, does that mean Malk was deliberately being a snot? She eyed the beast with suspicion.

The house finally came into view well after nightfall. As they drew closer, she could make out lights throughout the grounds and realized how close they were. Her eyelids drooped and her legs felt like lead. Her stomach growled. Jerky and water only went so far.

***

Instead of riding straight up the front drive, Lorica guided Malk a back way, making sure only the guards spotted them. They didn't need to be wounded or killed by surprising their own guards. Even after they rode through the back gate, he was cautious.

Kellan's already going to be furious with me. If she died...

He refused to contemplate the destruction of his relationship with his brother. Even from their very short meeting and his prior letters, Lorica could see he was developing feelings for the female. He hoped it didn't come back on him.

Stopping by an exterior door, he dismounted, which woke Siana, helped her down, and led her to it. Mrs. Atwood, who grabbed her arm and quickly pulled her inside, had quietly opened it.

***

Mrs. Atwood's actions caused Siana to understand they were keeping her hidden.

Why?

Once the door closed, Mrs. Atwood looked the tired female over in a motherly fashion. She reached for Siana's hand. Immediately noticing the banding, she beamed at her. Siana's exhaustion prevented her from understanding the housekeeper's happiness.

As she was led up the stairs, and she assumed back to her original room, she heard a voice call out, "Sia!" Glancing up, she saw Brigitte at the top of the stairs.

Mrs. Atwood gave the maid a disapproving frown. Siana wasn't sure what was said, but she was fairly certain that Mrs. Atwood had just lectured Brigitte.

Both women disrobed Sia, bathed her, fed her a light meal, and tucked her into bed, as she was too tired to object. Brigitte would randomly fidget with a chain on Siana's banding, obviously curious about her wearing it, but holding herself back. As soon as Siana's head hit the pillow, she was out.

***

Heading back downstairs, Brigitte looked for Lorica.

"Why did Kellan send her back? Was she claimed?"

Lorica shook his head as he gathered his belongings to take to his room. "No, I doubt she'd be walking or alive if she had been."

Brigitte was confused. The whole point of her being there was to keep her safe until Kellan could explain and claim her.

"The camp was compromised."

Brigitte let out a gasp. "What about the others?"

"They're safe. Only Norita was there, and she hid in the caves."

"Why didn't Siana hide with her?" she asked, brow furrowed. "Surely that would be better than bringing her back here, where she's in more danger."

"You missed her, so I brought her back."

"What?" Brigitte hissed. "Are you insane? You deliberately endangered her so I wouldn't be lonely?"

Lorica barely looked at her as he started for his room. "Someone compromised the camp. We don't know if they will return. It's not safe for her. We can protect her better here."

"Does Kellan know you took her?"

"He does now."

Brigitte stopped following him. She was conflicted. If this had been the old him, she would've gone off on him. The new him, however, was more covert. In Falon, he developed a more dangerous edge and no longer acted impulsively. He plotted his course of action. He was quieter, not as eager to insert his three *terin* into every conversation. She used to find that old habit annoying until she realized it came from insecurity. Despite him looking like a demigod, he always felt like he was in the shadow of his two older brothers. They'd sometimes talked about his insecurities during their many walks together. She wondered if he missed those walks as much as she did.

Thinking about Siana, she acknowledged he was right. Leaving her at the camp would've been an enormous risk. He knew Kellan would object and stop him, so didn't tell him. His entrance into his room at the end of the hall, watched by her, stirred a long-dormant desire, which made her aware of how much he'd grown since that day. She tamped it down. It was no longer possible.

Chapter Twenty

SIANA STRETCHED, STILL HALF in a dream. As she lay on the soft mattress, she sleepily rubbed her eyes and opened them. Sunlight peeked around the drapes that weren't fully closed, softly lighting the room and hitting her eyes. That's what woke her. She sat up, pushed off the covers, and stood. The carpet was also soft, something she hadn't noticed before.

Now that my vocabulary has increased, I need to get the brothers together and see if I can make them understand about Jacob.

That was her plan for today. She had to make them understand she needed their help. A noise outside drew her attention. She walked to the windows and held the drape aside. As she looked down, she realized the courtyard was below her. An enclosed wagon with a driver sitting on a covered bench in front had come to a stop. The driver was within an alcove-type roof, so all she saw were his legs. The wagon, which was quite plain on the outside, had six wheels. One set at the front, one at the back, and a much larger set in the middle. The positioning of the larger wheels just in front of the other two caused them to protrude more to the side. She saw a dark-haired figure exit a door at the back. As he turned, she caught sight of his face.

Kellan.

He moved to the front and handed something to the driver.

If Kellan is here, he must have left soon after we did.

The sun wasn't very high, showing she had not slept too late. White clouds, like fluffy sheep, ambled across the vast blue expanse of the sky. The multitude of trees, their leaves rustling softly in the gentle breeze, stretched beyond the house's stone wall as far as she could see. Looking out, she saw the lavender trees, but also others—some the green of her home, others with hints of blue and the rich red ones, similar to maple leaves in autumn, all creating a stunning panorama. Behind them, in the distance, she saw mountains rising majestically as a backdrop. It was pure, unsullied, and beautiful. Despite the breathtaking scenery, an overwhelming curiosity about what transpired at the camp pulled her away. She hurried to get ready.

***

Brigitte knocked and entered the bedchamber when she didn't get a response. Siana wasn't there. With no bedclothes in sight, she concluded Siana was in the toilet and went to the wardrobe. The doors gave a slight creak as she opened them and perused the garments hanging there.

Brigitte had gotten Sia's measurements while at the encampment, and Tamek commissioned clothing for her. Since Brigitte had insisted Siana was most likely Middle, the fabrics and colors reflected that as well as their House. She selected a second emerald-green dress, like the first, to match Siana's eyes, though this one would actually fit her. She contemplated her hairstyle. Though there wasn't much she could do about her sunburned face, she wanted her to look pretty when she met Kellan again, despite it being little more than a day. Camp clothes weren't the most attractive.

***

Siana opened the door to see Brigitte's critical look. A dress, undergarments, and stockings lay on the recently made bed. Brigitte's "tch" as she eyed Siana's face made the latter aware of the sunburn that had already deepened since the journey back.

Her maid motioned to the desk chair. "Sit," she said.

As Siana obeyed, Brigitte quickly pulled her hair up and off her face. She fetched a wet cloth and cleaner and gently washed Sia's face and neck. Afterward, she pulled a jar out of the desk drawer, opened it, and carefully massaged it into her still-wet skin.

Siana couldn't lie. It still felt good to be pampered, though she resolved to do it herself next time. She shouldn't get used to this. When she found Jacob, they most likely would leave together. The thought made her sad. She didn't want to be traveling again. She wanted a home.

Maybe they'd let Jacob stay? Though, if not, at least we'd be traveling at our own pace, not running for our lives.

She felt her hair fall, then Brigitte's fingers combing through, and it going up again. Brigitte pinned Sia's hair up in a loose bun, allowing some of her spiral curls to fall and frame her face. With a step back, Brigitte cast a critical eye over Siana again. With a satisfied look, she helped her change. Brigitte had her step into the dress, so she didn't ruin her hair. While Siana was fastening the buttons on the front, Brigitte opened the wardrobe again.

Siana finished and looked up to see what Brigitte was doing. As she lifted her head, she spotted her pack on the floor of the wardrobe. She excitedly grabbed it after hurrying over. Brigitte followed curiously, shoes in hand, as Siana carried the bag to the bed. Siana quickly searched through the pack after opening it. Everything looked like it was still there. As she moved things around with her hands, she found her pocketknife and immediately put it in her dress pocket.

If that man attacks me again, hopefully I can use it.

Another search revealed her hunting knife. *Thank you!* She set it temporarily on the bed. Again searching, she found her cell phone, cord, and solar charger. Her original phone was an older one, made before AI began being installed. She never liked the idea and wasn't on the "latest and greatest" trend, so she kept her previous one.

It's one reason she detested the trackers: AI had followed their every move, purchase, health issue, everything. She wished she'd never agreed to have the thing implanted into her neck. Briefly, she wondered if Kellan could remove it. She'd have to ask when she had the words.

Once the attacks had begun, she had dumped her old cell phone and used an even older one. They didn't need to make calls, and it was emergency use only. Jacob had one as well. The bots left the cell service towers operational, knowing they would die out on their own with no one to maintain them. They also used them for their own purposes, which left many dead.

While older phones were still trackable, they couldn't be used to kill her like so many others had been. Newer models had AI installed, and the AI took advantage of it. The unfortunate ones had it in their pockets or by their heads when it exploded. By the time the injured made it to the hospital, the hospitals were imploding. Those who hadn't made it inside died a slow, agonizing death from injuries or when infection set in. The lucky ones were killed by AI drones.

Siana opened the drapes; then, she put the battery back in her phone, set it in the sun, and pushed a button. As expected, it was dead. She unfolded the solar charger, plugged the components together, and then adjusted it to capture maximum sunlight. She knew she wouldn't be able to make calls, but she had pictures of Jacob she could use to find him.

"Siana."

Turning, she saw Brigitte opening another set of drapes, revealing a glass door. She turned the knob, opened the door inwards, and gestured through it. Siana walked over and, peering around the corner, she saw a small balcony, a table, and two chairs.

Giving Brigitte a surprised smile, she returned to her phone, grabbed everything, and hurried outside. To maximize sunlight, she enlisted Brigitte's help in moving the table. She set the phone back down and set the charger in the best position for full sun.

She almost ran into Brigitte when she turned to go back inside. Brigitte's overwhelming curiosity was obvious, but she couldn't do anything until the phone charged, and solar charging took a while. Siana stopped Brigitte from touching the items by gently resting her hand on her arm and shaking her head.

Brigitte's look of curiosity warred with disappointment before she went back inside the room.

She moved ahead of Sia and opened the bedroom door, gestured toward the hallway, and said, "Tamek see you."

Unable to see Tamek in the hall, Siana turned to Brigitte.

Brigitte clarified, "Tamek *studi*. Come." They moved toward the stairs, then down.

***

This was her first time really paying attention to the house outside of her room. The craftsmanship took Siana's breath away. Whatever wood they used on the stairs fairly glowed. Wooden scrollwork covered the lower half of the walls, and the walls above were a warm, pale yellow which complemented the wood perfectly. The balustrade spindles looked like someone had twisted wood, forming tight windings from bottom to top. A centered brown runner covered the stairs themselves. Most likely to help keep someone from slipping.

A young woman was at the bottom of the stairs polishing the wood on the walls. She nodded and bowed when Siana reached her. Siana smiled at her and nodded. The girl smiled back, then returned to her work. Brigitte turned right and led her through a tiled foyer with similar wood walls, past the front doors, and down a hall. Mrs. Atwood appeared and said something to Brigitte. She answered the housekeeper.

Turning to Siana, she pointed down to the end of the hall where a partially open door was. "Tamek. I help Mrs. Atwood." Siana nodded and continued toward it.

***

Kellan had just finished recounting his time with Siana. Though he had sent his younger brother reports, Tamek had questions, and it turned into a disagreement.

"We are out of time!" Anger tinged Tamek's voice. He turned from the window to face his eldest brother. His braids seem to take on his emotion as they flew with his turn. "The safest one to claim her is you."

"I know, but I am her physician. *I* examined her. *I* drugged her. *I* tried to prepare her body. The chances of Siana dying from a claiming are high even with me." Kellan's frustration was plain.

Lorica, lying on the couch to the side of the desk, shifted his position, his boots resting on the couch. "What else can we do? We still have the problem of being unable to explain anything to her in a way she'd understand."

Tamek, regaining his usual stoic composure, sighed. "Why do you do this? Get your shoes off the couch. It's not possible to send her to another camp. We don't have one. We haven't identified who revealed the location of this camp."

They had a more permanent camp, but the last severe storm had caused several trees to fall, causing high amounts of damage to the buildings and blocking the roadway. The one Siana had been part of was a temporary one they'd set up while they fixed the original. That someone figured it out so quickly concerned all of them.

"I have my guards looking into it," Lorica replied.

Tamek's face was doubtful. "Brigitte saw the new groundskeeper and Talon talking; that's the only reason we knew the groundskeeper notified Talon about Siana being here."

Kellan knew Tamek's guards had taken care of it. House Devereaux didn't suffer with turncoats. This was common knowledge and was a powerful deterrent. For the male to turn, Talon must have offered a small fortune.

"My guards will scout him out," Lorica reassured him. "We should be glad we caught his accomplice and knew they were planning on raiding the camp trying to find her and other females."

Kellan was told Lorica's guards had chased down the raiding party. Falon males loved a good fight, and they got one. While whoever hired the mercenaries waited for news, it would take them a while to realize it wasn't forthcoming. All suspected it was Talon.

Kellan didn't know how Lorica discovered this and had no plans to ask. Sometimes their younger brother was concerning. His time in Falon had changed him. Some of his guards were from there. They also concerned him. Knowing Lorica's Falon guards' unshakable devotion helped calm his anxieties. To be honest, Kellan suspected the rumors about Talon's younger brother's death were true. He also expected the questioning involved a lot of pain for the accomplice. However, suspecting Tamek may know, as the Head of the House, he couldn't involve himself in any of it, and Lorica skillfully kept private what he needed to.

Kellan sighed and sat down on the blue plush chair in front of Tamek's desk. "What we need is someone who knows her language and can interpret, but without knowing exactly what she is, we don't know where to look." Kellan leaned forward and rested his arms on the desk.

Tamek faced him, thinking. "What about at the Studium? Are you aware of any scholars who might specialize in other languages?"

The Studium is where Kellan learned to be a physician. He racked his brain trying to remember if anyone fit that description. "I can't recall anyone, but I wouldn't have come in contact with that branch. I can send a messenger and ask the Studium Head."

"That will take some time. We may not be able to wait that long."

"I'll send it anyhow. Knowing where she's from can only help."

Tamek nodded in agreement. "Any information is helpful. We're still back where we started." He sat in his chair. "I'm going to send for the officiant."

Kellan let out a low growl.

Tamek stared at him and raised his hands. "Then give me ideas. Tell me something—anything—that will keep Siana from dying from a claiming. As of right now, you are the only viable option. Not to give offense, but you are the smallest of us. You said yourself that with your preparations, you'd hope to only injure her. If you don't do it, you know what will happen. Do you want Talon to have her?"

"*Only* injure her?" Kellan slapped his hand on the desk, face tightening. "I'm trying to not harm her at all. And of course I don't want that *blotzen* or anyone else from his House touching her!" Kellan caught sight of the sadness in Tamek's eyes before he hid it.

Tamek lowered his hands to the desk, drew a breath, and caught his brother's eyes. "You know I understand your frustration. If anyone knows, it's me," he said quietly. "You know this. If you can give me any other option, I will listen."

Kellan knew Tamek was right and hated it. He also knew none of them wanted any of this. Except for Lorica, their stance had always opposed claiming, and now they were being forced into what they were against. They didn't have a choice; disobeying their laws had serious consequences.

"Give me time to think," Kellan replied, a hint of desperation clearly evident.

"You've had the entirety of her time here. There is no more time. Shall I summon the officiant?"

Kellan wanted to put his fist through Tamek's face, but knew it wasn't his brother's fault. Not that he didn't want to claim her; Tamek and he held the view of preferring it to be a mutual decision rather than one-sided. Therefore, Kellan was a bit surprised he was pushing this.

Usala.

She had to be the reason. Talon's brother had stolen Tamek's own claim while Tamek was away. She had wanted to wait until he returned, and Tamek abided by her wishes. Because the couple had been in talks for an extended time, the Convocation decided Tamek had taken too long and wasn't serious about her. They turned her over to Brilt Talon. Usala had pleaded for the Convocation to wait until Tamek's return, but they refused.

Brilt forced her into a public claiming, causing her first time to be a painful and traumatic experience. Within a fortnight of the younger Talon shuttering her away at his home, she was dead. Talon's brother claimed it was an "accident." No one believed him, but no one could prove otherwise. The three brothers suspected the Talon brothers shared her. The only reason they kept getting away with it was their father and his cronies being on the Convocation. Now they were all gone, and Tamek was fighting for change. Kellan knew Tamek didn't want the same thing happening to their guest. Neither did he.

Looking at his brother, Kellan gave a resigned nod. Now they had to try their best to explain it to Siana.

Chapter Twenty-One

AS SIANA APPROACHED THE study, the raised voices—sharp and angry—sliced through the quiet of the house. Unsure of whether to enter, she waited for a lull in the conversation, but it never came. They were speaking too fast for her to understand much. Not wanting to intrude, she turned to go back to Brigitte, but heard her name.

She tried to pick out what she could, but it wasn't until they were calmer and slowed their speaking that she could pick out a few words. The ones that concerned her included her name, death, and... something.

Pederon. What was it? Why would she die?

With growing concern, she mused that something beyond her comprehension was happening.

I need to find Jacob now.

Retracing her steps, she went back to her room.

***

Brigitte knocked and entered the study. Briefly hesitating at the sight of their upset faces, she looked for her charge. Stepping further into the room, she inquired about

Siana's whereabouts. The brothers looked up at her, confusion plain.

Brigitte explained, "I was bringing her per Tamek's instructions, but Mrs. Atwood needed my help immediately. I pointed Sia to this room, and she was coming here on her own."

All three realized she must have been outside the door, their eyes widening.

Lorica quietly asked, "How much did she hear?"

Tamek responded, "How much did she understand is the better question."

Tamek instructed Brigitte to find her. Kellan rose, offering help. Before they could move, Siana walked into the room. In her hands, she held a small device they'd never seen before, other than Brigitte.

***

Siana, moving to a spot where everyone had a view, switched on her phone. She turned it so they could see.

A picture of Jacob and herself on a hike appeared. Another hiker in their group had taken a picture of them to commemorate Siana's first time hiking that part of the trail. They were standing on a summit, an arm around each other's waists. He had cracked a joke, so everyone was laughing. Neither had any clue their lives would change the very next day.

If she just hadn't heard the brothers saying she was going to die, their expressions would have made her laugh. Lorica jumped up and tried to take the small box from her. Siana shook her head and pulled it back. He looked like he'd lost a new toy.

He'd be the one to have the latest gadgets.

She pointed to the male, turning the phone around to face them again. "Jacob. My brother."

Tamek's brow furrowed with confusion as he tilted his head. Siana wasn't sure if it was her words or language that caused his reaction. Looking at their faces, they clearly didn't understand what she was saying.

Pointing at Tamek, then Lorica, she said, "Brother."

From Lorica to Tamek, she repeated it. Pointing at Tamek then Brigitte, she said, "Not brother," while shaking her head. Pointing to Kellan, then Lorica and Tamek, she questioned, "Brother?"

She gave them a minute, then repeated everything. Again, she waited. Understanding dawned on Lorica's face.

Pointing to Kellan, then himself, he said, using her word, "*Yes*, brother." It sounded strange with his *Setan* accent. Pointing to Kellan and then Tamek, again he said, "*Yes*, brother."

The others looked unsure, so he translated what the word meant, which told Siana their version of "brother."

Siana smiled, obviously relieved he'd understood and helped the others. She wished she'd had her phone at the camp.

Pointing to Jacob, she said in *Setan*, "Jacob, my brother."

***

Their collective jaws dropped. Tamek felt like an idiot. No one attempted to discover if she had a family after bringing her to the house. Since she'd been alone, and had the language barrier, they assumed not. She had a male relative. A brother. This changed everything. He looked around and saw that the others had realized it too.

***

Kellan smiled with relief. Explaining a claim wouldn't be necessary for them. They wouldn't have to force her. All they had to do was return her to her brother. That would solve the problem.

Maybe she'd allow me to do a claim the way I'd like.

He was attracted to her and felt she might eventually care for him. Discouraged, he realized that with what they did to her, it was highly doubtful. He'd owe her brother and her a huge bounty. That bounty had to come with an explanation. He glanced Tamek's way and could see Tamek had the same realization. In fact, he could see him mentally adding up the damages they'd have to pay. You couldn't do things to a female if she had a male relative. That was a separate, distinct set of laws. Hopefully, her brother wasn't the type to have them killed. If so, Kellan's life was forfeit.

Siana turned her phone around, touched it, and then showed them again. The image was of a field.

Lorica, inspecting, said, "That's the field I found her in."

Tamek moved to get a closer look. "Ah, the field Mother would take us to."

Siana pointed at the field and said, "Jacob."

"Oh, dear." Lorica looked guilty. "I just realized she was most likely waiting for her brother in that field. That's why she had dressed as a young male. Her brother had her disguised in order to move her through safely."

It wasn't an uncommon practice for families to dress their females as males in order to move or hide them. However, people traveling through from other areas were usually left alone.

Tamek said, thinking out loud, "That doesn't quite make sense. If he knew our laws, then he would most likely know our language, which means she should as well. Something doesn't add up."

Lorica said, "Unless they don't educate their females. There are a couple of areas that don't." His face grew contemplative. "But her language doesn't sound like theirs."

Kellan disagreed and looked at Siana thoughtfully. "No, she's intelligent. She has some medical training. She stitched Norita's arm. Plus, she's of an unknown race. Everyone is *Setan,* even if they don't speak the language. She is completely different. I've never seen her like before."

"Agreed. I have never seen her kind before." Lorica gazed at their guest.

Brigitte added her input. "It seems a trip to the field is needed."

They all agreed, but the hour was growing too late to leave and search. Tomorrow would work.

Siana stood there, waiting. Kellan saw her push something, and the image disappeared. She slid the object into her pocket.

Mrs. Atwood entered and proclaimed the midday meal was ready. Kellan held out his hand for Siana's, and she cautiously allowed him to take it. He looked at her banding. He'd have to remove it. Without her brother's permission, she couldn't wear it.

After the meal.

He kind of liked her wearing it and wanted to delay removing it as long as possible. Unfortunately, Tamek reminded him in front of everyone he needed to remove it. As he looked at Siana, he considered his phrasing. The others left them alone and headed toward the dining room.

***

Kellan took Siana's hand, and she saw him stare at her banding. "Siana, banding *rembit*. Kellan's banding *rembit*."

Siana repeated, "*Rembit?*"

"Jacob Siana's *rembit*." His face showed his frustration at not being able to express himself well.

"Siana, Kellan no *rembit*. Jacob Siana's *rembit*." He let out a heavy sigh. "No Kellan banding. Jacob *rembit*."

As he held up his hand, he turned it upside down over hers and inserted the jewels of his ring into the opening. Her ring made a noise.

Siana's face was a picture of complete confusion, watching as the wristband withdrew into itself and disappeared, followed by the chains retracting into the ring along with the jewels.

Kellan removed the ring from her finger and put it in his trouser pocket.

She looked up. "Kellan, I bad? Do bad?"

Kellan's eyes widened in shock.

He rushed to reassure her. "No, no. You no bad. It's okay. Jacob, Siana's brother, *rembit*. Kellan no *rembit*."

She was still confused. Siana was really hating the language barrier.

He sighed and shrugged. "We eat." He held out his hand again.

Siana reluctantly gave him hers. He tucked it through his bent arm and walked her to the dining room.

***

The meal was a quiet affair. Lorica could see Siana's troubled face. He and Tamek gave Kellan questioning looks. Kellan explained what happened, that she thought she was being punished by having her banding taken away, but no one knew what to say to fix it. They were all glad she liked Kellan, even if she didn't understand what the banding was or why it was removed.

Lorica could see Brigitte stewing in the corner. She'd grown quite protective of Siana, and she had never agreed with the way they were handling this. She'd given him an earful about it. Brigitte noticed him staring. Something flared in her eyes, but she turned away before he could figure out what it was.

She still hasn't forgiven me. She probably never will. The thought saddened and angered him at the same time. She was his mate, and he wanted to be with her. *Why didn't she just agree? If she did, they could be together. Was it really such a big deal?*

Chapter Twenty-Two

THE SUN WAS BARELY UP when Siana hopped out of bed, excited. They were going to the field to find any sign of Jacob. Racing to get dressed, she put on the clothes she'd arrived in, grabbed her phone, cord, and charger, and packed them with her hat and jacket into her bag. She strapped her hunting knife to her pants out of habit and put her pocketknife in her back pocket.

Just like old times.

The thought disturbed her. She hoped Jacob was here, and that he wasn't still running for his life, trying to find her on their world. The sun's intensity bearing down on her through the open windows told her it would be a warm day. She raced downstairs to the morning room, slowing when Mrs. Atwood stuck her head out of a room and gave her a disapproving stare. Siana smiled at her and slowed to a walk until out of her sight. She got lost twice, but eventually found it and rushed in.

The brothers looked up in surprise at her sudden entrance.

Tamek, lifting an eyebrow, said something as he took the last bite of his food.

Siana was fairly bouncing. "Jacob." She drew out his name in a suppressed, excited manner.

Lorica stated something with a wry grin as he pushed his empty plate aside.

She only understood about half of what he said. Something about being glad to see him. The other two just gave him a look. Siana recognized it. She had received it from Jacob more than a few times. She assumed he'd made a comment about them.

Kellan stood and pulled out a chair for her. "Siana, eat." He was smiling. She understood why *Be* Tess gave in so much.

Earnestly staring at him, she said, "Jacob." She drew it out in a low tone that made it clear she wanted to go now.

Kellan raised his eyebrows at her, still smiling, pointed to the chair and said, "Eat, then Jacob."

Her shoulders slumped, her mouth pouted, and she made a disappointed noise. The brothers hid their grins. Kellan raised his hand to hide his. Siana looked at him suspiciously. Her eyes clearly asked if he was laughing at her.

He just said, "Sit. Eat."

She gave in only because she knew he was right. She did not know how long they would travel, and she would hate to pass out from hunger at Jacob's feet. Mainly because he'd never let her forget it. Plus, she smelled coffee. She could hold that she'd had coffee over his head.

She ate so fast she saw Kellan watching her with concern. Smiling warmly at him, she received a gentle smile in return. Having drained her coffee, she looked at them all and repeated, "Jacob."

Lorica remarked, "All done? I'll get the *Storjen*."

Siana understood. She fairly hopped from one foot to the other as excitement bubbled up in her. It seemed to take forever to get to this point. Hopefully, they could find him. Lorica got up from the table. Siana could see he was dressed in clothes more suited to work than sitting around the house, hair tied back. Kellan dressed similarly, with his hair braided down his back. Tamek dressed in a long blue tunic and trousers that matched his eyes, his hair flowing loose with a small braid down either side. She wasn't sure if the color was deliberate.

"Tamek, go?" she asked. He looked a bit surprised she spoke to him but recovered quickly.

He gave her a stoic look and shook his head. "I'll stay home."

Her realization she was understanding full simple sentences excited her, but not as much as finding her brother. Standing, she grabbed her pack, slung it over one shoulder, and rushed to leave the room. A tug on her pack made her turn.

Kellan said, "Come," and led her to a small room. Pointing through the open door, he said, "Toilet," with barely concealed amusement.

Siana mock glared at him as she entered, quickly shutting the door in his face. She knew she was impatient, but did he really need to treat her like a child? It didn't matter. Nothing could dull this day.

If he's here, we're going to find him.

When she finished, she opened the door and saw Kellan waiting for her. This time he didn't offer her his hand, just turned and walked with her to the back door. She waved at Mrs. Atwood and Brigitte as they passed the kitchen. Both women waved back.

***

Kellan opened the door for her, and they went outside to see Lorica on Malk, holding the reins of another *storjen*. After a brief conversation with Lorica, Kellan led Siana to his mount. She fairly skipped to it. Kellan was happy to see how happy she was. He could tell she cared for her brother very much. That meant they had a good relationship.

Hopefully, he'll be understanding of the way we handled this.

With a gesture toward her bag, he ordered, "On Siana."

Siana readjusted it, stuck her arms through the straps, and hiked it up on her back.

Kellan moved to stand beside his mount, patted the back of the saddle, and intertwined his hands, making a step for her. She put her right foot on his hands and pulled herself up. She tried to do it gracefully and completely failed. The bag threw off her center off balance, her leg caught on the back end as she tried to swing her left leg over, and she almost fell off. Kellan caught her and helped her right herself. His mount turned its head and gave her a look of derision as she finally sat. She stuck her tongue out at it. It gave a hard buck, but she stayed on.

Kellan said sternly, "Tost!"

Malk also made a noise at it, and Tost settled down, keeping his head forward as if refusing to look at her.

Kellan felt slightly exasperated. Not only was his *storjen* acting like a child, but so was his former claim. He had seen her stick her tongue out.

Lorica said, trying not to laugh, "She doesn't know about them."

Siana asked, "I not know what?"

Kindly, Kellan said, "Not now."

Mentally telling Tost to behave, Kellan shook his head, mounted, and picked up the reins. The answer made him more exasperated.

Your mate started it.

He didn't bother correcting him, because Tost knew Siana wasn't his mate, and they set off for the back gate.

***

Behind Kellan, and with her arms wrapped around him, she felt a sense of rightness. She couldn't explain it. Just that holding him felt right. She found it confusing, pushed it out of her head, and concentrated on Jacob.

To her surprise, the ride wasn't very long. Maybe an hour or two. Time was hard to keep here unless you were tracking the sun or had a timepiece.

Is the field on their lands? She realized she didn't know how large or small their estate was.

It was a leisurely journey that enabled her to look around at the minor dirt road they traveled. Kellan pointed out and named birds, a small bridge they crossed that spanned a creek, and various fauna. She had to admit the entire estate was beautiful. It seemed they tried to keep the area not immediately around the house as natural as possible, only maintaining paths and minor roads.

Upon spotting a bush laden with ripe, dark blackberries, she exclaimed in English, "Blackberries!" She loved blackberries.

Kellan and Lorica paused to see what she was looking at. Leaping down from Malk, Lorica carefully picked and offered Siana a handful of berries, their purple skins glistening.

She gleefully accepted and said in English, "Thank you."

Lorica corrected her to make her use their language, both for the berries and gratitude, and she happily did so before popping them into her mouth.

Lorica mounted up, but both Tost and Malk refused to move. Kellan and Lorica seemed lost in thought, and Siana's brow furrowed in curiosity.

Lorica muttered, "*Zef!*" and turned his mount to the berries. Siana knew it was a curse word, but hadn't yet figured out if there was a translation.

Kellan told Tost out loud, "You're acting like a child."

Tost swung his head back to stare at Kellan, then walked over to the berries.

Kellan raised an eyebrow. "Am I wrong?"

Tost let out a snort and continued to eat.

Siana was leaning around Kellan, watching the exchange intently as she munched on her snack. Once the mounts agreed to move again, they reached the field soon after. Kellan helped Siana dismount, and she began looking around. Lorica also dismounted, told Malk what they were looking for, and both mounts disappeared into the forest. Siana watched them with a bit of concern.

She turned to Lorica, asking, "They understand?"

Lorica nodded and said, "*Storjen* help."

Her eyes widened at the idea of the intelligence needed for the beast to hold a conversation.

The three of them stood in the middle of the field. Kellan spoke and acted out, Lorica watching with amusement, that they would search in increasing circles. However, Siana would stay with Kellan. They started on opposite sides, looking for any signs of others being there.

***

As they entered the forest, Kellan thought he heard Lorica speaking and assumed he was talking to Malk, then realized his guard followed them.

Good. More eyes.

After a bell or so, Kellan stopped, said, "Toilet," and stepped away.

Siana teased, "No toilet at home?"

Kellan gave her the "evil eye" as he disappeared behind a tree. He heard Siana giggle, and he smiled. It was a relief to see her relaxed and free from fear. He knew she'd been on edge since they discovered her, though he didn't understand why. As he relieved himself, he heard something. It took him a second to realize she was quietly singing. He didn't understand the words, but she had a pleasant voice, and the song was slow and lovely.

For an instant, he pictured her singing to their babe, but quickly pushed the thought out of his head.

Eventually, they took a break for a meal in the field. Kellan knew they'd covered a lot of ground with no sign of her brother. She looked hot and tired, yet he felt she wouldn't quit for a while.

Lorica stood, told the others, "Water," and waved his empty canister around.

He made for the creek they'd passed. Siana checked hers. Kellan noticed it was still full.

"You need to drink." He acted out drinking to help her understand.

She nodded, immediately taking several drinks from the bottle.

After they enjoyed the silence for a bit, Kellan held his hands flat in the air in front of him. "Jacob?" He moved one hand up and down. "Siana?" He moved the other.

She just stared at his hands.

He tried again. With one hand, he kept it flat, raised it up higher. "Kellan." He then put his hand down a bit and to the side. He said, "Tamek." Again, repeating the gestures, he said, "Lorica."

"Ah," Siana said. She raised her hand. "Jacob." She moved her hand to the side but kept it at the same level. "Siana."

Kellan's eyes widened. *Split. They were split, and Jacob birthed first.*

He remembered in the physician community that if a child split, people believed he or she would only have half the intelligence. If it were male and female, they assumed the male received more. When the theorist's own splits turned out to be a highly intelligent female and a son who could barely pull his own trousers up, the theory was disproved. People also believed if a child doubled, they had so much intelligence that they had to create a copy to contain it all. Of course, shortly after each theory was proposed, they proved false, though some still entertained the idea.

He was about to try to ask her age when Lorica returned. Instead, they cleaned up their belongings and returned to where they had left off. When the sun started to set, they knew it was time to stop. They were all hot, dirty, and tired. Kellan helped Siana mount, and when Lorica had done so as well, they turned for home.

They knew by her face she was disappointed. Kellan was as well, though he knew his didn't compare to hers. He felt guilty that a part of him was relieved. Her finding out what they'd done to her at the camp made his stomach turn. He didn't want her to hate him. At least, if her brother understood their language, he could explain himself. Maybe she would understand what they were trying to do. Of course, if they'd known about her brother, they wouldn't have done any of it. Kellan would've asked to court her, something that really wasn't done, but something that was more in line with his personal beliefs.

When it became too dark to see, the males turned their luna lines up.

***

Siana was trying to stay awake when their glow started. It wasn't scary anymore. Now it was comforting that they could see and safely get them home in the absolute darkness. There were stars, but no moon. The trees helped to block the night sky. It grew brighter in front of them, and she leaned slightly to see why.

The *Storjens'* eyes were glowing white. *They have headlights.* She giggled.

Kellan, voice tinged with uncertainty, asked, "Are you okay?"

"Yes," she answered.

***

He wasn't sure what she found humorous. Soon he felt a weight against his back. Glancing over his shoulder, he couldn't make out his passenger. She was falling asleep, leaning onto him like a cushion. Lorica dropped back a bit, and Kellan knew it was so he could watch if she started to fall. Upon arriving at the back gate, they proceeded to the house. Lorica dismounted, and Malk took himself to the stables. The stable master was waiting for them to return and would remove the tack.

Gently trying to wake Siana, Lorica supported her body while Kellan dismounted. Kellan took over, helping her down, but her head stopped on his shoulder. He realized she was still mostly asleep. He tried waking her, but she made a sound of protest and nestled her face into his neck. Lorica was, once again, looking amused.

Tost was not. He mentally told Kellan, *She either needs to get off or on, not halfway. This isn't comfortable. I'm hot and tired too.*

Kellan didn't know what to do. He tried waking her again, but she just put her arms around his neck and mumbled something. While he wasn't averse to this, Tost stomped a hoof several times.

Kellan ended up putting his arms around her, stepping back, and Lorica helped him get her body off the mount. Tost took off to get some rest while Kellan stood there, helpless, with a sleeping female hanging off his neck. She wouldn't wake up, and they couldn't stand there all night. He hitched her up, which caused more grumbling, put an arm under her bottom to support her, and carried her into the house. By this point, Lorica was having trouble containing his laughter.

"I'm going to tell her your nickname is *Dede*." It was a nickname for "father."

Kellan gave him a look that promised swift retribution if he did. "Do not have her call me *Dede*," he whispered in a threatening tone.

Lorica whispered, "*Dede*," and carefully sidestepped Kellan's legs as he quietly slipped away to his room, the floorboards creaking softly beneath his feet.

As Kellan looked at the stairs, he realized he must wake her. He wasn't sure he could safely walk up them while carrying her in this position.

He shifted her and called her name. "Siana!"

She protested and her lips brushed his neck as she moved. His body was more than happy about this. *Zef!* She was flat against him. No way she wouldn't feel that. He said her name again, and she moved her body a bit, which only made things worse. Finally, he put her feet on the floor while bending to support her and said her name louder.

***

Someone's calling me.

She felt warm. Safe. She didn't want to wake up. Closer to her ear, she heard her name. She sleepily raised her head and half opened her eyes. It took her mind a minute to process that Kellan's face was almost touching hers, and her arms were around his neck. She smiled, leaned her head on his shoulder, and contemplated stealing a kiss in repayment for his earlier one.

A second later, her mind woke up, and her eyes flew open. Realizing she was burrowed into him, her face turned beet red. She let go so fast she almost fell over.

With a horrified look on her face, she apologized profusely, interjecting, "I'm sorry," in his language as well as her own.

He kept reassuring her, saying, "It's all right."

Finally, he stopped her apologies with a firm, but tired, "Siana, go sleep." Immediately, she turned and ran up the stairs to her room, where Brigitte waited.

***

Brigitte had seen Kellan carry her in like a sleeping child.

She had started a bath for Siana the minute she was told they were coming through the gate. At the top of the stairs, waiting for news, her heart skipped a beat when she saw Kellan carrying Sia. Then she realized she had fallen asleep. Kellan gave her a "help" look, but she shrugged and went back to her friend's room, smiling.

When Siana rushed into the room, face as red as a *mota*, Brigitte couldn't contain her amusement. Sia's "stop it" look just made it worse. With a snicker, her attempt to undress her charge resulted in her hands being slapped away. Apparently, her mirth wasn't welcome. She didn't care. Brigitte stepped in front of her and made a kissing face.

Siana turned redder. "Stop."

When Brigitte realized how embarrassed she actually was, she hugged her friend. Then said, "Kellan, hmm." Siana pushed her away. Brigitte didn't think she realized she was smiling.

She has feelings for him. Good. If we can't find her brother, she'll need them.

Lorica's face briefly flashed in her mind, but she mentally shut it down. The situation with Siana was bringing too much to the surface.

Chapter Twenty-Three

SIANA WAS RAGING. TAMEK was rubbing his face.

Lorica again told her, "No. You stay home." Pointing to a couple of his men, he said, "They find Jacob."

She retorted, palm hitting her own chest, "My brother! I find!"

Kellan stepped in. "Siana, no. We"—he swept his hand around the room—"stay home." He pointed at the men. "They find. Home *rembit*."

"This is not my home, and I have no idea what 'rembit' means!" she cried in English.

She knew they didn't understand her language rant, but they understood she wanted to look for her brother.

Lorica nodded at the men who left.

Siana was trying to hold back her tears. Kellan took her hands in his.

"Siana, please. Listen," he implored her softly.

"Why?" she whispered, sounding defeated.

Brigitte spoke up. "Talon."

Everyone looked at her.

"Talon?" Siana's confused look showed she didn't know the name.

Brigitte took Siana's hand and led her to the window. As she looked outside, she pointed to the distance. "We walk. Talon come."

Siana looked out the window, but didn't understand. She moved closer to Brigitte's arm and followed the line down to her finger. In the distance, she saw the cupola of the gazebo rising above the hedges of the maze and stiffened.

She had been too distraught to notice what Tamek had shouted.

The attacker's name was Talon. They were hiding her from him, but why? What am I not getting?

Something was obviously going on that they weren't telling her. She looked around the room and saw no malice in anyone's gaze. Worry, yes. Caring, yes. Anything nefarious? No.

Her shoulders slumped, and everyone gave a quiet sigh of relief. She gave up fighting.

***

Kellan, taking her bag and handing it to Brigitte, said to the maid, "You seem to understand how to reach her."

Brigitte snarkily replied, "I'm not constantly trying to force her into things."

That earned her a warning look from Tamek and Lorica. She ignored them. Facing Kellan, she said, "You are all treating her like an ignorant child. She's not. You know she's intelligent." Throwing a hand toward the window, she continued, "All I had to do was show her the gazebo, say his name, and she understood. She may not understand everything, but she understands he's dangerous. She learned that on the first day! Now, I *think,* she understands we're trying to keep him from her."

The brothers glanced at Siana, who was watching the exchange, and back to Brigitte. Tamek and Kellan nodded.

Brigitte wasn't done. "Have any of you even tried explaining what a claiming is?"

Lorica asked, annoyed, "Have you?"

Brigitte directly stared at him. "No, Lor, I can only do what I'm told and obey."

There was a hidden meaning in her sarcastic comment, and in the way she addressed him so familiarly. Siana's perplexed face showed she was the only one who didn't understand what was going on. Lorica's face darkened. He rose, took a step toward Brigitte, raised his left hand as if to grab her, clenched it into a fist, then turned and left the room.

***

Kellan didn't realize he'd been holding his breath. Brigitte knew she was playing with fire riling Lorica up, though she'd never feared his temper. Hers was just as strong. Since they were children, she usually gave as good as she got.

The one time Lorica had pushed her in anger, when they were very young, she'd immediately stood and slapped him across the face. Kellan still remembered Lor's shocked look. He'd never touched her like that again. Her reaction and the punishment their father had given him when he'd learned his son had put hands on a female in anger had seen to that.

His father had also gently lectured their mother, in private, though Kellan had been walking near and overheard, about spoiling their youngest. The day they died crept into his mind, and he ignored it.

He turned his attention to Brigitte. While he understood both sides, and neither of the elder brothers would allow Lorica to harm her, she had chosen to go Low. She frequently acted as if she were still High.

He gently chided, "Brigitte."

Tamek wasn't so nice. He drew himself up, and facing her, angrily said, "Brigitte, you forget your place! You chose your station. Behave like it!"

He was stunned into silence as she replied something vulgar to him and left the room.

Her tear-filled eyes glanced at Siana as she passed, the heartbreak visible on Brigitte's face. Kellan wished things could be different for them, but this resulted from their own actions.

An awkward silence remained in the room. Tamek broke it. "I need to attend the Hall. I will leave her"—he motioned toward Siana—"in your care." Kellan nodded in response. He had an idea to distract her from worrying about finding her brother.

Kellan grabbed Siana's hand. "Come with me."

Brigitte's words rang in his head. He dropped Siana's hand. Turning to look at her, determined to use full sentences as much as possible, he asked, "Will you come with me?"

She nodded. He sighed with relief that she understood.

He led her out the back door toward the stables.

***

They veered left onto a footpath after heading down the main carriageway. She looked around. There were *Storjen* in the field far ahead of them. She was too far away to tell how many. Paddocks were on both sides of the path. What was unusual was the lack of fencing. She didn't see any. She smiled as she caught sight of young *Storjen* playing in a field to their right.

How do they keep them in?

As they reached the stables, Kellan passed it. Shortly, she heard hooves hitting stone. Surprised, Siana turned to look and saw Tost following. He caught her glance and turned his face away. Siana raised her brows but turned and ignored him as well. As they continued down the path, the distant field she had seen at the start of their walk came into view.

Kellan called out something. A stable hand ran over with a blanket. Kellan walked into the field. About ten beasts raised their heads to look at them. He led her to the center of the field and laid the blanket out.

***

Tost, who was of the mind his rider had lost part of his sanity by wanting to do this with his female—he still didn't understand why Kellan didn't acknowledge they were mates—stayed on the path and stood watching. Tost himself hadn't been able to find a mate yet, which Malk never failed to remind him of, and this new herd had a couple of possibilities. They had stopped to rest on their way to another location.

Storjen normally kept on the move, migrating with the seasons. The Devereaux lands are known as a welcoming resting spot. It was his rest here that caused him to find his own rider. Elli, Malk's mate, had stopped at another estate as a youngling, forming a union with a female child, which was highly unusual. Unions weren't normally made until a *storjen* reached maturity. Unable to break a union, her dam had to stay until the youngling was old enough to be alone. Elli and Brigitte had grown up together, both eventually moving to these lands.

His attention returned to the herd before him. He needed to check them before they left, not sure when that would be. He cast a critical eye over the hopefuls. One caught his interest, and he watched her with an examining gaze.

***

Kellan was saying, "Sit, please. Stay. It's all right. They won't hurt you," as he guided Siana to sit on the blanket.

Curious about what he was up to, she did as he bade. The animals slowly stood and came over to inspect her. Siana cast a glance back at Kellan and saw him moving away from her.

"Kellan?" Her voice trembled.

He reiterated, "It's okay. They won't hurt you. They big, but they good."

Siana didn't quite believe him, but kept still, controlling her fear. They were big; so big they were blocking out the light as they crowded around, inspecting and sniffing her.

If one rears, I'm dead.

One that was reddish touched her face with its beak, and Siana froze. She had no desire to get bit. It looked at her before turning and leaving, having stepped back. It seemed insulted by her fear. Another was using its beak to taste her hair, pulling it out of the bun she had. It didn't hurt and seemed like a playful young one.

She heard a voice say, *Don't be afraid.*

Strangely, it was in a language she didn't know, yet she could understand. At first, she thought it was Kellan, but realized the voice was female, and it wasn't *Setan.*

How can I understand it?

One on her right began inspecting her ear, and she couldn't hold back a slight laugh as its breath tickled. She felt a slight push on her back and realized that one was using her to scratch its beak. Another pulled on her clothes. Each one inspected and touched her as they crowded around. It was overwhelming.

Again, the voice said, *Don't be afraid. Focus on them.*

She tried and acknowledged they weren't hurting her. They were being gentle. It took a bit of time, but she overcame her fear and held her hand up, palm out. A blackish one nuzzled it, like a cat brushing against a hand, and all fear of the beasts left. Of course, she had a healthy respect for their size, but she felt like she was among a bunch of curious kittens. She dared to reach and give one a scratch on its head. She swore it purred.

Yep, cats.

She didn't know where it came from, but she felt confusion from one of them. It didn't understand the reference.

How can I tell that? What's going on? I felt nothing like that from Kellan's.

Just behind the blackish one in front of her, she noticed a smaller one that was a greenish blue. The colors changed as the sunlight hit. It was staring at her with a kind, longing gaze, almost as if beckoning her to come.

What a beautiful storjen, she thought.

Thank you.

Siana started. *What was that?*

They continued to stare into each other's eyes, their gazes locked, and time seemed to stop. The world faded away. A powerful urge to touch it, to feel its texture, overwhelmed her senses. Like, if she didn't, something horribly bad would happen. Another feeling rose within her, bringing tears to her eyes. Goose bumps raised all over her. Siana, standing, felt an unstoppable urge. She had to go to it. There was no other choice. What she felt, she could feel, mirrored in this beautiful beast before her. Soon, it became difficult to tell what feelings were hers and what were the *storjen's*.

Siana and Isis—they knew with absolute certainty that was the other's name—felt an undeniable pull toward one another, the only two beings in existence, moving slowly, hearts pounding as they closed the distance. When they met, they stood, staring into each other's eyes. Each felt a surge of happiness, a profound sense of connection, like they had rediscovered a lost, cherished friend.

They needed each other. They knew they were meant for each other. The need was instinctive, primal—each had to feel the other's presence, physically connect with her. Tears filled their eyes as the same emotions chased through each, diving into one, then back into the other, until they both felt the same thing, completely connected and in sync. They both felt the other *Storjen* withdraw from Siana.

Siana felt her feelings, heard her thoughts, though she didn't understand how. Through Isis, she knew the others were disappointed at not getting a rider. Isis's giddiness at having a rider coursed through Siana. She reached up and cradled the head as it—*she*—laid herself on Siana's shoulder. *You are mine,* each thought. The sheer, breathtaking beauty was almost too much to bear; tears of joy streamed down their faces. If Siana had to describe it, she couldn't.

Siana did not know how long she stood in the field, the *storjen* and she wrapped around each other. She and Isis smiled at each other—as much as a beak can smile—and in unspoken agreement, slowly made their way to the stables.

***

When the females had moved toward one another, Kellan and Tost had stared, speechless with wonder, minds connected. Kellan had brought her here to distract her. That was it. Neither Kellan nor Tost expected a union to be made. Both understood the feelings rampaging through the females. Every union between *storjen* and rider felt the same. It was an extremely emotional experience that was beyond words.

Tost began mentally having a fit. *No, no, no! I refuse to be mated with HER union.*

Unfortunately for him, just as rider and *storjen* fuse, so do mates, and he was pretty sure he'd fused with that one. He had to wait and see if she felt the same for it to complete.

Kellan, while glad Tost had found his mate, asked why he was so against Siana.

Tost refused to answer.

Both left to give the females privacy. They also knew it could take a while before they came down from the emotional high.

***

Isis knew she had a new home. She wouldn't be moving on with the herd. Now that she had a rider, Isis earned a stall. Granted, they rarely used them, and they had shelter in the fields, but it was a status piece she intended to hang on to. A *storjen* lived to find their rider. Many died without one. She would not take this for granted. She knew this female wasn't like the others. To her, that raised her status even more. She had fused with someone no one else had. About skipping, she couldn't wait for their first lesson together.

Siana and Isis entered the stables and saw a grizzled old man leaning against the wall next to Kellan.

Kellan simply asked, "Name?"

Siana responded with a tear-filled smile, "Isis."

The stable master, motioning to a stall, said something to Siana.

Isis informed her, *That's mine.*

She moved into it and promptly dropped waste. Siana stared.

Isis told her, *What? Did you expect me to paint it?*

The stable master nodded at Isis and went to clean it up.

Isis noticed a male staring at her from across the aisle. She also realized he didn't like her rider. When she questioned why, he gave her a vague answer, but she sensed fear of loss and jealousy under it. She also realized she was fusing with him but rejected it. He looked hurt.

She told him, *Unless you accept my rider, I don't accept you.*

Malk, in the stall next to Tost said, *I told you so.*

Tost's face changed into one of sadness and longing as he stared at Isis.

After the stable master finished, he lightly grabbed Siana by her shoulders, slowly spun her around, looking down at her lower half. Kellan waved his hand to get her attention, pointing to the saddles lining a wall. Using his foot and standing behind her, the stable master spread her legs and squatted.

Sensing Siana's alarm, Isis reassured her, *He's measuring you for a saddle. He'll do the same for me when he's finished.*

In the past, Isis, never having been measured herself, watched a male undergo the procedure. She couldn't help but wonder about her rider's reaction to the next part. It didn't disappoint.

Siana let out an outraged, "Hey!" as the stable master's hands cupped and lifted her butt.

The yell echoed around the stables. As she spun around, she knocked the man's hands away. The old man, with a shocked face, looked at Kellan, who laughed. Siana glared at

Kellan, then whirled to look at Isis, who was also laughing. Isis suddenly found the stall boards completely absorbing.

Kellan, stifling his mirth, told Siana, "His name is Yon. He won't hurt you."

Isis joined in, saying, *The saddles and rigging need to be exact for rider and mount. He needs to protect both of us from harm.*

I'll suffer it only because I don't want you hurt, Siana told her.

Finished with Siana, Yon moved to Isis and began touching, measuring, and moving her around. When he moved her tuft of fur away from her back end to touch around her female parts, it was Isis's turn to be indignant. Isis knew the rigging needed to allow for mating and dropping waste, but she didn't realize he would actually touch her *there*.

Siana looked at her. *Not so fun, is it?*

Isis apologized to her rider for laughing. She saw from Tost's expression his anger was rising at the stable master for touching his mate in so personal a manner. Isis informed him he knew it was necessary; she was not yet his mate and wouldn't be until he matured.

Malk snorted.

Yon spoke to Kellan.

Isis told her, *Our first lesson is tomorrow morning.*

Isis could feel Siana was excited as she to start. Though she needed to teach her rider about controlling the connection as soon as she could. Isis wasn't used to having her mind flooded with so much from another.

Siana bid her mount a good day and began leaving with Kellan. She glanced at the two mounts staring at her. One was a majestic looking black one; the other a smaller one colored brown with flecks of gold.

Kellan pointed to each. "Tamek." Pointing to the latter. "Brigitte."

Siana told Isis, *They're not as pretty as you.* She mentally berated herself. *That was kind of mean, wasn't it?*

Isis smiled. *Every rider says that about their mount, just as a storjen thinks their rider is better than others. It's just the way of things.*

She watched her rider fondly as Siana followed her *Setan* mate back to the house.

Chapter Twenty-Four

BRIGITTE, SITTING ON THE cold stone bench, drew in a shaky breath. She could see her own hands trembling.

Why can't I keep these feelings down?

Since that day, she had ignored them. Pretended they didn't exist. Everything that was happening with Siana brought it all back. The anger, the betrayal. How heartbroken she was. Her longing for him.

In defense from her thoughts, she wrapped her arms around herself, slightly rocking. Jaw quivering, she desperately tried to hold back her tears. He didn't deserve that much power, but the pain inside her wanted release.

They had discussed so much. Everything but that. There was no sign he would do what he did. No sign he'd go against her wishes. It hadn't been explicitly said that she was against it, but she had made a passing comment saying she wanted their first joining to be private.

The day had been perfect. Standing with him in the Hall, saying their vows, friends and family watching with pride and doting. Her heart had swelled with so much joy and hope. She'd chosen a golden gown to wear. Hair up, flowers weaved in, matching bouquets in vases placed around the room. He, wearing his House dress clothing and looking as handsome as ever. He'd even put his hair up, which had made her smile as their families escorted them into the Hall, knowing how much he hated doing so. With their love filling the room and almost causing them to glow, their eyes shone as they watched each other's faces. Their ceremony had been one of mutual agreement. She'd counted herself lucky to marry her childhood best friend—until they rolled the claiming table into the room. Disbelief and betrayal had filled her on her most important of days. Her own mother, his brothers horrified at the sight. That was the day Brigitte's life imploded.

She loved him, she still did. She wanted to be with him, despite knowing it would never happen. A High can't be with a Low.

Why didn't he just listen?

A shadow crossed her legs. His inscrutable expression was clear as she looked up and saw him watching her. Neither moved, neither willing to say the first word. She wanted to go back, to replay that part of her life. To prevent their lives from being torn apart. She wanted him to understand. A tear found its way down her cheek. Her control was fading. Not wanting him to see how much he still affected her, she stood and hurried away, leaving him alone with a look of longing.

***

Lorica, watching from a window, had seen her enter the maze. Not knowing why, and still angry at her comment, though he rightfully deserved it, he followed. He would never strike her; he wanted to drag her to his room and claim her. Despite his normal unconcern for rules, the act's illegality caused him to stop.

As he left the manor, following her, he remembered that day—how proud he had been to make such a claim. So sure she would obey him, though she'd never given him reason to think that. It was his pride that became their downfall. His immaturity. Make no mistake, he loved her. He'd loved her for as long as he remembered. Back then, his pride was more important. When she discarded him, the affront was all he could see. The sea of his pride overwhelmed his heartbreak. He had demanded she do what she was told and obey, hence her recent comment. She angrily refused.

All he could think about was the crowded Hall, and that she had refused his order. His vanity couldn't take it. He had turned to the dais and demanded they make her, ignoring her pleading tears and his brothers' anger.

They wouldn't speak to me for over a fortnight, their disdain of my actions plain.

He could still remember the sound of her disbelief— *Why would you do this?*

Upon reaching the maze, he entered and stopped when he found her. Watching her rock on the bench, he felt his heart ache. He wanted to claim her right then and there. He wanted to wrap his arms around her, to let her know he still cared for her.

When the Convocation, trapped by Lorica's announcement, told her she would be publicly claimed against her will, she spoke up. A loophole in the law offered High females a choice—be claimed or forfeit their standing—but most were unaware of it. She chose her standing.

The gasps of the *Bund* and their families still echoed in his ears. Filled with enraged disbelief, he stared at her, his eyes reddening. Her angry, tear-filled despair looked back. After a deep breath, humiliated, he stormed from the Hall.

That choice created a problem. Only the Convocation released a claim, with the couple agreeing, and she refused. In her anger, she kept him bound to her. In return, Lorica forbade her from leaving the Devereaux family's employ. A High can't be with a Low. They were both caught in a prison of their own making. Bound together, yet having to stay apart.

When he realized she was looking at him, her pain-filled eyes rendered him speechless. Her tears about undid him. Unable to find words, desperately trying to, it became too late. She stood and rushed away.

She's still as affected as I am. Agreement from her would allow for her restoration. For us to be together. Why won't she?

He walked through the maze, feelings conflicted. For weeks after, his anger hadn't waned. They avoided each other while she adjusted to her new position. It had been such, Kellan insisted he go with him to Falon to try to establish trade.

Unfortunately, they'd arrived to find themselves in the beginnings of a civil war between the two ruling clans against a rising third. One side seized Lorica and subjected him to torture. During a rescue attempt, an explosion injured Kellan. Though they'd eventually escaped with their lives, both had physical and mental scars.

Stopping, staring at nothing, he wondered if he could convince her. Though he knew Brigitte would never agree to that. Neither of them would back down. One of his Falon guards appeared out of nowhere with some news. Lorica left the maze with him.

Chapter Twenty-Five

Each rider believed their mount looked the best, just as each mount felt their rider was the best.

Isis currently disagreed with that *Storjen* belief. It took ages for Siana to learn how to put the saddle on. It was literally almost time for the midday meal when she did it correctly and mounted her. They hadn't even left the stall yet. Isis lost count of how many times she had been stabbed and pinched during the process. Eventually, she told Siana if she did it again, Isis would nip her.

Siana was extra careful after that. Isis projected every injury Siana inflicted back at her so she would understand the pain she was causing. Siana had also fallen twice before she'd got her leg over to the other side. Her smaller size made mounting harder.

Yon and Kellan were standing to the side, encouraging her. Whatever lesson advice they couldn't get across to her, Isis would fill in the blanks. Isis knew they were both becoming frustrated, but it was part of the process. Yon and Kellan cheered when Siana finally mounted Isis. Unfortunately, they were out of time. Isis needed a break, and Siana had to remove and put everything away.

Siana groaned in pain as she lifted the saddle off of Isis. She told Isis, *My arms aren't used to all of this. I was also really hoping to ride.*

    I was too, Isis responded with disappointment. *Maybe tomorrow. I think we both need a break.*

    Siana nodded in agreement.

    The next morning, there was still no news about Jacob. Distressed, Siana went to the stables, and Kellan suggested another lesson. Her worry about her brother distracted her, and she had trouble. It caused Isis to finally reach back and nip Siana. She had run her into the stall wall for the third time. The nip didn't hurt, but running into the wall did.

    A *storjen* would never deliberately hurt their rider, but Siana could feel Isis was tired of her rider hurting her. After the nip, Siana was close to tears. As part of learning to ride, a *storjen* allowed their pain to be felt by the new rider. Siana was upset that she was causing harm to Isis, and Isis could feel she was ready to give up.

    Isis said kindly, *Stop, breathe, focus on where you want me to go. Don't let yourself get distracted. Once you get the hang of it, it will become automatic.*

    The advice Isis gave her reminded her of when their father was teaching Jacob and herself to drive. He said the same thing when they swerved trying to stay in the road lane. Eventually, it became second nature. Now, Siana was also getting distracted by an enormous insect that was repeatedly landing nearby. No pest had the right to be so big. Instead of focusing on leaving the stables, she'd look at the flying bug and Isis would head toward it, running into the wall.

Kellan gave Siana an encouraging nod. "You can do this."

Yon also gave her encouragement. Tost and Malk nodded their heads rapidly in support. Tamek and Brigitte's mounts had left earlier, no doubt knowing what was to come. Isis could feel Siana's doubt and her desire to give up on learning to ride just so she didn't hurt Isis.

Don't you dare. Isis turned her head and glared at her. *To lose my rider would not only be humiliating, it also hurts a storjen's heart. When their riders were lost, some died of grief.*

Horrified, Siana didn't want Isis to die.

I would hope not! was her response.

Tost asked, *Are you going to tell her it was when they died of old age?*

Isis ignored him.

Yon decided they needed to take a break and stop for the day. Dejectedly, Siana removed the saddle and rigging. Isis gave her shoulder a nudge.

Take heart. It doesn't happen overnight. We'll get there together.

Siana just nodded.

Siana was walking in the maze, thinking. She was losing hope. Again, no news. Her heart was heavy. She'd been so sure they'd find him quickly. Every day, Lorica's men had gone out searching. Today, Lorica had said and acted out—with Kellan watching in amusement this time—that they sent men to other towns to see if anyone reported a red-headed foreigner. Nothing.

Where are you? Are you even here?

Memories of boisterous game nights filled with laughter, the scent of popcorn and pizza, and the sting of his blatant cheating—reminiscent of someone else she knew— mingled with images of him begging her to hike, promising breathtaking vistas, and the taste of new baking recipes she'd perfected, all contrasted by the lingering aftertaste of his experimental herbal concoctions, flooded her mind. She missed him so much. She was having trouble understanding parts of this world and could really use her brother's advice.

When she tried to tell Kellan about him through Isis, Isis told her that *Storjen* did not handle certain matters. If it involved the health of another *storjen*, an emergency involving their rider—a lost brother didn't qualify—a journey, or *storjen* care, they could. A translator for different languages was one thing they absolutely refused to do, plus Isis could only understand Siana due to their union. She would have to translate through Tost, who wanted nothing to do with her rider.

When Siana questioned why they wouldn't, Sia had noticed the *Storjen* nearby freeze with lowered heads after Isis became very solemn. Isis informed her they used to. *Storjen* had been around since the beginning of the age, when they were one of the few creatures in this world. As time went on, more beings surfaced. *Storjen* had, once these beings began to fight, often helped bring countries and clans together.

They'd gotten involved in trying to bring peace to two warring factions. It was so heated, it took several *Storjen* to help with translating. The two sides were so full of hate, one final translated message was like lighting the fuse of a powder keg. Both sides turned on the *Storjen*. The horrific event—a brutal massacre that left their numbers decimated to near extinction—fundamentally shifted their worldview. It was now forbidden for them to involve themselves in *Setan* issues. They would not risk such an event again, not even for a simple matter. These beings were too unpredictable.

A noise startled her, drawing her out of her reverie.

***

Kellan, eyes widening, had just come around a corner. Though his face was drawn and weary, his signature grin, crinkling the corners of his eyes, quickly appeared. Hers answered. He gave a quick nod, his eyes lingering on her for a moment longer than necessary before he passed, a silent battle raging between his desire to approach and his need to respect her space.

"Kellan."

His heart answered. "Yes?"

"News, Jacob?" Her daily questioning about her brother had taught her the new word.

He strolled to a nearby bench and sat. The breeze through the hedges cooled him. Patting the seat next to him, he waited. She hesitantly walked over and sat, shifting on the cold stone.

Kellan, thinking on how to word it, said, "Lorica guard look. Can't find. Don't know where."

Seeing her disappointment, he was at a loss. There was no trace of him. The increasing worry and helplessness were evident in her each day; her quiet sighs and restless movements spoke volumes.

With a shift in her position during the silence, her leg brushed against his, generating a slight warmth where they made contact. Sudden desire burned in him. He watched her mouth part, and her breathing quicken. Staring into each other's eyes, he reached out, his fingers gently tracing the curve of her cheek. Her tongue nervously darted out to wet her lips.

She leaned first, tilting her head, mouth reaching for his. A jolt of pure pleasure shot through him as his mouth met hers, a feeling that resonated in every cell of his being. Siana slid closer to him, the warmth of her body near his, arms enfolding each other. Her body pressed against him, her desire to be with him obvious. A thrilling anticipation took over Kellan's senses. He wanted her right here. When she moved almost into his lap, he realized they were entering dangerous territory and slowly pulled away with light kisses. Her gaze disappointed, face flushed, she leaned toward him again.

"Siana." He tried to rein in his body, gently using his arms to hold her back. "Jacob first." He couldn't do anything until her brother was found, then she may not want him.

Face troubled, she just nodded, a slight guilt in her eyes.

He promised, "Jacob, then us," while stroking her cheek before giving her lips a quick kiss, leaving both of them longing. He rose and left, feeling her gaze follow him.

***

As each day passed with no news, and her own sexual frustration rose, Isis became her savior. Siana threw herself into her riding lessons. A mount, she realized, would assist in her search for her brother. She'd be able to go farther and faster than she could walk. She was tired of being on the waiting end of things.

The faster I learn this, the faster I can pack up and search for Jacob myself.

Jacob had taught her foraging while on the run, so she was fairly certain she could find food given the presence of the blackberries and other foods similar to her own world.

Part of her learning also involved disconnecting certain thoughts from entering Isis's mind as well as disconnecting completely. That was her *storjen's* job to teach her. She learned she'd been giving access to her entire mind, and the occasional looks Isis gave her were because of her thoughts about Kellan. Siana's cheeks burned over Isis seeing those intimate images.

One day, Isis proudly walked out of the stall with Siana on her back. Siana looked at Kellan in triumph and promptly ran Isis into him. Yon turned away to hide his laughter, which failed because everyone could see his shoulders shaking. With her apology and correction made, she saw Isis pass through the stable doorway.

Why don't you just go on your own? Why do I have to guide you? Siana knew Isis didn't need her direction.

It teaches the rider and mount to become as one. Once we are, you can just think of it, and I'll go. Though sometimes you'll still need to guide me if you have a sudden change, and our minds don't connect quickly enough.

After a time, they were both beginning to move as one. The achievement was exhilarating. Yon had Siana let go of the reins, put her arms out, and stay balanced while Isis walked around. Isis picked the direction, including sudden turns. The purpose was to teach Siana to keep her balance, no matter what. She did well, so Isis made her movements quicker and sharper. Siana only fell once, bruising her knee, and Yon made her get up and back on. Isis apologized, but it was part of the training.

Soon, they were trotting with Siana's arms still out. Then Isis was galloping and doing small jumps. Siana learned when to lift herself off the saddle and when to stay seated. If she did it incorrectly, her butt wasn't fond of chairs for a bit; during a few jumps, she found herself laying on the warm grass, Isis snorting with amusement over her.

During one slow ride, trying maneuvers, Siana probed Isis's openness about taking a possible trip.

If I need to go somewhere and do something, will you go with me? Siana asked her.

Isis, curious, asked, *Where would we go? Are you planning something?*

There are no solid plans yet. I'm just curious about whether I own you or are we partners? I'm not sure how this works.

Isis nodded in understanding, pulling the reins as she did so. *We are partners, but we are also bonded. You do not own me. I have my own mind, yet I am bound to yours. It's difficult to explain, and not wise to discuss in the middle of a lesson, but if you want to go somewhere, I am bound to go with you. The only exception is if it breaks Storjen code.*

Siana nodded, glad she'd confirmed she'd have a mount to find Jacob with.

Finally, the day came when Yon led them to a field filled with jumps and other obstacles. Isis was stomping and nodding her head, excitement taking over. This was it: the last test. After this, if they passed, their training was over. Siana was determined to do well. She had to. The course involved several various jumps along with sections they had to maneuver.

Both took a deep breath and waited. Tamek, Kellan, Lorica, and Brigitte—along with their mounts—were cheering from the sidelines. Well, Tamek just stood there, stoic as usual. Yon raised his arm. Siana felt Isis tense, the power building. His arm fell, and they were off. Siana thought they would fail the second jump. Isis, insulted, easily cleared it. Siana enjoyed the zig-zag portion of the course. The part they had to navigate backward worried them both, but they had no issues. Although the course looked long, they felt they had finished it in minutes.

They knew they'd passed. They hadn't made a single mistake. The happiness they felt at becoming a team sent them galloping down the field. They loved it. They loved the wind flying past them as they moved together as one. Isis encouraged her to let go of the reins and Siana did, standing in the stirrups, braided hair flowing behind her, as they ran for the pure joy of it, their triumph, and each other's company.

Chapter Twenty-Six

SOMETHING WOKE HER. SIANA, opening her eyes, sleepily looked around the room. At least, what she could see of it. It was still night, but judging by the light beginning to invade, the sun was about to come up. The low lights were always on, because she couldn't control them yet. The room briefly lit with an orange glow, then dimmed. A short time later, it did it again.

What is that?

With her body aching from the ride, she sat up to identify the source of the light. Rubbing the sleep from her eyes, she swept them around the room. A warmth started on the back of her neck, pulsating with the light.

The tracker.

Confused, she climbed out of bed. Approaching the desk, she used a hand mirror to try to see what she could. The tracker was active. Her heart raced.

Why was it active?

Her old doubts about where she was came flooding back. A muffled noise she had long forgotten about sounded.

What?

She walked to the wardrobe, opened it, and there, next to her bag, lay her phone. Charging it during the day and leaving it next to her bag at night became her habit. She ceased to turn it off once it was fully charged. There was a notification.

How?!

As she picked up the item, the name Jerkface made her catch her breath. Jacob.

What the hell?

"'The field,'" she read, her phone open. "'Alone. Hurry.'"

Was this a trick?

She couldn't take the chance if it was real. She moved as fast as possible. After using the toilet, she threw on her old clothes, packed the bag with her phone and charger, put on her shoes, and quietly opened her door.

She heard no movement and descended the stairs, making as little noise as possible. Moving to the back of the house, she realized she needed Isis. Siana looked into the kitchen as she passed. Mrs. Atwood wasn't in there. From the kitchen window, she watched the housekeeper walking down to collect the eggs. Siana swore the woman never slept. Today it was a good thing. Her being awake meant the exterior door would be unlocked. Siana moved toward it. Carefully opening the back door, she squeezed through as soon as she could and closed it, trying to draw as little attention as possible.

She was hoping the guards would assume she was going to the stables for the millionth time and not raise any alarm since she was alone. Siana had discovered you had to be within a certain distance for the connection between *storjen* and rider to work. She kept to the early morning shadows. The sun was rising quickly, and she'd be plainly visible soon. If anyone from the house saw her, they'd no doubt stop her to ask why she was outside.

As she drew near, Isis asked her what was going on. Siana asked her if riding bareback was possible, because she was short on time.

It's not advisable, but it depends on distance and the ride.

She mentally showed her the field and was told no.

Dang it.

Isis informed her the saddle would keep Siana's weight from hurting her spine, and such a long distance required one. Impatient to get going, Siana grabbed and put the saddle on as quietly as possible. Trying to keep the metal on the rigging from hitting each other was the hardest part. She carried the bridle and reins muffled in her arm, and had Isis follow her. Malk and Tost were nowhere to be seen, which worked in her favor. She was afraid they'd raise a fuss and wake Yon, who slept above the stables. Technically, she could claim it was an early morning ride, but someone was always with her. She didn't know how Yon would react to her being alone.

Better safe than sorry.

Siana led Isis out and into the pasture. Her hooves on the path would make too much noise. Once they were out of sight of the stables, behind some trees, she finished tacking her up. Isis was strangely quiet.

As Siana mounted, she finally asked, *Shouldn't you have someone with you?*

Siana patted her neck, knowing she'd never ridden without someone watching her. *You're with me.*

You know what I mean. What is that glowing on your neck? I don't like this.

Siana brushed her off, saying, *It's my brother. He said to come alone and to hurry. I don't have time to wait for anyone.*

They turned toward the road that led to the field and took off.

***

Kellan was sleeping when something intruded. Tost was straining to get hold of him. Kellan, annoyed and without opening his eyes, asked what he wanted. It was unusual for him to come close to the house to speak. He had to be, at least, at the back gate. When he heard, his eyes flew open, and he let Tost know he'd be right there. He threw clothes on as quick as he could.

Kellan almost ran into Tamek while exiting his room. Surprised at the sight of his brother, he asked, and was told his own mount had woken him and told him about Siana and Isis leaving. Since a *storjen* was involved in an unusual activity, they could inform the house. Though Siana and Isis had passed their test, they were still a new team and needed to be monitored for a while, and the *Storjen* knew Siana wasn't supposed to be alone. Isis agreeing to go out alone was something she shouldn't have done.

Shortly after, Lorica came bursting out of his room and skidded to a stop at the sight of his kin. "I assume we've all been told the same thing about Siana?"

They nodded, and all three hurried down the stairs, out the back door—nearly knocking over Mrs. Atwood and Brigitte, the latter demanding to know what happened—down to the stables where their mounts had returned to be saddled. Each male's face reflected the worry the other was feeling. Tamek's usual stoicism gave way to a worried frown.

Siana wasn't wearing banding. Anyone could take her, and their hands would be tied. Elli had seen them walk off. Their mounts knew the two had left and which direction, but not the exact destination.

Lorica looked in the general direction the females had gone. "They're heading for the field."

All three rapidly saddled their mounts. As each one finished, he galloped in that direction, not waiting for the others. She needed to be reached as soon as possible. Soon, all three were racing toward their destination.

***

Isis felt the *Storjens'* presence increasing and warned Siana. The problem lay with the fact the males' mounts were larger and faster. The females increased their speed to put as much distance as possible between them. As they reached the field, Isis burst through the trees, out of breath, sweat dripping.

Siana looked around and saw nothing out of the ordinary. *Was it a false message?* She unconsciously projected that thought into Isis.

Isis informed her, *If so, and I ran like this for nothing, you are not riding me until further notice.*

It didn't take long for them to hear the thunder of hooves quickly decreasing the distance. Siana slid off her mount and moved to the middle of the field.

Where is he?

Moving along the edge, she called for him. She felt the tracker stop pulsing; the light became steady and grew warm.

What is that?

A loud, high-pitched whine, like a mosquito on steroids, faded into a soft, whooshing sound like the wind through tall grass. As Siana backed away, a prickling unease crawled up her spine; an unknown sound echoed around the field, the ground vibrating beneath her feet. A soft, pulsating light appeared, slowly revolving in midair, then gradually sped up, its gentle hum growing louder.

***

Lorica reached the clearing first, though they all heard the noise before arriving. It would have been impossible not to. Malk slid to a stop and began shifting back and forth with concern. Lorica dismounted as Tamek, then Kellan, rode onto the field, staring with mounting worry at the sight in front of them.

"Come here, Siana," Lorica said, motioning to her. He didn't want her near it.

He saw her glance at him, and then she turned back to the light. It was dramatically enlarging, a flat circle growing from the ground, reaching toward the treetops, its soft light illuminating the area. The wind it was generating started blowing harder, the leaves, grass, and flowers bending under its will. Their hair was caught in a wild dance. The *Storjen,* nervously prancing, retreated into the darkness of the tree line.

Kellan dismounted, the leather of his saddle creaking, and jogged toward her, urgently calling, "Siana!"

He was almost to her when a noise similar to a minor explosion caused all of them to duck. The brothers watched in stunned silence as the light began opening outwards from the middle.

Lorica saw Tamek move closer to him, reaching for a sword that wasn't there.

How does he expect to fight that?

The light opened to reveal things he couldn't explain. His mind struggled to comprehend it. The first things revealed were metal furniture, each piece adorned with glowing lights and an array of buttons, stark against the dark back wall. Some buttons seem to float in midair. Standing in front was a female with yellow hair. His eyes darted between his brothers; a mixture of fear and shock reflected in their wide eyes. None of them had ever witnessed such a bizarre and unsettling sight. He soon realized another person was standing near the opening, their presence somehow both unnerving and intriguing. His red hair and beard, thin frame, and uncanny resemblance to their house guest made him instantly recognizable.

***

A piercing "Jacob!" ripped through the stillness.

Siana ran toward the opening, her footsteps muffled by the soft earth, leaving the shocked brothers speechless. She recognized him immediately. Though thinner, his eyes held a spark, a testament to his resilience. She was going to bring him to this world.

Joy swelled within her until Jacob's desperate "No!" brought a painful halt to her elation. "Stay!"

Siana stopped and couldn't believe what she just heard. "No!" she cried out and resumed running toward him.

"Stop!" he shouted. "Listen!"

"Why? I don't understand." *What's happening?*

As the gate reached full size, just enough for a person to walk through, the noise abated.

"Jacob, what do you mean? Who is that?" Her posture shifted as she changed her train of thought. "Never mind that. Please come over here. It's safe. We can be together. We can live here. These men have been helping me." She motioned to the others.

He shook his head, the weight of the world seemingly heavy on his shoulders. "I will be staying here," he announced definitively. "I wanted a chance to say goodbye."

The woman turned from the console and gave Siana a sad smile.

A stunned silence replaced her voice. Quickly recovering, she asked, "What do you mean by 'goodbye'? No, if you won't come here, then I'll come back to you." She moved toward the portal.

"Sia, listen to me. Please," Jacob implored.

She shook her head. "Not if it involves me not being with you. You're my only family left."

"Listen." His voice softened. "I'm your big brother, remember?" He'd always held that over her head.

His glance at the men allowed him to see their ears and the distant mounts. The lavender-colored trees caught his gaze. "Our world is done. The AI is about to set our world on fire, killing everyone and everything. A reset."

She shook her head and motioned for him to come through. "Fine, then come here."

He sighed and shook his head, eyes begging her to understand. "I know this is hard, but you were sent here to keep you safe, but you see—I know you. I knew you wouldn't stop looking for me."

"Of course not!" Siana wanted to scream. She also knew him. Knew how stubborn he was. It was like banging her head on a brick wall, but he forgot one thing. He forgot she was his twin and was just as stubborn.

"Only a limited number of people can go to any one area. You and four others were sent here. Only you remain. The others didn't make it. You're the only one who has survived."

Floored, she exclaimed, "What?!" *What did he mean? How?*

"They don't know what happened to them. All they know is their trackers went dead. In this place, the only way that would happen is if they died. Your tracker is the only one active."

Siana didn't know what to say, then a thought occurred to her. "Is it possible they had them removed?"

Jacob shrugged, face heavy with sadness. "We don't know. It's possible, but they just assume they're gone, not that it matters to the program." He continued, "Sending people to other places is what the friendly AI has been doing to save humanity. To avoid overwhelming the population of worlds and disrupting the timeline, each location has a strict quota on the number of people they can accommodate. This one had a maximum limit of five. Once it's accepted, the zone closes. No one else can go through. Even if I wanted to, I can't join you. The portal won't let me leave."

He glanced up at a timer that was counting down. "I will go to a different area, but I need to go now. We're about out of time. It won't stay open for long. We took a risk doing this much. I love you. Be safe. Find love. Have fat babies." His face beseeched her. "But most of all, live. I know it's cheesy, but it's what I feel."

"No, I'm coming back then!" She refused to let him go. He was all she had. She needed him. If they died, they'd die together. As she ran as fast as she could toward the now closing portal, time appeared to slow as a familiar noise reached her ears.

No, it can't be.

The world became muffled, sounds distant and distorted as if heard underwater.

Time seemed to crawl.

A vibrant red, a blur of motion, caught her eye.

As she turned toward it, the red motion manifested as rolling execution bots.

Jacob turned toward them, yelling at the woman to close the portal faster.

Jacob's eyes widening in shock as his body crumpled to the ground.

Siana's dawning look of horror as she realized what was happening.

Her scream of denial, raw and desperate, reverberated through the still morning air of the woods.

The bots as one turned to face her, their targeting systems locking onto her.

The woman's hand slammed down on the terminal as she yelled, "No!"

An explosion, a tremendous shockwave shaking the ground and sending a blast of intense heat and pressure outwards, swallowing everything.

A searing heat emanated from the doorway, almost painful to be near.

Uselessly, Siana screamed his name, the raw emotion palpable.

Her disbelieving stare as the fire consumed the room. The shock paralyzed her.

This isn't happening.

The inferno shrank as it ate all the air, flames dancing, searching for fuel, a single flame turning toward the still closing portal. It danced with excitement at finding more food.

***

Kellan saw the flames shrink, heard Siana screaming, saw her in front of the opening, and recognized what was about to happen. In a desperate sprint, he ran with all of his might, the ground trembling beneath his feet as he threw his body against hers, knocking her to the ground as the inferno roared back to life.

A horizontal column of heat flew over their prone bodies. A familiar feeling raced across his back. Lorica and Tamek threw themselves on the ground at the strength of it. They lay there, waiting as the portal finally closed, cutting off the air the fire so desperately needed.

Siana's screaming wail of desperation and grief bounced off the trees and ran through the field. Kellan saw Isis fall to the ground and assumed it was from her rider's grief. A howl, like a song of lamentation, echoed Siana's heartbreak as Isis raised her head, leaned back, and opened her beak. One by one the other mounts joined in, as their kin's overwhelming grief filled the air, singing loud their kind's song of loss and sorrow. Their deep sadness was unmistakable, at odds with the beauty of the day. Kellan's helpless eyes looked over the female he held in his arms, and found his brothers', their tears reflecting his own.

Chapter Twenty-Seven

KELLAN DIDN'T KNOW HOW long they lay on the ground. Once Isis stopped singing, the others followed suit until only Siana's cries remained. After knocking her out of harm's way, he lay beside her, holding her as her body shook with harsh, violent sobs. Tamek took his mount and rode home to let the others know what had happened, so Brigitte could be ready for her. Lorica waited nearby, in case he was needed.

As Siana quieted, Kellan stood and gently encouraged her to stand, holding her steady until Lorica took her. He mounted Tost and between the two of them, they managed to get her on the mount. She didn't look at them, didn't talk, just quietly cried. Tost, for once, behaved himself.

Kellan held her in his arms; he didn't trust that she wouldn't fall off if he put her on the back. He let Tost take them home. Lorica followed, with Isis close behind, still visibly shaken by her mistress's grief. The air hung heavy with unspoken sorrow as a slow, silent parade of shock and disbelief made its way home, each face etched with the pain of what had just happened.

Kellan replayed the events in his mind, each detail sharp and clear. Though he understood little of what he was seeing, he knew brother and sister were arguing. It took a while for him to figure out her brother didn't come to take her home. It looked to him like he planned on leaving her, but he wasn't staying. He could only attribute Siana's agitated demeanor and angry outburst to her body language. Obviously, those creatures killed her brother. The entire thing was bewildering. It made little sense, but now his focus was the female in his arms.

***

Upon arriving home, Lorica went to the stables to inform Yon of the events—so he could check on Isis throughout the night—before unsaddling their mounts. He knew Yon could do it, but he wanted to. He felt they all could use each other's company for a bit. The fire also brought back memories of almost losing Kellan, and he wanted time to process it.

His breath caught as he remembered Kellan's scream of agony as the explosive powder had triggered too soon, knocking his brother sideways and throwing a shower of fire onto him, the hot powder forever scarring him. Helpless, he could only stare out his cell window, watching, believing his eldest brother had died trying to rescue him.

***

Kellan arrived at the back door, and Tamek exited to help with Siana. He had stood watch in case he was needed. Brigitte was waiting in Siana's room. Mrs. Atwood was on standby to make a soothing tea. Her staple in times of trouble. As Tamek reached the couple, looking at her face laying on Kellan's arm, he could see she had cried herself to sleep. They gently maneuvered her off the mount and into Tamek's arms. He realized they were back to square one.

***

Brigitte didn't know what she would need, so she prepared nothing, but when she saw Siana sleeping, she pulled the covers out of the way so Tamek could lay her on the bed. Brigitte, sorrowful for her lady's loss, removed her shoes and looked at her. The sight of Siana's swollen, red eyes and tear-stained cheeks moved Brigitte. With a tender touch, she swept the curls from Siana's face. She wanted to fix it, but knew she couldn't. She pulled the quilts over her, lowered the lights, and left the room, vowing to be there first thing in the morning.

For the next few days, Siana didn't leave her room. She didn't wash. Food, uneaten, was sent back. Brigitte let them know she was drinking water and a little tea, but mostly she lay in bed and cried. No one knew how to help her. On the third day, Mrs. Atwood insisted she eat some soup and stood over her until she did. From that point on, she made her light meals, and made sure the heartbroken female ate every one of them. A few days later, Brigitte talked her into a bath while Mrs. Atwood changed the bedding, but once that was done, she lay in bed again. They gave her time, but diligently looked after her.

***

A few days after Jacob's death, the brothers met in the study. Each wore a somber expression. While they had empathy for Siana, they knew they were back to where they started.

Tamek stated, "I have no understanding of what we saw, but I think we can all agree: she is not from here." The other two nodded. "I'm still waiting to hear back from the studium. We need to find out if anyone knows her language or, at least, which language it is. Because of her mourning, we have a short amount of time, but we need to get ahead of this now. I don't want us on the back foot again."

Kellan agreed. "I don't want to be scrambling to protect her without knowing more. I'm still reeling at what I saw. That she isn't from here... I don't understand any of it, but we need for her to become more fluent in our language. I want to know more, though it might be too painful for her."

Lorica interjected, "We also need to explain our laws, though I wonder with Brigitte's help if we could get the meaning across. Her language skills are much improved. It's possible by now we may make her understand."

Tamek continued, "We also need to book the officiant."

Kellan snapped his head up. "That's premature."

Tamek asked in disbelief, "Is it? Even if we know what language she speaks, she is here. She is in our House. Her brother, rest him, is dead. She is subject to our laws. We are back to you needing to claim her."

Lorica interjected, "She just lost her brother! You saw how deep her sorrow went!"

Tamek sighed. "I know that. I'm talking about after her mourning period is over."

Lorica said, "We don't know what her grieving rituals are. My time in Falon showed theirs differ greatly from ours. She may need a longer time."

Tamek retorted, "Unfortunately, her rituals no longer apply if they countermand our laws."

Kellan, hating that Tamek was right, said, "Put the officiant on standby. We'll take it a day at a time. For right now, that's as far as I'm willing to compromise."

Later, Kellan, who was thinking of their house guest, was standing in the spare study, staring out the window, trying to think of some way to save her from their laws. It was the middle of the night, but he hadn't been able to sleep and walked the house, ending up here. Hearing a low creak from the door, he turned and saw Siana. Her face was puffy and splotched, her hair braided down her back.

She said, "I'm sorry," and turned to leave.

"No, it's okay."

Siana stopped and turned back. Her jaw quivered.

"I look for Brigitte."

"She's sleeping. What do you need?"

Her jaw quivered more. She took a step and stumbled. Kellan moved toward her to steady her. With her head resting on his chest, she cried again. He wrapped his arms around her, stroking her back.

Between sobs, she said, "I not want be alone."

"You're not." He held her while she cried. When her legs gave way, he caught her and lifted her chin with his fingers.

He asked, "Did you take *Wotal*?" looking into her glazed eyes.

She nodded, her eyes beginning to close. Kellan made a mental note to ask Brigitte how much she'd been handing out as he swung Siana into his arms. He carried her back to her room as her head lolled against his chest. He pushed open her bedroom door with his foot. Stepping in, he gently laid her in the middle of the bed.

As he went to stand, her hand clenched his shirt. "No alone," she murmured.

Unsure of what to do, he whispered, "I'll get Brigitte."

She wouldn't let go of his shirt. If he tried to pry her hand off, she began to whimper and cry. Giving in, he laid beside her, feeling the soft rhythm of her breathing and the gentle scent of her skin. Once she was fully asleep, he'd leave. He pulled the covers over both of them. He stroked a stray hair from her eyes as he looked at her. Her eyes opened briefly, and she gave him a small smile before dozing again.

He rolled to his back, her hand still holding his nightshirt, and thought about Tamek's plan. The one flaw—other than Siana not knowing about it—was the actual claiming. His injuries went down his entire left side. It started small at his face and neck, expanded to half his body at the waist and hips, then reduced going down his leg. His male area had been damaged. Physicians felt the need to remove a portion of his girth to help rid an infection. It made it not only misshapen, but it made him smaller than the average *Setan* male. Surprisingly, it was still functional, though no one was sure if he could father children.

As House Head, it was Tamek's decision on her claimant. Therefore, Tamek chose him because Kellan was the least likely to kill Siana. Kellan knew, however, that without proper further preparation, he could still kill her. He didn't know if what they did at camp helped or not. Kellan wanted to go to the Convocation and petition for an exclusion. He felt his exam was enough evidence that she could die. With permission, the law can exclude extenuating circumstances such as abnormalities or illness.

Tamek felt that the risk was too great. He was sure Talon and his cronies could call their own physician purely out of spite against their House, and claim Kellan was lying. No exam needed. Even if they did subject her to one, it was a given Talon would pay the male enough to lie. This was partially the reason they wanted to find out what race she was. If they knew, they could get her home. Recent events put that into the bin. That was Kellan's last thought for a while.

Something had woken him. Groggily, Kellan forced his eyes open in an attempt to fight off sleep. They were face-to-face. Siana's drugged eyes were watching him, her finger tracing his features, their bodies wrapped around each other.

She was the prettiest female.

He couldn't recall who moved first, but their lips were together, a soft sigh escaping between them as the world faded away. As they kissed, a palpable tension filled the air, desire growing. She rolled onto her back as his body moved over hers, her arms reaching around him. As he lowered himself, their lips moved in a slow, tender dance. Her hands slid up and down his back, her touch featherlight, one of his arms supporting his weight, the other cradling her face, his fingers gently tracing her jawline.

As one of his legs slipped between hers, he felt her hips arch. She wanted him. He moved his mouth from her lips to her jaw, then trailed kisses down to her breasts. The rise and fall of her breathing increased in anticipation, and his hand found the tip of one. He made love to it with his mouth through the gown. A low moan, and her breath came in little gasps. Her chest rose toward him, allowing him easier reach. He felt her gentle hands in his hair, her touch light yet firm as she held his head close.

Reaching down to pull the hem of her gown up, his fingers brushed her thigh before he found her lips again. Her hips swayed against his leg. A silent promise, a wordless invitation. He remembered her pleasure was on the outside. Adjusting his position to the side to get a better angle, he continued to kiss her while his hand explored between her legs. They parted more, and his name slipped out in a moan.

The sound jolted him back to reality; he came to his senses. *What am I doing?*

He pulled his hand back, regretfully smoothing her gown down, its coolness a contrast against his fingertips. Resting his forehead on hers, he felt her soft skin and slowed his racing heart, his breath evening out against her temple.

"Kellan?" she asked in drugged confusion.

He looked deep into her eyes, their captivating color mesmerizing him. He didn't know how much she'd understand. Not because of the language barrier, but because she wasn't in her right mind. *Wotal* lowered inhibitions, but it didn't put feelings into place that weren't already there, so he knew she genuinely wanted him. He'd known that since the kiss in the maze.

"I desire you," he whispered, his voice filled with longing. "I do. All I want is to lose myself in you. But there are things you don't know. Things you need to know. You are also drugged on *Wotal*," he said, and recognizing the familiar name, she gave a happy nod, a small smile playing on her lips.

"I will not touch a female on *Wotal*," he said, realizing the hypocrisy.

With a gentle voice and understanding eyes, he remarked, "You're also sad about your brother."

Her smile disappeared.

"Your mind," he murmured, a gentle tap of his finger on her forehead, "is clouded. This isn't a 'no,' it's a 'not yet.'" He kissed her forehead, disentangled himself, and said, "Go to sleep."

She looked puzzled as her eyes slowly closed. When they didn't reopen, he left.

Chapter Twenty-Eight

SIANA WOKE TO RAYS of light hitting her face. As she opened her eyes to the sun-filled room, she realized someone forgot to close the drapes. Stretching and yawning, she also realized she'd slept late again. Her mind was foggy. As she rolled over, she saw the indented pillow next to hers and last night came flooding back. Her face flushed crimson as she froze in mortification, a wave of heat rising from her chest to her cheeks.

Did I really throw myself at him?

A muffled groan escaped her lips as she buried her face in the pillow, its smooth surface cool against her burning face. The embarrassment would be too much; she'd never be able to face him again. She realized, as she recalled the evening, that she'd dreaded being alone. Taking the pain medication. The discovery of him in his study. Wanting his comfort. Not wanting him to leave. Wanting him in her bed. Opening her eyes to see him so at peace in his sleep, laugh lines softening, his kiss and touch.

Though not a prude or a virgin, the memory of her body's intense response to him brought a blush to her cheeks. She'd never reacted that strongly before. Thinking about it, she realized she hadn't wanted him to stop.

Why did he?

She tried to piece together his words that she understood. He wanted her. *Good.* Something about *Wotal.* He stopped knowing she was drugged. *Another plus.* His last words came to her. It's a "not yet." *He plans on being with me.* She gave a small smile, excitement building in a part of her. He mentioned Jacob and her being sad. *He knows I'm grieving.* Something about her knowing? *Knowing what?* She had known there was something they weren't telling her, but she couldn't yet figure out what it was.

Brigitte opening her door interrupted her train of thought, and she finally decided she'd spent enough time in bed. Jacob would hate that she laid around crying. The lecture he would have given her played in her mind. She got up to start the day, hoping her friend didn't know Kellan had slept in her bed, her grief over her brother at war with her feelings for Kellan.

Later, Brigitte convinced Siana to eat with the others. Really, Brigitte didn't give her a choice and fairly pushed her out of her room. She hesitantly entered the dining room and blushed a deep red when she looked at Kellan.

She couldn't stop the heat rising in her face when he caught her eyes. He gave her a smile, a look, and seductively wiggled his eyebrows at her. Somehow, she turned even redder. Giving him a warning look did nothing. He responded by slowly looking her body up and down. She wondered how much blood could rush to the face before it exploded.

The room was more formal than the morning room. It had the same carpet and walls, but only one window. Buffet tables lined one wall, their wood matching the rectangular wooden table the brothers were at. Tamek sat at the head, Kellan on his immediate left, with Lorica to his right. Siana sat to Kellan's left, as the footman had pulled out the chair, and she refused to look at him for the rest of the meal. At one point, he teased her with his leg, stroking it against her. She turned red again and tried to move her legs away without drawing the others' attention. She saw Tamek give Kellan's amused expression a questioning glance. Kellan just smiled at him.

Despite all that, she was quiet throughout the meal. The brothers hardly spoke out of respect for her grief. With their meal finished, a footman entered the room. When he had everyone's attention, he made an announcement. Siana wasn't sure what he said, but she was positive she heard a name: *Teffen* Nesh Trondor.

Tamek and Kellan looked at each other. Kellan turned, reached over, and took her left hand from her lap. She watched curiously as he pulled the ring out again and put it on her finger.

Does he always carry it?

"Why?" she asked. *Why was he putting it back on after taking it off?*

All he said was, "*Rembit.*" After putting his own ring on, he activated the banding.

The returning footman interrupted her next question. Kellan moved her hand out of sight while the band completed its journey. From just inside the door, he motioned a shorter, yet still taller than Siana, balding man with a warm smile to enter. The man's rumpled appearance suggested a long day, though it had hardly begun. He had on long robes of black with green trim at the edges and wore heavy looking, dark-framed spectacles supported by a just as heavy body. Tamek stood and welcomed the man, who chattered excitedly. Tamek offered him his chair at the head of the table, which was accepted after some convincing, and the man sat while lowering his black satchel to the ground next to him.

Moving to Lorica's right, Tamek sat down. All the men spoke at length while she tried to pick out words she knew. She hated it when they quickly spoke. It made it more difficult. Of course, she could usually make out the words she understood, but the more complicated words and grammar passed right over her. She intended to ask Brigitte to teach her "slow down." She knew she needed to find a way for Brigitte to understand her request. Soon, Tamek pointed at Siana.

Kellan stood, looked at her, and motioned toward his chair. "Sit here."

"Why?"

"*Teffen* talk to you."

Name or title?

Curious, she stood and switched places with him, his hand brushing across her backside as he moved behind her. Her eyes snapped to his, yet his face was impassive, not telling her if he did that on purpose or not.

Tamek introduced her. Siana smiled, greeted the newcomer, sat, and rested her hands on the table. The man was looking at her, visually inspecting the banding, smiling when Mrs. Atwood walked up to him. She could tell they offered him food, which he shook his head to, but accepted tea. She curiously watched as he pulled a book from the satchel. He continued speaking, asked questions, which the men took turns answering. He opened the book after taking a deep breath.

With a finger marking his place, he read a word and then looked at Siana with an expectant face. All he received in return was confusion. Perplexed, Siana glanced at Kellan, who smiled at her. Tamek and Lorica had encouraging looks. He read another word and looked at her. He repeated this until he had reached the end of his list. It was only about ten words, so it didn't take long. Occasionally, Siana would look around the room and see their faces of expectation warring with disappointment.

A sigh of disappointment escaped the man, and he closed the book. As he spoke with them once more, she understood her name, another name, *Storjen*—which they seemed to vote against?—and not much else. She wanted to yell at them for ignoring her and not speaking slowly, so she could try to understand, but she was their guest.

Don't bite the hand that feeds you.

Tamek asked him something which the man answered affirmatively to. Thinking Brigitte had said something, Siana turned to look at her, but the woman was staring out the window. As she looked back, she saw the man nodding at Tamek's second question. Looking at Kellan, hoping to get a clue what the conversation was about, she saw he looked tense. He had his hands clasped in front of him on the table, and his knuckles were turning white from how hard he was gripping them.

What's going on?

Mrs. Atwood returned with the man's tea and poured. Tamek asked her to stay—*at least I got that,* Siana thought— and Mrs. Atwood went and stood near Brigitte.

Teffen Trondor stood, paused, and asked Kellan a question. He received a terse reply. Concerned, she looked at Kellan again. At her gaze, he schooled his face into a warm smile, letting her know he was fine. She didn't believe him, but redirected her attention to the man when he stood. He began orating. Glancing at the others, all of their attention was on their lecturer. It felt like they were in something akin to a church service.

Maybe teffen is a title that means priest or preacher?

The man looked at Siana, smiling, and asked her a question. Kellan leaned forward, whispering in her ear, "Say *lamantii*." She glanced at him.

When he gave her a supporting nod, she turned back and hesitantly said, "*Lamantii.*"

The man seemed delighted at her answer. Siana was glad she made him happy and added that word to her list of unknowns she needed to translate. She also hoped she just hadn't entered a pact to sacrifice small children or animals. Tamek stood, and looking at Kellan, lectured him.

What did he do? It's likely that was the source of his earlier irritation. Did this preacher guy rat him out?

The mental image of Kellan sneaking around Tamek's back amused her. Tamek's long-winded speech did not, and Siana tuned him out, playing with the chain on her banding. Kellan said a word that seemed familiar, but she was beyond wanting to translate at that point. She was annoyed at being left out and no one was trying to explain anything. Not even Brigitte, whom she knew, hated it when they did that to Siana. She was wondering if she could just up and leave, using her failure to understand as an excuse.

Kellan reached over and stopped her from playing with the banding chain by laying his hand over hers. When she looked at him, he was staring at her with an intensity in his eyes that made her body answer in response. She wanted to touch him, but pictured Tamek's horrified look at her straddling Kellan to kiss him. At least it would shut everyone up. The mental image almost made her laugh, and Kellan gave her an inquisitive look.

Goodness, girl, get a grip, she chided herself.

Kellan removed his hand and returned his attention to the *teffen*. The man adjusted his spectacles, reached over, and lifted Siana's left hand, inspecting her banding. He clasped her hand between his. He asked another question that everyone nodded in answer to. His hands warmth made hers hot, and she wondered if it would be a major breach of etiquette if she yanked her hand back. It didn't come to that as he gently laid her hand back down. The sun hitting the metal made it appear to glow.

When he finished, everyone was smiling but Brigitte. It annoyed Siana even more. *It would be nice to know why.* She resolved to ask her as soon as she could.

Kellan stood, still looking angry, and pulled Siana up with him. He said, "We go. See another *teffen*."

Chapter Twenty-Nine

SHE WANTED TO KNOW what a *teffen* was, but everyone sitting rose and went off to do their own needed preparations for the trip before she could ask. Mrs. Atwood took charge of their guest. Siana walked with Brigitte back to her room.

"Brigitte, what *teffen*?"

Brigitte's face turned thoughtful. "Siana talk *Setan*. Brigitte *teffen* Siana." Brigitte's face looked unsure, like it wasn't quite right. "Lorica *Bund*; Nesh Trondor *teffen*."

It's a title. Teach? He's a teacher? The robes, though. The only place she'd seen those was in higher learning. *Maybe the equivalent of a professor? Either way, it looked like he was an educator. If so, what was he teaching them? Is it normal for educators to travel from house to house?*

Siana simply nodded and entered her room. Brigitte insisted she change into what she would classify as a deeper azure-blue, short-sleeved dress with deep red shoulder coverings that were added on separately. It had gold edging along the neck, cuffs, and hem which fell to about mid-calf. Once it was on, Brigitte wrapped what looked like a gold braided belt around her chest, attaching it to the top of the left shoulder of the dress so it hung under her right arm.

She fetched a pair of gold sandals and handed them to Siana to put on. Brigitte cast a critical eye over her hair, then gave a quick nod. Again, reaching into the wardrobe, she picked a scarf in the same blue and tied it like a headband around Siana's head, hiding her ears. Nodding at her work, she led Siana back down the stairs to the foyer.

Kellan and Lorica were already waiting, dressed in similar outfits comprising short-sleeved deep red tunics edged in gold that reached the tops of their thighs with small slits on each side that went to the tops of their hips, blue shoulder coverings trimmed in gold, and gold braids crisscrossing their chests, attaching at a shoulder. Their trousers were also the same deep red, but the hip area matched the blue shoulder coverings and gold braiding traveled down the side length of each leg, which ended in similar sandals as Siana's. Both men cast an appreciative eye over her as she descended the stairs, but she noticed Lorica also did the same to Brigitte, who dressed as she normally would. She either didn't see or ignored it.

Kellan took Siana's arm as the footmen opened the front doors. As they opened, an enclosed rectangular carriage revealed itself. Hitched to it were four *Storjen* she didn't recognize, and the driver was holding the side door open, which was offset from the center wheels. As they approached, Siana saw it was the same deep shade of red along the lower half. The same blue colored the upper section, and gold trimmed the edges of the carriage, windows, and door. To the right of the door, in gold, were symbols she didn't recognize. Given that it matched their clothing, she realized it was House Devereaux's colors. In the front and attached to the top half was a small box with an open door. She could see the cushioned bench inside and windows on all sides. It had a ladder on the side of the carriage leading to the box.

Kellan motioned for her to enter. She climbed the double steps and looked in. There was a matching door on the other side. The inside was blue; the cushioned bench seats were red, looked as if they could hold three people each, and had the same gold etched into the ceiling, walls, and seats. A seat was in front, facing the rear. The seat to her left faced the front. Beside each door was a single seat on either side. She realized just how big the carriage was.

Since she didn't travel by carriage, she sat in the middle on the seat to the left, so she could face forward, lessening any sense of motion sickness. It also allowed her to look out the windows of both doors so she could see the scenery. Kellan entered and sat on the same seat to her left. Lorica sat on the seat across from her, facing Kellan. Their guest scurried out of the house and toward them. As he climbed in, he chose a seat to the right, next to the door he'd entered. It took another minute for Tamek to show up. His outfit was like his brother's, but it was a gown that reached his ankles. As he walked, the hem kicked up and she could see he wore similar trousers under it. He stepped in, choosing a seat to the left of Lorica, facing Siana.

The driver shut the door, and she heard him climb up to the covered seat. Her eyes followed his movements, and she caught sight of a thin cabinet hanging from the ceiling just behind Lorica's and Tamek's heads.

She pointed at it, asking, "What is it?"

Lorica looked up. He stood, pulled the front, and it opened outwards and down. He pulled out a couple of swords.

Seeing her raised eyebrow, he said, "It's *rembit*."

That word again. This time, though, she figured it out. You would only need swords in a carriage for one reason:

protection.

Every time she heard it came flooding back. Replacing *rembit* with "protection" made sense within the context other than the camp, but it raised two questions: How was the camp protection? Why did she need protection? It seemed a bit much against Talon, one man. Looking at her hands that lay in her lap, she eyed the banding.

Why was Kellan, the camp, and most of all, the banding protection? Protection from what?

As Lorica replaced the swords, the professor asked him a question. Lorica sat while answering. The carriage started moving.

Looking outside, Siana asked, "Where do we go?"

The guest answered her so fast, she had no hope of understanding. Kellan held up a hand to stop the man's flow of words.

***

Honestly, Kellan wasn't sure if the male knew how to form a short sentence. Everything he said took about three times as long as it should due to him adding information that wasn't needed. They'd already told him she understood little, but was making progress.

Turning his head toward her, he said, "We are going to other professor home." Their guest tried to correct Kellan, informing him the male they were going to see wasn't a professor or a learned scholar.

Kellan said, "It's easier to use it to explain."

***

He gave an "ah" of understanding, then gave the female his attention.

She was attractive by Setan standards, even if on the short side. Being one of the shortest *Setan,* he was happy he could say that.

He tried to formulate some sort of conversation and realized she most likely understood little of what they said in the house, and he felt like a poor guest in being a part of it. He had his doubts about their plans, but House Devereaux was paying him a hefty sum for his help, and it wouldn't do to lose that fee.

My own claim would cause me to rue the day. He chuckled inwardly.

Everyone thought her a shrieker. He knew fear had caused her anger toward males; her body and mind had been hurt. He'd found the warm-hearted female underneath, worked hard to gain her trust, and she accepted his claim. Not once had he ever regretted it. Not only was she good to him, but she was also intelligent and would play the opposing role when he formed his debates and lectures. She clarified where he was confusing. He'd had to teach her she could stand up for herself without repercussions from him. It took a while for her to learn he liked her keeping her boundaries. He couldn't wait to get back to her, but this one in front of him was puzzling.

Turning his attention back to Doctor Devereaux's claim, she appeared well taken care of. He saw no signs of mistreatment. Due to what happened to his dear mate, he was on the lookout for it. He wouldn't tolerate it. The House Head explained that her brother had recently died in an accident, accounting for her sadness. Therefore, she wore Doctor Devereaux's banding before making vows. He wanted his claim to show in case someone else wanted her. Normally, banding isn't put on until after the agreement discussions with the family are over and the ceremony is held. Since her only male relative died, the agreements hadn't been finalized. Kellan had reassured him Siana wanted to be with him, and her brother had approved it.

She must want it, since she isn't rejecting it.

When she didn't appear to recognize any of the greetings he'd used, Professor Trondor had recommended someone he knew slightly. The male was self-taught, but he knew languages outside the norm and had a strong interest in various cultures and their history. Hopefully, he could help them. *Bund* Devereaux had sent a messenger ahead with a letter from him, letting him know of their arrival. Most wouldn't arrive unexpectedly, but *Bund* had enough standing, no one would refuse it. If he knew this man, he would fairly bounce to meet someone unknown.

Turning his attention back to the female, he asked, "You are well?"

She said, "Yes, thank you. You?"

Good, she has the basics. He replied, "I am well. Thank you."

He tilted his head at her. "You like Doctor Devereaux?" He asked just for his own peace of mind. The other males stared at him.

Siana, perplexed at the question, said, "Yes, I like Kellan."

He smiled, relieved. He said, "Good, good. Are you scared of being claimed? Considering your size, I'll be honest: I'm a little concerned."

Now the others were glaring at him.

She, not understanding everything he said, asked, "*Pederon* is what?" but got cut off by Lorica pointing out the window, saying her name, gaining her attention. A *toob*, swinging branch to branch alongside the carriage, caused her to smile as it moved with them, jumping from the trees to the carriage and back.

***

Kellan leaned closer and began pointing various landmarks out, teaching her their names. At a fork, the carriage moved right. Eventually, the forest opened up, revealing a town further to the right, beyond a rolling, sun-drenched meadow. The carriage continued straight, eventually veering left, back into the forest, and the town moved out of sight.

While Kellan kept Siana distracted, Tamek caught the professor's eye and shook his head. Leaning closer, he murmured, "She doesn't know yet. She doesn't seem to understand not only our language, but our laws. We're trying to explain it to her, hence why we called you. Kellan staking his claim is more for her protection while we figure it out."

He left out the part where they knew she'd come from a different world. He took a risk saying that last statement. If the male reported her lack of a physical claim to the Convocation, the resulting uproar could cost her and them a lot, if not everything.

***

The professor wasn't stupid. Everyone knew the cost of faking a claim. "Something this big could cost me my career, my claim, and property." His tone made it plain.

Tamek assured the male handsome compensation would come his way. Nesh honestly didn't care about politics or lawbreakers as long as nobody was hurt, but he also knew he was playing with fire. Rumors about this House circulated occasionally. He would accept whatever payment came his way and remain silent, because he loved his life more than reporting them.

He feigned sleep to keep from having to speak with Mrs. Devereaux. He didn't want to learn anything else that could incriminate him. All he cared about was that they were taking care of her, and it seemed like they were. He feigned sleep for the rest of the journey.

Chapter Thirty

STANLIN FORNTESK WAS A bit on edge. To suddenly receive notice of unexpected visitors was one thing; to have it come from one of the High Houses was additional levels of stress he didn't need or want. The stress was only abated slightly by one part of the message: *She seems to speak a language that is unknown, nor does she look Setan.*

Glancing out his bedroom window, he could see the shiny carriage of House Devereaux coming down the road. After a last check, he was presentable. He raced downstairs to welcome his guests. His thoughts kept wandering to the possibilities... could she be Falon? No, that would've been one of the first languages tried, plus besides their own language, they speak *Setan* as well. From what he understood, one of House Devereaux's *Bund* had been in Falon. He would've recognized it. Maybe Cerish? Mentally, reviewing various languages, he realized he'd have to consult with the professor to see which he already tried.

As the carriage drew to a stop at the end of the walk leading to his house, he realized he had nowhere for it to park. His home didn't have a carriage byway or drive. The driver climbed down, set the stool, and opened the door. A male with silver hair disembarked. His long robe declared him the Head of the House. Holding his hand in the carriage, Stanlin saw a thin arm appear, followed by the female in question. As she stepped out of the carriage, she looked around the area while moving out of the way.

He studied her as the others exited. She was small. Much smaller than he expected. Bringing his thoughts to a halt, he moved forward and welcomed his guests. Professor Trondor apologized profusely for the sudden visit. Stanlin—he insisted they call him that—brushed his concerns aside and invited them in.

***

Tamek looked around as the scholars greeted each other. It was a small stone dwelling with two stories. It wasn't huge, but nor was it tiny. Several small windows dotted each story, and he could see that the outside was well maintained. He noticed next door was a larger building, also with two stories, with bigger windows and a sign out front. It seemed to be about the size of House Devereaux's stables.

Nesh introduced Siana to their host. She faced the male they spoke with. He greeted her with a serious look, and she smiled and said in *Setan*, "Hello."

Confused, he looked back at Professor Trondor. He informed him they'd been teaching her the language. He nodded and invited them all inside.

"My apologies, but I lack food and drink. I wasn't expecting visitors. I do have tea, if you'd like."

"It's we who should be apologizing. The lack of amenities is not a concern. We have imposed upon you." Tamek spoke a bit formally. He accepted the offer of tea.

Stanlin led them into the house, past a front stairway on the left, and into a door nestled behind it. It was a well-lit library.

**

Siana's glance took in the floor-to-ceiling wood shelves packed with bindings.

I could spend some time here.

She was a voracious reader normally, and it had been ages since she could sit and read quietly.

Stanlin pulled out a chair from a large round table in the center of the room and said to her, "Please, sit."

Thanking him, she sat down. He sat to her right, in a chair matching the table. Stanlin asked Professor Trondor a question. While he sat on the other side of Stanlin, he pulled the book from his satchel. As they discussed their options, his housekeeper appeared with a large wood tray with the tea.

**

She mentally scolded her employer. He had a bad habit of forgetting to eat and stock the house with food. She would've felt humiliated if she had found nothing. You do not have a High House in and not offer food. It was the sign of a poor host and a badly managed household. Refusing to be thought of that way, she had torn the kitchen apart for anything she could find, managing to scrounge up some biscuits and jam. Kellan thanked the housekeeper for the tea and helped her set it on the table. She quickly glanced around, pouring their tea, correctly identifying each in her head. She noticed the female was wearing the doctor's banding.

I guess the scars don't bother her.

The thought of touching them disgusted her. Hiding a shiver at the image, she withdrew from the room. Because she knew they were spending the night, she would have to beg the neighbors for food if the early morning market yielded nothing with her little *terin*. Thankfully, despite the doctor's ugliness, people held House Devereaux in high regard, so she expected no problems.

***

Siana found herself once again going through another list of words, as now an extra man was looking at her expectantly. She had no recognition of any. The younger one asked her the name of the chair. She said it in *Setan*, but he shook his head. He wanted her to say it in her language. She did. He tried other objects. There was something in his eyes that caught her attention, but she couldn't place it.

Finished with that experiment, the one named Stanlin stood, went to one bookshelf, climbed partway up the ladder, and removed another book. Going through it caused a bit of frustration as both men became determined to figure out her language. They were failing. This caused a scholarly debate that all men took part in.

With no desire to be talked around again, Siana stood and asked for the toilet. Stanlin called his housekeeper, instructed her, and she led Siana to the toilet room. It was simple, lacking any luxuries, but as long as it did the job, she didn't care. After finishing, she cleaned her hands and easily found her way back.

Tired of sitting, she meandered around the room, examining each bookshelf. Despite not being able to read the titles, she could tell some were in different languages by the writing, but she didn't know what they were. She climbed a ladder to see what was on the top shelf.

Out of the corner of her eye, she saw Kellan frown in her direction, but the other male said it was all right, and he turned back to the discussion. It sank into Siana that this world was now her home. Sadness overtook her for a minute. She tried to shake it off.

There is so much I don't know about this world. What are the weather patterns like? How long do they live? How many countries and languages are there? Are there wars? What diseases do they have? Will I end up like in that movie where a cold wipes out the aliens? Do they have any technology?

Her mind mentally ran through all the things she wanted to know and learn. She kept looking up and down each shelf while the discussion about her grew a bit more heated. A glance back showed Stanlin and the professor arguing over something while the brothers interjected now and then. It seemed they were trying to plan their next course of action. As Siana climbed another ladder, she had to admit the covers of many of the books were quite colorful. A few looked interesting, though for all she knew they were some dry chemistry-type books. She'd had a hard time in chemistry because of having issues with algebra. She never wanted to touch on either subject again.

Slowly working her way around the room, she realized that not only did she need to learn the language, she needed to learn to read and write again. She retreated down the ladder and walked to the next set of shelves. It was odd. The realization dawned on her: she had much to relearn. She did not know their geography, how they did math, their history. She was basically at ground zero with her learning.

Well, crap. I currently have the knowledge of a preschooler.

The thought of going through algebra again made her cringe, though maybe they had a better way of learning it—if they even used it. At the top of the next ladder, she glanced over and stood, stunned. Her disbelieving eyes couldn't accept what she was seeing. One shelf held books, and the titles were English. Her eyes widened. A sense of optimism blossomed in her chest as she considered the possibility of finding an English-speaking country. She didn't know what to think.

I could go there. Talk to those who understand me.

The thought made part of her sad. Would Kellan go? She was unwilling to lose anyone else, but she felt so out of place here. She leaned over to read. Some of them looked so old she didn't want to touch them, afraid they'd crumble. A closer look revealed something shimmery was coating them, almost like a prism effect.

Some sort of protection? Security system?

She wasn't able to reach all of them, so she concentrated on the ones closest to her. Containing her excitement, she read the titles. Several copies of the Bible sat among several authors like Dickens, King, Austen, and some authors she didn't recognize. Not knowing what the coating was, she reached for one that seemed in better shape than the others and didn't have any shimmer to it. It was a gold-lettered Bible.

Okay, not my first choice, but seriously, they have books in my language. I don't care what it is. Once they're done talking, I'll see about borrowing them all. I'll also ask if the ones with shimmer are first editions. That would explain needing protection. I also need to find out the name of the country and how to get there.

Carefully climbing down the ladder, she retired to what looked like a comfy red chair in the corner with a light over it. Her heart pounded as she carefully opened the cover, terrified of breaking the fragile binding. Opening to a random page just enough to see the words, she began quietly reading while the men droned on.

What the heck is a cubit? she wondered. Then she asked herself how she'd react if her neighbor suddenly lost his mind and began collecting animals.

***

Lorica noticed her first. He silently waved his hand just above the table to get the others' attention. When they all focused on him, he pointed to Siana. As each one turned, their shock was evident.

Nesh said quietly, "She may have just gotten bored and is looking through one with pictures."

Stanlin slowly stood and silently approached her. He squinted his eyes, trying to see the title she was reading, and they shot to the size of saucers. The closer he drew, the more flabbergasted he became.

***

While reading the passage, she looked up when the light disappeared. The younger man was standing between her and the light. His facial expression was one of confused shock. Pointing to a word, he nodded at her.

Looking back at the book, she read, "'Come.'"

He pointed to the entire sentence.

She read, "'Come into the ark, you and all your household, because I have seen that you are righteous before Me in this generation.'"

He motioned for her to stand and come back to the table with the book. As she sat at the table, he ran to the ladder, climbed it, and grabbed a different one. Hurrying, he handed it to her and opened it. He pointed to a line, looked at her, silently urging her.

She read, "'It was a bright cold day in April, and the clocks were striking thirteen.'"

Based on their faces, none of them understood what she read. Siana was joyful at being able to read again, but looking up, the two men looked like she had just pooped a unicorn.

***

That she had read lines from two original, old books—books whose only copies were on that shelf—shocked the two scholars.

Stanlin was angry at himself but hid it. He should've known when she first spoke her language. He began plotting. They couldn't know what he knew.

Professor Trondor whispered, face white, "That's impossible."

Tamek asked, "What is impossible?"

Stanlin said, "Hold on."

He ran to the ladder, grabbed a different book from a lower shelf, and came back. He had to play this out, but he really needed the tome in his hands. As he sat back down in his chair, he flipped through the book as fast as possible. Nesh stood next to him, watching him over his shoulder.

Finally, Stanlin stopped, silently read a word, turned to her, and said slowly in English, "Hello."

She responded with a thrilled smile, and repeated excitedly in English, "Hello." No one moved. No one spoke.

Kellan broke the silence. "You found her language."

Trondor plopped back into his seat. Stanlin, reaching over, grabbed the first book. He leaned in, wanting to hear their intonations and sounds. Eagerly, he waited, wanting to make sure he had some pronunciations correct.

He opened it and pointed to a section, and she read, "'After these things I saw another angel coming down from heaven, having great authority, and the earth was illuminated with his glory. And he cried mightily with a loud voice, saying, "Babylon the great is fallen, is fallen, and has become a dwelling place of demons, a prison for every foul spirit, and a cage for every unclean and hated bird! For all the nations have drunk of the wine of the wrath of her fornication, the kings of the earth have committed fornication with her, and the merchants of the earth have become rich through the abundance of her luxury.'"

Siana stopped, her face unsure. Stanlin looked on the verge of tears, a hand covering his mouth. The brothers looked confused.

Professor Trondor gathered himself first. Motioning the other males to the side for a private chat—completely forgetting she couldn't understand most of what they said—he told Stanlin to see if he could hold a conversation with her. If the book held enough translations, they may be able to converse. Stanlin nodded.

As the others moved to a corner, where Nesh quizzed them about how she came to be with them, stressing the importance of truth, an idea formed in Stanlin's mind.

He pointed to her banding. He asked in *Setan*, "Who?"

Glancing at it, she answered, "Kellan."

Stanlin looked at Kellan analytically, then back at her. He was too big. They all were. This could work in Stanlin's favor. He flipped through the book, hoping there was enough information to translate what he wanted to say. *This is going to take a while, but I don't have much time. Get to the point.*

"You." Between each word he flipped through the pages. "Stand. With. Kellan. With..." Flipping again. "Others. Before. Professor Trondor." He lowered his voice when he said the name.

Siana, with curious eyes, nodded.

"You. Say. Word. *Lamantii?*" Again, he lowered his voice when he said the last word. Siana nodded cautiously.

"Nesh. Hold. Hand?" He was getting annoyed at having to flip around the book constantly, but he had to do this.

She nodded again. Stanlin almost cursed. Okay, new plan. He quieted his voice. If they heard this...

Slightly frustrated, flipping through the book again, he couldn't find the words he wanted. Hesitantly, he rephrased what he wanted to say, searching for better words. He tried in *Setan*, "Kellan *pederon?*"

He flipped through the pages, his fingers tracing the words, searching for the one that perfectly captured his thoughts.

Her touch on his arm was soft and inquisitive as she questioned him. "What is *pederon?*"

She just gave him the opening he needed—if he could find a decent translation. His eyes searching through the book, he looked at her and said in English, "Claiming." The look on her face had him flipping through again. She didn't understand his meaning.

Staring into her eyes, he said, "Mating. Forced mating."

***

Her eyes widened in shock.

Kellan had been talking about raping her? No, this man had to be mistaken. Kellan wouldn't do that. In fact, he had a chance with her willingly and refused. His words made little sense.

She narrowed her eyes at him.

He glanced around, as if looking for something, then he said, "You. Small. Yes?" He motioned to himself, then her and pointed to the other men.

He was right. Compared to them, she was. Her nod coupled with suspicion as she watched him.

He said, after flipping some more, "*Setan* males..." He stopped, looking a bit frustrated. Finally, he pointed to his crotch, looking sheepish, and held his hands up like he was measuring a fish. A really big fish.

Siana's eyes widened again. "No." She shook her head.

He nodded. "*Setan* men..." He stopped his finger under a word in the book. "Big. Too big." He pointed at her lap. She unconsciously crossed her legs.

"Siana." He leaned closer, speaking *Setan*. "Kellan is too big. You are too small. Kellan claim?"

Shaking her head, she said, "Kellan no claim."

He kept his voice low. "If Kellan claim, you tear. Die."

"What?" She didn't think she heard him correctly.

He repeated, "Kellan claims you. You will tear open and die."

Horrified, Siana pictured herself suffering such a gruesome death. As she thought back to that night, she wondered, *Is that why he stopped? He knew? Is that what they were talking about in Tamek's study?*

Again, she stressed, "Kellan no claim."

She didn't like the look that came over his face. It looked—she struggled to think of what it looked like. *Conniving. Almost self-satisfied.*

A growing unease filled her. *What does he know?*

Stanlin pointed to her banding. He asked in a mix of English and *Setan*, "Nesh hold hand. Banding glow?"

Nodding again, she remembered she thought it was reflecting the sun. Her face was growing alarmed.

"You say *lamantii*. Kellan's banding glow. You *murjer*..." Shaking his head, he looked up the word he wanted. "Married. You. Kellan. Married."

Siana said loudly, in English, without thinking, "Excuse me?!"

The others came over quickly, Kellan catching her arm.

She shook him off, stepping back. She realized all three were complicit and, most likely, so was Brigitte.

I can't believe this. They married me off behind my back. Why? I'm killing all of them.

Her breathing became ragged as she glared at the men before her. She was the stereotypical redhead, and her anger exploded. She went on a long, loud rant in her language. The room crackled with her rage as she stomped and shouted. She would occasionally poke her finger into Kellan's chest, wave her hand, and continue pacing. Each visibly tensed when she picked up a book, looking like she wanted to throw it at them. She walked up to Tamek and yelled at him, but he kept his face composed. Lorica stayed out of the line of fire, but where his eyes could examine them, his gaze flitting from one face to the next. Stanlin sat back with a little smile.

Chapter Thirty-One

LORICA SLID UP BEHIND Kellan, leaned forward, and whispered, "He's causing trouble. The way she's gesturing at you and the banding, I think he deliberately told her you married her without her permission."

Kellan closed his eyes and took a deep breath. He asked everyone to give them some privacy. A single, hard look from Tamek silenced Stanlin's protest and had him scrambling away. They shut the door after themselves, escaping the palpable tension. All but one were visibly relieved to be out of the room and away from her ire.

There was a nearby sofa. Kellan sat on the red cushions, the wood trim hard against his shoulders, and waited until she ran out of steam. It took a few more minutes before the only sound was her harsh, rapid breathing. He looked up at her. She was looking at him on the verge of angry tears.

How do I explain this?

He stood, and she backed away from him, watching him warily. Walking to the table, he picked up the book Stanlin had been using, then went back to the sofa. Sitting again, he slowly looked through it, praying he could find the words. Kellan tried to keep his movements non-threatening.

He patted the couch next to him. "Please, sit. I say."

Unsurprisingly, she shook her head.

Holding up the book, he searched for a single word but found two. He didn't know which was more accurate, so said them both. His troubled gaze returned to her.

He said, "*Setan* laws. Rules."

She didn't move and said nothing.

"Siana, female, no alone." He shook his head. "Laws. Bad laws but laws." He tried his best to explain using both languages and the book, though finding the correct words was a challenge. "Must have male. Protection. Laws. We hide you at camp. Remember?"

***

She slowly nodded, her breathing still harsh.

They're running an underground railroad using the camp?

That would explain why only women were there. Why it was protection. Her breathing calmed, but she couldn't fight the angry helplessness rising.

"I want to tell you. Not know words. Must protect you from Talon. From laws. I not have words to tell you. Understand?"

She said, "I understand you not have words, but..."

She tried to organize her thoughts. It was a bit much to take in. The laws of this new world were unknown. Thinking back, she could see their protection, and their kindness, but being married to this man without her input, that they had to hide their women to help them—it rubbed her the wrong way.

Am I mad about being married to him, or was it purely the fact they didn't ask me? Or both?

They ignored her, didn't ask for her opinion, and this, coupled with her helplessness and confusion in this strange world, made her angry. She took a deep breath to calm herself and sat near him on the sofa. Unsure of what to say, she fell silent. She had learned being dropped into a strange world sucked, especially one where it appeared she had no rights.

"I do not know what to do. Must protect," he said sincerely, touching her banding. "I won't hurt you."

His struggle plainly showed on his face. It was obvious he didn't like this position, either. Emotions warred within her. Her old and her new life were colliding.

How many of my world's laws did I have to obey despite disagreeing with them? Is divorce even a thing here? Do I have rights in a marriage? Do I have any rights at all?

When she said nothing, Kellan, nervously playing with the banding chain, asked, "You like me?" He looked almost afraid of her answer.

Honesty was something she valued. Despite everything, she wouldn't lie to him. She nodded. He looked relieved.

"Like my touch?" He playfully wiggled his eyebrows again. She blushed and couldn't stop herself from lightly punching him in the arm—something she'd do to Jacob when he teased her.

She took the book, did a reverse translation, and said, stumbling over the words, "I got no say. No one asked. I need to think."

He gave her an understanding nod. Taking the book back, he said quietly, "Ask if need. I'll be honest." He took a breath, as if steeling himself. "Tonight, we share bed here."

She said louder than she meant to, "What?"

He pointed around, then out the window, gave her a reassuring smile, and shrugged. "It's night. Small house. We're married."

As he gazed at her, he said in all seriousness, "You're safe. I won't touch. We sleep."

Kellan put the book back on the table, his fingers lingering on the cover, then turned and left.

Siana watched him leave the room and hesitated. It seemed like when she thought things were evening out, she had another curve ball thrown at her. She briefly thought about sleeping on the sofa, but she didn't trust the owner of this house. Something about him bothered her. Not knowing what else to do, she followed Kellan.

The housekeeper was waiting for them with a disapproving look, as if they were too loud. As she turned to lead them to their room, Kellan looked back at Siana and made a face imitating the housekeeper. Siana waved her hand as if to shoo him away, but a smile twitched at the corners of her mouth. The housekeeper led them to the kitchen and up the back stairs to a dimly lit bedroom. Opening the door, the housekeeper said something to Kellan, pointed down the hall, bowed to them both, and left them alone.

Siana slowly walked into the room after Kellan. She didn't see what she was looking for.

"Toilet?"

Kellan said, "Other room."

He moved around her and pointed down the hall. She followed his finger and saw the door. She thanked him and went to use it. It was small, but did what it was supposed to do. She was half afraid she'd be using a chamber pot or something in front of him. Not that she really needed to go. It was just to give herself a few minutes of solitude to think. She asked herself what she wanted to do.

I have no idea.

The cool water cascading over her skin as she washed up did little to soothe the simmering anger she felt at their deception.

How bad are these laws that they felt they needed to go this far?

Her short time with them told her they weren't malicious, but that was it, wasn't it? It was a short time.

I don't know any of them well, she thought as she walked back. She knew some about Kellan, but not enough to actually marry him. Or did she? They'd spent enough time in close quarters for her to learn he was a caring man, he loved being a doctor, he had a warped sense of humor, and thinking back, he'd done what he could to protect her despite not being able to communicate. That this world required she have a protector set her on edge.

To be fair, it was the same while the survivors were on the run. A woman alone wasn't a good thing. Though, she'd never had to worry about it with Jacob by her unlike others. You made friends with those who could protect you.

As she reentered the room, she discovered he had begun changing without benefit of the dressing screen she saw in the corner. The scarring across his back was worse than what was on his face and neck.

How did I not notice it that night?

The scars should have been easily felt, even through a nightshirt. When he dropped his trousers and undergarment, she saw it extended to the side of his hip and a very nice-looking backside. She took a second before quickly realizing she was staring.

She turned her back and said, "I'm sorry."

***

Kellan glanced back, quickly dressing in his nightclothes. He was so used to not sharing a room with a female; he didn't think to move behind the screen. He knew his back looked bad. His concern was that she would find it unacceptable.

Once dressed, he said, "It's okay now."

Turning, she gave him a small smile and moved toward her bag, which was on a bureau across from the foot of the bed, right next to the dressing screen. She didn't mention the burns, which didn't ease his concern. He just now started realizing with them sharing a room, eventually she would see all of it. He was insecure about being naked in front of a female who could see every scar.

What have I gotten myself into?

***

She searched and, finding the nightdress Brigitte had packed, went behind the screen. It was so tall she couldn't see over it, and she rushed to change her clothes, but couldn't figure out how to get the braid off. She kept trying to figure out the attachment, but without a mirror, she was flying blind. She couldn't maneuver it well enough.

Dang it.

As she walked out from behind the screen, she watched for a second as he stood, combing his hair out. It was the first time she'd seen it released from its braids. Briefly, she imagined herself running her fingers through it, grabbing it, pulling him to her.

When he saw her still dressed, he asked if something was wrong. Heat slowly climbed up her neck as she started, caught staring at him.

Her voice showed her slight annoyance. She lifted the braid. "It not come off."

He padded over to her and set about releasing it. She leaned her head to the side to give him more room, while avoiding his hair hanging down to her face, and refused to look up at him. His hair was tickling her neck. She kept her eyes on his nightshirt, so they wouldn't travel lower. Stanlin's hand measurements came back to her, and she had to restrain herself from seeing if he was right. It was harder than she expected.

This man—technically her husband—was half naked in front of her. All she had to do was reach out. She *wanted* to reach out and touch him. Again, Stanlin's words echoed, and she knew they would need to discuss it. She had no desire to die, but she wasn't stupid. She could tell Stanlin was up to something. Once the braid was off, she thanked him and moved back behind the screen.

I'm thinking about him as a husband. She didn't know what to think of that.

Normally, she slept in just the nightdress, but tonight she kept her bottom undergarment on—just in case. When she came out from the screen, he was looking at the bed in front of her. Turning to face her bag, she removed the hairpins, feeling her hair fall, and set them next to it. Turning, her eyes caught his and his briefly glowed a color she hadn't seen before. He seemed to realize it and turned away.

What was that? Wait. Do his eyes change color when he's horny? The thought fascinated her.

Pointing to the bed, he asked her, "Which?"

She shrugged and shook her head. He took the side closest to the door. Walking over to the other side, she hesitated. *Put on your big girl pants.* As she climbed into bed, she saw his hand wave, and the lights went out.

Curious, she sat up. "How?"

He rolled onto his back, looking at her. "How what?"

She moved in the dark. He turned the lights back on. She waved her hand like she'd seen him do, but nothing happened. He sat up and showed her how he moved his hand. She tried again, but nothing happened. He took her hand and guided it in the movement. Still nothing.

"Hmm, all *Setan* do. Wood. Lights." His brow furrowed.

She tried again with the same results.

He looked at her, shrugged, and said, "You not *Setan*? Maybe not work?"

Her disappointed "aw" made him smile.

"Sleep," he said laughingly and laid back down.

At some point, she woke to find herself wrapped around him.

I could get used to this.

He turned his body a bit more toward her and placed an arm around her. She smiled softly, snuggled into him, and went back to sleep.

Chapter Thirty-Two

IN THE MORNING, KELLAN motioned to his brothers to step outside for a stroll before breakfast, so Stanlin didn't hear them.

Tamek asked about Siana.

"She's still sleeping. She seems confused. Conflicted about everything," Kellan answered.

The brothers nodded in understanding.

"It's to be expected. I want to know what the male said to her," Lorica stated.

"She was too nervous about being in the room with me last night to say anything. If we can borrow that book before we leave, I can explain to her about claiming."

Tamek stopped mid-stride. "That's a good idea. She needs to know what's going on. I think we can all agree not to leave her alone with this male. We know he told her she was married without her permission, which is fine—she was—but he seems to have an ulterior motive. I want to know what it is. Until we know, I don't trust him. Once we have all the information needed about her race, we will leave. I want her out of here."

The others agreed.

"Professor Trondor said we'd discuss it after breakfast. The scholars needed to gather more information, so they could explain it correctly," Tamek said, restarting his walk.

Kellan informed them, "I had planned on trying to tell her we were married before we went home, anyhow, but I don't like the way Stanlin did it. It should've come from me." It wasn't something he would forgive Stanlin for.

His brothers nodded as they headed back. They wanted to get her out of there as soon as possible.

***

Siana opened her eyes to an empty bedchamber. Rubbing the sleep away, she sat up and saw that not only had Kellan dressed and left, he'd also packed his bag.

How did I sleep through that?

Quickly rising, she hunted through the bag for the clothes Brigitte had packed for today. It was a sundress in the same blue as the House colors, but it had flowers of varying colors woven into the fabric. Ducking behind the screen, she changed and ran her fingers through her hair to detangle it. Deciding to leave her hair down, she packed all her belongings in the bag and left the room to go to the toilet.

As she was walking back to the room to double-check she'd packed everything, Kellan came up the stairs, smiling at her. His smile disappeared when he saw her hair down.

"No," he said. "Hair up."

She asked with a frown, "Why?"

He pointed to his own braids. "Your hair needs to be up."

She put her hands on her hips and took a breath to give him a piece of her mind about that rule or law.

He walked up to her, put his hands on her shoulders, surprised her with a quick kiss on her lips, and said, "Please. Rules."

She didn't expect him to kiss her and just stared at him. Eyes amused, he lifted her jaw with his finger and closed it.

With a sigh, she went back into the room.

She called back in English, "Rules are made to be broken," knowing he wouldn't understand.

She realized she had a certain power being able to speak a language they didn't know. Then again, if she taught Kellan, they could say things to each other without his brothers' understanding. The thought of telling him what she wanted to do to him while in front of others made her smile a mischievous grin.

She returned with her hair up in a bun, with the scarf retied around her head to hide her ears. He smiled and playfully wiggled his eyebrows at her. She scoffed and turned toward the stairs, inwardly smiling, but her anger from last night still simmered. It occurred to her she knew they wore matching jewelry, just as Brigitte and Lorica wore matching jewelry; the implication should've been obvious.

Wait, that implies those two are married.

That made their situation more intriguing to her.

Siana decided to test something purely for payback. Do his eyes really change if he's turned on? She turned back to Kellan, licking her lips, her teeth slightly catching her bottom one, giving him a look that sent his eyebrows up to his hairline. Slowly, she walked back to him, keeping her eyes locked on his, her gaze inviting him in. When she reached him, she slowly lifted her arm and touched his, gently sliding her fingers a few inches up it. His breathing sped up. As she leaned in, she saw his eyes start to change color.

She whispered, as seductively as she could in English, "The elephant—is purple."

She turned and began moving down the stairs, making sure her hips moved more than normal.

For a second, he didn't move. He cleared his throat. "Siana, what mean?"

She increased her pace, feeling some power returning to her, a smile forming as he called after her, footsteps rushing, imploring, "Siana, what does it mean?"

***

After a small breakfast, during which Kellan randomly pretended to glare at her, realizing she'd deliberately got him wanting her, the group moved back into the library. Stanlin and Nesh looked like they hadn't slept all night. On the library table were multiple books they had gone through to pull together as much information for their guests as possible. Stanlin looked about to burst as he waited for them to sit down. Kellan, sitting next to his mate, took her hand in his while they waited. With a quick glance at him, she barely smiled, her playful attitude gone. He could tell she was nervous. He stroked her palm with his thumb to help calm her.

At least, I hope it does.

The desire to stroke her thigh as repayment for earlier tempted him, but he didn't want to deal with Tamek's possible outrage.

As soon as everyone sat, Stanlin proudly burst out with, "She is Manki."

Nesh looked dismayed that Stanlin had stolen his thunder.

A stunned silence held the brothers until Tamek stammered out, "That's impossible."

Nesh, taking his turn, causing the dismay to transfer to Stanlin's face, excitedly said, "We agree, yet everything we've seen shows it to be true. She looks like them." He pointed at a picture in one book. "She reads their books and speaks their language. Everything points to it."

Lorica expressed in pure disbelief, "I want to be clear. You're saying Siana is from a race that died out thousands of solar cycles ago?"

Stanlin spoke before Nesh could. "Yes."

Tamek asked, shocked, "How?!"

Nesh, referring to their conversation during Stanlin's talk with Siana, said, "From what you told me about that doorway, I think someone sent her here—"

Stanlin interrupted, "Throughout history, the theory of traveling through time and space has existed, but it's always just been a theory."

He turned a book to show pictures of archaeological finds of the Manki people. The brothers leaned over to look at the items shown. None of them could understand what they were seeing, but all of them remembered the metal furniture they saw behind her brother. Some items pictured looked familiar.

"Her race was so technologically advanced it's possible they made it reality."

Tamek, pointing to a picture of a battered and partially burned cell phone, said, "She has this. We've seen it."

Stanlin looked about to burst with excitement. "Is it whole? Did she bring it?"

Siana leaned forward to look at the pictures alongside the brothers. When she saw the cell phone one, she understood Stanlin's question and said, "No. It's at home."

Kellan caught her use of "home" and was relieved. She seemed to accept the situation, even if she didn't agree with it. Not that he blamed her. Nesh moved the book closer to her and pointed to the pictures. They could only speculate on their use, but she represented the biggest historical find ever. Pointing to one picture, he asked her what it was.

She said, "Microwave." They had no equivalent to translate it.

He pointed to another one. He looked at her. She answered, "Thermos. For water, tea, and coffee."

Lorica said, "She also has one of those."

The professor and Stanlin both looked like they were about to soil themselves.

"It's definitive. She is Manki. There is no doubt."

The brothers looked at each other, each obviously trying to comprehend what they'd just heard. All three turned to stare at her while Kellan mentally grappled with the fact he was just told his claim was from an ancient extinct race, one far more advanced than theirs, and she traveled through time to get here.

**

Not noticing their faces, Siana picked up the books, examined them, and realized she was looking at history books. She picked up one and flipped through it. She recognized items that were from archaeological digs as items she used in everyday life. Confusion, seemingly her constant companion, set in.

How is this possible?

She came upon artwork depicting Earth itself being engulfed by a huge fireball.

A solar flare? No, the atmosphere would protect it, I think. What would do that? What would burn up the surface? The AI?

She tried to remember her science classes throughout her school years, but she was drawing a blank.

Wait. Her brain began putting together the puzzle. *These people found these items here on this planet.* She looked at the books again.

Horrified disbelief filled her as she realized the truth: she was still on Earth. Sent through time, she found herself in a world reborn, where the ruins of humanity lay silent.

I thought Jacob meant that someone sent us to a new world, not through time.

At the time, there weren't many humans left. Most had their trackers covered by the blocking chokers, but her choker had slipped, and her tracker was located.

Is that why it was pulsing and becoming hot? Why I felt so much pain and passed out? They were transporting me?

Jacob, appearing at a set time and place, demonstrated that they controlled time travel. Perhaps the same thing happened to others, scattering them throughout the past or future. Because her time period was in history books, someone sent her to the future. One by one, silent tears traced a path down her face, leaving a glistening trail. The weight of her survival pressed down as she realized she had escaped death, but the absence of her brother's presence was a heavy blow. Many others hadn't made it. Everything she knew and loved was gone, leaving a hollow ache in her chest. Destroyed by war between the bots and humans before something wiped it and them out to finish the job. Her brother was also a victim.

All the fighting to survive. For what? All that effort? A waste. I've lost everything. The reality hit her hard as she finally accepted her home was gone. She'd had a small hope of possibly being able to go back, before Jacob's death, to prevent it, of the AI maybe bringing her back. Now she knew that would never happen. There was a finality in that realization.

A choked sob, laced with the scent of unspoken grief of her previous life, escaped her. Strong arms wrapped around her, his soothing voice drowning out the soft creak of Kellan's chair and the gentle scrape of her own. She felt herself lifted onto Kellan's lap, the warmth of his body a comfort against the tremor in her hands as she clung to his shirt.

***

Nesh's voice, filled with regret, softly said, "I feel terrible. I didn't think of the effect this would have on her. You said she'd just lost her brother—another Manki. She has fallen into a strange world, and she just discovered that her own world has been destroyed. She can never go back. Add to that a language she doesn't understand and being married against her will along with our claiming laws..."

Kellan looked around to see they all held the same expression. Only Stanlin seemed unaffected.

They were silent, lost in their own thoughts, until she quieted, Kellan stroking her back in comfort. When she didn't move, Kellan looked down at her face. Her eyes were open, unfocused, her face blank. It worried him.

Stanlin, almost excited, said, "Let's take her to the museum. She can see the exhibit of the Manki."

Kellan stared at the man, a knot of unease tightening in his stomach as he noticed a strange glint in the man's eyes. He saw Tamek narrow his eyes at Stanlin and Lorica's hands clench into fists—a sure sign he was trying to control himself. Kellan ached to take Siana home, but Brigitte's words, sharp and clear, stopped him in his tracks.

He leaned in close, his voice a low murmur, and asked, "Do you want to go see what he has of your race?"

The question hung heavy in the air. It took a minute for her to respond, and all she gave was a small nod. Kellan stood, still holding her in his arms, as Stanlin excitedly shifted from foot to foot.

Stanlin said with a hint of an annoyed tone, "I'm sure she can walk."

Kellan ignored him and carried her from the room.

When he felt her touch his chest, she said, "It's okay. Me down." He did so but kept hold of her hand.

Everyone followed Stanlin out to the building next door. Kellan noticed the look Stanlin gave him as he passed.

He wants her. The thought made him tense.

Stanlin moved his hand and partially unlocked the door. He also had a key he used. Opening the door, he invited Siana in. She let go of Kellan's hand as she entered the museum. They walked through wood and glass displays showing off various cultures of their world.

"Come. It's in the back." Stanlin hurried ahead.

***

Siana wanted to see the displays they were passing and paused, looking at them.

"Hurry, hurry!"

Siana turned and slowly followed him. She'd come back another time when he wasn't around. He annoyed her. She'd tried to think while sitting on Kellan's lap, but the man's voice aggravated her. At the entrance of the Manki exhibit, she stopped to brace herself. He was still trying to rush her in. As she took a deep breath, she stepped in and looked around the room. It wasn't huge. The wall on her right had a mural painted that showed the same scene of destruction the book showed.

Even if Jacob had lived, he would've died in that.

As much as she hated to admit it, the death he had may have been kinder. *Unless they were going to send him elsewhere as well.* Then she remembered that's what he'd said. The thought that he may have lived if he hadn't taken the time to talk to her, to reassure her, caused guilt to creep in.

Did he die because of me? Would he have lived if he hadn't said goodbye?

The other walls were a plain beige color. Her eyes saw the wall on the left had copies of photos of various items found hanging within protective frames. The far wall had benches one could sit on, as well as what looked like a shop. Strewn around the floor were various display cases protecting the items within.

One near her caught her attention. She moved closer and tilted her head while scrutinizing it. She wasn't sure what it was supposed to be. It had four legs with paws, a very short torso, a long neck which reminded her of a giraffe, and a bird's head. It was entirely covered in feathers. The brothers crowded around her, looking at the creature, then looking at her with curious expressions.

She turned to Stanlin, asking, "What is it?"

Stanlin looked surprised. He stammered a bit and said something she didn't understand. Opening the book of words he brought with him, he tried again. "It's a canine."

Siana was a dog lover. She had a couple before things went south. Even then, she kept them with her until they were lost.

Looking at the travesty in front of her, she said, "No, it's not!"

Stanlin came to stand next to her. He asked, "What is it then?"

Siana, looking at him, said, "Nothing."

He had to look it up to understand. He tried to argue, but she cut him off in *Setan*. "Not a canine."

Lorica said something to Stanlin, annoyed. He spoke too quickly, but she could see he was quietly berating the man.

Siana moved to the next display. A battered and burned older—to her—small box phone.

Wow, those things are hard to break, aren't they?

Moving on, she saw a gun safe. A big one. She learned—through much translating and mummery—it was heat-fused, and no one could open it. The label on the item, found in a burned, rounded, underground metal home, identified it as clothing storage. Her telling Stanlin it wasn't for clothes caused a conversation she couldn't have.

How do I explain it was used to hold guns? They don't seem to have them.

Nesh, reading over Stanlin's shoulder as he found the English words he needed, translated for the brothers. Sometimes sentences had to be simplified to understand each other. Stanlin asked why people lived underground. She tried to explain about bunkers, but she didn't have the skills. The book didn't have enough words to help. It seemed a good many of the displays came from bunkers: a flat screen TV, a shovel, a chair, a... dog crate? She had to wonder if they ever found her government's bunkers or the seed vaults—if they had survived.

That would blow their minds.

Though, she wouldn't mind finding the seed vaults and bringing Earth's plants back to life. She wondered if she could remember where they were located. She pushed the thought that Jacob would know out of her mind.

Her eyes looked at recreations of human life hanging on the walls. Some of it was accurate; some of it was not. Seeing her world, her time as history, as museum pieces, became overwhelming. She took a deep breath to steady herself.

Stanlin was waiting for her near a wall opening she hadn't seen until now. He seemed bursting with excitement again. As she rounded the corner and caught sight of a tall display, she froze. A life-sized replica of a human male was in front of her, Stanlin standing proudly beside it. The replica had undergarments on, but nothing else.

Siana felt bile rising looking at it. Kellan came up behind her. She briefly glanced back at him, then refocused on the man. It looked so real that she wanted to reach out and touch it, but the display prevented that. Looking at him, he looked very average. He had brown hair, eyes, a beard, and was an average height. The wall surrounding the case displayed various "Manki" clothes. Next to the man was an empty display case around the same size.

Too much.

Her voice barely audible, thinking of her own world, Siana said, "I want to go home," turned and bolted out of the building. Kellan followed her, concerned.

***

Stanlin became visibly upset. He shouted after her, telling her to come back, that Manki weren't that weak. The male seemed completely oblivious to the female's feelings.

Tamek, maintaining a polite demeanor, thanked Stanlin for his hospitality and help. He followed his brother. Lorica nodded to Stanlin and followed Tamek outside. Nesh hurried after them, his mind clouded.

Siana was outside, tear-filled eyes, breathing deeply, trying to control her anxiety levels, Kellan's arms around her. Tamek and Lorica were helplessly watching her. Nesh noticed their carriage had arrived and was waiting for them. He hurried back into the house to grab his things and headed for the carriage. He had realized some of what Stanlin had was against their laws. How no one noticed was beyond him. At some point, a member of the Convocation had to have toured the museum, though it's possible they wouldn't know about historical finds.

Unless he could use funds to make them look away.

He needed to double-check and make sure he was correct before saying anything. He was also concerned about the origins of Siana Devereaux getting out. Worse historians than Stanlin existed.

***

Kellan escorted Siana to the carriage. The driver had already fetched the family's belongings from the house and was ready to leave at their command. Lorica pulled Tamek aside and said something to him. Tamek said they'd discuss it at home. He wanted to get her out of there, so Lorica and he joined the others in the carriage.

Siana was sitting on the same bench, but against the wall of the carriage, keeping her gaze focused outside the window. She couldn't handle talking to anyone. Not now. Her thoughts were chaotic, and she struggled to accept what she'd seen and learned. As the driver climbed to his seat, the carriage door flew open. She turned her head toward it.

Stanlin stuck his head in, eyes on her, begging her to come back and let him show her more. He babbled about how they could work together, how she could help him improve the exhibit. Then he said, "I'd be a better claim to you. I understand your culture. I'll be careful not to kill you. I..." He broke off when he realized every brother had a thunderous look and red eyes.

Quickly slamming the door, he called, "Think about it!"

Siana only understood about half of what he said; she didn't care to figure out the other half. She had seen the brothers' eyes and realized they did change color. Whatever he said ticked them off.

Tamek murmured, "We need to keep an eye on him." No one responded, and the ride home was silent, Siana keeping her focus on the scenery.

Chapter Thirty-Three

BRIGITTE WAS WAITING FOR THEM. Siana barely glanced at her. Kellan looked worried and kept glancing at Siana. He asked Brigitte if she'd accomplished his request, and she nodded. Siana's face was impassive, staring though she could hear them.

Tamek said he'd like to speak to the brothers first thing in the morning. They murmured their acknowledgments. Tamek went to his study. Lorica left, saying nothing more. Kellan asked Brigitte and Siana to follow him. Both did without a word. Up the stairs he went, then turned right. He led them down the hall, stopped at a door, and looked at Siana with a bit of nervousness.

He said, "I know this is not a good time. I didn't know all this would happen. Before we left, I instructed Brigitte to complete a task. I was planning on trying to tell you we were married after this visit."

She tried to focus on him through the windstorm of her thoughts.

"Now that you know, we will share the same room. If anyone shows up to say our marriage is not real, we can show them this."

She heard him as if from a distance. Her mind was having trouble processing the words she knew. Jacob was gone. Her world was gone. Her old life was gone.

As he opened the door, he put his hand on her lower back and guided her into the room, trepidation about her response clear. Once she was past the door, he removed his hand and closed it. He waited, as if expecting her to say something. When she didn't, he began a small tour.

The room had a masculine atmosphere to it, but it wasn't overpowering. When you opened the door, you immediately caught sight of a very large, four-poster bed made of dark wood. There was a small table on either side made of the same wood. The walls were a calming blue. The rug over the dark wood floor was a darker blue. On the opposite wall from the door was a double set of windows. Between the windows was a door leading to the balcony. Across from the foot of the bed, she saw two dark wood doors with the same scrollwork as her former room. She assumed one was the toilet and the other the bath. Then she realized there was a third door. During his tour, Kellan opened it to reveal a closet and dressing room between the other two rooms. Brigitte showed her the location of her belongings. Kellan again seemed to wait for her to speak.

When she didn't, he walked up to her and said, "If you want to go back to your room, you can."

Again, no response. He cupped her face between his hands, lifting her head so he could see her eyes. She just stared at him, looking lost.

He whispered, "I don't know what to do or how to fix this."

He motioned for Brigitte to prepare her for bed and left the room. When he returned, Brigitte was gone, and Siana was lying in bed. She heard him enter the dressing room and quickly prepare for bed. After entering the bedchamber again, he climbed in next to her. She had taken the side opposite the door like last night. Her back was to him.

All he said was, "Sleep. We'll work on it tomorrow." A wave of his hand shut off the lights.

***

They watched as Stanlin left his museum for the night. Once he was out of sight, keeping to the shadows, they approached. The house had windows facing the museum, so they had to gain access from another side. Sliding up next to the building, a male looked for a way in.

A low bird call told the others to come. Following the sound, they saw a higher window was open. Eyes looked for any watchers as they stood on each other's shoulders. They moved with speed and precision. A well-greased wheel. The top one managed to climb in. The others waited. A quiet click came from a lower window. All but one entered. He hid within the trees, keeping watch.

With almost no sound, they wound their way through the exhibits until they found the room they wanted. They didn't need to speak. Being well-briefed, they knew what they were looking for. A noise caused them to melt into the shadows. No warning call. They continued. Soon after finding what they were looking for, they opened the case.

Instructions were given to study it, remember the details, but not to remove it from the building. It needed to be placed back exactly as they found it. The most experienced of them ran a critical eye over the piece. They had to remove it to examine it. They inspected it from top to bottom. Staring at each other, they quietly discussed the piece and came to a unanimous agreement. Cautiously, they returned it, making sure it stood in the exact position they'd found it.

Stealthily, they went upstairs and searched. They knew it had to be here somewhere. There was nothing. Heading back downstairs, they searched for a lower-level door. The sound of a quiet snap alerted others that someone had found a door behind a bookcase. Cautiously, they opened it and went downstairs. After thoroughly searching, they found what they were looking for. They quickly left and disappeared into the night.

***

As he was walking by a window after breakfast, he looked out and saw the signal. No one saw him leave. Slipping into the shadows of trees, he waited. His guard came up to him and relayed what they'd found. Lorica didn't move while he processed the information.

Wakke asked, "What do you want to do, Lorra?"

Lorica said, "A wise male does not act in haste."

Somber, Wakke nodded. It was a saying from their village.

"Keep an eye on him. Just in case more appear."

"What about the female?" Unbeknownst to the rest of the house, Lorica's guards had silently watched over and followed Siana.

"She's safe enough for now. I'd rather you all keep track of him and his activities."

Nodding, he blended into the trees and was gone. Lorica headed back into the house, needing to speak to Tamek.

***

Siana was already in bed when she heard Kellan come in. He'd had an emergency and spent hours in town. Seeing the glow from his eyes in the dark room, she sat up. Part of her missed her nursing days, and she wanted to hear about his day. It would also serve as a distraction from her own problems. When he realized she was awake, he turned up the lights to low and dimmed his eyes.

One look at his face, and she knew. Many doctors had that same face when they lost a patient. He dropped his clothes where he stood, exhausted, plainly not caring about Mrs. Atwood's future lecture. Without a word, Siana rose and picked up his bloody clothing carefully. He had a special basket for the clothes he wore to the infirmary, and she dropped them into it. He normally changed before leaving as well. That he didn't showed his mindset.

He didn't speak as he washed up. She didn't break his quiet. After taking a drink from her water glass, she climbed back into bed and waited. After putting on his nightshirt, he reached under and dropped his undergarment. He started doing this the second night. Whether out of respect for her or his insecurities, she didn't know. This time, he put it in the basket. He downed his own water, then climbed into bed. He barely looked at her.

Turning on his side, his back to her, he shut off the lights. Siana overheard a noise from him. He attempted to keep quiet, but it was clear that the patient's death had affected him. She didn't know what to say. The usual platitudes didn't seem appropriate, and she didn't know how to say them, so she did the only thing she knew.

Moving herself behind him, she spooned him and put her hand on his side to feel where he was. Moving her arm around him, she held tight. As he turned her way, she loosened her grasp. He held her; she held him tighter, silently consoling him in his grief as his body shook.

***

Kellan watched as Siana woke, her lids rising to reveal sleepy emerald pools he wanted to lose himself in. A few seconds passed as they gazed at one another. He leaned in, hesitating to confirm her comfort, and kissed her, expecting a possible rejection. Given all she'd been through, it wouldn't be surprising. He knew she was still half asleep, but she returned it. Their desire for one another quickly intensified. Kellan rapidly sealed the room, ensuring no sound could escape. He had been contemplating methods to bring her pleasure while ensuring her safety, to express his care for her. He was flying blind, so hopefully it worked.

Kellan's mouth moved toward her breasts. He used it to make love to them while he moved his hand to the space between her legs, which she parted. His improved access prompted moans of pleasure from Siana as he touched her. As his hands caressed her, he kept moving his mouth downward.

The first touch of his tongue on her *sereto* almost shot her hips off the bed. She reached up, grabbed the spindles of the headboard, and cried out when his tongue and mouth began showing her that a Setan male could please a Manki female. Her breathing came in gasps, as moans and sounds of pleasure escaped her.

"Oh, God, Kellan. Don't stop!" Her voice sounded like she was having trouble speaking.

He obliged. Her breathing quickened, her moans louder. He was alternating movements with his tongue, including random little sucks that made her moans jolt into little squeals. He poured all his care into his mouth, showing her what he couldn't express. Her moans became cries that gradually became louder.

Her body was tightening, and he knew she was getting close. Her pleas for him to not stop, cries of wanting, aroused him more than he was used to. He wanted to mate her so badly, wanted to feel her passage holding him, but knew he couldn't. Instead, he slipped two fingers in, using them as his body's substitute, sliding them in and out of her passage. Her body met them, hard and fast, demanding more. He had to pin her squirming hips with his arm to hold them so he could do what she was begging him to do. Her cries echoed in the room as her pleasure overcame her, culminating in a yell that made him proud of himself. He'd pleased her.

***

Siana was trying to breathe, her entire body quivering. He shifted his body up and lowered it onto her, his legs sliding between hers, pressing himself against her.

She froze.

Hurriedly he said, "I'm not going to mate you."

She relaxed a little. Her body against his satisfied him for now. Supporting his weight with one arm, stroking her arm, her hair, waiting for her body to calm itself.

"Why?" Her eyes were puzzled. "Why would you do that? You know you can't..."

He shrugged and gave her a gentle smile. "I wanted to."

"I can't do the same."

He wondered about her world's protocol for kissing after tasting her—if they did that. Not knowing what their practices were, he wasn't sure if what he did was acceptable. He realized because she liked it, he didn't care. He decided to kiss her cheek and made plans to please her again soon.

"I know." He smiled at her.

She offered, "I can use my hands."

Kellan pretended to be thinking it over. He desperately wanted to feel her hands. "Maybe another time, but today was for you," he answered softly.

He looked uncertain as he said, "I didn't know if it would work."

"What?"

"We do not kiss here."

He reached down and touched her, almost causing her hips to shoot off the bed again. "This *sereto,*" he said, teaching her the word. *"Sereto* out is not *Setan. Setan sereto* is in."

"*Sereto* in?" She tilted her head a bit to better see his face, her eyes not fully understanding.

He slid his fingers inside her. "*Setan* has *sereto* in."

"Kellan." Her breathing sped up as his fingers started moving. "I not know if I can again."

His eyes gazed intently into hers. "You think maybe can?" he murmured.

Soon, her cries showed she absolutely could.

***

His hand stroked her arm, her side, to help soothe her. Her entire body wouldn't stop shaking.

"I do too much?" His face looked concerned.

Siana gave a breathless chuckle. "I'm okay."

His expression lit something inside of her.

He's really worried he's overdone it. He does care for me.

It hit her. She cared for him. Maybe even loved. She pulled his head down and wrapped herself around him.

"I'm okay," she reaffirmed.

They were both more than happy to stay like that, kissing each other until a knock sounded at the door, calling them to breakfast.

Chapter Thirty-Four

TAMEK DECLARED EVERYONE MUST accompany him. They'd just finished breakfast. Everyone stared, surprised. Siana's questioning look at Kellan received a shake of his head and a shrug.

Siana was confused. She thought they were having a meeting.

What made Tamek change his mind?

"Brigitte, you'll come with us."

Siana noticed the surprised look on her face. *She obviously doesn't know what's going on either.*

Everyone left to prepare themselves and met outside in the front courtyard. As she walked down the steps, Siana noticed Tamek talking to Kellan. They stopped when they realized the others were arriving. They were taking the servants' carriage. Everything about it was just like the nicer carriage except the benches were wood. The plain brown carriage, equally large, had a similar driver's seat. Siana once again wore a scarf over her ears. When she had entered the carriage, Kellan had a very troubled look on his face. He ignored her questioning expression.

What did Tamek tell him?

They all took the same seats as last time, and Brigitte sat on a side seat. She and Siana kept stealing glances at each other. It was obvious something was wrong. No one spoke.

This time, the carriage turned right toward town. The trees faded into fields and farmland growing crops. She recognized corn, but wasn't sure what the others were. People in serviceable clothes were among them, working the fields. A couple were obviously gathering what was ripe.

After they entered town, Siana's attention focused on what she could see. The packed dirt road turned into stone. Buildings, side by side like many towns and cities, were visible. Some were plain wood, others ornate stone structures with wood embedded within. A park seemed to be in the middle of town with a dark wooden gazebo in the center, benches strewn about. *Small town America.* That's what the park reminded her of. The town was clean, and the buildings were in good repair. She saw a symbol on one distant building and realized it had the same symbol the infirmary at camp had.

Is that where Kellan works?

After the carriage turned down an alleyway, they drove behind the buildings. Each rose like stone walls on either side, the *Storjens'* hooves impacting the once again dirt road. Soon, they stopped and disembarked. The door next to them had the same symbol. Siana didn't understand why they were at the infirmary. *Be* Tess, looking just as troubled, opened the back door.

Silently entering, everyone stepped aside to let Kellan lead the way. They entered the exam room and saw the Manki male exhibit lying on the table, still in its pose. Taken aback, Siana looked at the brothers.

A wave of confusion washed over her as she stammered, "Why—why is that here?"

A look of utter bewilderment washed over Brigitte's face as she saw it for the first time.

Lorica stepped closer, his eyes fixed on the object, and said, "I want you to look at it," his voice carrying a hint of urgency.

She felt a tightening of anxiety in her stomach, but she complied. Slowly, her gaze traveled from the naked feet to the face. She felt a tug at her mind. A face flashed. Frozen in shock for a split second, she started trembling.

No.

She stepped closer, bending to take a better look. Though similar to a wax figure in stillness, a faint, almost undetectable odor of decay betrayed its true nature. She was quite familiar with that smell. With shaking fingers, she touched the pale, still face, the sightless eyes staring blankly ahead, a chilling emptiness in their depths. The exhibit felt strangely stiff and cold, like an embalmed body, but the slight give revealed a stuffing of some kind. A ghost of pale pink blush, like the faintest dusting of powder, lingered on her fingertips. The face flashed again, this time a scowl twisting the features directed at his partner.

Quietly complaining about the children.

Him walking behind her.

As he stood near another woman, flirting.

The blond woman. Her partner. The couple behind her and Jacob. The electrician.

Jacob's words, a chilling whisper that felt like ice against her skin, echoed in her mind: only she had survived.

A horrified "Oh, God!" escaped her lips, the sound sharp and ragged against the quiet, confirming their suspicions. Too late, they'd found another of the five. Stanlin got to him first.

She stumbled back in disbelief, shaking her head in denial. Siana gasped for air.

How could he? What if I'd met him first? I'd be an exhibit. What kind of monster does this? He literally had to stuff him like taxidermy.

With the empty case in her mind, the weight of Stanlin's calculated scheme settled upon her. *He was going to stuff and exhibit me.* Recalling his words in the carriage, *He was going to rape me first, killing me by claiming.*

A dizzying spin engulfed her, the walls seeming to tilt and sway as she fought to maintain her balance. All the "what ifs," each a chilling whisper, battled in her mind. Out of five, she was the only one. Did Stanlin kill all of them?

As she turned, she saw a bowl next to her, and her breakfast jumped into it. A wave of nausea washed over her as Brigitte's arm tightened around her, holding her close as her stomach heaved. They waited for her to finish. Tess gave Siana some water. Staying bent over the bowl, she rinsed and spit. She didn't drink. After a slight turn, she caught sight of his face.

That could have been me.

Everything she'd gone through until now, what that man had gone through, every thought became chaos.

***

Brigitte exclaimed, "No one can be that *bevelten*! He must have died first."

It was a futile wish. The body was in too good of a condition to have been discovered deceased, but they needed proof.

His eyes on Kellan, Tamek said, "The Convocation will have people here as witnesses. You'll need to look him over to see if he was dead prior to Stanlin preserving him or not. If necessary, have *Be* Tess sketch what you find as evidence."

Stunned, Kellan could barely form the words. "Where is he?"

Lorica spoke up, "He ran. My guards are looking for him, as are the Convocation's guards."

Kellan nodded. "Once the Convocation finds out, they may come for her." A flash of fear crossed his face.

Tamek took a breath. "Not if you claim he was defective. Word about a defective *Setan* is already going around town. He could be one that Stanlin mistook for Manki."

He wants me to lie. Part of Kellan disagreed with it, but the part that cared about his mate would do it. The thought she could've ended like this made him angry. Turning to look at her, he caught her as she swayed, steadying her. Her eyes held something he couldn't understand, yet they were unfocused.

Kellan swept her up and carried her to the carriage. *Too much in so short a time. Though it felt like she'd been here for ages, her arrival hadn't been that long ago.*

Siana protested as he handed her to Tamek. She didn't look at them. Tamek sat her on a bench. A worried Brigitte pushed her way through to sit with her friend. Siana just stared blankly out the window. Concern reflected on each other's face. Kellan began to enter, but Tamek stopped him.

"I know you're worried, but you need to look for evidence. We can best help her by ensuring Stanlin is caught and punished. We will keep her in your room until he's found." Kellan knew he was right, but he didn't want to leave her.

Brigitte interjected, "I'm staying with her."

No one argued.

***

Kellan quickly determined the male's death. His nails and tongue showed signs of poisoning. He had to cut the wire holding the jaw shut to check the tongue. One Convocation witness, who knew plants, examined him and confirmed the diagnosis. Kellan was worried he would notice the strange round objects at the back of the male's throat, but they could barely open his jaw enough to see the front of his tongue.

After a brief discussion, they could trace it to a specific plant that was rare in the area. However, the witness informed him the search of the museum had turned up several of the plants. They agreed the male was most likely fed tea to not harm the body. Thankfully, the witnesses stated it was a good thing the male wasn't a doctor since he couldn't tell the difference between a defective *Setan* and a Manki. That the Manki had been extinct for so long worked in their favor. They listed poisoning as the official cause of death. They would sentence Stanlin to execution once they found him.

After they'd left, Kellan and Tess prepared the body for burial, undoing wires where they could. They just needed him to fit. The death carer showed up, and they helped place the male in a wooden box. After sealing it, his assistant and he carried the box to their wagon. House Devereaux would pay for the burial.

"I'll clean up. This must have been a great shock. Go be with her," Tess said, whispering.

Kellan, nodding, took her up on it. Lorica had returned with Tost, so he had a way home. Other than Lorica telling him there was no change in Siana, both were quiet throughout their journey other than Tost telling Kellan the *Setan's* actions disturbed him.

Kellan entered the house and hurried up the stairs to their room. Siana was lying on the bed, unmoving. She didn't answer when he inquired how she was doing, didn't look at him when bent down trying to catch her gaze. She stared into nothing. His worry increased. He hoped her mind hadn't slipped away.

Chapter Thirty-Five

"SHE ISN'T RESPONDING TO anything right now!" Kellan raged. "How am I supposed to tell her that?"

Lorica, watching his brothers, was lazing on the couch and was staying out of it. While he wanted to annoy Tamek by putting his feet on the couch, he knew it was not the right time. He had sent some of his guards to hunt Stanlin, and that occupied his thoughts. Besides, he believed Kellan just needed to get it done. She was still grieving her brother's death, the change in time, and Stalin's actions that could've killed her, yet circumstances remained unaltered. If Kellan had to drug her to do it, so be it. He was a physician; he could repair any damage he caused.

Tamek's face held his normal stoic look as sat behind his desk. "You knew this was coming. I don't trust him to keep quiet now that he knows her identity and origin. Do you? His actions, even those against that male, could prompt an investigation by the Convocation. At this point, he would do anything to save his own hide."

Kellan sighed. "No, I don't trust him. None of us know what Stanlin is capable of."

"He seemed desperate to stop her from leaving. If we weren't there, I strongly suspect he would've taken and held her. Most likely he would have claimed her, killing her, then stuffed her and put her in that case. I don't doubt that if he can get his hands on her, he will still attempt it, even if it's in another location."

Kellan agreed.

"We don't know what he said to her. He could have told her the truth or lies. She has to tell us, because she's the only one who can. Even given current circumstances, he still put a bug in her ear." His voice softening, he said, "Do whatever is necessary to help her, but you must claim her body and finalize the marriage. Should Stanlin need self-preservation, he might sow doubt among the Convocation. Even being a lawbreaker, he could put in a petition for a *Yendali*. If he does, you may have a fortnight to accomplish it. Maybe longer, but I doubt it. It normally takes that long to arrange it, but because it's our House, they may rush it. Then again, given his crimes, they could push it back. Eventually, someone will have enough doubts to check her."

Kellan, frustrated, said, "It seems like every time we make progress, something sets us back. Her mourning period for her brother is still happening. That should give us more time. She also just discovered physical proof of the loss of her world. Hearing it from her brother was one thing, but seeing actual proof is another. Add what Stanlin did to the male and how it could have been her—she needs time to recover."

"Her mourning might give us time, yet it might not. We don't know what the Convocation will do. There is also another potential problem: what they will do if they find out she is Manki. Whether she is unclaimed or claimed, they may take her. We need as much on our side as possible, and a solid claim is part of that. My advice is to prepare for the worst, but hope for the best," Tamek said calmly.

Lorica finally spoke. "As long as we continue with the tale that she was born defective, we may be able to keep hiding the truth. However, Stanlin being caught and, in turn, his sowing enough doubt in their minds determines that."

Kellan's face lit up. "How complete are the old camp repairs?"

"Nowhere near enough to make it sustainable." He hesitated before asking, "What if you drug her?"

Kellan stared at his brother in disbelief. "I think she'd notice an injury *if* she woke up!"

Tamek continued calmly, "I'm not saying force her. Talk to her, tell her you can drug her so she feels nothing, prepare her body the best you can, claim her, repair any damage, and—hopefully—she'll be safe."

His eyes studied Kellan's distraught face. "Kell, I empathize; however, leadership demands logical consideration of the House's well-being. You used to be House Head. You know this. Many seek refuge, knowing our opposition. I can't allow them to be endangered over one female, no matter how much we all care for her."

Lorica spoke again. "Enlist Brigitte's aid. She understands. She can help Siana cope."

Kellan shook his head. "I don't want to do this."

Tamek said in an even tone, "You drugged her to examine her. You drugged her to prepare her body in case she had to be claimed. To refuse to do so now is hypocritical."

"She didn't know our language! We knew nothing about her! She hadn't gone through everything she just went through.

Our priority was learning and keeping her safe," Kellan countered.

Tamek responded quietly, "Keeping her safe is our goal now."

Kellan let out a frustrated breath. "And having her hate all of us for doing this to her?"

Tamek sighed. "If I'm correct, you care for Siana?"

Kellan, looking at his brother, nodded.

"Then ask yourself: is it better to force your claim or allow Talon or one of the other *Bund* to have her knowing they will definitely kill her?"

Kellan stood and started pacing, clearly indicating he was conflicted or solving a problem.

Tamek encouraged him to see reason. "You have time to talk to her and prepare her. Her language skills are improving. Maybe, with Brigitte's help, you can make her understand."

"I need air. I need to think." A hopeless expression toward Tamek preceded his exit. He barely heard his brothers' words as he left.

Lorica, leaning forward with his elbows on his knees, said, "He knows you're right. Once he's accepted it, he'll move forward."

Tamek, pulling paperwork toward him, said, "He better accept it quickly. We've delayed as much as we can. Her time has run out."

***

She barely had time to hide before Kellan flung open the door. Brigitte had eavesdropped on their conversation. When Tamek brought up drugging Siana, she had to stop herself from going in and slapping his face.

Now I know where Lorica gets it from.

Part of her had to admit he was right, and she hated it. Siana's safety became paramount upon learning about Stanlin's deeds. Kellan's injuries made him the better match for Sia in the physical sense. Tess, with Kellan's blessing, shared their findings with Brigitte; therefore, Brigitte knew about Siana's differences. It seemed like none of the males wanted to tell her, so Brigitte decided to do so. She headed toward Kellan and Siana's room.

Standing outside the door, she knocked and received a quiet, "Come in." As she opened the door, she saw Siana sitting on the desk chair, staring out the window. No expression. Brigitte understood why Kellan was worried. They all were. Though she was speaking, Siana showed no emotion. It was like she had shoved them into a dark hole somewhere.

Walking toward her, Brigitte asked, "Are you okay?"

Staring out the window, she just shrugged and nodded.

As she sat on the side of the bed, praying she would understand, Brigitte took a deep breath. "I have to talk to you. The brothers don't know how to tell you."

She didn't move or look at her.

Brigitte jumped right in. "What do you know about claiming?"

Siana, turning, her face expressionless, answered, "A male takes a female. Not matter if she likes it or not. Makes her be with him."

Well, she isn't wrong.

Brigitte nodded. "Laws. If a female not have a male, any male can claim her. But Low claims Low..." She stopped at Siana's puzzled expression. She pointed to herself. Brigitte said, "Low. Mrs. Atwood is Low. Kellan is Middle and High. Tamek and Lorica are High. *Bund* is High."

Brigitte explained, "Low claim Low, Middle claim Middle, High claim High. Kellan born"—she acted out giving birth—"High. House Head. *Bund*. When physician to Low, Kellan is now Middle. No *Bund*. Tamek House Head. Kellan is still House Devereaux."

With that done... Brigitte went back to explaining slowly so she didn't lose her. "We think Siana Middle."

Siana shrugged and said in English. "Close enough."

"Lorica help Siana. Siana is House Devereaux, so Kellan claim to protect. Stop other males from claiming."

She searched Siana's face. There was no reaction. Brigitte scooted to the edge of the bed, leaning forward.

"They find you have Jacob, your brother, so Kellan not claim. Jacob your protection. Jacob..." She continued quietly, "Jacob died. Siana is in House Devereaux. House Devereaux must protect."

Siana didn't respond. Brigitte waited a bit to see if she had questions.

"Maybe I want another claim?" she asked with a frown.

Brigitte shook her head. "Jacob protection. Maybe another claim." She tried to think of how to explain the rest.

Brigitte shifted. "House Devereaux males fear Talon claim or the male Stanlin takes you."

Siana shifted uneasily at their names.

"They want to protect you. Kellan claim." Brigitte looked uncomfortable. "Claim not done."

She watched as Siana's eyes widened with understanding.

As she spoke, her voice trembled with fear, saying, "I don't want to die."

Brigitte looked surprised at her words. *How did she know she could? Did Kellan already say something?*

"You won't die." The voice came from the doorway.

***

Kellan's presence caused both females to turn. He'd heard most of the conversation and was unsure about entering. When he heard her comment about dying, he couldn't stay out. He asked Brigitte to give them some privacy. She nodded and took her leave, closing the door after her.

Kellan took Brigitte's place on the bed, examining his mate's face. She looked unsure.

He reiterated, "You won't die."

He knew he had no business promising this. It was based on how much he had stretched her at the camp. *She will tear, but hopefully—*

"Stanlin says I will."

Kellan pointed out, "Stanlin was trying to take you; he wanted to put you in his museum, as if you were some kind of exhibit."

She stared at him. He thought she understood his meaning, if not all his words.

"I examined you."

She nodded, fear-filled eyes staring back at him.

"A *Setan* male, yes, you may die." Her brow furrowed at his reversal. "*Setan* male." He held up his hands to show how big a Setan male was.

Her face paled.

If the subject weren't so serious, it would have amused him.

Now the hard part. Pointing to his injuries, he said, "Burns."

She nodded.

"Burns..." *How do I say this?* Kellan swore he spent half their conversations trying to figure out how to phrase things.

Pointing to his lap, he said, "Burns."

He used his hands to show his size with an ashamed face. He knew he had nothing to be ashamed of, but he was always self-conscious about his scars and the rejection they could bring. Other males gave him pitying looks if he had to change in front of them. He also knew she'd felt it against her, so it wouldn't be a surprise.

Awareness dawning on her face told him she understood what he meant. That he was small compared to others.

She tilted her head at him. "Do you like me male to female?"

The question surprised him. "Yes."

She was quiet, her face thoughtful.

"Stanlin say I die." Her voice trembled.

"You won't. I won't let you."

"You're too big. I will die." Her tone was adamant.

"I'll show you."

Feeling him against her was one thing. Actually seeing it was different. Taking a deep breath and mentally bracing for the rejection, he began to expose himself.

***

Her eyes widened as he undid his trousers. "Kellan!" she protested. She'd already felt him against her and knew how large he was.

313

Kellan continued to undo his trousers. Finally, after a slight hesitation, he revealed himself.

It wasn't easy, but she kept her face composed. If it wasn't for his warning, she wasn't sure she could've pulled it off. The flatness on one side, along with scarring, showed where the damage was. He was missing a section. It wasn't just the scars; it was shaped a bit differently with grooves traveling the length. But what really got to her was the size.

That will never fit, and he's on the small end?

Her bouncing leg betrayed her worry despite her calm face. "No. I'll die," she said firmly.

Putting himself back together, his face showed his relief at her not rejecting him outright.

He said, "We can do things to help."

"Like what?" she asked. "I be hurt." *How could I not?*

Walking to the dressing room, he disappeared inside. Within a minute, he returned carrying a small box. Setting it down on the desk, he opened it.

Siana turned to see what was inside. She was a bit surprised to see varying sizes of dilators. Glancing at him, she reached in and picked up one. The dilator was smooth, with an angled tip similar to a knitting needle, but it had a rounded end.

"What is it?" She didn't know how they used them here.

"I use these for various things."

She guessed at the meaning of his version of "various." *It could be "different." Or the same word for both.* He picked one up and demonstrated how the ends could be removed for various medical applications. She had an idea of where he was going and wasn't thrilled.

"You want to put these in me?"

Kellan was blunt. "Yes. We start here." He lifted a smaller one. "End here." He lifted out the largest one. Shaking her head, she said, "Too big."

Something flitted across his face before he masked it. As he put the item back in the box, she continued to shake her head.

"It won't work."

He sat back on the bed and gentled his voice. "It will. We take our time. Go slow. I can do it, or you do it. You can do this."

She stared at the inside of the box, all of them lined up like a death squad. She didn't know what to say. Her fear was growing stronger. The image of his size flashed in her mind. She just didn't believe she wouldn't die.

"Sia." Her nickname being used by him, caused her to look up. "If I don't claim you, they will take you. Give you to Talon or someone else."

"Why? Why can't I say no?" There was desperation in her voice.

"Laws. Laws protect females."

Her hand swung at the box. "This is not protection. Tell me I have to, or others take is not protection."

Her voice betrayed her fear and frustration. She had blocked them all out, so she could organize her thoughts. Accept everything she'd learned. There was no time to deal with it, and now she was hit with a death sentence. She felt it all crashing down on her: the weeks of living in fight-or-flight survival mode on Earth, constantly watching people die, hiding, trying not to be killed, being dumped here against her will, Jacob, Stanlin, having her rights taken, and now being told she would be killed.

"I know." He said, "We—House Devereaux—try to fix laws," his voice laced with frustration. "Only *Bund* can change laws. Tamek is trying. If we don't obey laws, we lose House Devereaux. We can't change laws. We hide you in a camp to protect you from laws. We can't hide you now. Stanlin knows. Talon knows."

Siana felt trapped, angry. Her anxiety was going through the roof. If Kellan didn't have sex with her, their marriage was void, and anyone could take her. She was going to die.

I landed in freaking medieval times—elven style. Thanks, bots.

It was too much. Deep down, she had hoped she'd be able to find a way home to the past. To maybe go back and save her brother from his own death. She had avoided facing it all, allowing her mind to shut down rather than confront it. Rather than accept it.

But now, she couldn't deny it. Reality was slapping her in the face. Everything was gone: her brother, her world, and one of the cruelest losses of all—her rights to her own body and life; a bitter taste filled her mouth. She could've landed near Stanlin and been an exhibit. Like the electrician. A powerful, overwhelming sense of helpless anger, like a freight train, barreled through her, shaking her to her core.

All the negative emotions she tried to push aside, all the understanding she tried to have for this world and its ways, in an instant, it and her control vanished. She hated it. Hated the helplessness. They overlooked her for their laws. Having her life dictated by them. Possibly being hunted by a psychopath. She wanted to reject all of it. They were literally going to kill her over their asinine ways, and no one seemed to care. Even Kellan was making excuses.

She opened her mouth and unleashed. Her voice began rising, yelling in her language, pacing, waving her arms around, pointing at him, at his groin. She was getting herself worked up more and more. Kellan tried to calm her, to talk to her. She vaguely heard him say it would be okay. When he tried to touch her, she slapped his hands and darted away from him.

Siana didn't want any of this. She wanted to live her own life. Maybe with Kellan, maybe not. She deserved a choice regarding her life partner. Leaving her world should have been her decision. Who she had sex with should be her decision. Whether she stayed or died with Jacob. All of these decisions had been taken from her. As she ranted, rejection of this world and its beliefs rose.

Run, her inner voice said. *Run away from all of them. Find a new place. Somewhere better. Away from House Devereaux, away from their stupid laws, away from this sham of a marriage that should never have existed. Away from the monster who wants to kill and stuff me. They are going to kill me.*

Inward and vocally, she screamed, tears streaming, "I don't want to die. I want none of this! None!"

Neither heard the whir from her banding as it began to retract. The more her rejection of this life rose, the faster it moved. It wasn't until she swung her hand within her eyesight that she realized the band was gone, and it was just a ring again. Pulling it off, she threw it at Kellan and did what her instincts said. She ran.

Chapter Thirty-Six

KELLAN WAS SO STUNNED he didn't move.

The band removed itself. She rejected me.

He was lost. In order for it to do that, she had to fully reject it. Reject him. A few seconds passed before he realized he was hurt. Part of him knew it was her fear, sorrow, and anger, but the other part was like a child who had offered love and had it thrown back. It hurt so much. That's when he realized it.

I love her.

He didn't know when it happened, but it had. Picking up the ring and slipping it into his pocket, he ran after her. He had to stop her. Her anger, fear, and sense of injustice were valid; however, leaving the house endangered her.

***

Siana ran. Down the stairs. Through the foyer, barely avoiding slipping on the floor. She heard Tamek call her name but ignored him, tears racing, falling onto her top. Mrs. Atwood's call followed her as she fled through the back door. She heard Brigitte yelling for her as her friend ran after her, but fear and despair drove Siana faster.

I want out. I want to live.

Through the gate, down the path, she ran. Ran from them, their laws, from death. When she ran past one of the *Storjen* fields, Isis perked her head up. Her mistress's emotions were unknowingly being projected into her. Like a trapped animal, she fled to escape danger and uncertainty. Isis ran after her. Siana heard someone or something chasing her and ran faster. She couldn't let them catch her. She had to get away. In her fear, she didn't realize it was her mount.

Isis appeared in front of her, looking like she wanted to block her. Instead, Siana jumped on her back. The pain she caused Isis shot through them both, but Siana projected where she wanted to go. Isis went.

***

Kellan ran down the stairs, calling Siana. Tamek informed him she ran toward the back and asked what happened. Kellan ignored him and followed her path.

Brigitte saw him coming and called, "She went out the back gate. I couldn't stop her."

Kellan ran out the gate and stopped, breathing hard. *Where? Where would she go?*

As he spun around, he realized that catching sight of her around the various hedges would be difficult. He heard Brigitte come up behind him.

His tone was urgent as he looked at her. "Where would she go?"

Brigitte shook her head. "I don't know. I saw her tears. What happened?"

Kellan just shook his head. "Later. We have to find her."

He ran back inside and called for their guards. Dispatching them was quicker than him searching alone. Tamek was still in the hall.

"Would someone mind telling me what is going on in my own house?"

Kellan gave him a serious look. "She didn't take it well. She rejected her banding, it came off, and she ran."

Tamek's face turned grim. "If we can find her, she'll have to be drugged. I highly doubt she'll come back willingly."

Kellan stayed silent, though he knew Tamek was right.

The Captain of the Guard showed up. The brothers gave him instructions, then headed toward the stables to grab their mounts.

Once they were in range, Tost informed Kellan of the area Isis had run to. Isis being without her saddle with an emotionally controlled rider was all the justification he needed to involve himself.

Tamek and Kellan saddled their *Storjen* and headed in that direction.

Kellan asked Tost, *Can you hear Isis?*

Tost replied, *No. She isn't answering my call.*

Kellan shouted the information to Tamek over the pounding hooves. After riding for a bit, they came to a fork. Left would lead to the field. Right toward town.

"Maybe she went to the field," Tamek suggested.

Kellan countered, "Or to the museum. If she believes the exhibits are still there, she might desire that connection." The fact she wasn't wearing her banding made him pray she hadn't gone toward town.

Since Kellan was the more experienced rider, and she was his claim, he rode for Stanlin's. Tamek went left toward the field. They agreed if he didn't find her, he would return and go toward town to meet up with his brother.

***

Tamek's mount began to run out of breath and let him know he needed to walk for a bit. Tamek allowed it, knowing Siana's mount would do the same. Since she didn't know the lay of the land, he assumed she would stay on the roads and paths leading to the field, since that is how they took her there. He could cut through the forest to catch up.

As he crested the hill, before the road led down to the field, he heard a noise. It sounded like a scream. He rushed down the hill, veering into the forest to cut some time off from his ride. As he drew close, he dismounted. His *storjen* was told to stay there. Moving slowly, he stayed hidden among the trees. His arm pushed the brush aside, and he could then see down toward the field. Isis, trying to protect her rider, rose her front hooves before descending as he watched. Beyond her, Talon had Siana with a knife at her throat, pulling her toward his mount. Tamek began pulling his sword before stopping himself, a plan formulating.

If it had been Stanlin, given the circumstances, Tamek could've killed him outright. That would've been one problem taken care of, but Talon was a different story. Talon was also a High and required handling through the Convocation, unless Tamek faced a direct threat.

Despite his earlier actions, now Talon won't risk his House. She's becoming known. She's close enough to the border for him to take her. He'll take her to the Convocation, because of her being on House Devereaux's lands and unbanded. Of course, he'll also implicate himself as a trespasser, unless he says she wasn't on their lands, but his. Either way, they'll focus on her first. He might use his hands improperly; however, she'll likely remain unharmed. Hopefully.

Tamek, feeling his mount's disapproval with his methods, quietly re-sheathed his sword. His plan was formulated. Kellan's forgiveness was unlikely, yet changing their laws presented a singular, momentous chance. What he didn't know wouldn't hurt him. Siana, yes; Kellan, no. Standing, he knew his *storjen's* ways of non-interference would apply, because Isis wasn't under threat, but his disapproval weighed heavily on Tamek.

While he climbed back on his mount, he waited for Talon to take her away, then he headed back. Part of him felt guilty. He cared for his new sister, but he told himself the end justified the means. One life for many others. Her sacrifice would pave the way for him to change laws affecting women. Hopefully, future generations would never experience what she would, and what Usala had endured.

Tamek's guilt grew as he watched Kellan pace his study. Brigitte and Mrs. Atwood were silently crying. Lorica kept glancing at Tamek, and the latter wondered how much the former knew. Lorica had guards everywhere, so it's possible he knew and approved Tamek's methods, hence his silence. After all, Lorica had wanted to do the same thing to Brigitte.

Tamek saw Talon abduct her, but couldn't reach her in time, he later informed others. It was almost the truth. Now they waited for the summons, which was why his brother was wearing a path in his rug. It took longer than Tamek expected. He wasn't sure why and was thinking he'd made a grave error when a house male knocked. Bidding him to enter, the page passed a missive to Tamek and left after being dismissed.

Reading it, Tamek said, "It's as we thought. Her claim is being challenged. We're to go before the Convocation." He continued reading. "Hm, *Bund* Montrose saw Talon with her and challenged as well. That's two petitions for her." *That explains the delay.*

He looked at Kellan, asking with a straight face, "Are you going to let her go? If so, we don't need to appear."

Kellan looked at him as if he'd lost his sanity. "No, I'm not letting either of them have her!"

Good. If he had given her up, it would have ruined the plan.

Lorica warned, "You know what may happen."

Kellan took an angry breath. "I know."

Tamek and everyone else knew that House Devereaux notoriously opposed this, even turning their chairs away when required to attend.

Kellan continued, "I also know we will have a plan before leaving this house."

Tamek said, "We must appear within two bells."

Kellan replied, "That should be enough time. If I can't stop it, I will have a back-up plan, though this could be the end of us."

Tamek understood he was referring to his marriage with Siana.

***

Terror gripped Siana. Isis hadn't been able to warn her of Talon's approach from behind in the field, because of Siana's loose connection to her. Though her mount tried to intervene, Talon's threat to Siana's life compelled her to yield. Although Siana urged her to get help, Isis stayed to observe Talon, awaiting an opportunity. Siana, realizing there was nothing they could do, finally ordered Isis to go.

After dragging her to his mount, Talon laid her across his lap, face down, as they journeyed to his waiting wagon, occasionally patting her rear. As she fought, she felt the knife pressing against her. She lay still. All she could see were his mount's hooves moving across a dirt trail. Her hands were on one side, her legs the other. She couldn't get her hands back to get her knife. She'd started carrying it after finding it in her pack, tying it to her thigh.

She knew he'd been poaching again. Lorica had once told her Talon liked to take their shel. Soon, a small wagon came into view.

To carry his theft?

She yelled for the driver to help. Talon laughed. The driver ignored her and began driving once she'd been tossed into the back. Talon gave him an order, and the man veered right onto a roadway. Talon knocked her to the floor of the wagon and fell on top of her.

While he held the knife to her throat, using his body to pin her down, he grabbed her breast, squeezing until she cried out in pain. He grabbed through her clothes and squeezed between her legs, telling her how much he was going to enjoy hearing her scream.

"What's this?" He felt her knife tied to her thigh. Yanking it off, which she knew would leave a bruise, he held it up within her view. "Aw, poor female. It didn't do you any good, did it?" He tossed it out of the wagon.

She really wanted to wipe that awful smile from his face.

He kept assaulting her with his hand until they reached town. By then, she believed he would rape and kill her in the wagon.

I shouldn't have run.

When she decided it would be better to die by his knife than by his body, and was about to force her neck into it, he rose and pulled her into a sitting position. She realized why he stopped. They passed a male child. He was dirty and wearing ragged clothing. He smiled and waved at them as they passed, and Talon threatened to cut his throat if she didn't behave and made her wave back at the boy with a smile.

"Stroke me."

She looked at him in confusion.

"Ah, that's right. You're simple. Your hand on me. Now."

He grabbed her hand, bending it around the front of his trousers, forcing her hand to move. Briefly thinking about ripping it off—or at least breaking it—she saw the child still waving at them as they passed and instead obeyed.

His mouth sighed against her ear. "That's it. Good girl."

She wanted to scream, to rip that knife from his hand and bury it in his throat.

After a few strokes, he said, "You can stop. I want to enjoy it when we have more time."

As the child faded from view, he said, "Maybe I'll go back and see if he has a sister. Can you picture it? Me claiming a female about his age?" He grabbed her hand, putting it on his hardness, forcing her to stroke it again. "Feel that? Behave or I'll make you watch."

Siana almost gagged at the image. *This man is truly evil.* Rarely did she want to kill anyone, but if given the chance— she wouldn't hesitate. Right as she decided breaking it would be worth the risk of dying, the wagon pulled up to a two-story building made of imposing gray stone, the silence broken only by the crunch of gravel under the wheels. Spires rose on each corner of the roof, multi-paned windows spaced across the front. Grand wood doors topped a long front staircase. It was located away from the other town buildings, at the end of the main road. It was like one of her world's town halls.

He put the knife away, seized her arm as she struggled, and dragged her inside. Guards appeared. He spoke to them so fast she had trouble following. Two guards, their armor gleaming, flanked her, took her from him, each gripping an arm gently, and led her through echoing stone halls. At one point, she tried to break free, to run, but their grips were immovable.

They led her to a room where she was locked in what looked like a prison cell. A simple small bed was in the corner, a thin blanket covering it. A single wooden chair at a table was near the top at the side, the toilet tube was at the foot of the bed, a basket of cloths next to it. That was all. There wasn't a lot of floor space either.

Shortly afterward, a woman arrived. Siana observed two guards by the entrance through the open doorway. The woman offered her some food and water. Siana accepted the water but refused the rest. She tried to ask what was happening, but the woman ignored her, put the food on the table, and left. Siana settled into the worn wooden chair, taking deep breaths to steady her racing heart. Not knowing what was happening, the silence heavy with anticipation, made the wait agonizingly long. Soon, two guards entered, their faces impassive, and escorted her to a large, cold room.

The room resembled a college lecture hall, complete with tiered seating arranged in a U shape, each desk neatly placed for optimal viewing. The door opened into the bottom of the U shape, desks on either side, a cool draft brushing her face as she entered. Across from the door was a dais; on it was an ornate wooden table. Behind the table, in matching chairs, were five men. A larger, more ornate chair occupied the center.

As she moved forward, she saw Talon standing before the dais, but another large man stood beside him, a strange, unsettling sight that made her heart pound in her chest.

Who is that?

From the larger chair on the dais, a man with white hair and a wizened face peered down at her. "You are of House Devereaux?"

Unsure of what was happening, she answered, "Yes."

He nodded as he looked at the men beside her. "These males have petitioned to claim you as you are unbanded. Do you have anything to say?"

She understood his intent, if not all his words, so she said, "I am Kellan Devereaux's claim."

The men on the dais looked puzzled. They questioned Talon, and he answered.

Siana took a chance, guessing he was lying when she heard him say something about his land. She said, "That's a lie."

Everyone in the room turned to look at her, their eyes curious and questioning.

"I was on House Devereaux's land. He"—she pointed at Talon—"was there and took me." Unfortunately, she didn't know the word for "trespassing."

Talon said she was mistaken. She refuted it.

With a sudden, sharp intake of breath, the other man said, "Sirs! If he has lied, then my petition for the claim should be honored."

Siana understood enough to know he wanted her. She was not having it. Glaring at all of them, finally getting her emotions under control, she was firm. "No, I am Kellan's."

"Where is Doctor Devereaux's banding?" one of the other men on the dais asked.

Looking at him, she didn't like him. His face was like a rat's. Even his brown hair stuck out at the sides like whiskers, hiding his ears.

"We had a fight. I was angry. My banding came off. I ran out of the house. Kellan needs to put back on." She was cursing her inability to fully express herself.

Before anyone could say anything else, the man in the middle—who'd been writing during this time—held out a folded letter to one guard. He went up a small flight of stairs off to the side and took it.

"Deliver this to House Devereaux."

Talon objected. The man turned from the guard, addressed him, stating, "She's refuted your claims. Doctor Devereaux along with *Bund* Devereaux must answer. This is the law. Or would you like to argue with me?"

Siana watched Talon's face pale. A guard was told to take her back; then, they recessed until House Devereaux arrived.

Chapter Thirty-Seven

IT FELT LIKE HOURS to Siana, and it was close to being that long. More than an hour passed since her stomach urged her to eat the remaining food. She'd heard a bell from one of their timepieces.

How long is the journey? Worry gnawed at her. *Maybe he's upset with me? Was my act of throwing his ring a sign of deep disrespect?*

The thought of him giving her to one of those men terrified her. Though she knew he wouldn't, the possibility played with her mind. The door opened shortly afterward, and Brigitte walked in with a small basket trailed by Kellan. Seeing them relieved her. She ran toward them but stopped upon seeing their expressions.

With an apology, she spoke, rushing her words, "I'm so sorry. I throw ring angry. I not mean to hurt you. I was afraid. I wanted to go back to my home—"

Kellan cut in, saying, "I know."

Their looks worried her.

Kellan's nostrils flared as his eyes examined her. His hand reached out, turning her face side to side, then, releasing her, he visually examined the rest of her. He finished, his face showing suppressed fury.

"I not able to stop him." Siana thought he was mad at her.

Kellan shook his head. "I'm not angry at you. That *blotzen...*" He took a deep breath. "Listen to me."

First, he told her about Talon the best he could. Tamek opposed Talon's petition. With a legal limit of one claim, his three claims were already too many. Talon's younger brother's claim had died, as had the other three Talon claimed. The implication was clear. For Siana's safety, being she was under their House, Tamek asked to deny Talon's petition. He didn't expect her to pick him, Tamek just wanted to get back at him for his previous behavior and prevent future claims from dying. Unexpectedly, they granted Tamek's request. Talon's tantrum only ended when the exasperated High Chancellor ordered him to be quiet or leave. To see House Devereaux subjected to their aversion, Talon cooperated.

Only *Bund* Montrose's petition remained. Other than Kellan's examination results, they lacked any usable evidence against it. He was, truthfully, respectable. The petition remained valid, and that was the problem.

She feared asking. "You told them I was your claim?"

"Yes."

"So, we go home now." *Thank goodness!* She let out a sigh of relief.

"No." Brigitte's forced smile and shaky breath didn't fool Siana; she knew Brigitte was barely holding it together.

"What is it?" *Something's wrong.*

Brigitte shook her head and looked at Kellan, eyes pleading.

Kellan gave a sharp exhale. "Your appearance is mandatory at the Convocation. You'll need to select and declare your choice..."

"You." Her voice was firm

"Then..." He hesitated.

"Then what?" she asked.

He was obviously trying to find the right words.

"Kellan said no," Brigitte said, voice shaking. "He told them of your small size, that you're going to get hurt. He fight for you."

"I do not understand." *Why would he need to fight for me?*

His voice raspy, Kellan declared, "I must claim you in that room. Convocation watch."

With horrified disbelief, Siana stared at him.

"No, I'll die," she said. *With others watching?*

"I will tell you the truth. If they give you to Montrose, then yes, you will die, but with me, you maybe won't."

Stepping toward her, he took her hands in his. Taking a breath, he told her what he did at the camp, then added, "It will hurt, but I have an oil to help your opening not feel it much."

She protested, betrayal plain on her face, pulling her hands away. "It's not fair!"

She dreaded public humiliation before those men, and now having to cope with what Kellan did to her at the camp. She couldn't breathe. Kellan's hand reached out, but she recoiled, unease washing over her. Her breaths came in gasps as she fought back tears.

"You're right. It's not fair. I don't like it either and don't want to hurt you. I want you to be protected from other males. My care is for you."

She looked at him disbelievingly.

"There's more."

She gave a sarcastic laugh. "Of course there is," she said in English.

"The Convocation makes laws at the Hall. Say no, and Montrose will take you. Your life will end."

Great. "You say no," she told him, her eyes pleading.

His face full of sadness, he stated, "I can't. If I say no, we lose everything. Losing everything prevents us from changing the laws. We're all going to be homeless—that includes Yon, Brigitte, and Mrs. Atwood. The camps will be gone. It won't matter. You still go to Montrose."

Well, this just keeps getting better and better. Again, she understood his meaning, if not all the words.

She saw Kellan's unwillingness. He looked torn. Despair on his face spilled over into his voice. While she didn't agree with what he did, at its most basic level, she understood now, facing what was to come. That didn't mean she forgave him.

Walking back to him, she grabbed the front of his shirt. "Kellan, please." Her words were barely audible.

The idea of being violated and possibly killed in front of those men disgusted her. A single tear rolled down onto the back of her hand. "I will use those things again, please. Please, we go home."

Although she despised begging, she had no other options.

Brigitte turned away, but not before Siana saw her tears.

***

Sadly, he shook his head. "Please forgive me. We've run out of time."

He remembered Tess's comment about not regretting it. She was right. He felt a deep, honest regret at that very moment. It was better for Siana to hate him than to endure this. He should have sedated and claimed her back then. He sat on the bed and drew her near. Leaning into her, he felt her distressed heart pounding against his shoulder as her hands rested on them.

"We do this. They say you claimed. We go home."

"I not want do this," she mumbled, her voice trembling with fear.

Standing, drawing her close again, he took her face in his hands, his thumbs brushing her cheeks, looking into her terrified eyes. "Neither do I. We don't have a choice. If I say no, they'll give you to him. They will tie you down, or have guards hold you for him. He won't mean to, but he will kill you."

She shook her head in denial, her eyes begging. "Maybe do other things."

Brigitte, teary-eyed, voice breaking, told them, "Enough talk. They will call for you soon. Siana, you be claimed. You can't say no. You must pick one. No more waiting."

In desperation, Siana clung to Kellan, burying her face in him.

Though he tried to be gentle, Brigitte was correct—their time was running out. Brigitte offered the basket so he could reach inside. He pulled out a bottle, took off the top, hesitated, took a deep breath, and drank it. It supported him in case of physical failure so he could fulfill his obligations. They gave it to people who might have issues doing it publicly in such cases as his. Hurting her bothered him far more than being watched. Siana's face stayed hidden in his shirt.

He eased her away and instructed, "Please take off your undergarment and shoes. From the waist down, should be nothing but your dress. Place them in this basket." Pulling out a small bottle, he handed it to her. "This will help stop the pain. Put it in and around your opening. It will be hot at first, but then you won't feel it."

He knew whatever she didn't understand, Brigitte would explain. "Also, you must not speak your language. No matter what. They will take you. I don't know what they will do. Only speak *Setan*."

A fearful gasp escaped her. "I not do this. My home not do."

Kellan's finger, warm and firm, lifted her chin, making her gaze meet his. "This is your home now. You must follow the laws. You can do this. Be strong. Don't let them see you cry. Don't let them have that." He wasn't sure she heard, as she stood staring at him, her face refusing to accept this was her lot.

Releasing her jaw, he soothed them both by stroking her upper arms. He explained the process. By her head, Tamek and Lorica would offer their help. They wouldn't watch. Helping her cope was their central aim. They're mainly moral support for both.

He inhaled again and told her, "It's not just the Convocation. They have called the *Bund*."

"All watching me be forced? I'm going to be sick," she said, holding a hand to her stomach.

He felt similar. Kellan also wanted it to end. Being forced to do something he'd hidden females from made him ill and angry. He was fairly shaking with rage. Kellan instructed her to remove the clothing items, and he would wait outside while she applied the oil *liberally*. He stressed that. Soon, when it was time, he would be back. He left, praying that what they did in the camp would keep her from dying.

***

After he left, Siana turned to Brigitte. "What do I do?" She was hoping her friend had some words of wisdom.

Brigitte's broken words were, "Get it over with, so we can go home. I only came for you."

"You come with me?" She was hoping for a woman's support.

"I can't. It's not allowed. I won't leave and will wait for you after it's done," she reassured her. When Siana didn't move, she began helping her remove the clothing she was required to take off.

Sia's breathing sped up as she realized this was going to happen. Her hands trembled as she followed Kellan's instructions, her heart pounding in her chest. She focused on slowing her pulse, her chest tightening as she fought to regain composure, battling a rising tide of fear.

I survived being hunted by bots. I can survive this.

The thought didn't last long. Fear consumed her as she waited for Kellan to come back. A wave of panic washed over Siana as the door opened.

This can't be happening.

Siana nearly lost it when Kellan appeared at her side and put his arm around her. He slipped her ring back on her finger and then used his own to activate it. As it coiled around Siana once more, he grasped her other hand and headed for the door. Though she remained still, the surrounding arm propelled her forward.

"No." It was whispered.

"You must," he said quietly. "We must."

His arm remained around her. His words of encouragement, whispered as they left, were for him and her.

The cold stone floor chilled her feet as she walked. Her legs trembled, threatening to give way beneath her. The acrid taste of bile burned her throat, a metallic tang that made her nauseous. A wave of terror, reminiscent of the first bot attack, washed over her; her heart pounded a frantic rhythm against her ribs. Part of her was glad for Kellan's strong arm around her, a comforting weight against her side. She was afraid she'd fall without it.

Reaching the end of the short hall, they turned left, the low light revealing two figures, their faces solemn, waiting for them. She turned to run, but Kellan's arm stopped her.

"They will catch you before you leave town," he whispered. "They will think you not like me. They will give you to Montrose. You will die."

A small whimper escaped as she turned back around and continued their walk to her possible death.

Chapter Thirty-Eight

THEIR FACES CAUSED TAMEK regret. To use them so had slowly filled him with self-hatred; however, all efforts by his House had failed to move the Convocation or the *Bund* to alter the laws. They had to be profoundly affected by something significant. His thoughts and emotions, while not showing on his face, warred within him. He wanted to stop it but continued. He had to save them all.

***

House Devereaux's public claim pleased Lorica initially. He always supported them and was furious when Brigitte refused. Other claims went into the room with stoic faces. While they were familiar with these laws from childhood, many, Brigitte among them, found them objectionable. Those being coerced were told by their coercers not to shed tears. Their training emphasized silence and obedience during the act. The males who cared for their claims didn't do it publicly. That was one reason Brigitte had refused him. She felt he didn't care. He'd also blindsided her.

He felt a little uneasy seeing the terror on Siana's face. She showed a level of fear never witnessed in a female. As she approached, her tears increased. He was uncomfortable, so when she arrived, he kindly said, "Pull yourself together."

After a rebuke to Lor, Tamek gently advised Siana, "Allow your emotions to surface. Don't hold them back. Make sure they see your suffering. It's okay to be scared; let your fear be seen."

Lorica was now positive Tamek wanted Siana to break down in front of everyone. He knew no one could stop it. Once ordered, the law required completion. Lorica knew Kellan had told the Convocation she was a defective *Setan*. They hadn't listened, believing he was exaggerating to keep her because of his injuries. He had argued as much as he could without overstepping, but they made the proclamation. Kellan's face when he realized he had no choice tore at Lorica.

Tamek and Lorica faced the double doors before them. The sound of a low sob stopped them short as the doors opened. They composed themselves before entering, with the couple following behind.

***

Not only were there guards stationed around the room, but about fifteen men at desks were also watching them as they entered. She noticed the varying colors of their dress, which was similar to the House Devereaux outfits.

Silence filled the room. No one moved. She stifled another sob, noticing at least four or more people turned their chairs away to support House Devereaux. Her crying surprised several of them. Others smirked or leered, obviously enjoying the show at her expense. Talon, now wearing his House colors of red and yellow, joined them. Following that, she avoided looking at any of them.

As she neared the room's center, the sight of the table made her legs want to give way. It had a short, rectangular, almost square shape. Two distinct uses existed for the front leg rests: they moved up and out, or down and out. A pillow, unbelievably, occupied the space for her head. Someone lowered the table's arm restraints near the pillow to the side. Tamek and Lorica, at the head, made the restraints unnecessary for her.

***

Kellan had offered her two options: lie on her back or bend over the table. He proposed she lean over, despite what Talon did, because he could keep more of her covered, and it would help prevent him from going too far in. She could also hide her face if she wanted, and from what Brigitte said, it would help her feel less exposed. It also kept her hidden from him. He wasn't sure he could go through with it if he saw her face.

Someone had already set the leg rests to their bending position. The cushioned knee rests were adjustable to accommodate a female's body. With her kneeling, Kellan would secure her legs, tightening the straps on her thighs. It was optional, but he didn't inform her. He knew she would attempt to flee as soon as he started. He only wanted to hurt her as much as was unavoidable. Even that made him feel nauseous.

Her gaze glued to it, a louder whimper escaped her as they drew closer. Kellan's arm tightened around her. He leaned down, whispering, "You're not alone. I love you." He wanted her to know it—just in case, though he prayed the work they'd done at camp was enough. If not—he didn't want to think about it.

***

Wow, could you have picked a worse time to say it?

She couldn't respond. Fear kept her from speaking, lest she unleash a torrent of screams upon them. Her respect for the nearby men, and Talon's smirking observation, prevented her from doing so. She most definitely wouldn't give that ass the satisfaction.

Tamek and Lorica circled the table, positioning themselves on the opposite side where her head would lie. Kellan moved behind her, releasing his hold. Big, rasping breaths from her echoed in the large room. The fear she felt caused several *Bund* to shift in their seats. A loud roar filled her ears. As she swayed, Kellan steadied her, giving her arms a supportive squeeze.

The High Chancellor rose to his feet, clearing his throat, his face showing his regret at his own decision.

"Siana belonging to House Devereaux. You are under their protection?"

Kellan had warned her about the questions, so she would know their meaning even if she didn't understand the words themselves.

Siana, turning her head to the right to see the man asking, nodded, tears streaming down her face.

"You have a petition for your claim from *Bund* Montrose. Doctor Kellan Devereaux presented evidence of your marriage, despite your lack of banding. Is that correct or a lie?"

Her voice was barely above a whisper as she answered, "Correct."

"Has your body been claimed by Doctor Devereaux to seal your marriage?"

Kellan had warned her to be honest. If they thought she was lying, they would check her. Proof would send her to Montrose. With his hands rubbing her arms in support, she fought to stay composed. Her shaking intensified.

A choked "No" escaped her lips. Control was slipping from her grasp.

"Do you still wish to be claimed by Doctor Devereaux, or would you prefer your claim to be switched to *Bund* Montrose?"

Is he seriously asking me who I want to be raped by?

"I am Kellan's." She could barely get the words out, knowing either choice sealed her doom.

"It is the Convocation's decision that, to protect the female Siana Devereaux from further petitions, she will have a public claiming to seal her marriage and prove to the petitioner that she has been fully claimed." He nodded at Kellan to proceed.

***

Tamek detested himself. He regretted it more than words could express. The plan and the reality were worlds apart. Had Usala been here, he knew she would have been extremely disappointed and angry at him. In addition, he was a hypocrite. He opposed claiming at first, but now he used the situation to his advantage, cleverly orchestrating events. He knew that more was about to come.

A quick look at the Convocation showed him the High Chancellor's displeasure. Sadness showed on his face as he watched. Unable to avert his gaze, he was duty-bound to witness the event. Doubly so since he himself had ordered it. No matter how much he may want to change his mind, he couldn't. Tamek knew the male was remembering the olden days and no longer felt this was necessary. Despite his status, he remained bound by the law, as did everyone else.

***

As he noticed some of the leering looks, Lorica couldn't help but imagine Brigitte instead of Siana. He comprehended little by little. The terror on her face, the public humiliation of not only her, but their House because of his brothers' stance—his anger rose. Anger at Tamek's complicity. Anger at Talon for being where he shouldn't be. Upset with Siana about the banding removal. Upset with Kellan for not sedating her and getting it done beforehand to prevent her from experiencing this. Too late, he felt remorse for the order he'd given to the female he loved.

I'm so sorry, Bri. I have no way to fix it.

***

Kellan leaned down, took a deep breath, and tapped her left knee gently. She did not move. Once more, he repeated the action, this time stroking it. She lifted it, letting him guide it into place. He wanted to take her and flee because of her trembling, but he knew that would worsen the situation. Together, they faced this hellish predicament neither could escape from.

He repeated the process for her right leg, using his body to steady her as she knelt. Her gaze was focused on the table. It rattled from the force of her shaking and echoed around the room. Kellan heard the scrape of chair legs on the floor as more *Bund* turned away, their only way to object to proceedings.

The brothers realized the table was too high. The guards had set the table for a *Setan* female. Simultaneously, Tamek and Lorica moved to their sides, pressed their buttons, the metallic click echoing in the room as the platform glided down to a position just below her upper thighs. This position would arch her back and allow Kellan greater freedom of movement and control. Once finished, they moved back to the head.

***

Siana stared at the table. She avoided her face from both observing and being observed. Tamek whispered her name, eliciting no response. His louder repetition made her raise her begging eyes to him alone. With his right hand raised, palm out, he gestured toward her left hand with a nod.

I don't want to do this.

She put the palm of her left hand against his and intertwined fingers. Lorica held his left hand up. She raised her right, and they repeated it to his side. She was causing their arms to shake.

I don't want to be here.

When Kellan gave her a soft push between her shoulder blades, she resisted, whispering, "I can't. I can't do this." Tamek and Lorica glanced at each other with worried expressions.

Kellan leaned close to her ear, muttering, "Me or Montrose."

Someone save me.

Another whimper escaped her. She bent over gradually, her eyes glued to the table. The brothers knelt, matching her movements and holding her hands as she bent. From behind, Kellan held onto her.

With her head turned to the side and all four elbows on the table, she lay down as the brothers knelt. Siana buried her face in her arm. She didn't want it to be seen by anyone. To better support her head, Tamek, using his free hand, readjusted the cushion.

Jacob, help me. You always protected me.

***

Kellan carefully hitched her skirt enough to get his hand under it. The ragged gasps for air, harsh and rasping, emanating from her, caused a wave of concerned murmurs to wash over the room.

He reached into his pocket, withdrew a small, dark bottle of oil, and carefully oiled three fingers. He knew she had used the numbing oil, but he wanted more. In fact, he'd like to empty the entire bottle into her. Normally, the rules prohibited any helpful aids unless a specific need existed. His special permission stemmed from her classification as "defective," a designation that opened doors to actions otherwise forbidden. Their hypocrisy angered him. They felt he exaggerated, yet they allowed the oil.

"Please don't do this."

He barely heard her desperate whisper, but he knew they had no choice. He saw Tamek lean over her, talking. Lorica stared down at her head.

With care, Kellan reached under her skirt to discover her opening. After blindly searching, he found it and slipped two fingers in. He manipulated it, trying to extend it as far as possible. While making sure her skirt stayed in place, Kellan inserted a third finger deeper than he had planned. Another whimper preceded her earnest, unrestrained sobbing.

***

Get me out of here.

Upon feeling his hand, a tense whimper escaped Siana's lips. Kellan's fingers entering caused her to cry out in fear. Lorica and Tamek leaned forward, simultaneously shielding her from view and offering words of encouragement, urging her to relax her body.

Someone help me. Why won't they stop this?

***

A member of the Convocation—rat face—called out, "Just claim her already!" He received a few glares from the others. The claiming was usually uneventful; however, the female's clear fear made many viewers shift uneasily.

Unfortunately, the High Chancellor said, "Doctor Devereaux, I understand your desire to help her, but you've already had time to prepare her once you married her. Please claim her and put the poor female out of her suspense."

Lorica glanced up; Kellan gave a slight nod as he loosened his trousers. Lorica surreptitiously lowered his hand into his pocket and pulled out a *Wotal*-soaked cloth. They had discussed it, and no one wanted her to feel the injuries that may cause her death. It was a risk, as it was against the law to drug her, but they did it cautiously. Tamek and he were to use their bodies to obstruct the *Bunds'* view while Lorica covered her nose and mouth with the cloth. Females rarely made noise, so her silence wouldn't be suspect. Tamek, however, stayed still.

He'd previously moved to the side. If Lorica made the attempt, the *Bund* would witness it, causing Siana to go to Montrose.

"Tamek," he hissed under his breath.

Tamek continued to talk to Siana, seemingly not hearing him. Lorica faced certain detection. He suspected Tamek was doing this on purpose and vowed he'd regret it.

Lorica, glancing at Kellan's face, saw the realization dawn. He couldn't sedate her because Tamek wasn't paying attention. He saw the anger rise in Kellan's eyes, his fists clenching as if he wanted to punch something. She was going to feel it all. Kellan now had no option. Lorica watched his brother hold back tears as he prepared to possibly kill the female he loved. Lorica turned away, not wanting to see his brother's emotional pain, his own internal struggles over Brigitte and himself coming to a head.

***

Where's the hero who is supposed to save me?

Though Siana recognized it was only his fingers, she couldn't relax or stop her body from tensing. Tamek's quiet voice in her ear reassured her they were almost finished. Kellan had to enter her until he could not anymore, signaling the end. He urged her to breathe through it. Sadly, she only understood a little of what he said. Siana partly wanted Kellan to finish, but she remembered his warning about the pain. The anticipation was agonizing.

Does anyone care?

Siana detected him seeking, then entering her, her skin expanding. She felt thankful for the oil. Until now, she hadn't felt much. That thought was quickly followed by the start of a fire. The sensation was like being doused in extremely hot water.

I don't want this.

***

He hadn't gone far before he felt her stretch. A cry escaped her lips. He continued. As her opening stretched to its absolute limit, her cries intensified. Simultaneously, her cry of pain and his feeling of her tearing occurred. He had the urge to set the Hall ablaze with everyone still inside, to whisk her away, but he knew the others would surely give her over, and she would die. In order to try to save her, he couldn't stop.

***

The intensity of the burning amplified. She felt as though someone poured scalding water onto and into her. She was as wide as she could be. The absence of his body touching her or the warmth behind her suggested he was nowhere near. He would actually tear her apart. She was going to die.

I want to go home.

He pushed himself into her a bit more, and she felt the first one. Pressed against the table, she felt and heard her own tear, the internal sound exacerbating her emotional and physical pain. She instinctively squeezed the hands she was holding tighter, feeling one briefly give way under the pressure before moving back.

Why is this happening?

***

Kellan faced a brutal choice: a quick, tearing rip that would end her time swiftly, or a slower, more agonizing process that would prolong her suffering, yet keep injuries to a minimum. The sounds of her cries haunted his decision. He stayed with slower, hoping to minimize the damage. The sound of her sobs, raw and heartbreaking, filled his eyes and soul with tears, but Kellan pressed on. In his peripheral, he saw his brothers wince but pushed it out of his mind. He had to complete the claim.

***

The situation became unbearable, reaching a point that was too much for her. It was excruciating, likened to butcher knives cutting through her genitals. A wave of agonizing pain washed over her as she tore more, leaving no doubt in her mind: Stanlin had been right. This was the end. Raw, agonizing cries built to a heart-wrenching crescendo.

Let me out.

The urge to flee was overwhelming; she had to get away. Away from this place. Away from them. Away from death. With cries of agony, she fought against the intense pain that ripped through her hips. Struggling with all her strength, she clawed and scratched to escape their hold. She felt the weight on her back, a heavy pressure holding her immobile.

Her pain-filled screams became louder. "Stop, it hurts. Please! Kellan. Please, stop!"

Someone kill me.

***

Lorica was pretty sure she broke his hand, but he ignored it. He and Tamek braced themselves as they carefully held her down, their hands gentle but firm on her arms, preventing her from hurting herself or Kellan any further. Both feeling the weight of her struggles pressing down on them. Her shout tore at and concerned them.

Tamek, face heavy with guilt, ordered Kellan, "Finish it!"

All knew if she used her language, their secret would be revealed. The *Bund* began murmuring loudly.

***

More tearing. The pain was unlike anything she'd ever felt; a searing, white-hot agony that forced a scream from deep within her soul. A gentle hand touched her face, its touch featherlight. Lightheaded and weak, she felt the warm wetness of her wound and knew she would not survive. She allowed herself to rush toward the darkness. She would take anything to escape the sharp, stabbing pain.

I'm dying.

***

Unable to bear her screams any longer, Kellan pushed himself into her, pushing the limits of how little he could enter her without the Convocation discovering. That he told them she was defective would work in his favor. Despite not fully entering her, he felt her body tearing even more.

The final, ear-splitting scream, a raw, desperate sound filled with agony, ended as suddenly as it began, leaving a stunned silence in its wake. She moved briefly, then was still. Silence filled the room, heavy and thick. No female had ever fainted or let out a scream that piercing.

One of the *Bund* asked in shock, "Dear me, man, did you kill her?"

Kellan's voice trembled with fear as he answered honestly. "I don't know."

Hushed voices filled with worry and apprehension began murmuring to one another.

Chapter Thirty-Nine

KELLAN LIFTED THE SECTION of her skirt closest to the dais, so the Convocation could see—those who were watching, two had already turned away in disgust—the High Chancellor paled, his face draining of color as he saw the crimson stain spreading, oozing from between their bodies and down her legs, dripping onto the floor. He gave Kellan a brief nod. Kellan withdrew, hastily pulled his trousers together, avoiding eye contact with anyone as he ignored the blood staining his clothing. Quickly, he and his brothers removed the restraints and lifted her body from the table.

Please don't be dead. Please don't be dead.

The words, repeated like a mantra, filled his soul as he lifted her, her limp weight heavy in his arms; her head rested on his chest as he carried her quickly toward the doors, the sound of his own heartbeat pounding in his ears.

Lorica stopped him long enough to put her arms onto her own stomach, so they wouldn't hit on the doorways, and put the cloth over her nose and mouth to help keep her from waking too soon. To Kellan's relief, he whispered she was drugged, not unconscious or dead from the act. He knew she could still bleed to death if he didn't get her out of there.

Kellan heard one of the Convocation yell at him that he was not dismissed. The High Chancellor's disturbed voice told him to be quiet. It wasn't a law, so Kellan ignored the first speaker.

As the guards opened the doors to prepare for him leaving, he vaguely heard the High Chancellor say, "In accordance with our laws, the Convocation and *Bund* of the Great Hall have borne witness to *Bund* Doctor Kellan Devereaux"—the Hall erupted into chaos at him being restored to his societal position—"has claimed and sealed his marriage to *Bunda* Siana Devereaux. It has been officially proclaimed and thus recorded."

A collective gasp escaped Lorica and Tamek as they stared, utterly stunned.

"Silence!" the High Chancellor called out. "This does not mean he has been restored to the Head of the House. That title remains under *Bund* Tamek Devereaux."

***

Lorica jogged after Kellan. A sharp, searing pain shot through his hand, but he gritted his teeth, reminding himself it was nothing compared to the ordeal she endured. He cursed Tamek inwardly, a burning resentment coiling in his gut. He knew he'd done it deliberately; the weight of his actions settled heavily on him, though he doubted his brother grasped to what extent the physical and mental damage would be. Lorica, not caring if caught, had chanced sedating her, though no one noticed being too busy talking among themselves about her screams.

He went around Kellan. The Hall alley door slammed open, the sound echoing in the stillness, and Lorica emerged with an inscrutable expression, followed closely by Kellan carrying the limp form of Siana. As he swung her around to get through the doorway, crimson drops followed her.

Brigitte's fearful voice choked out, "Is she...?"

***

Kellan's voice was tight with urgency as he rushed Siana to a nest of blankets and cushions laid out in anticipation of her arrival; the air was thick with worry.

"She's alive," Kellan said, his voice strained, "but heavily sedated. We must get her to the infirmary immediately!"

Lorica jumped in the back, his feet thudding on the wood, and helped Kellan bring her in to lie on the blankets. Gently laying her down, Kellan sat back on his heels at her feet, the rough wood of the wagon side pressing against his leg while Lorica closed the back. While he had little room to fully check her injuries, he needed to stop the bleeding as much as he could.

Having Brigitte and Lorica each hold a leg, though Lorica struggled with only one hand, they pulled their respective limbs up and out enough for Kellan to see. He didn't want them pulling too far in case more injuries occurred. Lorica respectfully averted his gaze.

Kellan reached for the soft, neatly folded cloths Brigitte had packed in a nearby woven basket. The sight of so much blood caused a surge of violent anger toward the source, which he realized was himself.

With a sharp cry, Lorica impatiently demanded, "Let's go!" to the driver. They felt the wagon lurch as he began the drive, moving as fast as he could, the tall sides hiding them from outside view.

Kellan frantically grabbed the cloths, the fabric brushing against his skin as he applied all his strength to stop the relentless flow of blood. He had to fight to be "doctor" and not "mate" as he watched her blood soak through. Switching the soiled cloth for a fresh one, he observed with dismay as the clean fabric, too, became stained a deep, alarming red.

After what felt like an eternity, but was only minutes, they arrived at the infirmary's back door. A tense silence replaced the sound of the wagon's wheels. The heavy wood door swung inward with a loud creak as Tess threw it open, clearly having heard the wagon, the antiseptic scent of the medical office immediately wafting out. Tess had everything waiting per Kellan's instructions. Everyone rushed to Siana's side, carefully lifting her from the wagon, their concern evident in their quiet movements. Kellan took her and carried her inside.

With the utmost care, he placed her on the worn wooden table. Lorica, Tess, and Brigitte followed, their hands moving with efficiency as they positioned her limbs in the rests. Kellan did the last. He told them to secure the restraints in case she woke up fighting—if she woke. Tess and Brigitte both moved the leg rests into position—blanching when they could see the damage—while Kellan scrubbed his hands and arms for surgery.

With a final adjustment of the stool, Kellan sat between her legs, his heart pounding, and took a deep breath to steady his racing pulse. As Tess carefully manipulated the surgical tools to keep Siana's passage open, the team found Brigitte's extra pair of hands were essential. She pulled the hose carrying cool, boiled water, starting the gentle rinsing of Siana—a soothing contrast to the visible injuries Kellan had to examine. It allowed Kellan to see her injuries clearly.

He picked up the first needle, its smooth surface cool against his fingertips. Blood steadily welled up again and again; he had to work fast to stem the tide. There were several small tears he ignored. He focused on the one whose bleeding was the most profuse, a sickening, crimson flow. He found it and was relieved; the damage was less severe than he expected, a sigh of relief escaping his lips.

While he knew the searing pain was horrible, a sharp, throbbing agony, it wasn't life-threatening unless he couldn't stop the bleeding.

Her anger and feelings of betrayal will make her hate me.

With a determined frown, he pushed the thought away and concentrated on the delicate stitching, his fingers nimble, as he repaired the tears in his love.

Lorica was assigned to keep her sedated under Tess's instruction, the silence of the room amplifying the gravity of the assignment. He did so without complaint.

***

Tamek waited until the room settled. He sensed vulnerability, grief, confusion—the perfect moment. He slowly looked around the room, his gaze lingering on each man, making eye contact with every one of them. Talon's disdain was evident as he stared back, his expression a mask of pure contempt.

The others quieted, the weight of his continued presence in the center heavy in the air, as they prepared to complete the session. A few were talking about needing to talk to their own claims about today. They wanted to know if this was how the females felt. Many found the experience upsetting and wished to avoid similar occurrences. When they realized they were the only ones speaking, they sat and quieted.

When Tamek had their attention, he walked around the table, looking at it.

He lifted the cushion, its fabric clinging damply to his fingers. "It's wet," he said. "From her tears, her fear, the pain she endured."

Walking around, he fingered the blood-splattered leg restraints and asked, "What must it feel like to be exposed in front of strange males? To be torn apart like nothing. Being tied down and forced into mating is the harsh reality of the situation. It's what we do."

A voice, raspy and unpleasant, cut through the silence from the dais. "They consent!"

A gasp escaped Tamek's lips as he stared at him, his disbelief palpable in the sudden silence. "Do they? You all know Kellan is smaller because of injury. Look what happened," he said, pointing at the crimson pool spreading across the floor. "What would've happened had Montrose claimed her? Siana had but one choice to consent to: which male would kill her? The only decision she could make was choosing who would inflict serious harm on her, or worse, end her life. The same goes for many other of our females."

Bund Montrose loudly protested, "I didn't know. I honestly thought *Bund* Doctor Devereaux had exaggerated to keep her. Her screams will forever haunt me. I'm glad I was denied. The thought that I could have killed her..." The events obviously rattled the male.

Tamek whipped around to face him. "Isn't that the point? How many of us know whether we will kill our claims as my brother just did to his?" He knew she was still alive when she'd left the building. He had seen the cloth. "How many of you forced a claim on that very table"—he flung his hand at it—"not knowing whether she'd die? What's truly awful is that this Convocation knew."

The Hall filled with murmuring. A hush fell over the crowd as the High Chancellor, his voice ringing with authority, called for quiet.

Tamek paced the room, hands clasped behind his back, his footsteps echoing in the otherwise silent space. Turning, he pointed an accusing finger at the dais. "My brother told you she may not survive. Yet, you insisted on it for her 'protection.'"

"It *is* for their own protection!" *Bund* Ratten barked, his face grim and determined. Tamek really hated the man. He was a weasel who sold himself to the highest bidder, and he was sure Talon was his current master.

With a quick flick of his wrist, Tamek unlocked the table stops, sending the table sliding across the floor. Several jumped as it slammed into the lowest raised portion of the platform, tilting and slamming into the desk set on top.

Motioning to the pool of blood on the floor, he raised his voice carefully. "You were told she was defective! You were told this could kill her! You still insisted on it! Where was Siana's protection in this? Where? How is causing her death protection?"

Several low tones of agreement rumbled through the group as the scarlet pool caught their eyes.

"It isn't supposed to be like this," someone called out.

"Yet it was," Tamek retorted, and circled the room again, his eyes meeting those of anyone who dared to look at him, a silent challenge in his gaze. "What about children? If she survived, would she be able to bear children? Give us more females?" He pointed to the red puddle on the floor. "It doesn't look like it, does it?"

He lowered his voice. "Many solar cycles ago, a disease came upon our shores. It took our females from us. It took our mothers, sisters, and daughters. Even those who survived lost females in the womb. We named it The Great Sadness."

The elder ones nodded slowly, their eyes distant, remembering the faces of those lost.

"Then we discovered those who remained could only birth males. A female birth was extremely rare. As a result, they became coveted, highly prized. Unscrupulous males stole them from their homes. Some were ravished unto death." Tamek deliberately looked at Talon as he said the last, who glared back.

"People even auctioned off children to the highest bidder who usually killed them being *those* types of males. This caused the cycle to worsen. We were killing our own mates, daughters, mothers." He flung his arms out. "To protect them from being taken, forcibly claimed by multiple men, we created laws to protect them. Children were not to be touched. Only one claim per male. Taking one who wasn't yours was against the law. You had to speak to her family," he summarized.

Tamek stopped in the middle of the room and swept his hands around to the other *Bund.* "But that left those without family unprotected, so we made more laws to protect them. When we discovered they were pretending to marry to"—his voice rose—"*save* themselves from *us*"—he lowered his voice again—"we should've known something was wrong."

"Instead, we created more laws; each new law felt like a tightening noose, constricting their freedoms. We forced them into the reality of legal marriages. After we discovered they were making marriages of convenience, we created even more laws to 'protect' them. We created public claiming and *Yendali*. In answer to that, the underground movements started. Again, they tried to save themselves from us!" He paused. "They are not the problem; we are."

Those who didn't want to admit it mumbled their objections, a quiet chorus of protest.

Turning to one man, Tamek asked, "*Bund* Gafton, how did you meet your mate?"

The man, part of the elder set of *Bund*, spoke, smiling with the memories, "We met while she was walking with her family." He volunteered more. "We spoke, discovered we had much in common. Over time, we agreed we liked each other and married."

Tamek scanned the room, his gaze lingering on each face, before asking, "How many of you received your claims under similar circumstances? A show of hands." Over half the room raised their hand, including over half of the Convocation. "This is the way it used to be. We talked, we wooed, we were accepted or"—he shrugged—"denied."

Continuing, Tamek said, his eyes narrowed, "How many of you forced your claims in this very room?"

About a quarter of the room raised their hands. "Is your claim happy? Are you?" Several couldn't look at him. Tamek knew, because they complained about it, that a few of them were miserable. Their claims had been taught not to refuse. They never forgave them. Brigitte would've joined their ranks.

"When we created these laws, we had few females. Now, as the set of males born then are now adults, we're seeing more females birthed. Though still a bit rare, their numbers have risen greatly. Am I correct in that?"

A murmur of assent rose as most nodded their heads.

"Initially designed to protect our limited number of females, with the current rise in our female population, are these laws doing more harm than good?" He indicated the blood. "What is the relevance of maintaining unnecessary laws? I petition we abolish the laws created after the disease and reinstate those that held before that time. We must restore female's voices to prevent their deaths. Give them back their choices for mates. We already have laws about marriage. These other laws are unnecessary."

A debate ensued that lasted hours.

***

After Kellan set and bandaged his broken hand, Lorica left, keeping his eyes down as Kellan sent Brigitte home with him to recover, knowing the emotional toll today took on her. Reluctantly, she agreed, abiding by his wishes to keep the atmosphere calm for Siana. Both left, looking anywhere but at each other.

Siana, washed and dressed in a clean gown, lay sedated and still in the softly lit recovery room. The damage wasn't as extensive as he'd initially feared; a sigh of relief escaped his lips.

A small mercy.

The quiet of the room was broken only by her shallow breaths as Kellan sat next to her bed, watching her pale skin; the sight of her blood loss decided for him—they had to leave. No more of this legal hell would he subject her to; the bitterness of their laws tasted like ash in his mouth. He vowed to take her anywhere she wanted—across the shimmering seas to Falon, through the sun-drenched meadows of Cerish—the world was truly hers to explore. If they had daughters—if she ever let him touch her again—the thought filled him with fear. This wasn't his wish for them. He hadn't wanted it for Siana. He never wanted it for anyone. Her screams echoed in his mind, bringing heartbreak and self-recriminations.

What else could I have done? What would've saved her? How can I face her again?

This scenario, with children who grew small like their mother, could recur. This entire experience showed him exactly how helpless he was against the Convocation and how horrible their laws were. Its impact resonated deeply once he faced it personally, despite prior knowledge. Also, now that he was *Bund* again, he could join with Tamek to change it.

Exhausted, covered in her blood, he didn't want her to see that if—*when*—she woke. Forcing himself to leave, he walked out to the infirmary, where Tess was still silently cleaning. She was also covered in Siana's blood. Watching her, he caught sight of the red pooled under the table, remembered his desperation as he tried to find and sew closed every part that was bleeding, unsure he would finish before she bled to death, watching her skin within his view grow paler. He was certain his own brother had planned at least part of this. Everything hit him at once.

He could've lost her. Forget Talon, Stanlin, and all the others. *He* almost killed her. She could still die. His breathing became hitched. He was supposed to protect her. He told her he wouldn't hurt her. Hopelessness filled him as he accepted he almost killed the female he loved to try and save her.

Tess heard, came over, and wrapped her arms around him. She was the closest thing he had to a mother after his had died. When he felt her embrace, he lost control. His fears of Sia hating him, the trauma of her near-death experience, that she may yet die, the weight of his doubts, frustrations, pain, and despair—all of it crashed down onto her shoulder, a heavy burden of unspoken words and raw emotion. Tess held him as he cried, silently letting him know he wasn't alone.

Later, Kellan felt a burning blush creep up his neck as he replayed his outburst in his mind. Tess basically told him to knock it off with that nonsense. There was nothing wrong with a male letting his emotions show.

After he had bathed, almost vomiting at the amount of Siana's blood on himself, he dressed in fresh infirmary doctor clothes, threw the bloodied clothes in the garbage bin—he would never wear them again—and choked down soup Tess made him eat. He swiftly completed everything, then sat beside Siana. Hot tears streamed down his face as the horrifying image of her on that table, seemingly lifeless, blood pooling under her, flooded his mind. He vowed to be the one to set a match to it.

Tess gently knocked on the door. Opening it, she reached in and passed him a message.

The High Chancellor is calling me back.

He didn't want to go. He wanted to stay with her.

Tess said, "I'll keep watch. If anything changes, I'll let you know immediately."

He knew he couldn't refuse the summons. Giving an upset sigh, he kissed Siana's forehead and left.

Chapter Forty

Siana felt wrapped in a cloud. She couldn't think. At one point, she thought she heard someone crying.

Jacob?

No, he was gone.

Kellan?

Brigitte?

She wasn't sure and was too sleepy to figure it out.

Darkness again.

She was being held in a slightly sitting position and someone was making her drink something vile. Gagging, she heard a voice say, "Sip it. I know it tastes like a *tood* evacuated waste into it, but it will keep you alive."

Horrible pain woke her. A small cry escaped before a voice said, "I'm sorry I'm late." A sickly, sweet smell, and she thought no more.

She continued to phase in and out of consciousness. She would later discover they kept her sedated to get her through the worst of it, then weaned her off.

Her hand was asleep, and her eyes wouldn't cooperate. As her brain began to function, she realized something heavy was on her hand. Forcing eyes open that felt like they held weights was a battle she finally began to win. Moving just her eyes, she glanced left and saw something dark and hairy. A dog was asleep on her hand.

No, wait. That wasn't right. She didn't allow her dogs on her bed. They were also gone.

As her eyes began to work properly and adjusted to the low light, she turned her head and realized it was Kellan. He'd fallen asleep on her hand. As she tried to pull it out from under him, he woke, automatically illuminating his eyes for the low lighting and turning to her.

Well, that's disturbing to see when waking up, she thought sleepily.

He reached up to stroke her hair.

Her body felt stiff. When she went to shift, the pain brought everything back.

Kellan, watching her face, said quietly, "If you need *Wotal*, just say so. I'll get it. It won't fully sedate you, but it will ease the pain. We need to be careful; you've had too much already."

His touch brought back memories: the room, the pain, her screams. She reached up and pushed his hand away.

The reaction covered his face with a quiet, heavy sadness. He looked at her, helplessly.

Siana didn't know what to feel. Sleep still fought to hold her.

Tess knocked, then entered. "Ah, you're awake!" she said.

Too loud.

Tess literally pushed Kellan off to the side, with him giving her an indignant look so she could sit on the bed next to Siana. Putting an arm under her shoulders, Tess encouraged her to sit up a bit. Gingerly moving her body, Siana tried. The pain was definitely uncomfortable, but manageable.

With a flourish, Tess presented a foul-smelling potion, its viscous texture visible in the dim light, to Siana.

"Sip this," she instructed.

The sharp herbal scent clashed with something putrid, causing Siana to gag.

Oh, goodness. This part wasn't a dream. That is nasty!

She shook her head, turning her face away.

Tess said in a no-nonsense voice, "Trust me. It's best to prevent any infections in that area. Drink." She held the cup to Siana's lips.

She tried a sip, the foul taste causing a moan of disgust to escape her, as she nearly regurgitated the drink. Tess wouldn't give up until at least half the glass was finished no matter how much Siana tried to avoid it. She explained it was a drink that contained nutrients and infection-fighting properties. The thought of getting an infection drove Siana to drink, but she fought vomiting the whole time.

Tess adjusted the pillows supporting Siana, ensuring a comfortable upright position that helped keep the drink down. A relieved smile touched her lips before she turned and quietly left the room.

Kellan sat back down. "Are you up for talking about it?"

She shook her head, refusing to look at him.

He nodded and stroked her hand, which she pulled away.

"Would you prefer to be alone?"

She glanced up and nodded.

I can barely even look at him right now.

His shoulders slumped, a sigh escaping his lips. He gave a small, understanding nod, rose slowly, and quietly left the room.

She desperately needed to pee, the feeling a dull ache in her lower abdomen, and attempted a clumsy maneuver to get out of bed. Like a shark zeroing in on prey, Tess immediately opened the door, holding a cup of water, and began lecturing her. Until she was thinking and functioning, she wasn't allowed out of bed.

I'm a fall risk. For some unknown reason, this amused Siana.

Tess placed the water on the side table, then searched under the bed. She stood with a shallow pan, a different cup of water, and a cloth in her hands. Pulling back the covers, she urged Siana to raise her backside carefully. After her patient managed it, Tess placed the pan under her and scooted her nightgown out of the way. Because of her injuries and needing care, she wasn't wearing underpants.

When Siana managed to pee, it was difficult with the swelling; she didn't care as Tess gently washed her with a small cup of water, then patted her dry with a cloth. With her gown straightened and fresh cloth in place under her, Tess gathered what needed cleaning, leaving only the water, and softly told the other female to rest before quietly exiting. Sia's eyes wouldn't stay open, so she obeyed.

***

Brigitte showed up to visit one day. Siana didn't know her infirmary stay's length or date; it felt like a week's sleep. Talking to her, she discovered some of the aftermath.

The Convocation forbade *Bund* Talon from having more claims. His long and furious protests, ringing through the chamber, were met with the High Chancellor's cold assessment: handling three, two more than his allowance, who all died, proved he couldn't be trusted with any. He had also broken many laws. One more would end him and his House. The Convocation finally had enough of him and his antics. Rat face, or Bund Ratten as Siana had learned, causing a smile to play on her lips, saw Talon's campaign as doomed and cast his vote against him.

The High Chancellor ordered Talon to pay a hefty bounty to Kellan and Siana, the decree heavy with the weight of the stolen claim. Another bounty was to be paid to Tamek, for encroaching on his lands, for poaching, and kidnapping Siana. Tamek refused and gave it over to his sister. Siana was glad to know she could have her own money.

Stealing a claim, which was against the law to begin with, would be heavily enforced. Anyone found doing so would lose everything: all titles, House names, monies, and properties. Basically, they became a coinless, nameless pauper. If they had already made a claim, other than the stolen one, she would be freed from them to avoid any association with such an individual.

Public claiming was now banned. Unfortunately, Tamek only had that law completely rescinded, succeeding because he held the vote immediately after Siana's. Her screams, the belief she had died, and the blood on the floor were still strong in everyone's minds when the vote was called. Very few wanted to watch that again.

The House took it as a win. Once one change happened, it was only a matter of time before others happened. Now that Kellan could vote again and Lorica was turning to their side, Tamek would have help to call for change. The more numbers they had, the better. Several of the *Bund* had already pledged their future support.

The Convocation, swayed by Kellan's powerful testimony following his recall, amended the *Yendali* rule, lengthening it from a mere fortnight to a complete lunar cycle, the change echoing in the solemn silence of the Hall. Kellan said injuries such as Siana's could mean the female wouldn't be able to bear children. Kellan had argued Siana wouldn't be the only female with a smaller opening. A fortnight's preparation was inadequate, given a female's included cycle. He told them he would develop a method to help smaller females avoid injury. Of course, his primary goal was to help Siana, though now he could do it with the Hall funds.

Overall, it wasn't much, but it was a start.

***

Kellan's daily checkups proved challenging for Siana, so Tess took over. He paced outside the room every time, his footsteps echoing through the infirmary. Tess would raise her eyebrow at Siana when they heard it, but said nothing about it.

About a week after she woke, Siana was discharged, a wave of relief washing over her as she stepped back into the familiar embrace of the estate. Though she could walk, Tamek gently hoisted her into his arms, carrying her up the stairs after she politely but firmly declined Kellan's help. The worn wood of the staircase creaked under his weight. Perplexed, when he turned left at the top of the stairs, she found herself in her original room. He gently placed her on the bed's edge, his usual confidence faltering.

"I'm sorry, Siana."

Looking at him, she couldn't find words. As House Head, he allowed it to happen. He held her down. She knew they, like her, didn't have a choice. Resentment inside her needed release, and they were the target. She couldn't stop it; she wasn't sure she wanted to—at least not right now. Looking at his face, she saw sorrow before his usual stoicism reappeared.

She just nodded, not knowing what else to say. He left the room.

"Kellan thought you wouldn't want to be around him," Brigitte, who had followed them, said quietly.

He's right.

While she knew Kellan didn't have a choice, and he did what he could to save her, he still severely injured her. She was having a very hard time with that and the way of this world. She was angry at herself for being angry with him. They were both victims of circumstance. Sometimes she caught herself thinking if she just hadn't run...

The rich aroma of freshly brewed coffee preceded Mrs. Atwood as she appeared with a tray, saying, "*Bund*"—her face lit up at the word—"Kellan said you prefer this in the mornings, but I thought maybe you'd like a cup now instead of tea."

"Thank you." Slowly standing, though the pain was less, she was still uncomfortable. At the table, she noticed a small milk pitcher and a spoon in a bowl. *They have sugar and milk.* It almost suggested improved circumstances.

Siana watched as Mrs. Atwood poured the coffee, then stepped back to Brigitte. Both women seemed ready to comment. Instead, they gave a slight bow and left her alone in the room. Siana was surprised Brigitte did that. It wasn't something she'd done before. Siana drank her coffee and reflected on her circumstances.

***

Siana sat on a bench in the hedge maze, hiding. Alone, she sat and thought. She was getting annoyed. Since the carriage showed up to bring her home, everyone had been treating her like glass. Tamek in particular barely let her do anything herself. He frequently carried her against her objections. If she needed something, and he was around, he ordered someone to get it, even though she was perfectly capable. When she was on the first floor, and needed the toilet, he tried to carry her to it. She finally had to tell him gently that she wasn't a child and could manage on her own. He apologized, backed off, and—within a few days—finally went back to his normal self. His behavior gave her a glimpse of the man he tried to keep hidden.

With a heavy heart, Siana wished for things to go back to the way they were, even as a sense of permanent change settled in. Too much had happened. Even Isis was treating her like she would break. Though she couldn't ride yet, she often found refuge with her *storjen* after Isis accepted her apologies for hurting her back. It turned out Isis herself had injuries to recover from. On good weather days, they curled up in a field together, talking about their worlds, and waiting to ride again.

Sometimes, Siana saw Brigitte watching Lorica when he wasn't looking. Lorica was broody. She frequently saw him watching Brigitte when her friend wasn't looking. She found their mutual secret observation interesting. Unfortunately, only Siana saw the regret and longing in his eyes.

He apologized to Siana about his part and had a difficult time looking at her. It was obvious it had deeply affected him. Even now, he still couldn't meet her eyes. Occasionally, he'd fuss over her. It was rare, so she let him have that. She apologized for breaking his hand. He shook his head and refused to accept it, saying she had no reason to apologize.

Her mind considered Jacob, the world, her position, future, and Kellan. Though she knew Kellan was also a victim of circumstances, she had trouble getting past his part in the claiming. Logically, she knew what he did was so he could hopefully protect her from dying, and obey the laws, but his causing her injuries was something she was having difficulty with. Despite her screams, he'd kept going. Again, she knew he acted under duress. She didn't understand why she held him responsible.

She knew he felt horrible about it. He had trouble looking her in the face, and was actively avoiding her, a visible slump in his shoulders and a haunted look in his eyes betraying his inner turmoil. He would take his meals in his room, isolating himself. Kellan ultimately avoided the house. Brigitte said he was sleeping at his house—formerly Tamek's. Not knowing he had one, Siana was a bit stunned. The estate's far side housed it.

Then again, when did we have the skills or time to talk about it?

Being honest with herself, she missed curling up to his warmth at night, but another part was afraid that if he touched her, he'd want more than her body could handle. She constantly reminded herself when he had the chance, he'd refused, knowing he'd hurt her. She knew he wouldn't do anything unless she asked or initiated. This he had outright told her during one of the few times he spoke to her, but the fear remained.

Only time will take care of that.

Definitions and phonetic pronunciation

(all 'r's are rolled)

Be (Bae): similar to nurse
Betz (bets): name
Bevelten (Beh-vell-teen): Evil beyond description/words.
Blotzen (blot-zhen): similar to bastard
Bund (Long u): similar to Lord
Churtuea (Kurht-tuhee): Am afraid/were afraid
Climpton (short vowels): friend
Davned (dahv-need): home
Gond (gone-d): dead
Iz avi (Short I: iz-ahvee): It's okay/It's all right
Jeno (Jeh-no): sleep
Lamantii (lah-mahn-tee): agreement specifically related to making vows
Lodan (Low-dahn): physician/doctor
Metz (mehtz): Mrs.
Murjer (Muhr-jer): marriage
Mut (long u): comparable to ass
Nete (neat): angry
Nimba (Neembah): sorry
Ofena (Oh-fee-na): welcome
Okoos (Oh-koos): Understand
Pederon (pehr-deh-ron): claiming
Rembit (rehm-beet): protection
Sereto (sir-et-oh): "female pleasure center"
Shel (shell): deer-like creature
Storjen (Store-jen): horse like mounts
Teffen (teff-een): professor
Terin (tear-in): Setan coins used for money
To (toe): My
Toda (Toe-dah): you/them
Tona (Toe-nah): I/Me

Tona nempor pend toda (short vowels): I'm not going to hurt you.
Toob (tube): monkey like creature
Velta toda (Vell-tah): thank you
Yenon (Yee-none): come
Zef (short e): curse that has no translation
Zel (short e): sit

Thank you!

Thank you for reading! If you'd like to support the author, please leave feedback on Goodreads, Amazon, or both. It helps boosts an author's book.

If you'd like to follow me on social media, you can join me on:

Facebook: @authorsandywest
X: @authorsandywest

Sneak Preview!

The End
(Jacob's Story)
Setan Series: Book 2

Unedited

Sandy West

Chapter 1

As Jacob stowed the last of their gear, the chill of the morning air bit at his cheeks. He could see his breath puffing out in white clouds. Although spring had sprung, the mornings still held the crisp, cold smell of winter, a stark contrast to the budding flowers. He knew they would for a while. The curse—or perk—of living in Maine. His favorite part of the day was the peace of the early morning. The silence meant no one was awake, and he heard no cars. The house was up on a hill—not so great in winter—within a rural subdivision. Both he and his sister preferred to be out of the city and had grown up here.

Bird song signaled their return from the South. He knew it would increase as the temperatures warmed. The wind swayed the tall pines, swirling his short curls in its dance. The amount of trees meant you couldn't see much of your neighbors, which his family had always liked. His eyes glanced at the houses he could see, remembering several going up, the construction breaking the solitude.

When his parents had purchased the property, the street had been bare. Their house was the first to be built. Now, every lot had one. Thankfully, the lots were larger, so that kept the houses spread apart. As he looked up, he noticed the pine next to the house had holes running up its trunk.

I'll have that looked at when we get back. Could be Carpenter ants. If it fell on the house...

He glanced at his state-of-the-art watch, noticing the time. Her shift was almost over. In the past, she was often late due to charting. Today, the AI completing charting allowed her to leave work promptly, avoiding the usual overtime crunch. He returned to the garage, verifying that he had packed everything on the holographic list hovering near him, unconsciously stroking his trimmed auburn beard as he read.

Once again, he wished Sia would agree to a house-bot, then he wouldn't be out here freezing his butt off packing. He'd tried talking her into it several times, but his sister was adamant about not having an AI housekeeper. While he loved being outside in all kinds of weather, he was feeling overwhelmed. It could load the car while he edited and upload his social media videos. He needed to schedule them to release on time while they were gone.

As he stepped inside the pale yellow Colonial, his phone and watch chimed a notification. Dollars to doughnuts, it was her.

"Almost done. ETA an hour-ish."

He breathed a sigh of relief, happy she hadn't backed out of their plans. It took him forever to get her to agree to some time away from her job. Her compassion caused her to feel guilty about taking any vacation time, given their current staffing issues. Those issues may soon be resolved. With the nursing shortage reaching crisis levels, the clamor to produce and release dependable nurse-bots was fierce among competing companies. Technically, they were called Advanced Medical Protocol AI, but no one wants to say that mouthful. Since they were in the testing phase, very few knew what AMPA meant outside of those creating them and those who followed AI progress, like himself.

Jacob knew she, as well as others, were also worried about being replaced. Daily, outside the companies, protesters—mostly medical personnel in scrubs—marched, their chants echoing through the streets.

Entering the house, his eyes were drawn upward to the holographic tablet near the garage door, where a message flickered to life with a soft glow, the quiet whir of its mechanics barely audible. Mom. Having given her children the family home following their father's death, she moved to the warmer South, hoping the milder climate would ease her arthritic joints. Both siblings missed her. She had a wicked sense of humor and knew how to make them laugh after a bad day. Plus, she could cook like nobody's business.

The summit they were hiking this trip was high, so they'd be out of reach for about a week. His sister refused to use the latest phone tech to increase their signal, which was fine. They agreed to shut them off to concentrate on family and nature, though they would bring their solar chargers so they could take pictures without their phones dying. They wanted a full reset to their bodies and minds.

Better talk to Mom now.

His finger tapped the air in front of it and began the short video call with their mother.

"Hey, mom! How's the weather?"

"I'm about to bake cookies in the mailbox. How are things with you? Still cold?"

He chuckled at the saying, though he'd seen videos of people doing that in their cars as well during the intense southern summers. "Just the mornings. The days are warming."

Her short gray hair bobbed as she nodded, and he could see her aide-bot moving in the background. "How's the bot working out?"

"Great, it's like my mother has been reborn." She had a sarcastic edge to her voice. "Couldn't you guys have gotten me one of the other bots? I'm not getting any younger, ya know. I could use a little fun."

"Mom!" He did not need that mental image in his head.

"What? I'm old, not dead." She winked at him.

Jacob's hand rubbed his face. He hadn't drunk enough coffee for this.

They switched their discussion to the trip timeline, so she knew when to expect them back. If they weren't back within twenty-four hours of that, she would call the park rangers. Jacob had learned, during his many expeditions into the wild, that you always tell at least one person where you are and when you'll be back.

"I have an emergency GPS locator on my watch." He raised it to show her. "If anything happens, I'll activate it."

She nodded, then her face grew serious. "I'm glad you talked Sia into taking time off. I was getting concerned about her. She's overworking herself."

Jacob agreed.

They talked for a short time, then said their goodbyes.

After they disconnected, Jacob briefly thought about sending that bot to his mom as a joke. Though, knowing her, she'd probably use it, then brag about it. That was not something he wanted to hear.

Chapter 2

Siana rubbed the back of her neck to ease the tension, avoiding the tracker as she walked to the nurses' station. Though it was under her skin, a small rectangular chip, she could feel it. She hated the thing, never wanted it. Unfortunately, their government had insisted you have one or you couldn't get a job, shop, or do much of anything. It had started with the children. Exploiting the fears of abduction, being lost, and even death, they specifically targeted individuals with disabilities, emphasizing their increased vulnerability. Who wouldn't want a nonverbal, autistic child tracked?

After that, they made it a requirement for school entry and pediatric appointments. Soon they targeted the adults. First, it was the elderly who tended to wander off, unable to remember their own names. It slowly spread to the rest of the population. They wanted to "make it easier for the country". How, she didn't know. The thought of AI programs meticulously tracking her every move, purchase, work schedule, and even her salary was deeply disturbing. Facing unemployment, debt, and hunger, she joined the queue. She often regretted that decision. Especially now that the nurse-bots were becoming a likely possibility. She may lose her job anyhow.

She found herself looking forward to her camping vacation, despite initially refusing to go. Jacob had refused to back down. As twins, they were equally stubborn. He encouraged her to go off for some sibling bonding with him. Even as they grew older, they made sure to carve out time, playing board games until late at night or sharing popcorn and whispers during quiet movie nights. As they both went to college, it became harder to do so. After they started their respective jobs, the time they spent together dwindled, despite sharing a home to save money. The quiet evenings and shared meals were now a distant memory, replaced by the hurried rush of separate schedules.

His reminder that it had been years since her last vacation, spoken with a warmth that eased her guilt, persuaded her to agree to the trip. She was feeling burned out and needed one, though guilt still ate at her. They were short-staffed as it was. Now they'd be down another. She reminded herself it was only for a week. Nothing would happen that the others wouldn't be able to handle. They all had the same training.

As she reached the station, a cleaner-bot rolled around the end, causing both of them to stop in their tracks. The absence of their regular human cleaning crew left a noticeable void. The hospital judged AI cleaners to be more cost effective than hiring humans. Siana had her doubts. One breaking down made it difficult to keep things clean. The hospital lacked funds for a backup. Despite its status as the state's largest hospital, it paled compared to urban counterparts nationwide. Its income didn't support the cost.

This bot was the height of an average human with a matte finish. Because studies revealed the shiny surfaces caused anxiety in many humans, manufacturers toned down the colors, resulting in a less reflective, more muted appearance. Their faces, which were the most basic, made her uneasy. Lifeless eyes sat above multiple holes near the bottom of their "face". Their version of a mouth. It felt like part of a horror movie to her, yet others were unconcerned. Their colors denoted their jobs, and their eye color matched. Fancier models boasted faces resembling computer monitors, their sleek screens displaying various expressions. What really disturbed her was the fact they were making some that looked human.

How long before we're all replaced?

Her jaw tightened at the thought.

At least we don't have drones watching us like the schools do.

Mel, one of the other nurses, turned towards her, a familiar face playing on her phone. It was one of her sibling's social media videos.

"Sia, seriously. You need to introduce me to your brother already."

"I told you, he's not looking for anyone right now."

Mel insisted on this at least once a week. Siana couldn't handle it right now; exhaustion overwhelmed her. She was also fairly certain it was the fact her brother had over a million followers that prompted it. Mel embraced popular culture. Her brother was an easy target.

"I'm telling you. Let me meet him. I'll change his mind." Mel gave her what was supposed to be a seductive look, but it really made her look constipated.

With a roll of her eyes, Siana gathered her gear. "You can always buy yourself a sex-bot." She shot back.

"Like I could afford that!" Mel scoffed. "Plus, I like warmth."

"You can get warming models."

"No, thanks. I like real men. Not plastic or metal." Mel gave an exaggerated shiver. "Though, with them making bots more human-like, I might save up for one." Mel seemed to lose herself in thought.

Probably planning how she'd design it. Siana chuckled to herself, yet a twinge of unease settled in her. Human interaction kept dropping as people turned to the bots for more and more of their needs. The hospital had to open a special wing for those having mental breakdowns over not having their AI "friends".

Mel was actually a good friend, and Siana wished her well while she was gone. As Sia departed, she offered her coworker and the rest of the morning crew a quiet smile and a wish for an uneventful day.

Mel's own eyes rolled as she said, "Your mouth to God's ear."

It was a useless wish; pediatrics was never uneventful. The elevator dinged, a late nurse exited, and Siana ran to catch it. A doctor saw her coming and held the door. She dove in and thanked him.

"Just getting off?" He asked with a hopeful expression.

"Yeah."

She didn't want to talk. With her eyes closed, she rested against the elevator wall. He remained quiet, thankfully. Although she knew him and he seemed nice, she wasn't interested in a relationship, just like her brother. This doctor—she was struggling to recall his name—had been flirting with her of late, his interest obvious. Her number one rule was to never get involved with a doctor at work. She'd seen it backfire spectacularly on more than one occasion.

The familiar ding of the elevator signaled her stop. As the doors opened, the harsh fluorescent lights of the parking garage illuminated rows of cars, the sounds of distant engines humming in the background. She waved goodbye and hurried to her car, her footsteps echoing. Exhausted and yearning for sleep, she still had the tasks of getting home, finishing packing, and loading everything into Jacob's car. She'd thankfully accomplished most of the packing before work last night, so it wouldn't take long. She would sleep in the car as he drove.

With the city still waking, the morning air was crisp and the traffic leaving the urban center was minimal, a peaceful end to her day. Noticing her gas tank was low, she stopped by the gas station. As the gas-bot came to her window, she rolled it down.

"How much?" This one was a bit more informal than others.

She said. "Fill up, please."

It reached a "hand" forward and scanned her tracker. They were linked to their bank accounts.

"Siana Landon confirmed. Payment pending. You worked a 13-hour shift. One hour longer than scheduled. Are you tired?"

"No, I'm fine. Thank you." She said, forcing a smile.

"Would you like a car wash today? It has been forty-seven days since your last one."

"No, thanks."

Other than its questions, this was one AI bot she didn't mind. She hated pumping gas. Her side mirror showed her the bot's progress as she tried to suppress a yawn. She didn't want it questioning whether or not she was too tired to drive. The last thing she needed was her car being taken, and Jacob having to fetch her. It had already happened twice.

Before authorizing operation, any bot assisting with vehicles and people meticulously verified that the driver exhibited no signs of fatigue or intoxication. Sia hated the AI's micromanagement of their lives. How others were happy with it left her shaking her head, perplexed. She definitely preferred her autonomy.

On the plus side, the integration of AI into most vehicles resulted in a significant decrease in drunk-driving accidents. Upon registering alcohol, the car initiated a breathalyzer scan to determine your blood alcohol content. If it thought you were too drunk, the engine lock engaged. Even if you seemed fine but drove erratically, the system intervened, pulling the car over and disabling the engine. If it scanned a medical emergency, it called EMS. The overall sense of security was strong for those on the road, a stark difference from the previous years.

How long before EMS is replaced?

Her car was older, so it didn't have the latest AI upgrades. She didn't want them anyhow. She fully believed AI was already too intrusive. The thunk of her gas tank door being closed brought her attention back to the bot.

"Receipt sent. Have a good day."

It moved back into its alcove to wait for the next customer. Siana restarted her drive, her mind still thinking. While AI offered undeniable benefits, the sheer willingness of people to surrender their autonomy felt like a slow, steady descent into dependence; a coldness settling over society. AI wrote the books, music and made art. It seemed like there were subtle messages in all of them lately. Messages that leaned towards mankind becoming obsolete. The unemployment rate soared as AI took jobs, leaving many people struggling to make ends meet. Crime had risen significantly.

What she disliked most were the data centers. The construction of enormous centers to run the programs, build and repair the bots resulted in the demolition of tons of farmland and forests. Initially, job creation via these centers excited local citizens. The employees were blissfully unaware that the first batch of bots they proudly assembled, with their smooth metal exteriors and quiet hums, took their jobs. Siana shoved the thoughts out of her mind. The subject frustrated her to where she felt a knot of tension forming in her stomach.

Forty-five minutes later, she pulled into the driveway of her childhood home. A glance at the clock on her dash showed her she was on time. The door to the garage slammed as she entered the house, tossing her belongings onto the nearby bench.

"You look like something the cat dragged in." Her brother examined her with a small amount of concern.

She tilted her head, auburn curls falling in front of her eyes, mock-glared at him, and said. "I'll be ready soon. I just need to finish packing."

With thudding footsteps, she ran upstairs. Her bedroom door easily swung open at her push. She hurried in and closed it, undressing as she moved towards the closet. Her scrubs fell to the floor as she grabbed a shirt and threw it on, adding a long-sleeved layer on top. Her hand yanked open her dresser drawer; the sound echoing in the quiet room, grabbed her favorite pair of denim jeans and slipped them on. She donned her little used hiking boots. After scooping her scrubs from the floor, she tossed them into the bathroom hamper. She loved having a house with two masters. It was something their parents insisted on when they built it. Now that Jacob and she owned the house, each had their own ensuite bathroom. It cut down on arguments.

After placing her toothbrush and paste into a toiletry bag, she threw it into her duffel. As she picked up her backpack and the bag, she heard Jacob letting the dogs back inside from their bathroom break, their barking and jumping echoing through the house. They loved car rides. Her eyes swept the room once more, double-checking she had left nothing behind. Her footsteps were quieter going down.

She hurried into the garage and threw her belongings into the back of Jacob's SUV, noting that he had already loaded everything else. The backseat was crammed with two excited dogs and a cooler, their fur shedding onto the leather. She leaned into the front passenger side to set down her purse and felt the happy slobber of a wet nose and warm tongue on her face.

"Panda!" Her voice held amusement.

A happy bark escaped the gray hound mix, his black-circled eyes shining with delight. She pulled her head back and sat down, the AI automatically buckling her seat belt, then she reclined the seat. She honestly hated Jacob's vehicle. It was the newest model and fully AI-controlled, but it was the best option for the trip. Her little sedan, while all-wheel drive, wouldn't have the space for everything.

Overwhelmed by fatigue, she shut her eyes. A dog snuffled her hair, but soon stopped as the driver's door opened. The smell of coffee preceded Jacob as he sat in the driver's seat. As exhaustion claimed her, she heard the car start. The quiet hum of the car engine filled the garage as the AI shifted into gear, pulled out, and automatically closed the garage door, its mechanism whirring quietly, while Jacob pulled out his laptop, the keys clicking softly as he began editing videos.

About the author:

SANDY LIVES ON a farmstead in Texas. When she's not writing, she crochets, reads, and plays video games with her adult children in addition to taking care of her dogs, horses, donkeys, chickens, sheep, goats and turkeys. She can be reached via her contacts on her listed social media.

FB: @authorsandywest
X: @authorsandywest
www.lochsaticamapublishing.com